# J.D.ROBB

# New York
# to Dallas

piatkus

PIATKUS

First published in the United States in 2011 by G.P. Putnam's Sons,
a division of Penguin Group (USA) Inc.
First published in Great Britain in 2011 by Piatkus
This paperback edition published in 2012 by Piatkus

A CIP catalogue record for this book
is available from the British Library.

ISBN 978-0-7499-5586-1

Typeset in Bembo by M Rules
Printed and bound by CPI Group (UK) Ltd, Croydon, CR0 4YY

Papers used by Piatkus are from well-managed forests
and other responsible sources.

 MIX
Paper from
responsible sources
FSC® C104740

Piatkus Books
An imprint of
Little, Brown Book Group
100 Victoria Embankment
London EC4Y 0DY

An Hachette UK Company
www.hachette.co.uk

www.piatkus.co.uk

# Eve Dallas – Personnel File

**Name:** Eve Dallas

**Nationality:** American

**Rank:** Homicide Lieutenant, New York Police and Security Department

**Born:** 2028

**Height:** 5 foot 9 inches

**Weight:** 120 lbs

**Eyes:** Golden brown

**Hair:** Light brown

**ID number:** 5347BQ

### Service:
Began police officer training at the Academy in 2046, aged 18.

### Family:
Between the ages of eight and ten, Eve lived in a communal home while her parents were searched for. Eve was found with no ID, no memory, and was traumatised having been a victim of sexual assault.

### Why Eve is a cop:
'It's what I am. It's not just that someone has to look, even though that's just the way it is. It's that I have to look.'

The Present is the living sum-total of the whole Past.

THOMAS CARLYLE

I wonder, by my troth, what thou and I
Did, till we lov'd.

JOHN DONNE

# 1

While a late-summer storm bashed against her single skinny window, Lieutenant Eve Dallas wished for murder.

As far as she could see, a good, bloody killing was the only thing that would save her from the torture of paperwork stacked like the Alps on her desk at Cop Central. Her own fault, no question, but she'd been just a little too busy investigating and closing cases to hunker down with budgets and expense reports and the damn evaluation sheets.

Telling herself it was part of the job didn't help when she actually had to do it – in bulk – which was why she'd closed herself in her office with lots and lots of coffee and wondered why somebody didn't just kill somebody else and save her from this nightmare.

Not really, she told herself. Or not exactly. But since people consistently killed other people anyway, why not *now*?

She stared at the numbers on her computer screen until her eyes throbbed. She cursed, sulked, steamed, then strapped on and squeezed, crunched, fudged, and manipulated until she could make the stingy departmental bottom line fit the needs of her division.

They were murder cops, she thought with bitter resentment. Homicide didn't run on blood alone.

She got through it, moved on to the expense chits submitted by her officers and detectives.

Did Baxter actually believe she'd bite on three-seventy-five for shoes because he'd fucked up his own chasing a suspect down a sewer? And why the hell had Reineke shelled out double the usual rate to a street-level licensed companion for information?

She stopped, got more coffee, stared out at the brutality of the storm for a few minutes. At least she wasn't out there, plugged like a wet cork into one of the shuddering airtrams, or shoving her way through the drowning hell of street traffic. She could be soaked, steaming like a clam in the endless stream of heat the summer of 2060 poured on New York.

Stalling, she thought in disgust, and forced herself to sit again. She'd promised herself she'd finish before the afternoon ceremony. Both she and her partner would receive medals. Peabody had earned it and more, Eve thought, as the catalyst for taking down a ring of dirty cops.

If paperwork was the drudgery of command, submitting Peabody's name for the Meritorious Police Duty Honor for Integrity was a boon. All she had to do was finish the grunt work, then she could enjoy the moment with a clear head and guiltless conscience.

She wished she had candy, but she hadn't settled on a new hiding place to thwart the nefarious Candy Thief. She wished she could dump some of this crap on Peabody the

2

way she had when Peabody had been her aide instead of her partner.

Those days were over.

Stalling again, she admitted, and raked her fingers through her short, choppy brown hair.

She hacked her way through the expense reports, submitted them up the chain. Someone else's problem now, she decided and felt almost righteous. No reason she couldn't start the evals later.

'Task complete. Shut it down.'

Unable to comply, the computer responded.

'I finished.'

Inaccurate statement. Previous command stipulated all listed reports and evaluations must be complete before system rest. This command by Dallas, Lieutenant Eve, priority basis, can only be countermanded at her order by fire, terrorist attack, alien invasion or an open and active case requiring her attention . . .

Jesus, had she really programmed that? 'I changed my mind.'

Previous command specifies changes of mind, fatigue, boredom, and other lame excuses not acceptable for countermand . . .

3

'Bite me,' Eve muttered.

Unable to comply . . .

'Fine, fine, fine. Computer, display previous evals, in alpha order, for all officers under my command.'

She worked her way through. She'd put the damn command in to keep herself in line – and because every single one of her men deserved the time and attention it took for a solid and judicious evaluation.

She finished Baxter, both Carmichaels, and had slogged her way to Jenkinson when the knock sounded on her door.

'Yeah, what?' She scowled over at Peabody as her partner opened the door. 'Is it an alien invasion?'

'Not that I've heard. There's a guy out here, pretty shaky, claims he can only speak to you. He says it's a matter of life and death.'

'Yeah?' She perked up. 'Computer, life-and-death countermand. Save and hold.'

Verification required . . .

'Peabody, tell this fucking machine there's a human being requiring my attention on a matter of life and death.'

'Ah, Computer, Peabody, Detective Delia, requests the lieutenant's attention on an urgent matter.'

Verification accepted. Saving data. On hold . . .

Annoyed, Eve gave the computer a rap with the heel of her hand. 'It's pretty pitiful when your own comp won't take your word.'

'You put all that in there so you wouldn't squirm out of the paperwork.'

'Still. Send life and death back.'

He came at a stumbling run, a skinny guy she judged as late twenties. He sported a tangle of messy dreads, baggy red shorts, gel-flips, a silver lip ring, and a dingy white tank that showed off his tattoo sleeves. Sweat ran down his thin, white face.

'You're Dallas. Lieutenant Eve Dallas, NYPSD. Homicide.'

'That's right. What's the—'

He burst into tears – loud, hiccupping tears. 'He said – he said – I could only talk to you. Had to come to you. He's got her. He's got Julie. He's gonna kill her if you don't come back with me. He said an hour, and it took me half that to get here.'

His words rolled on top of each other between sobs and shakes. Eve got out of her chair, shoved him into it.

'Suck it up and slow down. What's your name?'

'I'm Tray. Tray Schuster.'

'Who is he?'

'I don't know. He was just there, in my place. Our place. She just moved in last week. Just there when we woke up, and he tied us up. He ate breakfast, and he – doesn't matter. You have to come or he'll kill her. I forgot, I forgot. I'm supposed to say, "There's the bell for round two." Please, he's got

5

a knife. He's going to cut her. If you don't come, if I go to anybody else, he said he'd kill her.'

'Where?'

'My place. Our place, I mean.'

'Where's your place, Tray?'

'Two-fifty-eight Murray Street.'

The address clicked, and with the click came a twist in the guts. 'Apartment three-oh-three?'

'Yeah.' He swiped at his face. 'How did you—'

'Stay here, Tray.'

'But—'

'Stay.'

She strode out, into the bullpen. 'Peabody.' Scanned the desks and movement. 'Baxter, Trueheart, Carmichael, Sanchez. Whatever you're doing stop and suit up. Suspect is Isaac McQueen. He's holding a woman hostage, two-fifty-eight Murray Street, apartment three-oh-three. Suspect is armed and extremely dangerous. Additional data en route as the suspect has given a time limit on response. Carmichael, Sanchez, get the wit from my office. Keep him locked in your vehicle. Peabody, with me. Let's move!'

'Isaac McQueen?' Peabody scrambled to keep up with Eve's long legs. 'The Collector? He's in Rikers. Life sentence.'

'Check that. He's either out or somebody's posing as him. That was his apartment. That's where he kept . . .'

*All those young girls. So many young girls.*

'He's got this guy's cohab,' Eve continued, shoving her way

onto the elevator. 'He sent him to me, specifically. I took McQueen down, in that apartment.'

'There's no alert or notification . . . wait.' Peabody swiped at her PPC. 'Internal alert buried here. They haven't even informed command. McQueen escaped sometime yesterday. Killed one of the nurses in the infirmary and managed to walk out wearing his uniform and ID.' Peabody looked up from her PPC. 'He just walked out.'

'We're damn well going to walk him back in.' She jogged across the lot to her vehicle. 'Inform Commander Whitney. He can start knocking heads together at prison administration. He hasn't killed her,' Eve murmured as she peeled out of the underground lot. 'McQueen didn't escape just to slice up some woman. He's smart, organized, and he has an agenda. He has needs. He doesn't kill them – unless they break or dissatisfy. He collects. He's not interested in this Julie. She's over his age limit.'

Peabody finished the text to their commander's office before looking over at Eve. 'She's a lure. For you.'

'Yeah, but it doesn't make sense. He'd just end up boxed in, the way he was before.'

Didn't make sense, Eve thought again, but ordered Peabody to request uniforms for backup.

She used the wrist unit her husband had given her, engaged its communicator. 'Carmichael, I want you and Sanchez to cover the rear of the building. Uniforms on the way for backup. Baxter, you and Trueheart will go in with me and Peabody. Body armor. He'll be expecting us.'

7

She shook her head, ripped through the narrow opening between two Rapid Cabs. 'He won't be there. No way he's going to trap himself. He knows I'll come, and won't come alone.'

'Maybe that's what he wants you to think, and it's a trap.'

'We're about to find out.'

She studied the building, one of the cavernous homes that had survived the Urban Wars, and had been converted into apartments. It had seen better days – its better days had passed a century before – but it held up with its faded pink bricks and ornately grilled windows.

Its main entrance opened directly onto the sidewalk and had minimum security. Working-class neighborhood, Eve thought, as it had been during McQueen's reign. Most of the residents came home at the end of the day, settled back with a brew and some screen, and minded their own business.

So McQueen had been able to mind his for nearly three years. And the lives of twenty-six girls between the ages of twelve and fifteen had been forever scarred.

'He's got the privacy screen up,' Eve said. 'If he's up there, he knows we're here. He'd have made contacts, friends, in prison. He's charming, engaging, sly. It's possible he got his hands on something more long-range than a knife. Keep down. Move fast.'

She checked in with Carmichael, gave the go.

Blanking out memories, she moved, taking point up the stairs, weapon drawn. Throat dry, mind cold.

8

'Let me scan the door.' Peabody pulled out her PPC. 'He might've rigged it.'

'It opens on a living area, kitchen behind, eating area to the right. Two bedrooms, one right, one left. Bathroom attached to the one on the right. Half-bath left of the kitchen. It's a big unit, about five hundred square feet.'

'Scan reads clear,' Peabody told her.

'Baxter, straight back. Trueheart, Peabody, go left. I'm right.' She nodded to Trueheart and the battering ram. Counted from three down with her fingers.

The door crashed on its hinges, locks snapping. Eve went in low and fast, focused on the now, not the then. She heard the rush of feet as her team poured into the room.

She shoved open the bedroom door, swept with her weapon. She saw the figure on the bed, but continued to clear – left, right, closet, bath as she heard her team members call, 'Clear!'

'In here,' Eve shouted, and now moved to the bed.

'You're okay. It's okay. We're the police.'

She loosened the gag around the woman's bloody, swollen mouth. The sounds she made were incoherent moans and whispers.

He'd stripped her; his pattern there hadn't changed. Before Eve could give the order, Trueheart, his young, handsome face radiating compassion, lifted the thin bedspread from the floor to cover her shaking body.

'You're going to be all right now,' he said gently. 'You're safe now.'

'He hurt me. He hurt me.'

Peabody moved in, pulling the knotted sheet McQueen had used to bind the woman's hands from the hook screwed into the wall. 'He can't hurt you now.' Then she sat, drawing Julie against her to let her weep.

'He swore he wouldn't hurt me if Tray did what he said, but he did. He did. He raped me, and he hurt me. And he did this to me.'

Eve had already seen it, tattooed in bloody red over Julie's left breast, caged in a perfect heart.

'Bus is on the way,' Baxter told Eve. He angled away from the woman sobbing in Peabody's arms, spoke quietly. 'They'll have a rape counselor on the other end. Do you want me to call the sweepers to go through the place?'

It wouldn't matter, she thought. He wouldn't have left anything behind he hadn't intended to. But she nodded. 'Let the boyfriend know she's safe. He can go with her to the hospital. You and Trueheart step out, please. Peabody, get Julie some clothes. You can't put them on yet.' She stood at the foot of the bed, waited until Julie met her eyes. 'They'll have to examine you first, and we're going to have to ask you questions. I know it's hard. You should know Tray did everything he could to get to me as fast as possible, to get me back here.'

'He didn't want to leave. He begged him to let me go instead. He didn't want to leave me.'

'I know. His name is Isaac McQueen. He told you something, Julie, something he wanted you to pass on to me.'

'He said I wasn't right, wasn't . . . fresh, but he'd make an exception. I couldn't stop him. He hurt me, he tied my hands.' Quivering still, she held her arms out to show the raw bruising on her wrists. 'I couldn't stop him.'

'I know. Julie, I'm Lieutenant Dallas. Eve Dallas. What did Isaac want you to tell me?'

'Dallas? You're Dallas?'

'Yes. What did he want you to tell me?'

'He said to tell you that you owe it all to him. It's time to pay up. I want my mom.' She covered her face with her hands. 'I want my mom.'

It was foolish to feel useless. She could have done nothing to prevent what Julie Kopeski and Tray Schuster had endured. She could do nothing to change how that trauma would change them.

She knew Isaac McQueen's pathology, his particular style of torture. He was adept at instilling a sense of helplessness and hopelessness in his victims, at convincing them to do exactly what they were told, how they were told, when they were told.

She hadn't been one of his, but she understood the victimology as well.

She'd been someone else's.

It did no good to remember that, or to think about the girls she'd saved. Or the ones who'd been lost before, twelve years before, when she'd looked into the eyes of a monster and had known him.

Instead, she drew Tray aside at the hospital.

'They need to examine her, and Julie needs to talk to the rape counselor.'

'Oh God. God. I shouldn't have left her.'

'If you hadn't, she'd be dead, and so would you. She's alive. She's hurt and she's been violated, but she's alive. You're going to want to remember that, both of you, because alive's better. You said he was there when you woke up.'

'Yeah.'

'Tell me about that.'

'We overslept, or I thought . . .'

'What time did you wake up?'

'I don't know exactly. I think it was about eight. I rolled over thinking, "Holy shit, we're both going to be late for work." I felt off, strung out, like we'd partied hard the night before. But we didn't,' he said quickly. 'I swear. Julie doesn't even toke zoner.'

'We're going to need to screen both of you,' Eve began.

'I swear, we didn't use anything. I'd tell you. He gave Julie something, he said, but—'

'It's probable he drugged you both. We'll screen to see what he used. Nobody's going to hassle you about illegals, Tray.'

'Okay. Okay. Sorry.' He scrubbed hard at his face. 'I'm just screwed up. Can't think straight.'

'What did you do when you woke up?'

'I ... I told Julie to get moving, gave her a nudge, you know. She was really out. I kind of rolled her over, and I saw tape over her mouth. I thought she was pulling a joke, started to laugh. He was just there, man, that's all I know. He grabbed me by the hair, yanked my head back, and put a knife to my throat. He asked if I wanted to live. If I wanted Julie to live. He said there wasn't any need for anybody to get hurt. I just had to do what he told me. I should've fought back.'

'McQueen has a good seventy pounds on you, maybe more. He had a knife to your throat. If he'd killed you, do you think Julie would be alive?'

'I don't know.' Tears kept leaking out of his eyes, faster than he could swipe at them. 'I guess maybe not. I was scared. I told him we didn't have much money, but he could take whatever he wanted. He thanked me, real polite. That was scarier. He had some of those plastic restraints and told me to put them on, and to sit on the floor at the foot of the bed. So I did, and Julie's still out. He told me he'd given her something to make her sleep while the two of us got acquainted. He told me to hook the restraints to the leg of the bed, and handed me another set to put on my ankles. He put tape over my mouth. He said to sit and be quiet, and he'd be back in a minute.'

'He left the room?'

'I tried to get loose, but I couldn't.' Absently, he rubbed at the abrasions on his wrists. 'I could smell coffee. The bastard's

13

in the kitchen making coffee. He comes back with it, and with a bowl of cereal. He takes the tape off my mouth and sits down. He starts asking me questions while he has his freaking breakfast. How old am I, how old is Julie. How long have we been together, what are our plans. Have we had the apartment long. Did we know its history.'

Tray had to suck in a breath, let it out in a shudder. 'He kept smiling, and he's, like, earnest. Like he really wanted to get to know us.'

'How long did you talk?'

'He did most, and I don't know. It's, like, surreal, you know. He told me it was his apartment, but he'd been away a long time. He didn't like the color we'd painted the bedroom. Christ.'

He paused, looked at the exam room door. 'How much longer before I can go in?'

'It takes some time. Did Julie wake up?'

'He finished breakfast, and even took the dishes away. When he came back he gave her something else. I think I went crazy. I was screaming, I guess, and I tried to get loose. I thought he was going to kill her. I thought—'

'He didn't. Remember that.'

'I couldn't *do* anything. He slapped me a couple times. Not hard, just light taps. That was scary, too. He said if I didn't behave he'd, Jesus, he'd cut her left nipple off, and did I want to be responsible for that? He had one of these hooks Julie uses to hang plants and stuff, and he screwed it into the wall. He used the sheets to tie her up, and hung them over

14

it so she was sitting up when she came out of it. She was so scared. I could hear her trying to scream behind the tape, and she was struggling against the sheets. Then he put the knife to her throat, and she stopped.

'He said, "That's a good girl." He said to me that two things could happen. He could cut Julie, nipples, fingers, ears, little pieces of her could fall on the bedroom floor until she was dead. Or I could have one hour to go to the Homicide Division of Cop Central and speak to Lieutenant Eve Dallas, deliver a message, and bring her back. If I took longer, he'd kill Julie. If I spoke to anyone else, he'd kill Julie. If I tried to use a 'link instead of talking to you in person, he'd kill Julie. I told him I'd do anything he wanted, but to please let her go. Let Julie go deliver the message instead of me.'

He had to rub fresh tears from his eyes. 'I didn't want to leave her with him. But he said if I asked that again, or anything else, if I questioned him in any way, he'd take the first piece off her so I learned my lesson. I believed him.'

'You were right to believe him, Tray.'

'He told me what to say, made me repeat it over and over while he held the knife on Julie. He cut me loose, kicked some clothes and the flips over. Sixty minutes, he said. If it took sixty-one, she'd be dead because I couldn't follow instructions. I had to run. I didn't have money or plastic or credits, nothing for a cab, for a bus. Maybe if I'd gotten another cop, quicker, he wouldn't have had time to hurt her.'

'Maybe. And maybe he'd have slit her throat. That doesn't

take much time. She's alive. I know this man, and you can believe me when I tell you he could have done worse.'

She pulled out her card, passed it to him. 'You're going to want to talk to someone about what happened to you. Someone who's not a cop. You can tag me when you're ready, and I'll give you some names.'

She walked away, thinking of paperwork. She'd wished for murder, she remembered, and had gotten worse.

At Central, Eve used the bullpen for a brief, gritty briefing on Isaac McQueen.

'The subject is a thirty-nine-year-old male, brown and blue – though he changes both regularly. Six feet, three inches, at two hundred and twenty pounds. He has studied and is adept at hand-to-hand, including several areas of martial arts, and he kept in shape in prison.'

She flashed his prison ID on screen, studied the lines a dozen years in a cage had dug into his face. Women found him handsome and charming, she knew, with his slow, flirtatious smile. Young girls trusted his almost feminine features, the full shape of his lips, the twinkle of dimples.

He used that, all of that, to lure his prey.

'He favors knives as weapons and as a means of intimidation. His mother was an addict, a grifter of considerable skill who taught him the ropes. They had an incestuous relationship, often working a mark as a couple. She also fed his addiction for young girls. Together they abducted, raped, tortured, and subsequently sold or disposed of their victims until

Alice McQueen's body was pulled out of the Chicago River in the fall of 2040. Her throat had been slashed. Though McQueen never admitted to the murder, he is believed responsible. He would have been nineteen.

'He is also believed responsible for the abduction of at least ten minor females in the Philadelphia and Baltimore areas, and the murder of Carla Bingham, Philadelphia, and Patricia Copley, Baltimore. Both women, ages forty-five and forty-two, respectively, were addicts McQueen partnered with, lived with, and hunted with during his time in those cities. Both were found in rivers with their throats slit. Due to lack of evidence or lack of balls by the respective prosecuting attorneys, McQueen has never been charged with these crimes.'

But he did them, she thought. And more yet.

'Between 2045 and 2048, he used New York as his hunting ground, partnered with Nancy Draper – age forty-four, funky-junkie. During this period he'd refined his skills, added some flourishes. He and Draper lived in an apartment on the Lower West Side, financing their habits and lifestyles by running games and identity theft and electronic fraud – other skills he'd developed. He no longer sold his prey, but kept them. Twenty-six girls between the ages of twelve and fifteen were abducted in New York, raped, tortured, beaten, and brainwashed. He kept them shackled in a room in the apartment. The apartment itself was soundproofed, with the prison area shuttered. During his New York phase, he tattooed his vics, with the number indicating their abduction status inside a heart over the left breast. Twenty-two were found in that room.'

And she could see them still, every one.

'The remaining four have never been found, nor have their bodies been recovered. Even their identities are unknown as he often preyed on runaways.

'He is a highly intelligent and organized sociopath, a predatory pedophile, a narcissist with the ability to assume numerous personas. He uses his mother-substitutes for support, cover, for ego, then eliminates them. Nancy Draper's body was recovered from the Hudson River two days after his capture. She'd been dead for three days. It's likely McQueen was preparing to move on, either out of New York or simply to a new partner.'

She favored the new-partner theory, always had.

'He confessed to nothing, even after intense interrogation. He was convicted on multiple counts of kidnapping, forced imprisonment, rape, battery, and was sentenced to consecutive life sentences without possibility of parole on-planet, at Rikers, where the reports state he was a model prisoner.'

She heard one of her men give a sound of disgust and derision, and since she felt the same, made no comment.

'Right up until yesterday, when he slit the throat of a medical and escaped. Since that time he returned to his former apartment, bound the couple living there, threatened them, and after forcing the male vic to leave to find me, beat and raped the female, leaving her with the heart tattoo numbered twenty-seven.

'He left them alive because he wanted them to deliver messages. He's back, and he intends to pick up where he left off. This isn't homicide,' she added. 'It's not officially our investigation.'

She saw Baxter straighten at his desk. 'LT—'

'But,' she continued in the same tone, 'when a fuck like McQueen sends me a message, I'm going to pay attention. I expect every one of you to do the same. Read his file. Take his picture. Whatever you're working on, whoever you're talking to – a wit, a weasel, a vic, a suspect, another cop, the guy selling you a soy dog from the corner glide-cart, you show it. Keep your eyes and ears open. He's already hunting for number twenty-eight.'

She headed to her office – she needed a minute – and only closed her eyes briefly when she heard Peabody's footfalls behind her.

'I have to write up the report, Peabody, and touch base with the commander. Read the file.'

'I've read the file. I studied the case, in depth, when I was at the Academy. You were barely out of the Academy yourself when you found him. Still in uniform. It was your first major collar. You—'

'I was there, Peabody. I remember the details.'

Peabody's dark eyes stayed steady, her square face sober. 'You know who he is, what he is, how he is. So you know he broke pattern to send you a message. You cost him twelve years, Dallas. He's going to come after you.'

'Maybe, but I'm not his type. I went through puberty a

long time ago. I'm not naive, stupid, or defenseless. It's a lot more likely he'll consider it a competition – he needs to beat me. And there's a city full of young girls for him to pluck from to make me pay for those dozen years.'

Tired, she sat. 'He doesn't want me dead, Peabody, at least not right off. He wants to show me he's smarter than I am. He wants to humiliate me, at least for a while. That's how he'd see this, a humiliation for me when he starts his new collection.'

'He'd have studied you. He thinks he knows you, but he doesn't.'

'He will, before it's over. Look, we're getting tight on time. Go change into your uniform.'

'We can postpone the ceremony, start working the case.'

Though having a medal pinned on her chest was the last thing Eve wanted with Tray Schuster's grieving face and Julie Kopeski's shock-glazed eyes in her head, she shook her head.

'We're not postponing anything, and it's not our case.' But she intended to make a hard pitch for it. 'Now get out of my hair. I have to change, too. You're not the only one getting a medal today.'

'I know it's not your first. Is it still a big deal to you?'

'This one is. This one's big. Now go away.'

Alone, she sat a moment. Peabody was right, she thought, McQueen didn't know her. She wasn't humiliated. She was sick – in the heart and the belly, in the mind. And thank God, she realized, she was working her way toward pissed.

She'd work better angry.

20

# 2

In the locker room with its familiar perfume of sweat and soap and someone's cheap aftershave, Eve tied on the hard black uniform shoes. She hated them – always had – but regulation was regulation. She flexed her toes a moment, then pushed off the bench, reached for her uniform cap. Turning to the mirror, she fixed it squarely on her head.

She could see herself as she'd been a dozen years before, green as spring, with a shine on her shield and on those damned hard black shoes.

A cop, then and now, without any question, any hesitation over what she was meant to be. Had to be. She'd thought she'd known, but she hadn't known, really hadn't begun to know what she would see and do, what she would learn and come to accept. What she would live through and live with.

A lot of corners turned, she thought, and one sharp, jagged corner had been turned the moment she'd stepped into apartment 303 at 258 Murray one sweltering day in late September barely six weeks after she'd graduated from the Academy.

She remembered the fear, the coppery smear of it in her throat, and she remembered the horror like a red haze.

Would she do anything differently now, now that she did know, now that she was no longer green? She couldn't say, she decided, and wondered why she'd ask herself the question.

She'd done the job. That was all any cop could do.

She heard the outer door open, stepped away from the mirror, shut her locker. And when she turned, there he was.

She'd told him not to change his schedule, but then Roarke most often did what suited him. Seeing him settled her, brushed away the question she couldn't answer, dimmed the light on the past she wished she could will away.

He smiled at her – beautiful, just fucking beautiful in his slick business suit, the black mane of his hair gleaming nearly to his shoulders.

She knew every plane and angle of that amazing face, every line of the long, rangy body. And still, there were times just looking at him stole her breath as nimbly as the thief he'd once been.

'I love a woman in uniform.' Ireland wove through his voice like a shimmer of silver.

'The shoes suck. I told you that you didn't have to come. It's just a formality.'

'It's so much more, Lieutenant, and I wouldn't miss it for worlds. When I think of all the years I spent dodging cops, and never once considered how bloody sexy a woman could be in dress blues. Or maybe it's just my woman. My cop.'

He stepped forward, brushing his thumb over the shallow dent in her chin as he lifted her face. He kissed her, very lightly, and his stunning blue eyes searched hers. 'What's wrong?'

'It's just work.' He saw, she knew, what others didn't. 'Something came up.'

'You've caught a case?'

'Not exactly. I don't have time to get into it right now. But I'm glad you came. It won't take long. You'll only have to put off buying a couple third-world countries and listen to the mayor make a boring speech.'

'Well worth the price.' He kept his hand on her face a moment. 'You'll tell me later then.'

'Yes.' She would. She could. He was another corner turned, the biggest and the best. She'd met him at another ceremony, one for the dead, she the primary investigator on a murder, he a suspect with a shady past, a dubious present. A man with the face of a fallen angel and more money and power than the devil himself.

Now he was hers.

She took his hands, felt the shape of his wedding ring against her palm. 'It's a long story.'

'We'll make time for it.'

'Later.' She shrugged it off. 'You're right. This is more than a formality. It's important for Peabody, and for Detective Strong. The moment's more than the medal, and a hell of a lot more than the boring speech. They earned it.'

'And you, Lieutenant.'

She spoke her earlier thoughts. 'I did the job.'

She walked with him to the door. It opened even as she

reached for it. Peabody's main squeeze, Ian McNab, stood, not in the usual wild colors and patterns of the fashionable e-geek, but in spiffy dress blues. He'd even tucked his long tail of blond hair under the cap.

He said, 'Hey, Dallas, looking tight. Roarke, glad you made it.'

'Ian, I barely recognize you. You look very official.'

'Gotta do what you gotta. The shoes bite.'

'So I hear.'

'I swung in to let you know they decided to move the deal outside, front steps of Central.'

'Oh, shut up.'

Understanding glinted in his green eyes. 'The mayor wanted more exposure for the cops that took down Renee Oberman's ring, and for himself if you ask me. You figure it's going to get another big bounce in the media. Good cops against bad cops and all that. Anyway, Peabody's at her desk.' He jerked a thumb over his skinny shoulder. 'With her head between her knees. Maybe you could smooth her out so she doesn't boot when the mayor pins the medal on her.'

'Oh, for Christ's sake.'

She strode out, long and lanky in the uniform, into the bullpen, and over to Peabody's desk.

'Pull yourself together, Detective. You're embarrassing yourself, and more important, you're embarrassing me.'

'They're going to do it outside. In public.'

'So the fuck what?'

'Public,' Peabody said, head still between her knees.

'You're being honored by this department and this city for having the integrity, the courage, and the skill to take out a blight on this department and this city. Dirty, murdering, greedy, treacherous cops are sitting in cages right now because you had that integrity, courage, and skill. I don't care if they do this damn thing in Grand Central, you *will* get on your feet. You will *not* puke, pass out, cry like a baby, or squeal like a girl. That's a goddamn order.'

'I had more of a "Relax, Peabody, this is a proud moment" sort of speech in mind,' McNab murmured to Roarke.

Roarke shook his head, grinned. 'Did you now? You've a bit to learn yet, haven't you?'

'Sir.' With an audible gulp, Peabody got to her feet.

'Jesus, you're green and sweaty. Go splash some cold water on your face.'

''Kay.'

'Peabody. Damn it, you earned this. So suck it up, straighten up, and take what you earned with some pride. If you can't do it out of pride, then do it out of fear, because I swear to God I'll kick your ass hard and I'll kick it long if you—'

She broke off as she spotted movement, saw the faces. She thought, *Crap*.

'Don't let us interrupt,' Phoebe Peabody said with a breezy smile.

'Mom?' Despite the direct order, Peabody squealed like a girl. 'Dad. You came! You came all the way to New York.'

She launched herself at them, jumped up and down in their arms in her uniform shoes.

'We ran into traffic or we'd have been here sooner.' Sam Peabody closed his dreamy gray eyes and hugged his daughter hard. 'Everybody sends love. We wanted to deliver it.'

'You're here. You're here.'

'Where else would we be?' Phoebe tipped Peabody's face back, and her pretty face went soft as silk. 'Look at my sweet girl. My sweet, brave girl. We're so proud of you.'

'Don't, don't. You'll make me cry, and I'm not allowed to. Under orders.'

'So we heard.' Tossing back her long, dark hair Phoebe stepped over, gave Eve a hug and a kiss on the cheek. The quick laugh said Phoebe knew the display of affection embarrassed Eve. 'You look formidable in uniform. And sexy. Doesn't she, Sam?'

'She does.'

She got another hug and kiss, right in her own bullpen. Free-Agers, she thought, they just had to spread the love.

She could only sigh with relief when they turned their attention to McNab and Roarke.

'They never wanted me to be a cop,' Peabody said quietly, and drew Eve's attention. 'They love me, and they wanted me safe and home. But they love me, and they let me go. They came to see me get this commendation. I won't puke or pass out.'

'Good. Take off after the ceremony, spend some time with them.'

'But McQueen—'

'Not our case. Yet. Take the time, Peabody. Things could

be bad for a while, so take the good while you've got the chance.'

She stood on the steps of Central in air damp and steamy from the morning storm. Maybe she'd have preferred a more private venue for the ceremony – less media, less fuss – but Peabody deserved the moment. As did Detective Strong, who stood with them, braced on crutches.

They'd pulled the crowd the mayor hoped for, with plenty of reporters, fellow cops, family, the simply curious. She let the boring speeches roll over her while she scanned.

Nadine Furst, of course, front and center with the media corps. She wouldn't miss the story, or stint on friendship. She saw Mira, dressed in one of her lovely suits, and reminded herself to speak to the department's top profiler and shrink about Julie and Tray.

Peabody's parents, holding hands. Mavis, her oldest friend, stood with them, along with her husband and baby.

She hadn't expected them. Apparently playing down this whole medal business hadn't worked. Obviously, she thought, as she spotted Crack – hard to miss a giant, tattooed black guy with feathers hanging from his ears. And beside him stood Charles, the slick former licensed companion, along with his new bride, the dedicated Dr. Louise Dimatto.

She felt a flutter of mild horror as she watched Trina elbow her way up to Mavis, nuzzle baby Bella, then shoot Eve a narrowed, critical look.

Jesus, it wasn't as if anybody could even *see* her hair under the cap. Anybody but Trina, she decided. She suspected the hair-and-skin tech had X-ray vision.

Eve looked away, found Roarke, decided she felt more comfortable looking at him.

Who wouldn't?

Then she experienced sheer shock as she was damn sure she caught a glimpse of a bony figure in black. Summerset, Roarke's majordomo, pain in her ass, walking cadaver, here?

Maybe she was hallucinating due to interminable-speech boredom.

Every cop in her division attended, and as per her request stood on the steps. As did Feeney, her former trainer, partner, and current captain of the Electronic Detectives Division. His hangdog face remained sober, but she thought his eyes were a little glazed.

Imagined hers might be, too.

She tuned in again at the sound of applause, slid her gaze toward Commander Whitney as he joined the mayor. He, too, wore dress blues. She thought, as she often did, of the street cop he'd been before he'd taken the chair.

They moved to Strong. The mayor spoke quietly to her about her service, her injuries, fixed the medal on her chest.

The process repeated with Eve. She didn't have anything – particularly – against the mayor. But Whitney's handshake meant more than a politician's words to her.

'Well done, Lieutenant.'

'Thank you, sir.'

Now came the pride as the mayor spoke Peabody's name.

Integrity, honor, courage. She let the smile come – what the hell – as she heard Peabody's voice, just a little shaky, accept the congratulations and gratitude.

For a moment it was okay – the time, the fuss, even the round of photo ops. Because she stood with two good cops, and the man she loved so much it made her stupid was smiling at her.

The milling began – shoulder slaps, handshakes. She caught the glint in Peabody's eye, and fired one back.

'No hugging. Cops don't hug.'

Peabody tracked her gaze to Strong, currently being hugged by another cop.

'She sustained injuries.'

'Okay, but in my mind you're getting a giant hug and a big, sloppy kiss.'

'Keep it in your head or you'll sustain injuries.'

Feeney stepped up to her, his uniform cap pulled low over his explosion of ginger and silver hair. 'Nice work, kid.' He gave her the acceptable cop hug – a punch on the shoulder.

'Thanks.'

'Thought the mayor would never shut up, but all in all, it's a damn good deal.'

Peabody got her hug and big sloppy, with the addition of a pat on the ass from McNab.

'Yeah, it's a damn good deal.' She spotted Roarke making his way to her, and feared she'd get a hug – and more – despite her call for dignity.

But instead he simply took her hand in both of his. In his

eyes she saw something that made her own sting. She saw pride.

'Congratulations, Lieutenant.' He tapped the medal with a fingertip. 'It suits you. And to you, Ryan,' he said to Feeney, 'for your part in making her the cop she is.'

Feeney's color came up, as it did when he was pleased or embarrassed. 'Well, she had the raw material. I just had to kick it into shape here and there.'

'He did plenty of that,' Eve began. 'I think he—'

She broke off. She saw him, just a glimpse, just a flash. The handsome face, the jailhouse pallor. Sunshades, sandy hair slicked back, a smart gray pinstriped suit, royal-blue tie.

'Jesus Christ.'

She sprang forward, but the crowd swallowed them both. One hand on the butt of her weapon, Eve muscled her way through, craning her neck. Cops and civilians swarmed around her; the noise of downtown rolled over streets and sidewalk. An ad blimp blasted out a jingle for a sale at the Skymall.

Roarke snaked his way through to where she stood on the sidewalk, one hand still on her weapon, the other fisted in frustration.

'What is it?'

'I saw him. He was here.'

'Who?'

'McQueen. Isaac McQueen.' She shook her head. 'Son of a bitch. I have to report to the commander.'

'I'll wait. Go,' he said. 'I'll make your excuses to Mavis and the rest. And Eve.' He laid a hand on her arm. 'I want to hear about this – all of it – when you're done.'

Commander Whitney still wore the uniform, as did Eve, when she walked into his office. He stood behind his desk, a big man who carried the weight of command well on strong shoulders. His dark eyes, cop's eyes, measured her before he nodded.

'You're sure?'

'Yes, sir. He wanted me to see him, wanted me to know he could walk right through a sea of cops outside this house. He needs to insult and humiliate this department, and me in particular. I need to put a team together, Commander, *asap,* and find him.'

'He's being hunted, Lieutenant, by the NYPSD, and the FBI.' He held up a hand before she could speak. 'I understand you want him, and want a piece of the hunt. I'm not going to tell you not to use your considerable knowledge of McQueen, and your resources to aid the search. The fact is he wants you as much as you want him, and I suspect has given you a great deal more thought over these past years than you've given him.'

'I know him, Commander.' The frustration she'd felt on the street wanted to bubble back to the surface. 'Better than any cop in the NYPSD, better than anyone in the FBI. I made it my business to know him. I don't want to wait until he kills someone to make him my priority.'

'Do you believe he'll contact you again?'

'Yes, sir, he will.'

'Then we'll take it from there. In the meantime put together everything you know about him, run your probabilities, use your resources. I expect a full report from the warden, the chief administrator, the prison psychiatrist in charge of McQueen's case, and the guards on his block by morning. You'll be copied.'

'He has a plan. He always has a plan. He didn't walk out of Rikers without one. I want to interview other prisoners he had regular contact with, and the guards. I need access to his records, his visitor's list, his communications.'

'The prison's conducting an internal investigation.'

'Commander, he's been out for nearly twenty-four hours.'

'I'm aware of that, Lieutenant. I wasn't informed about the escape until this morning.' He waited a beat, nodded slowly. 'The mayor and I had more to discuss today than handing out medals, however well deserved. Prison administration has requested until nine hundred to conduct their investigation. They've been given the time. I can promise you at one minute past nine tomorrow, you'll have what I have.'

'They're playing politics and CYA. By nine tomorrow, he could have taken another girl. More than one.'

'I'm aware of that as well.' He sat now. 'Even after we're given what we need, we may not know anything to aid in this manhunt. His previous capture involved solid police work, Dallas, and a stroke of luck. We're going to need both to put him back where he belongs.'

★

32

She took time to change, to gather up all the file discs she needed, the old reports. Even then she could still taste the bitterness in the back of her throat.

As arranged, Roarke met her by her vehicle in the garage.

'Here, let's have those.' He took one of the loaded file bags she carried. 'I'd've helped to carry these down if you'd told me you were loading up.'

She wanted to say it was her weight to carry, but that sounded pompous. 'I didn't realize there was so much.'

Not entirely true, she thought, and let him take the wheel. There was more yet on Isaac McQueen, stored in her home office.

'First, I should tell you I declined a number of invitations for drinks, dinner – and/or a mag, drunken partython at the venue of your choice.'

The last would be Mavis, Eve deduced. 'Sorry.'

'No need. You have a lot of people proud of you today, and who understand you've work to see to. Peabody's parents plan to stay a day or two, and hope to see you again before they leave the city.'

'Yeah, that'd be good.' She drummed her fingers on her knee.

'How did it go with Whitney?'

'About like I expected. Less than I want.'

'From the heft of those bags, I'd say it's going to be a busy night.'

'I won't get data from the prison until morning. Isaac McQueen. He's—'

'I looked him up while you were with Whitney, so I have the salients. Twenty-six girls. And then there was you. I want to hear it, Eve, from you.'

'I'll tell you all of it. I guess I need to. But I have to clear my head. I have to settle it down. He could be anywhere.' She stared at the streets, the sidewalks, the buildings, the ever-moving crowds. 'Anywhere. I want to be out there, looking, but it's a waste of time and energy. I have to think, and I can't think until I get my head straight. I need to work some of this off, sweat a little. Take an hour in the gym.'

'With a sparring droid you can beat up?'

She smiled, a little. 'Not quite that much.'

'Take your hour. Then we'll talk.'

She remained silent until he drove through the gates, down the long curve of the drive to the beautiful house with its towers, its turrets, its unique style.

He'd built this, she thought. This house. This home. Her home now, too – and that was something else that could steal her breath.

'I didn't have anyone to talk to about it before. I hadn't started training with Feeney, hadn't met Mavis. I didn't think I needed or wanted anyone to talk to about it. I think now, this time, if I didn't, I might go a little crazy. I don't know if I could take going back alone.'

'You're not.' As he had at Central, he took her hand in both of his. 'And never again alone.' This time with his eyes on hers, he brought her hand to his lips. 'Take your hour. Go on, I'll get your file bags.'

He knew, she thought, because he'd read about McQueen, that she needed time and understood why. She wasn't sure what she'd done in her life to earn someone who understood her so well.

She stepped inside.

Then again, nothing came free.

Summerset stood in his stiff, funeral-black suit, his face stern as a headstone – and the fat cat, Galahad, squat at his feet.

'I find I can still be shocked,' he said. 'You're home nearly on time, and unbloodied.'

'Day's not over. You know I thought I saw a dead man walking a couple hours ago. Did you have to go downtown for some eye of newt?'

He lifted his eyebrows. 'I have no idea what you're talking about. I prefer doing my shopping uptown.'

'Must've been another corpse.' She strode by him, opted to take the elevator down to the gym.

Thinking the lieutenant had looked quite impressive in her uniform, standing on Central's wide steps, Summerset walked over to open the door for Roarke.

And lifted his eyebrows at the file bags. 'I take it any celebratory dinner is on hold.'

'It is, yes. An old adversary come round again. It's troubling,' Roarke said as he started upstairs with the cat trotting after him.

She ran three miles, hard, selecting an urban setting, so the program simulated the sound of her feet pounding on pavement, the buzz of traffic – street and air.

She set another program for weights and pumped until her muscles wept. When that wasn't enough, she showered off the sweat in the bathroom attached to the expansive gym.

She'd do a couple dozen fast laps in the pool, she decided, and burn off the last of this ugly frustration and sick fear.

She didn't bother with a bathing suit, but just grabbed a towel. More than the hour she'd asked for, she noted, but she wasn't quite there yet.

When she stepped out into the tropical paradise of the pool area, wound through the trees, the flowers, she saw him sitting at a table. He'd changed into a T-shirt and casual pants. He had a bottle of wine, a couple of glasses – and worked with apparent enjoyment on his PPC.

Waiting for her, she thought. Wasn't that a miracle? This amazing man would wait for her, would be there.

She hadn't needed the three miles, she realized, or the weights or the laps. All she needed was Roarke.

'There you are.' He glanced up. 'Better?'

'I took longer than I said. I got caught up.'

'No matter. I had a bit of work to finish up, and had a swim as well.'

'Oh. I was thinking you'd take one with me.'

'Well, I could, but I always enjoy watching you in the water, especially since you like to swim naked.'

'Pervert.' She walked to him. 'Why don't you come in? Unless watching's all you're up for.'

She let the towel drop.

'When you put it that way.'

Rather than diving in as was her habit, she walked down the steps, through the lagoon corner, ordering on the jets and blue lights as she slowly sank in.

'I was going to burn the rest off with some laps,' she said as Roarke shed his clothes. 'But I figure you can do a better job of it. Maybe.'

'A challenge.' He joined her in the water. 'Something else I'm always up for.'

She tipped her head back, shot her fingers in his hair, gripped it. 'Prove it,' she said, and dragged his mouth to hers.

She wanted hot and hard, like the jets pulsing in the blue water. No tenderness, no gentle caress, but greedy and careless.

He knew, he always knew. She set her teeth on his shoulder as his hands took, rough and ready, whipping her to the place where there was no room for thoughts, for worries, for a world of the cruel.

His mouth, his mouth, scorching her skin, devouring her heart right through her breast while his hand shoved between her legs. The first orgasm ripped her as he dragged her under the water.

Breathless, blind, she sank into the pool, into him and the battering sea of sensation. Only to surface on a wild cry of release when he pulled her up again.

She wrapped around him, slick with water, hot with needs. Her hands and mouth were as busy as his, as demanding and urgent. The trouble he'd seen in her eyes, the sadness he'd sensed coiled in her dropped away. With them went his worry, went everything but this mad, almost brutal wanting.

Snared in it, he shoved her to the wall. His fingers dug into her hips as he plunged into her.

Breathless gasps muffled against his mouth. He wanted to swallow them, swallow her in deep, dark gulps. The water slapped and slithered, sluiced off skin faintly and eerily blue in the light.

'Take more.' Steeped in her. Drowning in her. 'Take more.'

*Yes,* she thought, *yes. More.* Gripping the edge, she wrapped her legs around his waist. Arching up, arching back, she took until her cries echoed around the garden. Took until there was nothing left.

# 3

He knew if it was left up to Eve they'd have the conversation and what passed for a meal in her home office. Another case, he decided, where she needed more. As summer refused to retire for the season, he arranged for the meal on one of the terraces, where the gardens burst with color and scent.

There, with the air stubbornly holding the damp from the morning's storm, tiny lights glimmered, candles flickered against the dark.

'I've got a lot of research to get to,' she began.

'Undoubtedly, and we'll take all the time you need once I understand the situation, and you've got some food in you. Red meat.' He lifted the cover off a plate.

Eve eyed the steak. 'Playing dirty.'

'Is there another way? We've a barrel of salt for your fries.'

She had to laugh. 'Really dirty.' She took the wine he offered. 'You know my weaknesses.'

'Every one.' And he hoped the pretty table, the pretty evening would help her through what she had to tell him. 'I'll wager you missed lunch.'

She sipped, sat. 'I had to hack away at paperwork all

morning, and kept thinking if I just had a body, I could skate out of it. It's that *careful what you wish for* bit. Sucks that it's usually true.'

She told him about Tray and Julie, then of the prison administration dragging their feet on notification of McQueen's escape. Bookending the worst of it, she supposed. Building up to going back.

'He wants your attention.'

'And he's got it. He'll keep it until he's back in a cage. He should've been transferred to an off-planet facility six years ago when Omega was complete. But . . .'

She shrugged, continued to eat.

'They never charged him with the murders. His mother, the girls never recovered, the other women?'

'No. Not enough evidence, especially if you're a PA more concerned with your conviction rate than actual justice.'

'You were disappointed,' Roarke commented.

'I was green.' She shrugged again, but with more of a jerk. 'I figured we had enough solid circumstantial on the four missing girls, on the dead mother, partners. We had enough to try him on those charges, too. But that wasn't my decision. That's not my job.'

'You're still disappointed.'

'Maybe, but I'm not green now, so I'm realistic. And McQueen wouldn't break. Feeney worked him for hours, days. He let me observe. He even brought me into the box briefly, hoping seeing me would shake, or just piss off McQueen enough for him to say something, make some mistake. And I'm getting ahead of myself,' she realized. 'I guess I'd better start at the beginning.'

'Twelve years,' he prompted her, wanting her to talk it out, for both of them. 'You'd barely begun.'

'I'm trying to remember me, to see myself. To feel. I wanted to be a cop so bad. A good cop, solid. To work my way up to detective. I wanted Homicide, that was always the goal. Homicide detective. I didn't really know anybody in the department, in the city for that matter. Most of the rookies who graduated with me were scattered around the boroughs. I got Manhattan, and that was big. I needed to be here.'

He topped off her wine, gave her a small opening. 'I think of the photo you gave me for Christmas, of you at your desk at the Academy. Hardly more than a child, and your hair long.'

'I'd hacked it off by the time I graduated.'

'You had cop's eyes even then.'

'I missed things. I had a lot to learn. I was working out of the Four-Six, Lower West. A little house. Central absorbed it, I guess, about eight years ago. It's a club now. The Blue Line. Weird.'

She paused when a thought struck her. 'You don't own it, do you?'

'No.' But he filed it away, thinking she might enjoy owning her first cop shop.

She drew a breath. 'Okay. So. I was only a few weeks on the job, on patrol or doing the grunt work they stick rooks with. It was hot, like this, late summer when you're wondering if it'll

41

ever cool off again. There was a mugging that went way, way south. A couple, in town visiting their daughter. She'd just had a baby. They're walking back to her place, did some shopping for the kid.

'Junkie, crashing, and he's got a six-inch sticker. They don't hand everything over fast enough, and he gives the woman a jab to hurry them up. One thing leads to another, and the man ends up dead with a dozen holes in him; the woman's critical, but conscious. Manages to call out until somebody stops. It's a decent enough neighborhood, and it's freaking broad daylight. But there just wasn't anybody around. Bad luck. Feeney caught the case.'

'That would be good luck,' Roarke prompted.

'Yeah. Jesus, Roarke, he was good. I know the e-work is his thing, and he's the best. But he was a hell of a murder cop. He didn't look that much different – less gray, not as many lines. But even back then he looked like he'd slept in his clothes for a couple nights running. Just watching him was an education. How he worked the scene, read it, read the wits.'

Looking back, seeing Feeney in her head, she settled a bit more. 'I stood there, watching him, and I thought, "That's what I want." Not just Homicide, but to be that good. He stood on the sidewalk with the blood and the body, and he saw it. He felt it. He didn't show it, hard to explain.'

'You don't need to.' Because he'd stood and watched her with blood and body, and knew she saw. Knew she felt.

'Well. The junkie went rabbit, and the wits gave conflicting descriptions. The surviving vic was mostly out of it, but we had a general to go on. They called in some uniforms to canvass because one of the wits said they thought maybe he lived right there on Murray, or knew somebody who did. I was partnered up with Boyd Fergus, a good beat cop. We ended up at two-fifty-eight Murray. We weren't getting anywhere. Nobody'd seen anything, and most of the people who lived in that neighborhood were at work anyway. So when we got to that building, Fergus said we'd split up, and since I was younger and had better legs, I should start up on three. He'd take the first floor, and we'd meet up again on two. It was just . . .'

'Fate?'

'Or luck, or what the fuck. But I headed up to the third floor.'

And she saw it. Felt it.

The old building trapped the hot like a steel box, then mixed it with the smell of the veggie hash – don't spare the garlic – someone was stirring up for dinner on the second floor. She could hear the various choices of evening entertainments vibrating against walls and doors. Trash rock, media reports, canned laughter from some sitcom, soaring opera banged and echoed dull through the stairway. Over it she heard creaks, voices, and somebody carping about the price of soy coffee.

She could relate.

She filed it all away, automatically taking note of the size and shape of the hallway, the exits, the window at the far end of the landing, the cracks in the ancient plaster.

It was important to pay attention, take in the details, know where you were. She appreciated Fergus for trusting her to do so, trusting her to handle the knock on doors on her own, even if it was just another routine.

Routines made up the whole, formed the structure for everything else. Boredom was a factor, sure, in the routine of knocking, identifying, questioning, moving on, and doing it all again and again. But whenever boredom tried to sneak in, she reminded herself she was a cop, she was doing the job.

For the first time in her life, she *was* someone.

Officer Eve Dallas, NYPSD.

She stood for something now. For someone. She climbed the stairs in the stuffy, noisy building for Trevor and Paula Garson.

Two hours before Trevor had been alive, Paula healthy. Now he was dead and she was struggling not to be.

And one of those knocks might, just might, result in information on the asshole who'd taken a life, broken all the lives connected to it.

So she knocked, identified herself, questioned, moved on.

At the second apartment, the woman who answered wore pajamas and exhausted eyes.

'Summer cold,' she told Eve. 'I've been trying to sleep it off.'

'You've been home all day?'

'Yeah. What's this about?'

'Two people were mugged in this vicinity approximately two hours ago. Did you see or hear anything unusual?'

44

'You know, maybe. Head cold's got me, so I can't taste anything, brain's fuzzy, and my ears are plugged up. But I thought I heard somebody screaming. Figured I imagined it, or it was from one of the neighbor's screens, but I looked out the window. I did see somebody running, but I didn't think anything of it, just went back to bed. God, was somebody hurt? This is a good neighborhood.'

'Yes, ma'am, someone was hurt. Could you describe the individual you saw running?'

'Maybe. I didn't really get a good look. That window.' She gestured. 'I'd come out to get a drink – lots of fluids – and thought maybe I'd try the couch awhile. I heard something, and walked over to look.'

'Do you mind if I come in?'

'No, sure. Better keep your distance. I'm probably contagious. Honestly, Officer, I was pretty out of it. All the meds, but I did see somebody running. That way.'

At the window, she pointed west. 'It was a man. Long hair, um, brown, I think. He was running away, but he did look over his shoulder. I think. He had a scruffy little beard.'

'Height, weight, skin color?'

'Oh. White, I think. Not black. I guess he looked sort of skinny. Shorts! He was wearing shorts. Knobby knees. And he was carrying a couple of bags, shopping bags. I remember because I thought, "Wow, he's in a hurry to get home with his loot." Jeez, it was someone else's loot.'

'Was it someone you've seen before?'

'I don't really think so. I'm usually at work during the day.

45

I only moved in a couple months ago, and don't really know anybody yet.'

Eve took the woman's name, her contact information, thanked her for her cooperation. She stepped out, intending to tag Fergus, inform him of the lead and her status.

She saw someone at the door of 303.

He had two shopping bags – local market, she noted – and set them down to uncode his door.

She noted the door had serious security, unlike the standard she'd observed in the rest of the building.

She filed away his approximate height, weight, what he wore as she approached. 'Excuse me, sir.'

He'd just opened the door, reached down for the bags. He straightened slowly, turned. She saw a beat of blank before his face transformed into polite curiosity.

'Officer. What can I do for you?'

'Are you the resident?'

'Yes, I am.' Now he beamed a smile. 'Isaac McQueen.'

'Are you just getting home for the day, Mr McQueen?'

'Actually, I ran out a short time ago to do some shopping.'

'Were you at home approximately two hours ago?'

'Yes, I was. Is there a problem?'

Something off, she thought, but didn't know what or why. She kept her eyes level on his as she walked toward him.

'There was a mugging.'

Distress covered his face, but it seemed to her he slipped it on like a mask. 'Is that what was going on? I saw the police around when I walked down to the market.'

'Yes, sir. Did you see or hear anything else?'

'Not that I can think of. I really should get these groceries put away.'

Something off, she thought again. Just ... something. 'I'd like to ask you some questions, just routine. May I come in?'

'Really, Officer ...'

'Dallas.'

'Officer Dallas, I don't see how I can help you.'

'I won't take up much of your time now, and it'll save you from another visit later so I can complete my report.'

'Fine. Anything to help the boys – and girls – in blue.' He stepped in, let her follow.

Big space, she thought, nicely furnished. Plenty of windows, all privacy screened. And the door to the left had a security lock and two hand bolts.

Yeah, something off.

'I need to get my fresh fruits and vegetables in the cooler,' he told her.

'No problem. This is a nice unit, Mr McQueen.'

'I like it.' He carried his bags to the kitchen, began to unload.

'Do you live alone?'

'At the moment.'

'Employment?'

'Is that relevant?'

'Just details for my report, sir.'

'I do e-work, freelance.'

'So you work at home.'

'Primarily.'

'Nice and quiet,' she commented.

Quiet, she thought, unlike the rest of the building. Why would a freelance e-man soundproof his apartment? Why would he have a room locked and bolted from the outside?

'Were you working two hours ago when the incident took place?'

'Yes, I was, which is why I didn't see or hear anything.'

'That's too bad because the window behind you has a direct view of the crime scene.' She glanced left. 'Is that your office?'

'That's right.'

'Mind if I take a look?'

'Yes, I'm afraid I do.' He continued to smile, but annoyance slithered through. 'My work is sensitive and confidential.'

'Requiring you to lock it up, from the outside.'

'Better safe than sorry. Now if that's all—'

'You said you live alone.'

'That's right.'

'That's a lot of food for one person.'

'Do you think so? But then you're very thin, aren't you? Officer Dallas, unless you believe I mugged a couple of people on the street a stone's throw from my own home, I'd like to get my food put away and get back to work.'

'I didn't say a couple of people.'

He sighed, hugely. 'You must have. Now, I'll show you out.'

As he came around the counter, walked toward her, she

shifted her balance, instinctively laid her hand on the butt of her weapon.

'Mr McQueen, I'm wondering why you wouldn't report a crime, or at the very least contact nine-one-one when a woman was screaming for help.'

'I told you I didn't see anything. And if I had, some of us choose not to get involved. Now—'

'You don't want to put your hand on me, sir.'

He held his up in a gesture of peace. 'And I don't want to contact your superior and report this harassment.'

'I'll contact my partner downstairs. He'll come up and you can report us both.' Fergus would kick her ass most likely, but *damn it* there was something here. So she pushed just a little harder. 'And then you can explain what's behind that door.'

'Officer Dallas.' His tone, his expression transmitted mild annoyance mixed with reluctant amusement. 'Have it your way.'

His fist rammed fast and hard. She dodged, but the punch glanced off the side of her cheekbone, and her face exploded with pain. The single stumble back gave him the time and space to kick the weapon she drew out of her hand.

She pivoted, her right hand numb, her face throbbing, swung into a spinning kick, followed it with a back fist. She landed both, would have tapped her communicator for assistance, but caught the glint of a knife.

Fear coated her throat as she barely evaded the first vicious jab.

'Scream if you want.' He smiled, but she saw – somehow

49

recognized – the monster behind it. 'No one can hear. And your 'link, any com devices?' He jabbed again, almost playfully. 'They won't work in here. I've got jammers activated. You should have listened to me, Officer Dallas. I gave you every opportunity to leave.'

He blocked her kick, sliced out with the knife and scored her shoulder.

He outweighed her, had a longer reach and a weapon. Combat training, she judged, as she used her own to dodge, to weave, to land a blow or two.

Fergus would contact her, and unable to tag her come looking.

But she couldn't depend on backup. All she had was herself.

'You wanted to see what was in my workroom. I'm going to show you when we're done. I'll show you where the bad girls go.'

She threw a lamp at him. Pitiful, she thought, but it gave her a little room.

This time when he sliced, she went in low, plowed her fists into his balls, her head into his belly. She felt the knife catch another piece of her, but came up hard with an uppercut, jammed her knee into his already tender crotch.

She tried a body takedown, and he flung her across the room.

'That *hurt*!' Outrage reddened his face, stripped away all amusement. 'You skinny bitch, you're going to pay for that.'

Her ears rang. Her vision blurred. She thought, *no,* she'd

be damned if she'd die this way. She was going to make god-damn detective.

She shifted her weight and balance, came up with both feet. When he staggered back she scrambled up and behind a chair. Time to catch her breath. She was hurt, knew she was hurt. Couldn't think about it. He'd kill the hell out of her unless she evened the odds.

'I'm a cop.' She tasted blood along with the fear. 'Dallas, Officer Eve. And you're under arrest. You have the right to remain silent.'

He laughed. Laughed and laughed, with blood running from his split lip. He came forward, passing the knife from hand to hand. 'You're a feisty one, and entertaining. I'm going to keep you alive for a long, long time.'

For an instant she saw two of him and thought, fleetingly, she might have a concussion. Closer, she thought, let him get closer. Let him think she was finished.

Then she shoved the chair hard into his knees, and dived.

She rolled, came up with her weapon. As he leaped toward her, she fired. He jerked back, kept coming. She fired again. 'Go down, you fucker!' And again.

She heard herself screaming when the knife dropped out of his hand, when he slid, shaking, to the floor.

'Son of a bitch, son of a bitch, son of a bitch.' She got to her knees, weapon still trained. She couldn't get her breath. Had to get her breath.

Training, routine. Kick the knife away, get out your restraints. Secure the prisoner.

She straightened, swayed as pain and nausea churned through her.

*Jesus, Jesus, I'm hurt.*

She couldn't say why she did it. Even years later she didn't know why she'd felt so compelled. She searched his pockets, found the key.

She staggered to the locked room even as her mind reeled off procedure. Go out, contact Fergus, call for backup. Officer needs assistance.

Sweet Jesus, officer needs assistance.

Instead, she dragged the bolts clear, managed after three tries to uncode the lock.

And she opened the door to hell.

'There were so many of them. Children, just girls, shackled, naked, covered in bruises, dried blood, God knows what. Most of them were huddled together. Eyes, so many eyes on me. The smell, the sounds, I can't tell you.'

She didn't know if she'd taken his hand or he'd taken hers, but the contact kept her grounded in the now, and a desperate step back from the horror.

'He'd put a couple chem toilets in there, some old blankets. There were cams up in the corners so he could monitor them. I didn't see any of that, not then. All I could see were girls and their eyes. I can still see them.'

'Take a break.'

She shook her head, tightened her grip on his hand. 'All at once, that's better. For a minute I went somewhere else. I'd buried those memories of my father, and that room in Dallas so deep. It was gone, all of that was just gone. But for a moment, standing there, with all the girls, all the eyes, I went back. The dirty red light from the sign flashing against the window glass. The cold, so cold. And the blood all over me. Not me, a child, but the child was me, and the pain was mine. For that moment it just poured back, poison down the throat. I froze. Just stood there, with part of me eight years old and covered with blood in that awful room.

'I started to go, just slide away, just slide to the floor, just slide back into that place I didn't really recognize. But one of the girls started screaming at me. *Help us. Do something. You bitch,* she said, *do something.* Her name was Bree Jones. She and her twin sister, Melinda, were the last taken, only a week before. A week in that hell. Well, some of them had endured it for years.'

'As you had,' he murmured.

'I didn't know, or couldn't know. Or wouldn't.' Eve closed her eyes a moment, focused on the warm, firm contact – Roarke's hand holding hers.

'But she screamed and shouted, yanking at the chains. And it brought me back. *Help us.* That was the job, to help, not to stand there frozen and shaking and sick. The others started screaming, shouting, crying. It didn't sound human. I went in. I wasn't thinking straight. I didn't have the keys to the shackles. I had to find the keys.'

She let go of his hand to rub both of hers over her face. 'Procedure, routine. I pulled it out, dragged it through the hell. It got me through. I told them I was the police, told them my rank and name, told them they were safe now. When I said I had to go out, get more help, they went crazy. *Don't leave us.* Begging me, cursing me, wailing like animals. But I had to. I had to get Fergus, get more cops, get medicals. Procedure, routine. It's the foundation. I left them. McQueen was coming around. I didn't even hesitate, just gave him another shock. Didn't think twice about it. I stepped out in the hall, and got Fergus on my communicator. I told him to call for backup and medicals. A lot of both. Multiple victims, apartment three-oh-three. He didn't ask questions, called it in while he came on the run. He was a good cop, a solid cop. I heard him running up the stairs when I went back to the room. I heard him say, "Mary, Mother of God." Like a prayer. I remember that, then it gets blurry for a while.'

She took a breath, another drink of wine. 'But we found the keys, and he found some sheets, some blankets for the girls. He stayed so calm, like a good dad, I guess. Soothing. Then procedure. Backup, medicals, getting identification and information. Feeney.'

She looked over the garden with its glimmering lights, drew in the fragrance of flowers she couldn't name.

'Feeney came in, sat down beside me while the MTs dealt with the cuts. All that controlled chaos around us, and he sits down, gives me a long look. You know how he does.'

'Yes,' Roarke murmured. 'I do.'

'"Well, kid," he said, "you caught the bad guy today, and saved some lives. Not a bad day's work for a rook." I was a little punchy. They'd given me some tranq before I could stop them. So I said, "Fuck that, Lieutenant. It's a good day's work for any cop." He just nodded, and asked me how many girls. I said twenty-two. I don't know when I counted. I don't remember counting.'

She swiped at tears she'd just realized streamed down her cheeks. 'God. I wouldn't go to the hospital. Big surprise. He took my oral report right there in McQueen's apartment. Two days later, I was reassigned as his aide. Homicide, Cop Central. In some twisted way, McQueen got me everything I wanted.'

'You're wrong. In every way, Eve, you got it for yourself. You saw something in him others hadn't, and maybe wouldn't have for a long time.'

She took his hand again, needed his hand again. 'I saw my father. I saw Richard Troy. I didn't know it, but I saw him when I looked at McQueen.'

'And saved twenty-two young girls.'

'For twelve years that was enough. Now it's not. He's already hunting, Roarke.'

She brought her gaze back to his. 'He'll have a place. If he doesn't have his partner already, he'll soon find one. He'll have transportation, probably a dark van. He broke out through the infirmary, so he'll have drugs – tranqs, paralytics. He'll change his appearance a little. His hair was lighter when I caught sight of him today. He's too vain to change it much, but he'll do subtle alterations. He'll dress well, fashionably, but nothing overdone. He'll look safe, attractive. And he'll be eager to start again. Julie gave him a release, but she's not what he's after. He'll need a girl, twelve, thirteen, or a young-looking fourteen or fifteen. If she's with friends or family he'll find a way to separate her. He'll lure her into the van, or give her just enough tranq to make her compliant.'

She needed to work, Roarke thought. To utilize data, logic, pattern, and step away from the emotion.

'How?' he asked. 'How would he finance or acquire transportation, a place, suitable clothing, and so on?'

'If it's convenient or necessary, he'll steal. Pick pockets. He's as good as you.'

'Please.'

'Okay, maybe not, and I'm going on reports and history anyway. We presumed he had money or funds stashed. The clothes, the electronics, the food and wine in his place? He had to have money, more than we found. He grifted, and well, a long time, and the e-fraud was lucrative. EDD couldn't find a trace of an account attached to him, other than the standard he had under his own name with a couple thousand in it. It's possible they missed it, but we figured he kept a stash, as he'd been trained to do as a kid. Just dig in, take the cash, and go.'

'Multiple caches would be smarter. All the eggs in one basket makes an expensive omelette if broken.'

'You'd know. If he had funds tucked away in New York, he'd have access by now. But ...'

'But?' Roarke prompted.

'I could see a stash, or a few. Running money, quick cash. But he's smart, greedy, like I said, he wants good clothes, good wine, all that. He knows his way around electronics.'

'He'd have that account – or likely accounts, you're thinking. Investments, letting his money make money.'

'Yeah, I figure that. His other priority would be the partner. He needs that attention, support, and someone to run interference.'

'The visitor's list, communications. She'd be in there, wouldn't she?'

'Has to be. He might escape on impulse and opportunity, but if he hadn't had a plan in place, he'd have gone underground until he had one.'

She paused a moment, let herself think it through now that her mind had cleared. 'They're looking for somebody running, hiding, even scrambling. He's not. He deliberately sought attention, so he's confident, secure. He's not on the run. Getting a hit off the BOLO we've got out on him would be sheer luck. He kept his first New York victim in that room for three years. She was strong. He lived there in a working-class neighborhood, on the third floor of a well-occupied building, and managed to transport his victims in, and we assume transport the bodies or remains of the ones who didn't survive out, without anyone seeing him. He won't go down easy.'

'I don't question your judgment, but will add that this time it's more than feeding his need, more than the girls. It's you. It's showing you up, paying you back. And payback is a distraction. It adds an element of risk that wasn't in play before.'

'It's a factor,' she agreed. 'And the break in his pattern complicates things for him more than us. Still, he's had twelve years to think it through, plan it out, refine the details. I have to catch up.'

'Then we'd better get started.' He rose, took her hand to bring her to her feet. 'You didn't take him down all those years ago just because you were lucky. You were smarter than he was, even then. He was stronger, had the advantage, but you didn't lose your head or panic. And you didn't stop. He may have had this time to plan and refine, but you've had it to hone your instincts, to build experience. And you have something else now you didn't have then.'

'You.'

'See how smart you are?' He brushed a kiss over her forehead. 'It'll give me pleasure to use my considerable resources, not to mention skills—'

'You just mentioned them.'

'So I did. In any case, I'll enjoy using them to help you put him away a second time, and for good. And I can start doing just that by accessing his visitors and communications logs from the prison.'

She opened her mouth, a knee-jerk refusal on the tip of her tongue. It wasn't as if she hadn't bent the rules before, but it never sat quite right. 'Yeah. Yeah, you do that. They've got no business stonewalling until tomorrow while they work on their spin. I don't care about their spin or the politics. I need to know who he's talked to, seen. I need it all. A few hours' jump on this might save some kid from being taken.'

They set up in Roarke's private office, with the unregistered equipment, shielded from the intrusive eye of CompuGuard. He walked to the wide, U-shaped command center, laid his palm on the security plate. 'This is Roarke. Power up.'

And the controls glittered like jewels against the sleek black console. Nothing accessed here could go in any report, not until the data came to her by proper and legal channels. But . . .

One of his shades of gray, she thought. He had more than she did, a thinner and more adjustable line. Still, all she had to do was remember all the girls, all those eyes inside that obscenity of a room, to step over to Roarke's side of it.

She sat at the auxiliary comp, called up her files. She'd need to set up a board, she worked better with visuals. But for now she'd take the time to refresh herself on all things Isaac McQueen.

She steeped herself in it, in the photographs, the data stream, the psychiatric reports, court transcripts. She surfaced when Roarke set a mug of coffee on the console beside her.

'The medical he killed yesterday had a wife and a two-year-old daughter.'

She nodded. 'You think I need to justify what I'm doing, or letting you do. Maybe sometime down the road I will. Right now I'm clear on it. I'm sidestepping politics.'

She looked up at him. He'd tied his hair back — work mode. 'I've got no problem with that.'

'All right, then. I have his visitors log, and the record of all approved communications. I imagine you've considered he communicated with someone outside by non-approved means. If so, he didn't use any variation of his own ID, or send or receive by anyone using any variation of those on the approved list. I'll look deeper.'

He leaned on the console, sipped from a mug of his own. 'I programmed a search for key phrases, repetitions. So far all the e-coms are innocuous. Answers to messages from reporters, writers, an inmate advocacy group. There's very little over a twelve-year period, which weighs on the side he found a way to skirt around approval.'

Eve drank coffee and considered. 'He's got the e-skills. He wouldn't make a mistake there, and he'd be very careful what he put on a hard drive. We stripped down his electronics before. Next to nothing. He's very careful. The way to the partner, if he's lined one up, would be through visitation. Face-to-face contact. Privacy rules, thanks to prison advocacy groups, prevent monitoring prisoner visitation. It'll be a woman, between forty and ... adding the twelve years in, probably more like between fifty and sixty. Attractive, with some sort of addiction or vulnerability he can exploit.'

'Nearly all his visitors were female. Data's copied to your unit.'

Eve called it up. Out of twenty-six visitors, eighteen were women, and most of them repeat visitors.

'I get the reporters – after a juicy story, maybe a big book deal or vid. He'd probably string them along awhile, get them to come back, entertain him. Tell them nothing. But the rest? What did they get out of spending time with him, knowing what he'd done, what he is? I don't – Jesus, Melinda Jones.'

'Yes.'

'August, 'fifty-five. About five years ago. Single visit. I need to run her.'

'I did. She's a rape and trauma counselor, attached to the Dallas police department, where her sister is a cop who just made detective. They share an apartment, live only a few miles from their parents, and the home where they grew up. She's single, and she's clean.'

'Okay. She'd have been about nineteen when she made this visit.'

'Facing her monster.'

'Maybe. Probably. I'll have to contact her, see what he said to her. She's not his type now. Too old for his tastes, too young for partner status. A rape counselor and a cop. They made something out of what happened to them. It's good to know that.'

She scanned down the list. 'Multiple visits would be the highest probability. Not too many. No point in sending up a flag.'

She ordered the computer to separate out names of subjects who'd visited between six and twelve times. 'We'll start with these.'

'I'll take four.'

They ran them for data, put images on screen.

'Computer, delete subjects three, five, and eight. Too

many busts,' she told Roarke. 'He wouldn't work with someone who screwed up that often and got caught. And since subject two is now deceased, we can toss her out of the mix. Down to four,' she said as she paced. 'Number one, Deb Bracken, has a New York address, so we'll check her out in person. The other three are scattered around. Miami, Baltimore, and Baton Rouge. We'll have local authorities give them a look once we're cleared.

'There's something about this one. Number seven.'

'Sister Suzan Devon,' Roarke read. 'Recovering illegals addict. Two busts for possession, one for solicitation without a license.'

'Yeah, but the busts are in her misspent youth. Nothing since she hit thirty. She's the right age. Early fifties, not bad looking. Member of the Church of Redemption, based in Baton Rouge. Lists spiritual advisor as reason for visits. Bogus bullshit.'

'The last visit was more than a year ago.'

'That wouldn't matter if he managed to set things up, and contact her under the radar. She gives me a buzz, so we'll look at her, and number six — she hits the notes. So Bracken, because she's here, Devon and this Verner because they buzz, and the last of the four, Rinaldi, because she made the cut.'

She turned to him. 'If we correlate their geographical location at the time of the emails you dug up, can we identify their particular communications? The contact system they used?'

'I don't know about we, but I can.'

'Smart-ass.'

'I'll just sit my smart ass down and do that for you, darling. And you can get me a cookie.'

'A cookie?'

'Yes. I'd like a cookie, and more coffee.'

'Huh.'

As he sat his smart ass down, she decided she wouldn't mind a cookie herself.

# 4

When Eve walked into Whitney's office the next morning, she'd already decided how to play it. She had data, theories, and specific individuals who needed a good talking to.

How she divulged it was key.

The meeting with the feds, the prison rep, the lawyers, and the department's Fugitive Apprehension team could be a lot of blather, spinning, glad-handing, or a pissing contest.

Personally she enjoyed a good pissing contest, but not when she was pressed for time.

So she went in prepared to play the game with every intention of winning it.

'Lieutenant Dallas.' Whitney remained at his desk as he introduced her to the feds.

She judged the curvy brunette, Special Agent Elva Nikos, and her partner, Scott Laurence, with his boxer's build and shiny pate, as seasoned.

And hoped they weren't assholes.

'Lieutenant Tusso is heading the FA team. We're waiting on the representative from Rikers.'

'While we are,' Nikos began, 'I'd like to relay to you what Agent Laurence and myself have related to both Commander

Whitney and Lieutenant Tusso. We're not here to shut you out or step on your toes. We understand that the NYPSD apprehended the subject and built a case for conviction, and that you, in particular, Lieutenant Dallas, have a vested interest in locating Isaac McQueen.'

'Then let me relay to you I don't care who finds McQueen and slaps him back in a cage. You and your partner, Lieutenant Tusso and his team, or me and mine – or any combination thereof. I don't care if it's somebody's grandmother with a can of pepper spray and a good right hook.'

'I appreciate that, Lieutenant. You can be assured that any leads or information we generate during this investigation will be shared.'

'Ditto. I can start now, or wait until the prison rep decides to join us. Commander?'

Whitney watched her carefully. 'You have new information, Lieutenant?'

'I believe I've ... generated possible leads, yes, sir.' At his nod, she continued. 'I accessed the employment records of guards and other staff who most often came into contact with McQueen. As all of the staff can and would be considered suspects, this access fell into the boundaries of procedure. Executing standard runs and probability scans, I'd like to bring in Kyle Lovett, a guard assigned to McQueen's block, and Randall Stibble, a lay counselor.'

'What do you have on them?' Nikos demanded.

'I'm assuming you don't need to see my work,' Eve said, on the dry side. 'Lovett's done two rounds in a gambling addiction program. Since his wife left him eighteen months ago, I'm betting he needs round three. McQueen likes addictive personalities.'

She had more, but the access there dipped into shadow territory.

'Stibble counsels chemi-heads and alcoholics. He brings his own personal experience. He's been in and out of rehab since he was sixteen, did time as a juvie and an adult for illegals-related offenses. McQueen doesn't do illegals, drinks – wine is his choice – in moderation, but he attended Stibble's sessions regularly. He doesn't waste his time or do anything without a purpose.'

'You suspect either or both of these men aided McQueen in his escape?' Lieutenant Tusso asked.

'I think one or both did more. McQueen works with a partner until she bores him, screws up, or fulfills her purpose. He'd want someone on the outside. He'd need to get and receive communication from her.'

'He needed a liaison,' Nikos said.

'And has likely worked with more than one over the past twelve years. We're going to find his visitors list leans heavily toward females. We connect someone at the prison – and my money's on either or both of these men – we have a lead on the partner. She'll be an addict of some kind, likely have a sheet for grifting at the least. She'll be between the ages of forty-five and sixty. Attractive.'

Now it got trickier.

'I have a short list of names of women who fit the partner

profile, and have connections or associations with either Stibble or Lovett. We could get lucky and match one up with the visitors list.'

'That's considerable, and in a short amount of time.'

Eve merely glanced at Nikos. 'We don't have any to waste. He's already hunting.'

'We know McQueen prefers urban environments,' Tusso began. 'He most usually hunts and abducts his victims in busy areas, likes the crowds. Times Square, Chelsea Piers, Coney Island – those were his primary hunting grounds during his last spree.'

Eve wanted to say it hadn't been a spree. Sprees were fast, furious, often random. Just a thirst for violence and excitement. But she held her tongue.

'He's already hit in New York,' Tusso continued, 'and sent messages to Lieutenant Dallas through the victims. Our focus will be on his known hunting grounds.'

'We'll coordinate with you,' Nikos told him. 'Our probability scans and anals are heavily weighted toward McQueen moving out of New York and going under for a period of time,' she began. 'We're looking at public transportation, and doing facial recognition on toll scans.'

Eve held her tongue again as Nikos ran through the FBI's strategy. If the feds wanted to believe McQueen was on the run, let them.

'We already have officers in place at the high-probability targets,' Tusso continued. 'McQueen usually snatches his vics at night, but he's been known to work in daylight.

We'll have those areas covered twenty-four/seven until his capture.'

After a brisk knock on the door, Whitney's admin announced Oliver Greenleaf, the prison's chief administrator. Eve immediately dubbed him a weasel. Striding in at his side in a sharp red suit, Amanda Spring, the prison's chief counsel, carried a glossy leather briefcase the same shade of golden brown as her hair.

'Commander.' With a toothy smile, Greenleaf extended his hand as he crossed the room. 'I do apologize for being a bit late. We were detained by—'

'You're fully twenty minutes late,' Whitney said in a tone that, to Eve's private satisfaction, wiped the smile off Greenleaf's pale, pinched face. 'And I'm not interested in your reasons or excuses. You've already kept this department and agents from the FBI waiting more than twenty-four hours for information vital to our joint investigation.'

'Commander.' Spring nudged her client aside, and spoke in a tone equally stern. 'As legal counsel for—'

'I have not yet addressed you, nor do I intend to. Your facility is responsible for the escape of a violent pedophile, Greenleaf, and you've wasted the valuable time of the officers and agents working to apprehend him. I'm telling you, and the lawyer you felt it necessary to bring to this office, that if one girl is taken, is hurt in any way, you will have hell to pay. That's a personal promise.'

'Commander Whitney, threats are hardly productive.'

Whitney skewered the lawyer with a look. 'If you speak

again, I will have you removed from this office. You were not invited here. Your client has no need for legal counsel as he is in no danger, unfortunately, of being placed under arrest. Now, I want all the data and reports, lists and files this department demanded after being, belatedly, informed of Isaac McQueen's escape.'

'We have quite a bit of data for you. Unfortunately, our internal investigation is not yet complete. It's, of course, imperative that this investigation be thorough and comprehensive. We expect to have those reports finalized and in your hand by the end of the day.'

Whitney's stare could have melted iron. 'If you stall thirty seconds more, this is what's going to happen. I will hold a media conference, along with my lieutenants and these agents. I will announce not only that Isaac McQueen walked out of your facility after murdering a medical, but that you deemed it proper to delay informing the NYPSD of this escape for over eighteen hours. During which time, McQueen assaulted and raped a female victim, assaulted her male cohab. I will provide graphic details of these attacks.'

'Commander—'

'Shut up. I'm not done. I will further report that your facility has delayed another twenty-four hours in providing this department and the FBI with vital and pertinent data, and that charges of obstruction of justice are being considered. I will then have Lieutenant Dallas remind the public just what she found when she apprehended Isaac McQueen twelve years ago. You'll be lucky if they don't come for you with pitchforks.'

He waited a beat. 'I want everything you've got, and now, including your preliminary reports and findings on your internal investigation. Thirty seconds,' Whitney repeated when Greenleaf looked at Spring for guidance. 'Don't test me again.'

Spring opened her briefcase. 'Permission to speak,' she said, in bitter tones.

'No. Put the files on my desk, then get out. Both of you. If all the data required and requested is not within those files, Greenleaf, you're going to need a lawyer, as is your superior. Feel free to pass that information along to him.'

Spring laid a disc bag on Whitney's desk, then shook her head when Greenleaf started to speak again. She turned on her fancy heels, strode out with her client scurrying after her.

For a moment, there was absolute silence.

Throughout the ass-kicking, Laurence sat, silent and still. His face put Eve in mind of some African chieftain. Handsomely carved, fiercely stoic.

Now, a grin spread over those sculpted planes and angles. 'It's inappropriate,' he said, 'but I really want to applaud. One question, Commander, would you have done it? Gone public?'

'Lieutenant Dallas?' Whitney glanced at her. 'Would I?'

'You gave them more time than you wanted, than was necessary. They showed no genuine concern for endangering the public, or even for the murder of an employee in their facility. They decided they'd run the show – and illustrate it by being deliberately late to this meeting, and continuing to stall on the results of their internal. Had it been necessary, you would have gone to the media and roasted them. As it is, I believe you'll use whatever influence and contacts you have to see that Greenleaf, his lawyer, and his superior have their contracts canceled.

'In my opinion, Commander.'

'Lieutenant Dallas has just given you a brief demonstration of why she's one of the most valuable assets of the NYPSD. She observes, deduces, and reports with accuracy.'

Eve took her copies of the data files to her office, with a quick signal for Peabody to follow when she swung through the bullpen.

'How'd it go?' Peabody asked. 'It took longer than I figured, so I was starting to get jumpy.'

'The prison people kept us waiting, kept trying to stall. Whitney sliced and diced them like one of those Samurai chefs. It was beautiful. I think we got lucky with the feds. I'm not reading complete asshole, though I believe they're pursuing the wrong angles. And Tusso from FA's got teams in place at McQueen's known hunting grounds. Now sit down.'

'Uh-oh.'

'I have names, connections, and a plan of action already. I'm not going to tell you how I got the data.'

'Okay.'

'Officially, I gathered the data by standard means, maybe brushing the line a little. I've already passed what I could with those parameters to the other investigators. The feds will be talking to one of the guards. He's dirty. We'll take a lay addiction counselor. He's involved. I know this because I was able to generate a list of probable partners, and he's connected to several females who visited McQueen in prison. Four of them made my short list. One's in New York. We'll talk to her.'

Peabody puffed out her cheeks. 'The meet may have taken longer than I thought, but we're a lot further along than I figured.'

'Not far enough. He's had almost two days. The guard's a toss-away. Gambling addict, and though I wasn't able to pass it on, the feds will shortly find out he's got a not-very-well-hidden account where he's been making regular deposits of two large a month, for years. McQueen knew we'd track that, pull the guard in. He won't know anything much.'

'Which is why you gave him to the feds.'

'He has to be interviewed, sweated some. He may have more than I think. But it's Stipple who rings for me. He won't know McQueen's plans, not the fine details anyway, but he may know or have a good guess as to who he's hooked up with. The woman's on the way, so we'll take her first. I need you to run and analyze all the data the prison just handed over en route. Searches and anal fully on record now. Let's go.'

'How are we handling the coordination with the other teams?'

'We work independently,' Eve told her as they headed out, jumped on a glide. 'Share all results, hold a daily briefing. So far nobody's playing games. But . . . you should do a standard on the feds,' she said, and gave Peabody the names. 'Just to get a full sense of them.'

'How many men are you putting on the team?'

'I want to talk to these two possibles first, then I'll get down to that.' In the garage she got behind the wheel of her vehicle. 'I've gone around and around on it. I had some time and space to settle last night, think it through. The probability runs, given the current data, say McQueen's in New York. He'll hunt here, work to engage me. He wants me to be part of the investigation.'

'That makes the most sense.'

'I don't think so, because staying in New York is stupid, and he's not. He broke pattern, yeah, which means he's likely to break it again. But I've had twelve years to make New York my ground. He wants to take me on, and yeah, that plays. But why would he do it on my home ground? He could go anywhere.'

'Leave New York,' Peabody pointed out, 'lose you.'

'He's already given me a good shot. I don't know. It doesn't feel right. It feels too simple, too straightforward. He likes elaborate. He had years to put his plans together, and this is the best he can do? Maybe I'm overthinking, second-guessing.' She rolled her shoulders to loosen them. 'I need to consult with Mira. I'd trust her more than a probability run.'

'She was at the ceremony yesterday.'

'Yeah, I saw her.'

'It was nice, seeing so many friends. I owe you big for cutting me loose early yesterday.'

'Consider you won't be again until McQueen's back in a cage.'

'Even so. It meant a lot to my parents for me to spend real time with them. Dad took us out to dinner. A real restaurant, too. Not veggie, not vegan, not healthy choice for Free-Agers. We had actual meat. They were sorry you and Roarke couldn't come. They understood, but they were sorry.'

'It was nice to see them anyway. Give me data, Peabody. We're nearly there.'

'Special Agent Scott Laurence, twenty-seven-year vet. Recruited while he was in college. String of commendations. On the short list for bureau chief.'

'Interesting. He let her take the lead.'

'Well, she's no slouch. He's married – twenty-two years. Two kids. She's single, got eight years in. Degrees in psych, criminology. First in her class at Quantico.'

She looked up when Eve rattled up to a second-level spot on the street. 'Anyway, they look solid.'

'Felt that way. Bracken works nights. Tends bar at a strip joint where she used to peel it off.' Eve gestured. 'She lives above her current place of employment.'

Peabody glanced over. 'Handy.'

'Had her club LC license pulled when she tested positive on the regulation exam for illegals. She's fifty-one, no marriages, no official cohabs, no offspring. Spotty employment, a couple of stints for illegals-related charges. Nothing major. Her juvie records show consistent truancy, runaway, petty theft.'

'Sounds like McQueen's type.'

The neighborhood had probably seen better days, but to Eve's eye it looked as though it had always been dirty, dreary, and dangerous. The strip joint, cleverly named Strip Joint, hunched against the sidewalk like a gaudy toad. Some street artist had drawn excellently executed and optimistically sized male genitalia onto the naked and also optimistically endowed naked woman on the sign.

As it didn't look fresh, Eve assumed either the owners didn't give a rat's ass or thought it added interest.

She'd have used her master to gain access to the residential door, but the lock was broken. And that did look fresh.

She ignored the smell of stale zoner in the skinny entryway, and the far skinnier elevator. Peabody clumped up the stairs after her. 'Why do guys always urinate on the walls of places like this?'

'Expressing their disdain for the facilities.'

Peabody snorted. 'Good one. Disdain by pee. I bet she lives all the way up on four.'

'Four-C.'

'Oh well, I ate all my dessert last night and part of McNab's. I deserve to walk up four flights. I wasn't going to have dessert, but it was right there, all gooey and sweet. It's like sex. I mean, when it's right there, what are you supposed to do? I wasn't going to have that either – sex – with my parents bunking in the office, but, well, it was right there.'

'I'll tolerate the gooey and sweet, Peabody, but I'm not thinking about you having sex with McNab, especially in the same sentence as "my parents."'

'I think they had sex, too.'

Eve struggled not to wince or twitch. 'Do you want me to kick you down four flights of steps and make you walk up again?'

'I'd probably bounce all the way down, too, with all this gooey and sweet in my butt. So I guess not.'

'Good choice.'

No palm plate, no security cam, Eve noted, on 4-C. Just two dead bolts and a manual peep.

She banged her fist on the door.

'McQueen's partners always kept their own places,' she told Peabody. 'Usually worked full- or part-time. We only have information from the vics on the last. She helped him lure, abduct, restrain. She helped him clean them up if he decided to use one he'd had for a while. Then she liked to watch.'

Peabody's face went cold. 'Which makes her as much of a monster as him.'

'Yeah, it does.' Eve banged again.

A door opened across the hall. 'Shut the fuck up! People are trying to sleep.'

Eve studied the man glaring at her. He stood buck-naked but for a nipple ring and a tat of a coiled snake. She held up her badge. 'I'd call that indecent exposure, but it barely qualifies. Deb Bracken.'

'Fuck. She's in there. She sleeps like the dead.' He slammed the door.

Eve banged again, kept on banging until she heard somebody

cursing from inside 4-C. A minute later she saw the bleary eye through the peep. 'What the hell do you want?'

Once again, Eve held up her badge. 'Open up.'

'Goddamn it.' The peep flipped closed, bolts and locks rattled open. 'What the hell? I'm trying to sleep here.'

From the looks of her, she'd been doing a good job of it. Her hair, a short, sleep-crazed mess of brass and black, stuck up everywhere around a thin, slack face. She'd neglected to remove her enhancers so her eyes and lips were smeared with what was left of them.

She wore a short black robe, carelessly looped, that showed good legs and breasts too perky not to have been paid for.

'Isaac McQueen.'

'Who?'

'If you bullshit me, Deb, we'll have this little talk downtown.'

'Christ sake, you beat on my door, wake me up, hassle me. What the hell is this?'

'Isaac McQueen,' Eve repeated.

'I heard you. Jesus.' She gave Eve a hard, smeary-eyed scowl. 'I need a hit.' And turned, shuffled away.

Eyebrows cocked, Eve stepped in, watched Bracken continue to shuffle to the far corner of the messy living area where the kitchen consisted of a bucket-sized sink, a mini-fridgie, and a shoe box-sized AutoChef. When she stabbed at the AutoChef it made a harsh, grinding hum, then a clunk.

She pulled out a mug, downed the contents like medicine.

From the smell, Eve identified cheap coffee substitute. She waited while Bracken programmed a second mug, took a slug.

'Isaac's in the joint.'

'Not anymore.'

'No shit.' The first glimmer of interest passed over her face. 'How'd he get out?'

'Sliced up a medical and took his ID.'

'He killed somebody?' Bracken's scowl deepened. 'That's bullshit.'

'It's not the first time.'

'I don't believe that.' She glugged down more coffee, shook her head. 'He wasn't in for murder, so he didn't do murder. He's maybe a prick, but he ain't no killer.'

'Tell that to the medical's widow and kid. Has he been by to see you, Deb?'

'Shit no. I'm old news to him.' She frowned into her coffee. 'Prick.'

'You visited him in The Tombs.'

'Yeah, so what? It's not against the law. Some cop framed him, set him up so she could get some flash. So he liked kiddie porn. Everybody's got their quirks, right? Anyway, I just went in a couple times to talk to him, give him some company.'

'Eleven visits is more than a couple,' Peabody pointed out.

'What's the difference? I haven't seen him in, like, two years. He gave me the boot. Get that? He's in the joint and he gives *me* the boot. Prick.'

'How did you and McQueen get acquainted?' Eve asked her.

'What's it to you?'

At Eve's nod, Peabody took a file from her bag, handed it to Eve. She walked it over, set it on the tiny, crowded counter. Opened it. 'Take a look. This is what he kept in a locked room in his apartment twelve years ago.'

Bracken's face paled, but she shook her head again. 'It was a frame-up.'

'I was in that room. I found those girls.'

'You're the one who set him up?'

'I didn't set him up, but I took him down. And I will again. Here's what he did yesterday, so I'd know he was back in business.' She showed her the evidence photo of Julie Kopeski. 'She and her cohab live in that apartment now. McQueen broke in. He beat the crap out of her, raped her. I wonder, Deb, if he'll decide to look you up, renew your acquaintance.'

'I wanna sit down.'

'Go ahead.'

She made her way through the clutter, dropped into a chair. 'This isn't bullshit?'

'Do you want to see a picture of the medical he cut up?'

'No. Christ no. I liked the guy. I mean I really liked him. He talked to me like I was special, said real sweet things. And he's nice looking, you know? He just seemed so sad, and like he needed somebody to talk to, to care about him. It really hurt my feelings when he said he didn't want to see me anymore.

And he took me off the visitor's list, wouldn't answer my messages.'

'You didn't start visiting him out of the goodness of your heart.'

'See I was in this program. I had some issues with . . . substances. It was like community service, supposed to be good for me. And okay, I'm clean now. You can do a test. I've been clean for almost nine months. But maybe back then I still had issues, and I got a hundred for the visits. I did it for the money at first, but then I really liked the prick. You know?'

'Who made the arrangements?'

'I don't like to get him in trouble.'

'Deb, McQueen had a steady stream of women visiting him. Women like you,' Eve added, 'with issues. McQueen liked to work with a partner. A woman with issues.'

Spots of color bloomed on her cheeks as her mouth dropped open. 'Fuck me! I'd never do shit to a kid – to anybody. Okay, maybe when I had issues I skimmed a few pockets, ran a few games, but that was part of the issue. I never hurt anybody. I wouldn't have helped him do anything to a kid. Christ sake.'

'Which is probably why he gave you the boot. Who set *you* up?'

'Stib. That son of a bitch. I'll kill him. I don't mean for real,' she said quickly.

'Randall Stibble?'

'Yeah, yeah.' She shoved at the mess of her two-toned hair. 'He headed up the program, was like the counselor, and he did that stuff for inmates. I got messed up when Isaac cut me off, and I dropped out of the program, got sort of deeper into the issues awhile. I'm clean now. Swear to God.'

'I believe you. Did he ever talk to you about his plans?'

'Well, sometimes he talked about finding a way out, and when he did how he'd set the record straight with the cop who set him up. I guess that's you.'

'Did you ever smuggle anything in to him?'

'Look, look, I'm clean. Nine months clean, and I got a regular job. It may not seem like much to you, but I haven't been clean, not really, since I was fifteen.'

'I'm not going to hassle you about it,' Eve told her. 'But' – she tapped Julie's photo again – 'I need to know.'

'Okay, well, maybe, sometimes, I'd pass stuff to Stib, or to this guard—'

'Lovett?'

'If you already know why ask me?'

'What stuff?'

'Well, maybe, sometimes, some kiddie porn. He had a weakness, who was I to judge?'

'Is that all?'

'Maybe electronic stuff.'

'Such as?'

'I don't know – hand to God – I don't know much about that shit. He'd give me lists, and I'd go get it. Even paid for it mostly. *Prick!* He said how electronics was a hobby, and they wouldn't let him have the stuff he wanted inside. I mean, what was the harm? He was so nice. He called me baby doll.

Nobody ever called me baby doll. And he sent me flowers. Twice.'

'A real romantic.'

'Yeah. Yeah, I thought.' Slumping, she sulked into her coffee. 'Then he gave me the boot, and now you're saying he really did that to those kids. Maybe I should've known it, but I had those issues back then. You see things different when you're clean.'

'If McQueen contacts you, contact me. If he comes to the door, don't let him in. Alert nine-one-one and contact me.'

'You bet your ass I will.' She took Eve's card.

'Do yourself a favor. Don't contact Stibble.'

'I got zip to say to that son of a bitch. Jesus, I really liked the guy. Sick fuck.'

'Your take?' Eve asked Peabody as they headed back to the car.

'Same as yours. She was telling it straight. I don't think McQueen's given her a thought in the last two years. I can't see him paying her a visit.'

'No, but the thought he *might* will have her telling us anything else she thinks of, and it confirmed Stibble as the liaison.'

'And we've got a lot more than zip to say to that son of a bitch.'

'Bet your ass.'

# 5

They found Stibble in a shoe-box storefront he used for addiction counseling. He looked, Eve decided, even more like a ferret in person than in his ID documents. The short, curly beard he sported didn't do anything to soften his pointy chin, and the rose-tinted shades on his short hook of a nose only added an element of silly.

Those, the skinny braid down the back of his white, hooded tunic, and the pair of leather bracelets around his bony ankles combined to fall somewhere between affected Free-Ager and urban monk.

Which, she supposed, was what he'd aimed for.

He sat with three people on the floor in a circle. Some sort of pyramid-shaped paperweight stood in the center. Harps and gongs trilled and bonged.

He paused, beamed a welcoming smile at Eve and Peabody.

'Welcome! We've begun our visualization exercise. Please, join us. Share your first name if you feel comfortable doing so.'

'That would be Lieutenant,' Eve said, and took out her badge. 'And you can visualize taking a trip down to Cop Central.'

'Is there a problem?'

'Isaac McQueen's a big one. You arranging his auditions for a new partner while collecting a fee from the State's another big one for you.'

Stibble folded his hands at his waist. 'It sounds as if you have inaccurate information. We'll need to straighten this out. I have another forty minutes in this session, so if you'd come back—'

'Would you like to stand up voluntarily?' Eve asked pleasantly, 'or would you like me to help you? Class is dismissed,' she said to the trio on the floor.

'Hey, I paid for the hour.'

She studied the man who'd objected, the scruff of beard, the exhausted eyes.

'What's the damage?'

'Charge is seventy-five. Special introductory fee.'

'Buddy, you're so getting hosed. Peabody, give this gentleman the address for the closest Get Straight location. It's free,' she said to the man. 'They don't make you sit on the floor or look at pyramids. And they serve halfway decent coffee and cookies.'

'I really object to you insinuating I—'

'Button it,' she advised Stibble. 'I apologize for the inconvenience,' she told everyone else. 'Your counselor's required elsewhere.'

'I'm happy to reschedule.' As his group filed out, Stibble hurried after them. 'Please don't let this minor problem cause you to stumble on your journey to health and well-being!'

'Close it up, Stibble.'

'I have other patients due in—'

'His rights, Peabody.'

'Wait, wait!' He waved his hands in the air, danced on his toes, did a couple of agitated circles while Peabody recited the Revised Miranda.

'Do you understand your rights and obligations, Mr Stibble?'

'You can't arrest me! I haven't done anything.'

'Answer the question,' Eve ordered.

'Yes, I understand my rights, but I don't understand what this is all about. Isaac McQueen attended a number of my sessions. I've conducted them at the prison for years. I know he's escaped, and that's terrible. But it doesn't have anything to do with me.'

'Deb Bracken. Ring a bell?'

'I-I – I'm not sure.'

'She didn't have any problem remembering you, or the hundred dollars a visit you gave her after she agreed to meet McQueen. I've got a whole list of names, and I bet every one of them points a finger at you.'

'Human contact and talk therapy are essential tools in rehabilitation counseling. It's not illegal.'

'Taking a bribe from an inmate to set him up with women is. You didn't shell out a hundred out of compassion and generosity, Stibble. How did McQueen pay you?'

'That's ridiculous.' Behind the rose-colored glasses his eyes jittered with panic. 'I'm afraid Ms Bracken was under the influence of her addiction at the time. She's misremembering, that's all.'

'I'm about to charge you with accessory in the forced imprisonment of two people, the assault and rape of one of them.'

'You can't possibly be serious.' Panic morphed into fear as he backed up several steps. 'I've never laid a hand on another human being in my life.'

'McQueen has. You've been aiding and abetting him for years.'

'This is a big misunderstanding. I feel very upset to be threatened in this way. I think we should all take several deep, cleansing breaths.'

'Cuff him, Peabody.'

'Now wait, just wait.' He waved his hands around again. 'I did arrange for a few women to visit Isaac. For therapeutic purposes, and with full approval. Naturally, they – the women – needed to be compensated for their time. Rehabilitation requires many tools.'

'Cut the bullshit. How much did he pay you?'

'A small fee. Barely worth mentioning. Just to cover my own expenses.'

'A thousand a pop's a lot of expenses. We found your account, Stibble.'

'Donation.' It squeaked out of him. 'He donated to my center. It's perfectly legal.'

'How did you find the women? They're not all local.'

'I, ah, I've counseled many troubled people.'

'Who did he pick, out of those troubled people, to work with him?'

His eyes darted left and right, and Eve concluded she'd barely have to flex her fingers to squeeze the juice out of him.

'I don't know. I don't know what you mean.'

'Yes, you do. I see it all over you.' She moved forward just enough to infringe on his space, kept her face hard, her voice flat and grim. 'You knew exactly what he was up to, and you didn't give a shit as long as you collected your fee. He settled on one. I want a name.'

'I can't tell you what I don't know.'

Eve moved fast, had him against the wall, arms behind his back. She slapped restraints on him.

'No! What are you doing? You can't! I'm cooperating.'

'Not by my gauge. You're under arrest for taking a bribe while in the employ of the State of New York, for aiding and abetting a convicted felon, for accessory to that felon's escape, for murder, for—'

'Murder!'

'Nathan Rigby. McQueen slit his throat in the escape, and you're going down for it.'

'I didn't know. How could I know?'

'Give me a name.' Eve perp-walked him to the door. 'I want his partner.'

'Sister Suzan! It's Sister Suzan. Let me go.'

'Where is she?'

'I don't know. I don't know. I swear to God.'

She paused, just inside the door, slightly loosened her grip. 'How do you know he picked her?'

'I took messages in and out for them, after she told me he wanted to stop the visits. Memo cubes and discs. I don't know what was on them. He'd tell me where to send hers, different mail drops. That's all I know.'

'Oh, I doubt it, but it's a start.'

She muscled him out the door.

'I cooperated. You can't arrest me for anything.'

'Watch me.'


Eve planned to move him through processing, let him sweat, then hit him again. He had more to give, and she had little doubt he'd give it. While she worked him, Peabody could do a deeper search on and for Sister Suzan Devon.

But as she pulled into the garage at Central her communicator signaled.

'Dallas.'

'You're to report to Commander Whitney's office immediately, Lieutenant.'

'On my way.'

'Do you think something broke?' Peabody wondered.

'I'll find out when I get up there. Can you handle this asshole?'

Peabody glanced back at Stibble, who'd sobbed the entire way in. 'I think I can manage him.'

'Pass him off, then have him put in a box until I get there.'

He sobbed on the elevator, too. With absolute relief, Eve

jumped off at the first opportunity, shifted to the glides for the trip to the commander's office.

The admin showed her in immediately, shut the door.

'Commander. Detective Peabody and I took Randall Stibble into custody. He gave up the partner.'

'We'll get to that. Sit down, Lieutenant.'

Though she preferred standing, and he knew it, she sat, because his tone brooked no argument.

'Sir.'

'McQueen's surfaced. He's taken a hostage.'

'A hostage?'

'We assume hostage as she no longer fits his victim type.'

'No longer fits.' Her belly clutched. 'He's taken one of his former victims. He has one of those girls. I never considered – I should have.' She shook it off; tried to shake it off. 'How do we know she's with McQueen?'

'He left a message.' He paused at the knock, nodded when Dr. Mira came in.

Now Eve felt a prickle at the back of her neck.

'Eve.' Mira sat in the chair angled toward hers. Her face, as always, was quiet and lovely – but the worry in her eyes pushed Eve to her feet.

'Commander.'

'I want you to sit down, Dallas. I've asked Dr. Mira to join us as I – as we both – value her insight and opinion. I've already briefed her.'

When she obeyed, he brought his chair over – something

she'd never known him to do – so he sat across from her, at eye level.

'At approximately midnight, Central Time, Isaac McQueen abducted Melinda Jones, one of the twin girls and last victims he previously abducted from the Times Square area.'

'I know who she is,' Eve said quietly. 'She went to see him in prison when she was nineteen. I didn't follow up on it.'

Her mouth went dry now, and her heart began to thump. 'She lives in Dallas, she and her sister. The sister's a cop. They live in Dallas. My name.'

Because she'd been found there, beaten, brutalized, and unable – or unwilling – to remember.

'What was the message?'

'This recording answered when Detective Jones called her sister's 'link.'

Whitney kept his eyes on her, ordered his computer to replay the message copied to him by the Dallas police.

*Hello, Bree! I hope you remember me. Melinda did at our surprise reunion. Such a pretty young woman now, and you look just like her – even with the different hairstyles. It's your old friend Isaac. Melinda and I are getting reacquainted, and we've so much to catch up on. I hope to do the same with you. We hardly had any time together all those years ago as we were so rudely interrupted. Be a sweetheart, won't you, and pass this along to Eve Dallas – that's Lieutenant Dallas now.*

*Come and get me. If it isn't Dallas to Dallas – don't you love that – within eight hours after this message is received, well, I can*

*only say Melinda's going to be very unhappy with only nine fin-*
*gers. And that's just the start.*

*Eight hours, Eve. Round two starts now. Love, Isaac.*


'Did they trace the 'link?'

'In her vehicle,' Whitney told her. 'Barely a mile from her apartment.'

'What time did the sister try to tag the 'link?'

'At ten forty-three this morning.'

'It's still shy of noon. We're good on time.'

'We have no proof of life,' Whitney began.

'He wouldn't kill her, sir. Not right off the jump. He chose Melinda Jones for specific reasons. She confronted him while he was in prison. There are no visitor records listing any of his other victims or family members. In addition, he's gone to some trouble to set this up. He had to have ways and means to get to her, a place to keep her, and that means he's done his research and utilized his partner to make arrangements. No point in all that just to kill her.'

'While I tend to agree, it's very possible she's no more than bait – dead or alive – to lure you down. He wants you there, out of your element and without your usual resources. And we agree he's gone to some trouble, used a partner, with you as the target.'

He paused, leaned toward her slightly. 'Understand me, Lieutenant. I won't order you to go.'

'Wherever he wants to take me on, Commander, he won't stop until that happens.'

She'd known, Eve thought now. She'd known it wouldn't be New York, that he wouldn't wage this battle on her ground.

But Dallas. She'd never considered he'd use Dallas and a former victim.

And she should have.

'There are another twenty-one survivors from that room,' she continued, 'and he can pick and choose. And there are countless others who fit his needs. He wants to engage me. He'll torture Melinda Jones, and/or take other victims until he does. This isn't a negotiation. It's an either/or until I go where he wants me to go.'

No choice, she thought. He'd left her no choice at all. First strike to him.

'I'd prefer having your permission and support, Commander, and the cooperation of the Dallas PSD. But I'll go without it. I have personal time coming, and I'll take it.'

'I've spoken with Detective Jones's lieutenant. He's willing to accept your help, and include you in their investigation as a consultant. However ...' Whitney laid the palms of his hands on his thighs, tapped them twice. 'Dallas, we're all aware of your background, your history in that city. We have to assume McQueen knows parts of it.'

A small, hard ball of ice formed in her belly. 'It's likely he dug up the basics. That I'd been found there, my condition. It would only add to his determination to draw me back. You know him.' She turned to Mira. 'You know that would play.'

'Commander, if I could have a few moments in private with the lieutenant.'

His eyebrows drew together, but he nodded and rose. 'Of course.'

'We're wasting time,' Eve said the minute the door shut behind him. 'We all know I have to go, so there's no damn point in talking it all to death.'

'And I'll block you leaving New York unless you talk to me.'

'You can't.'

Mira's eyes, a mild, soft blue hardened to steel. 'Don't be so sure.'

'You'd let him torture, dismember, kill an innocent woman so, what, I don't experience some emotional trauma?' Eve shoved to her feet. 'I'm a cop. It's not your job to decide.'

'It's precisely my job,' Mira corrected with a rare flash of temper. 'You didn't blink. You didn't hesitate. And you'd better do both now, here with me. Or would you rather bull forward and go, then find yourself unable to deal with it when that innocent's – and your own – life is on the line? You were beaten and raped in Dallas.'

'Chicago, too. I remember it some, and a couple other places. Do I have to give you a list of cities so you can clear my travel?'

'You didn't kill your abuser in Chicago. You were finally able to defend yourself in Dallas, a child of eight, who – covered with blood, her arm broken, her mind frozen in shock – wandered the streets.'

'I know what happened. I was there.'

'And blocked it out for years, protected yourself from the memories of years of abuse as best you could. Lived with nightmares.'

'I don't have them anymore. I dealt with it. They stopped.' Almost entirely.

'Have you considered, even for a moment, what going back under these circumstances might mean? Going there, of all places, to hunt a man who abuses – physically, sexually, emotionally – children, just as your father did to you. Have you considered how this might affect you, personally and professionally?'

'Do you think I want to go?' It burst out of her, a quick flood of anger and heat. 'I went back once, to that room, to those streets, even to the alley where they found me. I got through that, and I promised myself I'd never go back. He's dead there, and here,' she said, putting her hands on her head. 'And I don't know if going there will bring him back again. God, I don't want to face that again, having him alive in my head. What do you expect me to do? Let her die because I'm afraid of him, of all of it?'

'No.' Mira spoke quietly now. 'I expect you to go, to do your job, to find him, and to stop him.'

'You just wanted me to break down first?'

'Yes, exactly. I care about you, Eve. You're so much more to me than another case file. I care about you as I do about my own children, and am perfectly aware those feelings can and do make it difficult for both of us from time to time.'

She let out a sound, a mix of sorrow and regret. 'A mother protects her child above all. She also has to let her go, but not without being sure her child is prepared and armed and ready. If you couldn't admit to yourself and to me those fears, those doubts, you couldn't be ready. Now I can let you go, even wishing I could stop you.'

'I don't want to go.' The breath Eve let out scraped at her throat like nails. 'I couldn't live with myself if I didn't.'

'I know. He'll use whatever he knows about your history, like salt in a wound. He'll play mind games, prodding where you're most vulnerable. I need you to promise you'll contact me if you need help.'

Eve walked back, sat. 'It makes it difficult from time to time, on my end, because my memories of a mother are twisted and ugly. She hated me. That's the foremost memory I have of her. The hate in her eyes when she looked at me. So I don't know how to respond when the offer of, I guess, a maternal type of affection and support is ... pure or whatever.'

'I understand that. It's something we can delve into deeper when you're ready.' Mira laid a hand over Eve's. 'Promise you'll let me know if you need my help.'

'I do. I will.'

Rising, Mira started for the door, stopped. 'You're stronger than you were, and you were always strong. You're smarter than you were, and you were always smart. You have more because you let yourself give and take more. He hasn't changed since you stopped him. You have. Use that,' she said, and opened the door.

'Commander,' Mira said when Whitney came back in. 'In my opinion, Lieutenant Dallas is clear for this assignment.'

'The choice is yours, Lieutenant.'

'You know I've made it, sir.'

'Very well. Lieutenant Ricchio has cleared you as well, and to take another investigator at your discretion. If you want Peabody, I'll have it done.'

'Peabody's needed here, Commander. She's studied the case files, already has the research and data on the partner. As well as a suspect in custody for accessory who may have more information. I want her to continue to work the case from here. To work it as primary.'

'That's your call.'

'I'll brief her. I'll take Roarke, as expert consultant, civilian, if he's available.'

'Make whatever arrangements you deem best, and contact me when you're in the air.' He drew a disc from his pocket. 'Data on Ricchio, Detective Jones, the other detectives and officers you'll most likely work with.'

'Thank you, sir. That's . . . thorough.'

'I know my cops,' he said briefly. 'It'll save you from running them. Good hunting, Lieutenant.'

She hurried back to Homicide. She'd have time to think, review, plan on the trip, but for now she had to move fast.

She spotted Peabody eyeing the dubious choices at Vending outside the bullpen. 'Peabody, with me.'

She went straight through into her office.

'I've got Stibble holding. I was just going to grab some lunch, then—'

'Grab it later. McQueen's in Dallas. He snatched Melinda Jones, one of his former vics, last night.'

'Is she alive?'

'Assumed. He left a message for her twin sister. I've been invited down there to play with him.'

'To—' Peabody broke off, shut the door. 'Does he know what happened to you there?'

'Undetermined.' As she spoke, Eve packed a file box. 'I'm leaving asap.'

'You mean *we*.'

'No, I don't. I need you here. I want you to handle Stibble. Wring him dry. Continue to find out anything you can on this Sister Suzan. She'll be in Dallas. She'll have laid the groundwork for McQueen. They've got a place, somewhere private enough to hold a hostage. She'll have a place of her own, close by. Use Baxter and Trueheart. If you need more manpower, let me know and I'll arrange it.'

'You're not going there alone.' Peabody shifted to block the door, and had Eve's eyebrows lifting.

'Were your orders unclear, Detective?'

'Don't pull that shit on me, Dallas. Just don't. It's a trap, and worse, it's there. It's where . . . it's there.'

'I know where it is, and of course he's figuring it's a trap. He'll want to string it out for a while, have some fun with it. That's a mistake.'

Now Peabody folded her arms, planted her feet. 'I'm going with you.'

'Peabody, I know you've been working on improving your hand-to-hand, but I can take you down in five seconds flat.' She took a breath as Peabody's face only tightened into fiercer lines. First Mira, she thought, now this.

'If I can't handle myself I don't have any business with this badge or this office.'

'That's not the point. This is different.'

'Every case is different, and how we deal with every case is different. But what's the same is we work it, we do the job, and we take the risks the job demands. That's it.'

She considered demoralizing her partner by moving her bodily from the door. Not only would it leave a bad taste in her mouth, but she needed Peabody on top, confident, clean-headed.

And under it, she just didn't have the heart to slap back the concern of her partner. Her friend.

'I'm going to talk to Roarke right now, see if he can clear some time to go along as a consultant. The commander cleared it with Dallas PSD. Don't question me on this, Peabody. I need to go, and I need to go knowing you're capable of taking charge of the investigation from here.'

'In charge? Me? But Baxter—'

'You studied McQueen, and you're familiar with all stages of the investigation to this point. You're a goddamn decorated officer of this department. And you *will* take the lead on the

New York end of this investigation as you've been trained to do. You will not let me down.'

'I won't let you down. Please don't go alone. If Roarke can't leave this minute, take one of the other men. Take backup that's familiar, that you know you can trust. You don't know the people down there.'

'I've data on all of them. If Roarke's not available, I'll consider hooking Feeney into it.'

'Okay. But if you need me—'

'I know where you are. Now I've got to go. He only gave me eight hours and it's ticking away fast. Send me whatever you get out of Stibble, whatever you get on the partner.'

'I'll stay in regular contact.' With some reluctance Peabody moved away from the door, followed Eve out. 'How do you want me to play Stibble? Should I—'

'You know what to do. Do it. Now brief the men.' Without another word she left.

She pulled out her 'link, tagged Baxter as she worked down the levels to the garage.

'Yo,' Baxter said.

'I'm headed out of town, following a lead on McQueen. Peabody's taking over here. I want you and Trueheart working with her. She's primary.'

'Copy that.'

'Don't give her too much grief, Baxter, but don't baby her.'

'How much is too much? Don't worry about it. Trueheart'll keep me honest. Just go get that fucker, LT.'

'That's the plan.' She clicked off, contacted Roarke's office.

His admin, Caro, smiled at her. 'Hello, Lieutenant. Roarke's just finishing up a holo-conference. If it's important, I'll cut in.'

'I'm on my way there. I need to talk to him as soon as possible. It's urgent.'

Caro's smile shifted to alert. 'I'll clear the time.'

'Thanks.'

And here we go, Eve thought, as she jumped into her vehicle and pushed the DLE Urban Roarke had designed for her to full speed. As she drove, dodging, weaving, hitting vertical to leapfrog, she plugged the disc Whitney had given her into the onboard comp, and began to familiarize herself with Lieutenant Ricchio and his unit.

When she stepped into the expansive black-and-white lobby of Roarke's headquarters, one of his security met her. 'We cleared an elevator for you. Straight up, Lieutenant.'

'Thanks.' She strode quickly past the moving maps, the banks and rivers of flowers, the crisscross of people bustling in and out of the shops and eateries.

Security escorted her to the elevator, then stepped back. 'It's programmed,' he told her before the doors closed.

She spent the time on the fast ride up, up, up, pacing the car, aligning her thoughts, working out what needed to be done and how to do it.

The doors opened again, directly into Roarke's office, and he stood waiting.

'What's happened?'

'McQueen's taken a hostage.' When he gripped her hand, she saw her mistake. He thought it was someone in New York, someone they loved.

'Who?'

'Melinda Jones. She's one of the twins, the last he abducted.'

'I remember.' But relief didn't register on his face. He remembered, she thought, everything. 'She's in Dallas.'

'He grabbed her late last night. I can fill you in on it later. He's given me a deadline to get down there, or he'll start cutting pieces off of her.'

'He wants you in Dallas?' Those beautiful blue eyes narrowed and sharpened. 'He specifically demanded this?'

'Yeah, in eight hours from the time the sister picked up the message. That was at ten forty-three, their time. It's twelve forty now. So I've got six hours to get there. Or . . . it's earlier there, so I lose an hour. Or gain it. Shit, I can't ever figure that crap out.'

'There's time enough. It isn't a coincidence he's there.'

'There are factors. We can get into them later. Right now I don't want to fuck around, give him any excuse to start cutting her up. I'm cleared to work with the locals, and to take a partner or aide, or whatever. I need Peabody to stay here, to run this part of the investigation.'

He nodded, and saying nothing more crossed the long space to his desk in front of the sea of glass that gave him New York. 'Caro, clear my schedule until further notice. I need a shuttle prepped and waiting at Transportation for a flight to Dallas, Texas. Right away.'

He clicked off the inter-office 'link. 'Sit down a minute,' he told Eve.

'I didn't ask you to go with me. I was going to, but you didn't give me a chance.'

'Do you think you could go there without me? Ever?'

She closed her eyes a minute. 'No questions? No objections? No 'You can't go back there'?'

'I'd be wasting my time and yours. Going will hurt you. Not going would break you.'

This time when she let out a breath, it shuddered. And she went to him, wrapped her arms around him. 'Yes. And going back without you? I don't want to think about it.'

'Then don't.' He drew her back, looked into her eyes. 'We'll deal with this, you and I.'

'Yeah, we will. I – we – need to get home, pack.'

He merely turned to the 'link again. A few seconds later, Summerset appeared on screen.

'Eve and I are leaving for Dallas on urgent police business. I'll need you to pack for both of us as quickly as possible, and have the luggage sent to my short-range shuttle at Transportation.'

'Right away. Will a week's wardrobe be sufficient?'

'That should be fine. I'll contact you with other instructions once we're on our way. Thank you.'

Even through the rush, the worry, she had room for a good scoop of appalled. 'Summerset's going to pack for me? Like, my underwear?'

Roarke glanced at her, smiled. 'You seem more disturbed by that than with the idea of facing down McQueen.'

'The first is humiliating, and I'm looking forward to the second. But I'll suck it up. It saves time.'

'Spend it sitting down. Take a breath. I need to go consult with Caro for a few minutes.'

'Roarke.' She remained on her feet. 'I know you probably think going with me on this kind of deal is part of the marriage rules.'

His lips curved in easy amusement. 'You do love your rules.'

'When I know about them, and understand them. I know I give you a lot of grief about owning the world, or buying up planets. It's not that I don't get how much work, time, responsibility it takes to run everything you run. I do. So I know you're putting a hell of a lot on hold for me. I don't take it for granted.'

'Eve.' He waited a beat. 'I once stood in a field in Ireland, alone, a little lost, and wishing for you more than I wished for my next breath. And you came, though I never asked you, you came because you knew I needed you. We don't always do what's right, what's good. Not even for each other. But when it counts, down to the core of it, I believe we do exactly that. What's right and good for each other.

'There's no rule to that, Eve. It's just love.'

Just love, she thought when he stepped out. She may have been going into her own personal hell to face a killer, but right at that moment she considered herself the luckiest woman in the world.

# 6

Eve spent the first part of the quick flight reviewing the rest of Whitney's data, then pacing. Thinking, working out an approach. Until Roarke completed whatever he was doing on his PPC and set the device aside.

'Tell me what to expect when we get there.'

'Can't be sure.' And it left her unsettled, edgy. 'Ricchio, Lieutenant Anton, is Detective Jones's direct superior. He runs Special Victims, so they deal with a lot of sex crimes and abuse to minors. Jones aimed her arrow right there.'

'And her twin aimed hers toward abuse and rape counseling. I imagine they've worked together.'

'Melinda counseled a number of vics in the SVU files,' Eve confirmed. 'Ricchio's a twenty-year man. Married – second time – twelve years. He has a son, eighteen, from marriage one, and a daughter, age ten, from his current. Comes off steady to me, gives his detectives some room. He's partnered Jones with his most experienced detective, Annalyn Walker. Fifteen years on, the last eight in SVU. Single, no marriages or offspring. She's got a good record. Those should be the main players we'll deal with.'

She broke off when her 'link signaled. 'The feds,' she said, reading the display before she answered. 'Dallas.'

'What happened to cooperation and sharing all data?' Nikos demanded.

Steamed, Eve thought. Very steamed.

'I'm working against the clock here, Agent Nikos. You can get all data from my commander and from Detective Peabody, who now has the lead in the department's investigation.'

'If McQueen's in Dallas, with a hostage, Laurence and I should be in Dallas.'

'Your travel and coordination with Dallas police isn't my call.'

'It's handled. We're about an hour behind you. You could've offered us a ride.'

'Look, Nikos, I've got just a little more important things on my mind than your transpo. McQueen's got a hostage, and he has every reason to inflict harm on one who got away. I'm not going to give him any reason to inflict that harm. We believe his partner is one Suzan Devon, current address Baton Rouge. My partner and her team are trying to track her.'

'I'm aware. We also have resources – considerable – and in using them have determined one Sister Suzan Devon didn't exist until about three years ago. The prints and DNA on record are bogus as they belong to a ten-year-old corpse named Jenny Pike. We're running face recognition on her to see if we can match her in our system.'

'She'll be in Dallas, with McQueen.'

'Maybe. Or he may have disposed of her by now.'

No, no, Eve thought. Catch up, catch on. 'He still needs her. He hasn't had time to hunt up a new partner. She's with him. Her ID as Sister Suzan went in the system before she met McQueen, so that's on her. He's got himself a player this time around. My partner's working Stibble, who set them up together. If he knows anything, she'll get it out of him. We're going to land in a minute. We'll continue this at Lieutenant Ricchio's house.'

Eve clicked off, looked at Roarke. 'Crap.'

'Because the FBI adds another factor?'

'Because I didn't think to inform them. It didn't cross my mind, and it should have. I promised full disclosure and cooperation.'

'If they're that close behind us, they got their disclosure quickly enough.'

'It should've come from me.' Shoving a hand through her hair she went back to pacing. 'Now I'm going to have to apologize. I hate that. And yeah, there's the other factor. Ricchio's not only swallowing a New York cop in his business, but the feds. In his place I'd be feeling a little put out.'

'You've got an hour's jump to convince him not to be put out with you. The FBI will have to handle their own diplomacy.'

She considered. 'There is that.'

Roarke snagged her hand on her next pass, tugged her into her seat. 'Strap in, Lieutenant.' Reaching across, he buckled her in himself. 'This is what you do.' He took her face in his hand, kept his eyes on hers as he knew she hated landing as much as takeoff. 'Where you do it is only one aspect.'

'It's a pretty big one.'

'You know your target and your objective. Those are bigger. And you know yourself.' He kissed her to settle himself as much as her. Because the shuttle glided in, touched down.

And they were in Dallas.

The minute she stepped off the shuttle, she frowned at the vehicle Roarke had waiting.

Amused, he opened the passenger door for her. 'I thought something discreet, without flash, would be most appropriate.'

'Just because it's not a solid gold, open-air zippy toy doesn't mean it's discreet. It looks like money. Whole big bunches of money.'

'It's a quietly styled sedan with all-terrain capabilities because you don't know where you'll have to go, do you now? And it's black.' He got behind the wheel, gave the on-board computer the location of the station house. 'In any case, a solid gold vehicle would weigh entirely too much. A nice gold veneer now, that might be appealing.'

'Trust you,' she muttered.

'You can, yes.'

He drove out of the station and straight into Dallas traffic.

She remembered this, from her previous return there. The thick traffic, the roads and streets that curled or angled off rather than forming a reasonable grid. And the buildings, she thought now – not like New York where old mixed with new, where brownstones spread and sleek towers climbed. But spears and towers, arches and wedges, all flashy to her mind.

Like a solid gold zippy toy.

She focused on them, on her instinctive dislike of the skyline, and refused to think about what had happened in a freezing room in a run-down hotel in the city's hard-edged sex district.

'It doesn't look the same, really, as it did when we were here. Not even two years ago.'

Roarke gestured to one of the many towering cranes. 'Something's always coming down and going up. It's a city in perpetual evolution.'

'Maybe that's good.' She shifted in her seat. 'Good it doesn't stay the same. Maybe I won't feel anything. It's like coming to an anonymous city. It's more off-planet than on to me anyway. Any city, anywhere. It's nothing to me.'

If it was, he thought, she wouldn't feel the need to convince herself.

'We've got a visitor's slot.' She read off a text. 'Level Three East, Slot Twenty-two. That's the same level as SVU.'

'Convenient.'

'They're being polite. They could've given us a slot on the other side of the building. So this is a good sign. I've got to persuade Ricchio to let me take the lead. He doesn't know McQueen, he's got no reason to. He'll have done his homework since the grab, sure, but he doesn't know this fucker.'

'Bree Jones does.'

'Yeah, but she's still got some green on her. And it's her sister on the line. You add that to the trauma, and believe me she's relived every second of it since ten forty-three this morning. I don't know if she's going to help or muck it up.'

Roarke turned into the garage, wound up the levels. 'You're nervous, anxious. Don't tell me you're not. I know you. They won't see it, but I can feel it.'

'Okay. I can hold that down.'

'No question. You might want to slow it down, follow Ricchio's lead, get a sense of him, and Bree Jones. Give them a chance to get a sense of you.'

'You're right. You're right, and I know that. I just want—'

'To get through it,' Roarke said, and parked in 22.

'Yeah, and that stops. Stops right now. If that's the best I can do, I should have stayed home.' She got out, looked at Roarke over the car. 'Priority one, get Melinda Jones out, safe and alive. Priority two, put Isaac McQueen, and his partner, in cages. The rest? It's just clutter.'

He walked around the car. 'Let's go clean house.' He took her hand as they walked to the interior doors.

'Hey! Consultants don't walk into cop shops holding hands with badges.'

He gave her hand a squeeze before letting it go. 'That's my cop.'

Security logged them in, cleared Eve's sidearm and clutch piece, then had them wait.

The white tile floors all but sparkled. The walls hit a soft brown, several shades richer and warmer than beige, and sported art with colorful geometrics framed in bronze. Benches under them held a shine. Nearby vending machines gleamed spotlessly clean.

Eve felt a nagging itch at the base of her spine that only increased when a couple of uniforms strolled by, smiled, and gave her and Roarke a cheery, 'Afternoon.'

'What kind of cop shop is this,' she asked, 'with fancy art on the walls and uniforms who give you a big smile instead of the beady eye?'

'You're the New York in Dallas.'

'What?'

'Buck up, darling. I'm sure somewhere in this facility someone's getting the beady eye.'

'The security officer smiled and said, 'Good afternoon, ma'am,' to me before I gave him ID.'

'It's a sick world, Eve.' He resisted taking her hand for another squeeze. 'A sick, sad world.'

'Yeah, it is. So why are these cops smiling? It's just wrong.'

He couldn't help it. He gave her a quick one-armed hug, brushed his lips over her hair. 'Cut it out, yes, I know,' he said with a laugh. 'But it seemed appropriate enough in a world of smiling cops. And here's one who isn't.'

Eve made Bree Jones the minute the detective stepped through the doors. For an instant, then overlaid now, and she

110

had a perfect image of the young face, bruised, swollen, twisted with rage and fear.

Then it vanished, and she saw a pretty woman, blond hair short, spiky, with soft features overset by a sharp, firm chin. Blue eyes dominated a face pale and shadowed.

She couldn't cover the fatigue, Eve thought, but she cloaked the fear. It barely showed around the edges.

She walked briskly to Eve, a small, compact woman in faded jeans, a white T-shirt, and brown boots.

'Lieutenant Dallas.'

The voice didn't quiver. There was an inherent drawl in it that made it sound lazy and overcasual to Eve's ears. But there was nothing lazy or casual about the handshake.

'Detective Jones. This is Roarke. He's cleared as consultant.'

'Yes. Thank you for coming. Thank you both for coming so quickly. I asked my loo to let me escort you in. I wanted a moment to thank you personally.'

'There's no need.'

'So you said before, but there is. And was. I'll take you in to Lieutenant Ricchio.'

'Are you working the case, Detective?'

'Lieutenant Ricchio is persuaded I'll be an asset.'

'Did you persuade him?'

Bree glanced at Eve, away again as they passed through the doors. 'Yes, Lieutenant, I did. It's my sister. I wouldn't have attempted to persuade him unless I believed, completely, I can and will be an asset.'

Eve said nothing. Bree walked like a cop – and excusing the drawl, talked like a cop. But the place? Everything glimmered clean and shiny. Treated glass on generous windows diffused the light, and the air hung steady at a pleasant temperature, belying the wet blanket of heat that smothered the city outside.

'Is this a new facility, Detective?'

'Relatively, Lieutenant. It's about five years old.'

Five years? Eve thought. Every cop she knew could've taken the shine off the place in five days.

They turned into SVU with its wide bullpen, its line of cubes for aides and uniforms. Cops at the desks, some in jackets, some in shirtsleeves, working the 'links, the comps. She wouldn't say every movement stopped when she walked in, but there was a beat.

In it she got stares close enough to the beady eye to put her at ease.

Ricchio used the traditional boss's attached office with unshuttered window. He stepped out immediately, held out a hand to Eve.

'Lieutenant Dallas, Mr Roarke, thank you for responding so quickly. Please, come into my office. How about some coffee?'

She started to refuse. *Let's get down to business*. But she remembered this was a world where cops smiled and said *please* a lot. 'Thanks, just black.'

'The same,' Roarke told him.

He programmed the AutoChef, and after passing out the

coffee, gesturing to his visitor's chairs – ones with actual cushions – he sat on the edge of his desk.

He wore a suit and tie, and had a lot of wavy brown hair around a face with a deep tan and lantern jaw. His eyes shifted to Bree, back to Eve.

'I expect you've read Detective Jones's statement and report.'

'I have. But I'd rather hear her account, if you don't mind.'

'Bree?'

'Yes, sir. I didn't get home until a few minutes after four this morning. My partner, Detective Walker, and I worked a long one. My sister and I share an apartment. I assumed Melinda was home in bed. I never checked. I went directly to bed, and as I'd taken the next day off, I slept late. I . . .'

She wavered a moment.

'It's my policy,' Ricchio said, 'when my detectives put in long hours, close a case, and have nothing hot waiting, they take a day to recoup.'

'Understood.'

'I didn't get up until about ten-thirty,' Bree continued. 'And I assumed Melinda had gone to work. There was a message from her on the fridge, as is our routine. She said she'd gotten a call, had gone out to meet with a rape victim she'd been counseling. She left the message at twenty-three-thirty.'

'Is it usual for her to meet a vic that late?'

'Yes, ma'am – sir. Pardon me, Lieutenant, I understand you prefer "sir".'

'"Ma'am"'s somebody's tight-assed aunt.'

113

It nearly got a smile from Bree. 'Yes, sir. It's never too late or too early for Melly. If somebody needs her, she'd be there. I didn't think anything of it. I'd have known if she'd left the message under duress. She didn't.'

'She didn't tell you who she intended to meet or where?'

'No, but that wasn't unusual, but ... if she'd come back, she'd have deleted the message, so it gave me a bad feeling. I decided to check in with her. When I did so, I got McQueen's message.'

As she said McQueen's name, Bree began to turn a silver ring around and around her finger.

'I checked the apartment, cleared it. I contacted my lieutenant and apprised him of the situation. He dispatched two officers and a Crime Scene Unit to my location, and put out an alert on Melinda and her vehicle. Her vehicle was found in the unsecured lot of a motel approximately three-quarters of a mile from our apartment. No one interviewed remembered seeing Melinda or McQueen.'

'Has the picture of the female we believe is McQueen's current partner been shown?'

'As soon as we received it from your department, Lieutenant. We didn't get any hits. We've run down or are running down everyone booked into the motel last night. So far, we've cleared everyone.'

'They didn't book,' Eve put in. 'They didn't stay there. They dumped her vehicle there, possibly transferred her to another. Most likely a van. You might re-interview asking about a van parked near where you located your sister's car.

Highest probability?' she continued when Bree took out a notebook. 'The female suspect met Melinda Jones outside of the designated location. Probably some sort of restaurant – down-scale, but busy. Café, diner, bar. Requests the vic to take her somewhere else, maybe quieter. She wouldn't want to go in with her target, be seen with her. The suspect's behavior is nervous, upset – as the vic would expect, and being predisposed to help she lets the suspect into her vehicle. Is that consistent with your sister, Detective?'

'Yes.' Bree paused in her notes, circled the ring again. 'Melinda would have taken her wherever she wanted to go.'

'At some point the suspect asks your sister to pull over, or maybe pull into an empty lot. She feels sick, or she becomes hysterical. It's smarter, simpler to incapacitate the – your sister and gain control of the vehicle if they're stopped. Suspect takes the wheel, McQueen joins them, or suspect drives to the motel, meets McQueen. They make the transfer, leave your sister's vehicle. Doesn't matter if you find it. It's better if you do, then waste time looking for them in that area. They're nowhere near that area.'

'If I'd checked when I got home—'

'It wouldn't have made any difference.' Eve cut Bree off. They didn't have time for the luxury of guilt. 'It wouldn't have mattered if you'd been home when she got the contact. She'd have responded, exactly as she did. She may have given you the name of the woman she intended to meet, but that wouldn't have mattered either because it's a lie. And within . . . I don't know the traffic patterns and routes around here, but I'd say in no more than an hour, long before you'd have felt any concern, she was secured in the location they had ready.'

Eve turned to Ricchio. 'That's the most likely scenario.'

'In your opinion, would he have taken her out of the city?'

'He's an urbanite – and he's been confined for years, away from the action, the energy, the movement. Neighbors tend to pay more attention to each other in the suburbs or out-lyings. Best guess is an apartment or condo, mid-level. Nothing too flashy. His partner would already be established there. Could be weeks or months, but she's got it all set up for him. It's soundproofed, has top-grade security, and plenty of room. In prior partnerships, the female maintained her own resi-dence. I don't see that changing. He doesn't want her in his space night and day. He likes his privacy.'

'You have an accomplice in custody.'

'Randall Stibble,' Eve confirmed for Ricchio. 'We'll call him a broker. For a fee he set McQueen up with potential partners who visited him in prison. My partner and another detective have him in Interview. If he's got anything more to give, they'll get it. Jones knew the female suspect, you said someone she'd counseled. You have her records?'

Ricchio nodded at Bree. 'We've accessed them, and we've run searches on every patient she's counseled in the last six months. We've found no matches on face recognition, DNA, or prints.'

'You need to go back further. It won't be that recent. A year, maybe more. They'll have put some distance between the alleged rape, the initial consults, and this contact and abduction. The ID she used to meet with McQueen is fake, good enough to beat the prison scans. Like McQueen, her appearance is probably altered somewhat. But they can't alter who and what they are.'

'I'd like you to brief my officers, give them profiles. Your experience with McQueen will be invaluable to the search for Melinda.'

'Agents Nikos and Laurence should be here within twenty.'

'Then we'll brief in thirty, if that suits you.'

'It does.'

'How is he financing this?' Ricchio asked her. 'The travel, the apartment, the transportation?'

'We always knew he had money. We just couldn't find it. He'll have funneled some to his partner for expenses on the setup. That'll give us a trail, once we find the crumbs on it. Our civilian consultant has a particular expertise on financials.'

She glanced at Roarke, nodded.

'He'll have multiple accounts,' Roarke began. 'Stibble and the guard he worked with both had secondary, buried accounts. Not particularly well buried. McQueen was able to transfer relatively small amounts out of an account – standard off-shore, registered to a dummy corporation – to theirs. He most usually used Stibble's email account to do the transfers. The off-shore account was easy to find once we looked, which tells me he has more. More and fatter. As he greatly depleted, we'll say this payroll account, he'll likely need to tap one or more of the others to cover his current expenses.'

'Why Melinda? Why here? I believe it's relevant,' Bree added. 'I'd ask even if she wasn't my sister.'

'You were his last, and you were a particular coup. Twins. He'd never, to our knowledge, taken more than one at a time. He'd only had you for a short period.'

'He could have tried for me. He should have tried for me,' Bree insisted. 'Taking a trained police officer has to be more of a rush than a crisis counselor.'

'I agree,' Eve said. 'But you didn't visit him in prison.'

'When?' Ricchio demanded. 'You're telling me Melinda had contact with McQueen before the abduction? Were you aware of this, Detective?'

'Yes. God.' A flicker of pain crossed her face as she pressed a hand to her temple. 'I didn't think of it, Lieutenant. I didn't remember, it was years ago. She didn't tell me until after she'd seen him. I was so angry. We had a terrible fight about it. I . . .'

'Sit down, Bree. Sit, for God's sake.' Ricchio rubbed his hands over his face. 'Why did she go to see him?'

'She said if she was going to help people who'd been abused, she had to deal with her own baggage. She had to see him, in prison, see him for herself, see him paying for what he'd done to us and the others. And she had to show him she'd survived it. Show him she was free and healthy and unscarred.'

She closed her eyes, took a breath. 'She didn't tell me before she did it because she knew I'd fight her on it. I'd have gone to our parents, done everything I could to stop her. But she was better after. She used to get headaches, debilitating ones. They eased off. So did the nightmares. She was better, calmer, happier.

'So I forgot it,' Bree said, bitterly now. 'Just let it go and forgot it.'

'Did she tell you what they said to each other?' Eve asked her.

'She said he smiled almost the whole time, so pleased, so charming. He said it was wonderful to see her again, how she'd grown into a beauty, crap like that.' Again, the ring went round and round her finger. 'He asked her questions she didn't answer, like if she had a boyfriend, if she was in school. He asked about me, wondered why I hadn't come to see him, too. She waited, just let him talk. Then she said it was wonderful to see him, too. In prison. It was wonderful to know, thanks to Officer Dallas, he'd be there for the rest of his life, that he'd never be able to hurt anyone ever again, to prey on children ever again. She loved knowing he was in a cage while she was free, living her life. And she left. He'd stopped smiling, and she left.'

'She taunted him, rubbed his face in it,' Bree continued. 'He wouldn't forget that. He'll hurt her. Like he did before.'

'Not yet,' Eve said quickly. 'Right now she's a tool, like Stibble, like the woman, like Lovett – the prison guard he bribed. She's just a tool and he needs to keep his tools. I'm his focus now. You said she mentioned me, specifically, as the reason he was in prison.'

'Yes, she – we – were so grateful.'

'As long as I'm his focus, he'll keep her alive.'

A female officer opened the door without knocking. 'McQueen's on Bree's desk 'link, blocked video. We're running it. He wants to talk to Lieutenant Dallas.'

'Show me,' Eve ordered. 'You don't.' Eve reached out, gripped Bree's arm as the detective bolted for the door. 'You don't give him another. You don't give him the satisfaction. Keep out of range, don't say anything. He doesn't see or hear you.'

Eve walked into the bullpen, crossed toward the empty desk. Remembered herself, glanced at Ricchio. At his nod, she stepped over, sat, and angled herself in full view of the 'link screen.

'A little ahead of deadline, aren't you?'

'You, too.' A smile radiated in his voice. 'How does it feel to be back where you started?'

'I didn't start here.'

'Didn't you? It's not easy accessing background on you, but I don't mind the work. You were a bit young for my tastes when you had your initiation. You bad girl. Still, I bet you were delicious. Tell me about it,' he invited with that smile in his voice. 'I'd love to hear the details.'

'Jerk off on your own time. Proof of life, McQueen, or I catch the next shuttle home.'

'Say please.'

'Fuck you. Proof of life or this conversation ends.'

He made a tsking sound. 'You were so polite when we first met.'

'You mean when I politely stunned you unconscious? Yeah, good times. One more chance or I'm gone. Proof of life.'

'If you insist.'

Innocuous hold music flowed out of the speakers. Making a joke of it, Eve thought. Getting a good laugh out of inflicting the emotional pain.

A moment later, Melinda Jones's face filled the screen. Glassy-eyed, Eve noted. Drugged. No sign of facial bruises.

'This is Melinda. It's Melinda.' Out of the corner of her eye, Eve saw the female officer stop Bree from rushing forward. 'He hasn't hurt me. I don't know where I am. She said, Sara—'

She broke off, cringing when the knife tipped to her throat.

'Uh-uh-uh! That's enough.'

'I want to see all of her,' Eve demanded. 'I came here within the time frame. I want to make sure you kept your end.'

'You have your proof of life, and she has all her digits. Block video.' The screen went blank.

'What do you want, McQueen?'

'Your blood on my hands and a pretty little girl in my bed.'

'Got a second choice?'

'Oh no, I'm sticking with the first. That's what I'll have when we're done. Meanwhile, I'll have the pleasure of watching you try to find me and, once again, save the girl. You won't, but I'll find you, then you'll end where you started.'

He gave a long, happy sigh. 'It's almost religious, isn't it?'

'We've got Stibble and Lovett,' Eve told him.

'Keep them. I'm done with them. Until later.'

'Location?' Eve called out when the transmission ended.

'Nothing.' One of the men at a nearby desk shook his head in disgust. 'He bounced the signal all over hell and back. Wherever it originated, our guys said it's jammed and layered in. We can't even verify he's in Dallas.'

'He's here.' She rose, turned her attention to Bree. 'Melinda's alive. He hasn't hurt her. If he had he wouldn't have her tranq'd. He'd want her to feel it.'

She saw the FBI come in. 'If I can have ten minutes with the feds, Lieutenant Ricchio, I'll be ready to brief your men.'

'Take my office.'

# 7

She updated the agents, and after a mild tussle won the argument. She'd brief the Dallas police, after which they'd add whatever additional data and findings they'd generated.

The briefing room held several big, shiny tables. They weren't surrounded by high-backed fancy chairs, but it still reminded her of a boardroom. Screens covered one wall, flanked by comp stations.

She had a podium, which she intended to ignore.

As the room filled with cops she signaled Roarke aside. 'Check in with Peabody, will you? Anything she's got, I want. Can you break down the bouncing and jamming? Because he's going to make contact again.'

'Given enough time, and proper equipment.'

She took another, flat-eyed, scan of the room. 'They've probably got the equipment here. They've got everything else.'

'I'd sooner my own. I'll work with EDD here if I must, but I don't know them. Neither do you. I can have what I need in our hotel suite, and link up with Feeney.'

She couldn't argue when she agreed. 'Do that. But we've got to play it straight with the locals. If you make headway, we bring them in. Financials and communications, they're on you.'

'I'll try to earn my exorbitant fee. Did Melinda Jones start to say a name?'

'That's my take. Sara – Sara something. I gave it to the feds.' She glanced over to where they were huddled with their PPCs. 'They're all over it. I'm going to give the locals everything I've got, then I need to set up my own HQ. I need my board, my book, my space. I need to think.'

She looked at the screens. 'How the hell do I work those?'

'I'll take care of that.'

'Good. The last thing I need is to flash up some cute little puppies instead of suspects.'

When she turned to the room, Ricchio walked to the podium. Shuffling and muttering silenced.

'Everyone here knows the situation. We've now formed a joint investigation with the NYPSD, represented here by Lieutenant Dallas, and Roarke as civilian consultant, and also with the FBI represented by Special Agents Nikos and Laurence. As you know, or should after the earlier briefing, Lieutenant Dallas apprehended Isaac McQueen twelve years ago and is responsible for the release of the twenty-two minor females he had abducted and held. Melinda Jones was one of the twenty-two.

'Everyone in this unit knows Melinda, has worked with her. I expect every officer in this room to afford Lieutenant Dallas, Roarke, Agents Nikos and Laurence every courtesy, and complete cooperation. Lieutenant.'

She stepped forward. 'Isaac McQueen is a predatory and violent pedophile. He's highly organized, intelligent, and goal oriented. He enjoys taking risks, feeds on them, but calculates them. He never intended to be caught, feels no remorse, but a sense of entitlement. His preferred target is female, between twelve and fifteen. Pretty girls. While he has targeted street kids, runaways, he prefers healthy, stylishly dressed targets – the middle-class kid.'

She looked toward the screen where Roarke displayed McQueen's image and salient data.

'He's an experienced grifter. He knows how to run a game. He enjoys them. Statements from the minor females after his apprehension told us he often forced them into role-playing. He adapts,' she continued. 'He blends. He is congenial, even charming, well dressed, well groomed, well spoken. He will live quietly in an urban setting, most probably a mid-level apartment building. He enjoys having neighbors – another kind of role-playing for him.

'He will go out. He'll be compelled to, especially after a twelve-year confinement. He will eat in restaurants, visit clubs, galleries. He'll shop, extensively and well. Shopping is a particular pleasure for him – acquiring. Collecting again. He'll know the city and his part of it very, very well.'

She glanced at Roarke, nodded. The next image came on screen.

'His mother, Alice McQueen, was a popper addict. She trained him in the grift, and she sexually abused him. It's believed this sexual relationship lasted until he killed her when he was nineteen. She is the prototype for the partners he acquires, uses, and murders when done with them. Older, addicts, attractive, smart enough to be of use, vulnerable enough to be used.'

She paused a moment until Roarke put the next image up. 'We believe this woman is his current partner. At this time, she is unidentified. Through a liaison, she was introduced to McQueen while he was in prison. We've determined they continued to communicate after the physical visits stopped. Once McQueen selected his target and location, she would have done the legwork. At some point she connected with Melinda Jones, posing as a rape victim. She would have been convincing, and would have developed a relationship with the target. We believe it's this woman who contacted the target and lured her to McQueen. According to pattern, she'll have her own residence, but visit his often.'

She stopped again, scanned the room. Cops taking notes, studying her, wanting to get the hell on with it and find the woman they all knew.

'Look, I understand your priority is to find Melinda, to get her home safe. I agree with that priority. But be aware, he will be compelled to hunt.'

This single thought lived in her gut like a parasite. There would be another victim, and soon.

'A day or two,' she continued, pressing the point, 'the juice of having Melinda, of screwing with me may be enough to satisfy him. But he's out, he's out eating, shopping – and he sees pretty young girls getting a pizza, window-shopping, running around with friends. He sees them, smells them, brushes up against them on the street. He wants – and he'll take.

'He held over twenty girls at one time. He won't have any problem holding one woman and a girl. She won't see it coming, so we have to. They'll work together. They'll use a van – something common, nothing new, nothing flashy. He most usually hunts at night, but not exclusively. Crowded places. Places girls of that age like to haunt. He'll use a pressure syringe, enough to disorient her. He'll need an apartment building with its own garage. If it has security, he'll jam it. He has excellent e-skills. For now Melinda's useful to him, and doesn't fit his victimology.'

'He raped an adult female in New York,' one of the cops commented.

Eve heard the bitter temper in the voice, as she turned to the detective. Late twenties, she judged, fit, good-looking, brown and brown.

And at the moment with a belligerent set to his jaw.

'He did that for my benefit. He doesn't need to prove anything with Melinda. He has her, so's already proven it.'

'You were confrontational with him during the 'link up.'

Eve angled her head, gave him a deeper study. Shirt-sleeved detective, hip holster, messy hair – hands scooping through it – tense face, hard eyes.

'Was I?'

'You told him to get fucked.'

'Is that confrontational around here?'

She got a quiet roll of laughter before Bree spoke up.

'You kept his focus on you – on you and him. Kept him engaged on that level, and a little pissed off – but at you. You and him. You are the target, so Melinda's the tool, the lure. So she's secondary. If he hurts her, deal's off and you go home. You made him hear that, you made him believe that.'

Okay, Eve thought, maybe Bree Jones would be an asset.

'And every time he contacts me – and he will do so again – I'll do the same. He expects it. He wants it. He gets off on it because he's convinced he'll have this second shot and it'll end differently. He didn't just get taken down by a cop, but by a rookie. Believe me, that's eaten at him, burned his ego. Believe me, too, he's no pussy. He'll gut you like a trout if he gets the edge. He's strong, and he can fight like a bastard. Don't make the same mistake I did. Get backup. Stun him to the ground if you have to. I didn't do either, and the son of a bitch almost killed me.

'Agents.'

As Eve expected, Nikos took the lead and – to her amusement – stepped to the podium.

'Special Agent Laurence and I would like to thank the Dallas Police and Security Department and Lieutenant Ricchio for the cooperation and assistance. The Bureau is committed to reapprehending Isaac McQueen, and to the safe return of Melinda Jones. We agree with the bulk of the profile, the data, and the suppositions Lieutenant Dallas related here. One point.'

She held up a finger, paused briefly.

'We do agree the subject is highly goal oriented, and as

such our analysis and probability ratio skews extremely low on the likelihood the subject will attempt an abduction of a minor at this time. Our focus will be on apprehending the subject with the safe release of his hostage.'

That's fine, Eve thought. You do that. And she noted Laurence continued to work as his partner addressed the room.

Nikos went on, repaving ground already covered, wasting time in Eve's opinion. Roarke edged closer, spoke quietly.

'They've arrested the prison guard, and they're working him and Stibble. EDD has all the electronics, looking for any communications to or from McQueen and the partner.'

'Good.'

'I've got better. Stibble let McQueen use his pocket 'link on several occasions. McQueen wiped it, but EDD's on that, too.'

'That's not better. That's excellent. I'd interrupt to update, but Nikos is having so much fun boring the cops.'

The faintest smile touched Roarke's mouth. 'She's a bureaucrat, and less boring than most. Laurence has something.'

Eve looked over, saw Laurence get to his feet. The movement shut Nikos up.

'Got her,' Laurence announced. 'Sarajo Whitehead, allegedly assaulted and raped by persons unknown October of last year.'

'I worked that.' Bree rose as well, looked at her partner. 'We worked that.'

'I've got that, too.' Laurence nodded. 'Subject was treated

at Mercy Free Clinic, Dr. Hernandez attending, and reported to this precinct's SVU. Melinda Jones as rape counselor.'

'Let's see her,' Eve demanded, then backed up. 'Sorry.'

'No need.' Laurence offered his PPC to Roarke. 'You look to be running this end. Can you interface?'

'I can.'

'She walked into the clinic,' Bree reported. 'It's open round the clock. Her clothes were torn and she had minor bruising on her arms and legs. Exam confirmed recent rough or forced sex, additional bruising on her thighs.' She glanced at her partner for confirmation.

'That's right.' Annalyn Walker nodded. 'She claimed she was assaulted after closing the bar where she worked – ah, the Circle D. It's about four blocks from the clinic. Said this guy grabbed her, smacked her around, had a knife. Made her take him back in the bar, raped her, took her purse and the jewelry she had on, left.'

'She gave us a description, but it was vague,' Bree continued. 'She claimed it was dark. Our investigation confirmed her place of employment and sexual activity on the floor inside the door. We found her empty purse in a recycler two blocks away. Melinda counseled her for several weeks. We never found the alleged rapist.'

'We'll need to see the case file,' Eve said. 'Interview her former employer, coworkers – because she won't be working there now – talk to regulars. We want to find the guy she had – consensual – sex with.'

'She had tearing,' Detective Walker pointed out. 'Bruises.'

'I'm sure she did. But she wasn't raped. She needed to look as if she was, report she was raped in order to hook up with Melinda.'

She gave Roarke the nod, angled herself for a good look at the screen.

'Minor changes in appearance from her Sister Suzan days. Went two-toned brown and blond, different eye color, a little fuller in the face, reshaped eyebrows.' Eve spoke half to herself as she studied the ID shot. 'Something about her rings with me, but I can't pin it.'

'Bogus ID again.' Roarke held up his own PPC. 'The woman with that name and those prints died three years ago in a vehicular accident in Toledo, Ohio.'

'You're quick,' Laurence commented.

'She's sticking to pattern and plan. She'll have a different ID now, a different appearance,' Eve added. 'She'll have used one other than this to set up McQueen's place here, to acquire the transportation. She may have changed yet again.' Eve nodded, eyes narrowed on the screen image. 'She's good, too. He picked well.'

'We know where she worked,' Ricchio said. 'Where she lived last fall. We start there. Annalyn, Bree, you've already talked to the people at the bar. Talk to them again, with this new information.'

'I'd like in on that, Lieutenant.'

Ricchio nodded at Eve. 'You've got it.'

'Laurence and I will take the residence.'

'I'm going to put some officers on the van and the real

estate,' Ricchio said. 'Look for purchase and registration of previously owned vehicles of the type profiled, and for rentals – apartments and condos with attached parking. Also purchases and installation of residential soundproofing. I'll see the file on Whitehead is copied to both you and the agents, Lieutenant.'

'Sounds like a plan.' Eve turned to Bree. 'We'll follow you to the bar.'

'Now,' Roarke said when he got behind the wheel, 'tell me what you really think.'

'They knew Bree was on duty – had the night shift – when they faked the rape. They wanted her involved. Get a look at how she works, how she is. And they'd play the very good odds she'd tag her sister as counselor. The woman sucked some joker into staying after closing to bang her – make it rough.'

'One of the oldest cons there is,' Roarke agreed.

'Yeah. She makes him suit up. She doesn't want his DNA, doesn't want to point the finger at him. Better if it's person unknown. Now she can connect with Melinda, play on Melinda's sympathies, engage her, involve her. Plenty of time since last October to watch her, get a solid sense of her routine – hers and her sister's. Drop away,' Eve added. 'I think that's what we'll find. The woman dropped away, stopped the counseling. Then she can come back after a nice time lag. She's had a relapse, or she saw her attacker. Hysterical, needs help. Please, can we talk? I know it's late, but I need to talk to somebody. The framework's a basic con. She'll have done something similar before.'

'It went too smoothly for her to have been a novice.'

Eve agreed. 'The sex is just a tool. I don't think he'd have trusted anybody to fake a rape who hadn't done it before, or used sex for blackmail and profit.'

Roarke glanced over as he negotiated traffic. 'Unlike Nikos, I don't agree with the bulk of your briefing, but with the whole. They wouldn't have acquired the van locally.'

'Again, same page. Gotta check, but she'd have found one out of Dallas, driven it in. Not until after they had the place. No point in it before that.'

Roarke shrugged as he swung around a pickup. 'I'll find it.'

'Will you?'

'She wouldn't have driven for days. Most likely she bought it in Texas. A big state, yes, but still just a state. In-state keeps the registration and transfer less complicated. And unless she's using up ID like candy, she may have used one we know about. Since she's going to toss it anyway, why not? I'd vote for Sister Suzan. She seems the used, inexpensive van type, doesn't she?'

Considering, Eve studied his profile. 'That's good. I hadn't worked that around yet.'

'You would have. This Ricchio likely will, too. He seems capable.'

'Yeah, he does.' She glanced out the window, noted they'd moved into meaner streets. Streets like the ones she'd wandered in shock as a child.

She turned away, tuned them out. When Roarke touched her hand briefly, she realized he knew.

'I'm not thinking about it.'

Oh, but he knew she was. 'No need to.'

'I dealt with it when we came back before. We both did.' She remembered he'd beaten his knuckles bloody on a speed bag when they'd come back from that room where it had happened. Where she'd remembered everything.

'Melinda Jones is what's important now,' she added.

'Do you believe he won't hurt her – or much – or was that for her sister's benefit?'

'I don't see why he would, unless he's bored, or loses his temper. He's got control, but he's also got a switch. That's what I saw when I stumbled on him in New York. How he is when the switch gets flipped. I'm going to try to keep him from being bored – and keep his temper on me. And if I can't, it's all the more likely he'll snatch a kid. Nikos is wrong there. An adult woman, an older partner, that's mommy sex, so it's habit, it's ingrained. But they can't give him what he really needs, and what he feels entitled to.'

'And again, what his mother helped acquire for him.'

'Exactly. Forty-eight hours, by my take – no more, and probably less. If we don't have him, he'll feed the need.'

Roarke pulled into a lot peppered with potholes, slid in beside the Dallas police.

'Entrance is around front,' Annalyn told them. 'She claimed he grabbed her out here, when she came out the back. Held the knife on her until she'd unlocked, then did her right on the floor.'

'There's a security cam.'

Annalyn looked up as Eve did. 'There wasn't. The owner installed one after the fact. The place isn't much, but he's a decent guy. He was pretty upset about the whole deal, and steamed that it happened in his place.'

They walked around front where, Eve agreed, the place wasn't much. When they stepped in she judged it as a bar for serious, no-frills drinking. Long bar, swivel stools, a scatter of tables with hard plastic chairs, crap lighting. No food service, and no amusements other than the ancient, flickering, and palm-sized screen hanging from a hook at the end of the bar.

It didn't lack for customers. She counted eleven, half of them in cowboy boots, and most of them solo drinkers.

The man running the stick had a gut like a whale and a bald streak straight down the center of his skull. He gave them a look, a nod, then came down the bar to meet them.

'Detectives. Don't tell me you found that fucker – excuse my language – who raped Sarajo?'

Bree took the lead. In Eve's estimation, her partner let her.

'The woman you knew as Sarajo Whitehead is wanted for questioning on another matter. It turns out she was using false identification when she worked for you, Mr Vik. And we now believe, on strong evidence, she faked the rape.'

'Goddamn it, excuse my language.' He shifted his feet. The enormous gut rolled like a tsunami. 'I gave her a week's pay after that happened, to tide her over. Felt responsible 'cause she closed the place for me that night, and I didn't have security on the back. Why the hell would she do something like that?'

'The thing is, Mr Vik, we think she had relations with someone here that night. I know we asked you, and everyone who worked that night before, but with this new angle, can you think of anyone she might have let in after closing?'

'Wasn't a regular, I'll tell you that. I grilled every last one of them my own self.' He swiped a rag over the bar. 'There was that guy, passing through. He didn't look nothing like the guy she said. She said he was big, had some Mex in him, dark hair and eyes. This guy was white as an Irishman's ass – excuse my language – and scrawny. Yellow hair. Talked too damn much to suit me. Here for his daddy's memorial, hated the old man anyway, and was heading back to Kentucky when it was over. I left about midnight. He was still here. But the flat fact is, he wasn't carrying no knife, and Sarajo could've squashed him like a bug if he tried anything. I never gave him a thought.'

'Did he mention his name?'

'Maybe did. Let me think.' Vik closed his eyes. 'Chester. Yeah, he said how he was named after the old man. Didn't say the rest, not to me. But he ran a tab, and I held the plastic like I do at the register. If he paid that way, I can find him.'

'It would really help us out, Mr Vik.'

'You hold on. Want a drink?'

'No, we're good, but thanks.'

'Laroo! Take the bar.' Vik and his massive gut wobbled their way to a back room.

'How white is an Irishman's ass?' Eve wondered aloud.

'You should know, darling.'

That got a snicker out of Annalyn. 'I dated a guy named Colin Magee way back in the day. He was mostly Irish. His ass was pretty white.'

'You dated everybody back in the day,' Bree said, but her eyes stayed fixed on the door to the back room, as if she could will Vik to return with what they needed.

'I've always preferred the sampler menu. Take a few bites, then try something else. So how's juggling cop and marriage?' she asked Eve.

'You're never hungry. Tell me, is this Vik's memory as good as he makes it sound?'

'Every bit,' Annalyn confirmed. 'He rattled off the name of every regular when we first came in, and his opinion on same. Detailed the work schedules, gave us former employees in case one of them had come back and done it out of spite.'

He waddled through the door again with a printout. 'Used the plastic. Chester H. Gibbons.'

He passed the printout to Bree.

'Thanks, Mr Vik. This is a big help.'

'She did what you say, I hope you get her good. After she didn't come back, I tried to get her on her 'link, even went over to her place. Worried about her – and felt guilty, too. She'd cleared out, and I figured she was too upset to stay.' He shook his head, eyed Roarke. 'You don't look like a cop.'

'I'm not, and thank you for noticing.'

'Irish, are you? Never knew a Mick – no offense – didn't know how to drink. You come back any time, we'll fix you up.'

'I'll keep that in mind.'

'I've got a couple questions,' Eve began.

'Now *you* look like a cop.'

'I am, thanks for noticing.'

Vik's smiled flickered in appreciation. 'But you ain't from around here.'

'New York. You've got an impressive memory, Mr Vik. When did Sarajo start working for you?'

'Would've been middle of August last year. She came in – Saturday night, it was, looking for work. Business was good, so I said she could work then and there. If she did good, I'd give her some hours. You could tell she'd worked bars before. She knew how to get the drinks out, when to talk, when to shut up. Good-looking. Even drunks like having a good-looking woman serve them drinks.'

'You didn't ask her any questions?'

'Not then, but sure, before I hired her on official. She said her man left her in Laredo, and she wanted a fresh start. She did the job. Wasn't especially friendly, but she did the job.'

'An observant sort such as yourself would've known she was a user.'

He lifted his shoulders; his gut flowed like the tide. 'Maybe I figured she gave herself a boost here and there. I didn't see it, and it didn't screw with her work. So not my business.'

'How often did she lock up?'

'Once, maybe twice a week. After she'd worked here awhile, she asked if she could work that shift a couple times a week, or more if I wanted. Two of the other waitresses, they got kids. She didn't. It worked out. What the hell you want her for? This isn't for crying rape or using some boosters.'

'No, but they both play. She won't come back here, Mr Vik, but if you happen to see her anywhere in your travels, don't approach her. Contact Detective Jones or Detective Walker. We could use witnesses like you in New York.'

'Couldn't get me there with a bowie knife at my throat or a cattle prod up my ass – excuse my language. Full of thieves, murderers, and lunatics. No offense.'

'None taken.'

When they stepped outside, Eve turned to Bree. 'I'd like to walk down to the clinic, talk to the doctor who examined the partner. I can take this one if you want to start working on finding Chester.'

Bree looked to Annalyn.

'Yeah, no point traveling in a pack. We'll let you know what we find when we find it.'

'Same goes. Since you're headed back, maybe you could update the feds.'

'Yeah, what the hell. The clinic's about four blocks, that way.' Annalyn gestured.

They separated.

'So,' Roarke began, 'you're looking for a woman of a certain age, an addict who knows how to run a con, doesn't quibble about hooking herself to a pedophile, knows her way around a hard-line drinking establishment, and plays the game well enough to fool Vik. And he's no pushover. She doesn't mind sex with strangers, and making it rough enough to simulate rape, and is just fine with aiding in the abduction and imprisonment of a woman who helped her.'

'Yeah, she's a princess.' Even the thought of her made Eve vaguely ill and bitterly angry. 'She's also organized enough to pull all this, and put things together on her own until McQueen got out.'

'In homage to our location, this isn't her first rodeo.'

'No. She's been riding for a long time.'

They stepped into the clinic, and she noted it did better business than the bar. The chairs lining the walls, more forming another back-to-back line in the center of the room, were full.

Babies squalled, kids whined. Several women sported bellies testifying they'd soon bring more squallers and whiners into the world.

Eve walked to the counter, where a woman in a floral scrub top worked feverishly on a computer.

'I'm sorry.' The woman didn't pause. 'The waiting time is two hours. There's another clinic—'

'I need to talk to Dr. Hernandez.'

'I'm sorry.' The woman didn't sound sorry. She sounded harassed and exhausted. 'Dr. Hernandez is with a patient. I can—'

Eve palmed her badge, waved it in front of the woman's

face. 'This is an urgent matter. I'll be as quick as possible, but I need to speak with Dr. Hernandez.'

'Give me a minute. God, what a day.'

She popped up, scurried down a short hall, turned left, and vanished.

'Why is everybody sick or injured?' Eve wondered. 'Thieves, murderers, and lunatics, sure. That's why we love New York. But it looks like Dallas has a plague.'

The woman scurried back. 'Listen.' She kept her voice low. 'Every exam room and office is occupied. If these people who've been waiting so much as see a doctor, I could have a riot. Can you talk to her outside? Out the back?'

'No problem.'

'I've got to ask you to go out the front, walk around. If I take you back—'

'Riot. Got it. Thanks.'

'Not a plague,' Roarke said as they made the trip on foot. 'More understaffed, likely underfunded, and the only free clinic for miles.'

'Okay, probably, but I've seen Louise's clinic. Free, and sure crowded, but not like that.'

'Louise's isn't underfunded, thanks to you.'

She hunched her shoulders. 'It was your money.'

'No, it was your money.'

'Only because you gave it to me.'

'Which, darling Eve, makes it yours.'

'Now it's Louise's, so it doesn't really matter. I don't like it here.' She rolled her shoulders when they reached the rear of the clinic. 'It's a run-down area, poor – and that's not what I mean. It's got a strong whiff of criminal underbelly. But you know, there's just no sense of character, or atmosphere. You feel like if some asshole came up to mug you, he'd have that accent, or cowboy boots, maybe the hat. How is that intimidating?'

'I do so completely adore you, and your chauvinistic New York mind.'

A small, dark woman darted through the door. 'Officer?'

'Lieutenant Dallas. I'm working with Detectives Walker and Jones. You had a patient, claiming she'd been raped last October – outside the Circle D. Sarajo Whitehead. Those detectives caught her case, and Melinda Jones came in as counselor.'

'Yes, I remember. Have you caught the rapist?'

'He doesn't exist. She faked it.'

'I sincerely doubt—'

'Don't. You can check with the detectives you know. This is a very dangerous woman who is working with a very dangerous man. You know Melinda Jones.'

'Yes, very well.'

'They have her.' As Hernandez stared, Eve pushed on. 'The faked attack was staged to make contact with Melinda, to connect. This woman lured Melinda out last night, and abducted her. We need everything you can tell us.'

'God, oh my God. I'm going to contact Bree. I can't just take your word.'

'Go ahead.'

Eve waited while Hernandez used her 'link, waited through the shocked words, the shakiness.

'I'm going to get you her files,' Hernandez said when she clicked off. 'I'll give you everything I have. I believed her. Her injuries weren't that severe, but her emotional state . . . I believed her.'

'No reason you shouldn't have,' Eve said. 'She's good at what she does.'

# 8

File in hand, Eve got back into the car.

'Back to the cop shop?' Roarke asked her.

'Have to. What I want to do is get to the hotel, set up my space, organize what I have, and *think*.' She scowled into space for a minute. 'I'm a team player.'

Roarke said, 'Hmmm.'

'I am,' she insisted.

'When necessary, yes.' He flicked her a glance. 'Especially if you're in charge of the team.'

'Okay, I'll cop to that – and that it's hard swallowing I've got to check with Ricchio – his house – the feds, figure out who to work with and how. Jones is sharp, but she can't be objective on this. None of them can. Maybe I can't either.'

'You have to adjust without having any time to adjust.'

'There isn't any time.'

'Exactly.'

'And he knows that. He's playing with that. Yeah. Yeah.' She tapped her fingers on her thigh as she chewed that over. 'The longer I'm off my rhythm, the longer he has to screw with me.'

'There are times when in order to get what you need, you have to work on two levels and integrate them on another.'

So speaks the business god, she thought – and accurately. 'Work with Ricchio and the feds here, with my people there. I guess the trick is the integration. We can all say it doesn't matter who does what or gets what, and it's mostly true. But cops are territorial. We have to be.

'God, I want coffee. And no, you're not having a supply sent down to Ricchio's department. It's just . . .' She wiggled a hand in the air. 'Adjust.' She nodded to herself. 'Gotta adjust.'

Adjusting, she took the medical files straight to Ricchio.

'Hernandez was very cooperative. I have her statement here as well. The gist is, the female unknown subject's injuries were fairly minor, but consistent with her story, as was her emotional state. She played the role well.'

'So she's played it before.'

'My take, yeah. We're looking for someone who's run sex cons. I understand you have people who can work with the data we have. So do I. I'd like to have some of my men working this in conjunction with yours. Different eyes, different angles. Whoever gets there first, we all win.'

'Overlapping ground takes time and manpower away from other potential leads.'

She wanted to stand, but sat. 'Look, I don't want to step on toes, but this is a tough balance for me. Imagine yourself called up to New York to work with an established unit.'

He smiled a little. 'I went to New York once, and I still

can't imagine it. Imagine yourself, in charge of an established unit, juggling in not only federal agents but a New York boss.'

'Tough balance all around,' Eve agreed. 'But the goal's the same for all of us. I'll get more done toward that goal if I'm able to tap my own resources as well as work with you and yours.'

She paused a moment. 'Straight out, I strongly believe the female UNSUB is the route to McQueen. She's done the legwork, and very likely continues to. She's the one who'll run the errands, and she's separated from him for periods of time. Her own apartment, potential other employment. She's been here for more than a year. Somebody knows her, has done business with her, sold her food, clothes, goods. She's an addict, and that's another angle. Where does she get her junk? She's attractive, and she's got a man to please. Where does she get her hair stuff, her face stuff, all that other woman stuff?'

Lips pursed, Ricchio sat back, nodded slowly. 'All right, you've got points. Focusing on McQueen sits easier with me, but you've got points.'

'If I may,' Roarke interjected. 'If you consider it a two-pronged approach rather than an overlap. Improve the odds.'

'Frankly, if I were in your position, I'd do what I felt I needed to do, regardless of the politics of cooperation. It's better if we all say we agree.'

'Works for me.' Her 'link signaled. 'Excuse me.'

When she stepped away, Ricchio turned to Roarke. 'As

the word is your particular area is electronics, you should meet Lieutenant Stevenson. He runs EDD.'

'Of course.'

'I'll have someone take you up when you're ready. We work with civilians, such as Melinda, in SVU routinely. That's not the usual in EDD.'

'Then I'll do my best to be unobtrusive.'

'My father recently retired as Deputy Chief,' Ricchio began in an easy, conversational tone. 'He was part of a task force, years ago, working on taking down a major weapons organization. Part of the investigation included a Patrick Roarke. I remember because my father spent a couple weeks in Ireland during the investigation. Any relation?'

'That would have been my father,' Roarke said coolly, 'which illustrates the world is a strangely intimate place. He had dealings with Max Ricker, as I'm sure you're aware. As you'd be aware that my wife is responsible for Ricker's current accommodations in an off-planet cage. A strangely intimate place indeed.'

'With interesting turns,' Ricchio agreed. 'Patrick Roarke was stabbed to death in Dublin, wasn't he?'

'If you're asking if I killed him, I didn't have that pleasure.'

He set aside irritation as Eve strode back. From the look in her eye, he knew she had something.

'Our female UNSUB traded sex with the guard we have in custody for contact with McQueen. He got her in three times in the last year under the radar, let them use one of the conjugal trailers. He swears the contact initiated with the woman,

147

not McQueen. She angled for a fourth, two weeks ago. McQueen instructed Lovett to tell her to wait.'

'She's in love with him,' Roarke commented.

'In whatever twisted way it works with her kind. She's hooked – addictive personality, and he's another drug. He won't keep her much longer.'

'He never confessed. It could never be proven, but the prevailing theory is once he disposed of his partner, he'd shortly dispose of any captives and move on.'

Eve looked at Ricchio, understood his guts would be in knots. 'Prior to New York, he was still evolving, finding his pattern, his rhythm. Added to it. He hasn't finished with me, so he hasn't finished with Melinda. Who do you want me to work with, Lieutenant? And do you have somewhere I can set up?'

'I've got a temporary office for you. It's not much. I'd like you to use Bree and Annalyn. Bree needs to keep her mind engaged, and she trusts you.'

Eve started to point out that Bree Jones didn't know her, but let it go. 'I'm good with that. Saves having to update them on what we got from the bar.'

'If you don't need Roarke at the moment, I'd like to have him acquaint himself with our EDD.'

'Best use,' she said to Roarke.

'Then I'll get back to you later.'

They went their separate ways.

'Not much' turned out to be twice the size of her office at Central, with a shiny desk outfitted with a data and communication center, a multiposition gel-chair, an AutoChef, a personal fridgie, an auxiliary station, two cozy visitor's chairs – and a large window she immediately shielded.

Too much space, she thought, too much comfort. Adjust, she reminded herself. Make it work.

She programmed what passed for coffee, made do with that while she began to set up a case board. She barely glanced over when Bree and Annalyn came in.

'I'm still setting up. I'll need you to share the auxiliary. Run an anal on all the data we have, specifically on the female UNSUB. And I want a time line up here on the board, starting with first known contact with McQueen right up to his last communication with me.'

'I'll start on the data,' Annalyn said. 'Bree, while the lieutenant's setting up, why don't you get us some eats? Use my code. My treat.'

'Sure. What would you like, Lieutenant?'

'Doesn't matter.'

'You a veggie?' Annalyn asked her.

'Not unless I can't identify the meat.'

'Texas beef, one of the perks. Hardly any filling. I'll spring for burgers, Bree.'

'Could use a Pepsi,' Eve added. 'Coffee's absolute shit.'

'I'll take care of it.'

When Bree left, Eve glanced at Annalyn again. 'Something on your mind, Detective?'

'She's a good cop, doesn't miss much. A little more seasoning, she won't miss anything. On a personal level, she can be a little intense, but she's not an asshole. Right now she's holding on by her fingernails. She'll keep holding on as long as she believes we'll find Melinda. She stops believing that, she's done. Not just for now. Just done.'

'Then we won't give her any reason not to believe it.'

'She needs to be part of bringing McQueen down.'

'I've got that, but that's your lieutenant's call, not mine.'

'You don't get you're her hero. Whether you want to be or not,' she continued, correctly reading Eve's face. 'You saved her life, and more important to her, you saved Melly. You know what he did to them, to all those kids, and you stopped him, you got them out.'

'I got lucky. If you read the files, you know I was lucky I didn't get us all killed.'

Annalyn propped her ankle on her knee. 'Not the way I read it – and besides, if it wasn't for lucky, half the cases we close would still be open. It doesn't matter how you did it, you did it. And you're a big part of why she can believe we'll do it again. Stop him, and get Melly out. If you've got doubts – and Christ knows I do – and you want Bree to keep hanging on, to be a useful part of the investigation, don't let her see them.'

Eve didn't hesitate, didn't need to. 'Let me make this clear. At this point in time, I don't have any doubts. What I have is data, facts, pattern, theory, and instinct. I don't believe we're going to get Melinda Jones home, and put McQueen and his partner in prison. I know it.'

Annalyn glanced toward the door. 'How do you know it? No, wait. If you mean that, tell us both when Bree gets back.'

'I'll do that. Get started on the anal.'

Having said her piece, Annalyn got to work without any more chatter. Eve continued with her board, had it nearly set to her satisfaction when Bree and the food arrived.

The smell of burgers and fries filled the room, and for a moment made the strange space comfortably familiar. Eve took her burger off the disposable plate, chomped in. 'Good,' she decreed. 'Okay, here's how I work, and how we'll be working as long as I'm here. I use visuals, like the board here, and if I'm sitting back with my eyes closed I'm not catching a nap. I'm thinking. If I kick you out it's because I want to think without your thoughts getting in my way. Detective Jones, if I refer to your sister as the vic, I don't want to see that look on your face I caught during the briefing. I know it's personal, and to a point that could be an advantage. But if it gets in the way, you're out.'

'Yes, sir.'

'Your partner understands you, and she's got your back. I don't want her distracted worrying that you're going to lose it at any point – any point – in this investigation.'

'I—'

'Don't interrupt. We're going to find McQueen and put him back where he belongs. I believe the most direct route to that end is the partner. We identify, locate, apprehend her, and bring her in, grill her like this pretty damn good Texas beef.'

She took another bite, swilled down some Pepsi.

'He had a long run before he went down. He chose his

spot and made it his sick, personal playground. He's not going to have a long run this time for very specific, very definite reasons.'

On another bite of burger, she leaned back on the shiny desk. Adjusting, she thought, and finding her rhythm after all.

'First,' she continued, 'I'm a hell of a lot smarter than I was twelve years ago. We have more resources and we know more about him than we did at that time. Second, because he's obsessed with getting to me, he's gone over the top pulling this off, involved too many people, left too many avenues – and we're going to squeeze all those people dry, take every one of those avenues until we find him.

'And the third reason.' She took another long drink of Pepsi. 'Melinda. She's a trained therapist. She knows how to talk to people, to get in their heads. She had the guts to confront him in prison, to know herself well enough to do that so she could take her life back. She had the stones to go into a career that would remind her, every day, of what he did to her. That makes her tougher and smarter than he is.

'If you don't believe that, all of that, then I can't use you here. Find something else to do.'

'I believe it, Lieutenant. All of it.'

'What's with the ring?' Eve demanded, and Bree stopped turning it.

'It's Melly's. I . . . I put it on this morning after this started. I wanted to have a piece of her, something I could touch, something to remind me I'm a piece of her.'

Eve nodded. 'Good enough. Do the time line.'

Eve studied the board, made some adjustments, some additions. She paced back and forth in front of it, frowning at the time line Bree created, mixing it in.

She needed to go by the female's former apartment, take a look at it, talk to the neighbors, the shopkeepers. Overlapping the feds, maybe, but she liked Roarke's two-pronged approach.

Might be something there, she thought. Some little crumb – something said, something seen. An impression. An opinion.

She wished fleetingly for more salt as she ate her fries. A lot more salt. She should just carry some in her pocket for fry emergencies.

An addiction, she admitted, like the coffee. Just something she craved and Roarke provided. That made him sort of her pusher, didn't it?

'Why does she fall in love with him?'

'Sorry?'

She shook her head at Bree. 'He's in prison. She goes for the money, the work – gotta live, gotta get what she needs. She's experienced, she's hard, she's self-absorbed. All addicts are. But she falls for him.'

She paced again, studying the two shots of the female, the picture of McQueen.

'Sure he's attractive. Maybe even her type. He's hard, too. He's been around, knows the score. But he likes little girls. Those small, supple bodies just budding. She's too old for his needs, too experienced sexually. However well she's kept her body, it's never going to be in first bud again. She has to know that.'

'He's charming,' Bree put in. 'When he raped me the first time, he was charming. I don't mean—'

'I know. You weren't charmed, but he put it on for you.'

'He flattered me. How pretty I was, how soft my skin was. It didn't matter that I was screaming. He kept saying things like that. He had candles lit, and music playing. Like it was romantic.'

Bree shook her head. 'You know all this. I told you all this before, when you talked to me in the hospital.'

'Doesn't hurt to be reminded. He charms her, flatters her. But that's not enough. Somehow she's convinced she's different than the others, that she has something with him. How do you train someone to do what you want, to follow complex instructions over a long period of time? To form the sort of attachment to you that would have them do whatever you wanted, even when you aren't there to make them. It's a con, just like any other. He can't control her with fear, so it has to be pleasure.'

'He gives her what she needs, promises more,' Annalyn said.

'The illegals. He provides.' Eve started to reach for her communicator. For Peabody. Two detectives in the room, she reminded herself. She needed to use what she'd been provided.

'I need names of inmates on his block. Look for an illegals connection and a release. Start with six months before his first contact with the female. Go back a year if you don't get any hits.'

'I'm on it,' Annalyn told her.

'Not all those contacts with Stibble's 'link were to her, I bet my ass and yours. Had to make arrangements to give his dog her bones. He's got someone on the outside who'd take care of that. Someone who either owes him a big favor, or who he has on his payroll.

'Too many people.' She nodded, felt the buzz. 'Just too many people. She's got a source in Dallas, too. Find the source, find her. Find her, find McQueen.'

'Jayson – Detective Price's brother – works in Illegals,' Bree began. 'He's the one who interrupted you during the briefing. He and Melinda just started seeing each other a couple months ago, so—'

'Don't care. Have him tap his brother. Really Fat Vik said boosters, but it's going to be more. She needs something to level out, keep it smooth. Can't just bounce on the high with all this going on. She needs to tune out, relax.'

'She'd think she's competing with girls, sexually, wouldn't she?' Annalyn commented. 'I'd add sex drugs. Erotica at a minimum to that.'

'Good point. Make it happen, Jones.' She considered Annalyn. 'You look good.'

'Thanks. I work with what I've got.'

'And you're single. You're out in the mix. You do the salon thing? The hair and all that?'

'Tough on a cop's salary, but once a month or so, yeah. I

see where you're going. She's got to look good for him. I bet she's had some body work since he hooked her. Lift the girls up some, laser off the lines, like that.'

'Recent, after she stopped counseling, before his escape. In Dallas, or close. She's thinking about seeing him, him seeing her, being with him, she might've gone for the works at some salon, and in the last few days.'

'Feels right.'

'Look, I'll take the inmate search. You and Jones know the city. Put together a list of most-likely salons, body work locations. Show both her ID shots. Let's get lucky again.'

'Are you going to update the feds with this angle?'

'Shit. Yeah, I'll take care of it.'

'Too bad,' Annalyn said, and grinned. 'Come on, Bree. Let's track this bitch down.'

Eve sat, started the search. Annalyn was right, she thought. It felt right. Felt good. While she worked she forgot the unfamiliar room, fell into a routine.

McQueen had mucked with his, she thought, and now his foundation cracked under the weight of too much fuss, too many additions.

It didn't surprise her to find so many cons, deemed rehabilitated, with connections to illegals.

'Prisons are full of bad guys,' she mumbled, ran each one.

'I like you, Burt, street name Thor, Civet. I like you a whole bunch.' She ran probabilities, smiled slowly. 'See there, the computer likes you, too. You're a popular guy. Contact Peabody, Detective Delia, NYPSD,' she ordered the 'link.

Peabody's face, showing a little wear, came on screen. 'Hey, Dallas. We've got Stibble and Lovett on hold. We think we've tapped them out, but we'll give them another go tomorrow.'

'I've got a line. Burt Civet, aka Thor. Did time with McQueen until he made parole about four years ago. His current address is listed on Washington Street. No current employment, so I'm just taking a wild guess he's dealing again. Find him, pick him up, squeeze him. Probability's high McQueen tapped him to supply the partner when she was in New York, keep her happy.'

'Got it.'

'I want everything he knows about this woman, Peabody. Everything. I want to know how McQueen handled the payoff. Make whatever deal you've got to make, but convince him it's in his best interest to roll over. He did five hard last time. Use it. He likes to sell to minors, tends to set up shop near playgrounds, schools, arcades.'

'Makes him a good match for McQueen.'

'I'm sure they bonded. I want McQueen's bitch, Peabody. Squeeze hard.'

'He's the lemon, we'll make lemonade. How's it going down there?'

'It's weird. They're too polite, they talk funny, and stuff has too much shine on it. But the coffee's worse than Central's, so that's something. I'm going to send you everything I've got, then I'm going to pull Roarke in from whatever he's doing at EDD. I want to work on my own at the hotel for a while. You can reach me on my pocket 'link.'

'I'll let you know when we've got him.'

Eve clicked off, sat back. She wanted to be there. She wanted to track down Civet, squeeze his lemons into lemonade.

She hadn't been able to intimidate, squeeze, or snarl since she'd left New York. It just wasn't right.

She tagged Roarke. 'I've got a couple lines,' she told him. 'I want to take what I've got and work at the hotel. I need to get out of here as soon as you can shake loose.'

'I'm right there with you. On my way.'

She copied and saved data, gathered what she wanted. Rather than contact the feds directly, she wrote a quick, down-and-dirty summary and shot it to their 'links as text mail.

When she walked out to inform Ricchio of her plans, Roarke intercepted her.

'I let the Texas lieutenant know where you'll be. Let's get the bloody hell out of here.'

'Problem?'

He took her arm to hurry her along. 'Let's just say I've gotten used to your cop house. This one's given me an itch between the shoulder blades.'

'How's the deal in EDD?'

'Not as charming to my mind as our own, but efficient and with a similar wardrobe – though with a southwestern edge. The commanding officer doesn't care for civilians in his space – something else I'm accustomed to. But I've dealt with that.'

'You showed off,' Eve said as they got in the car.

'It had to be done. I dislike being scowled at and insulted by cops. Present company excepted. And how was your day?'

'Progress.'

She filled him in as they drove.

'Your two-pronged approach seems to be working quite well,' Roarke commented. 'As does your focus on the woman. She's a chink in his wall. I agree with you, he won't keep her long. He has to know she's a liability, if not at this point, soon.'

'She could stretch it out if she plays him right – but I think she's probably emotionally attached, so she'll fuck up. And he has Melinda for company and conversation.'

'You think he'll use her after all?'

'I think that's low probability, which is why I'm worried he'll move on a kid, and soon. But she'll talk to him, at least I think she will. It's what she does now. She's trained. I want to believe she'll get through this, use that training, keep him from hurting her.'

He pulled up in front of the hotel, one of those slick, shiny spears in the city's arsenal. He said, simply, 'Roarke,' and handed the key code and what Eve assumed was a hefty tip to the doorman as the man all but bolted to the doors to open them.

'This isn't where we stayed last time. But it's obviously one of yours.'

'It is, yes, and I thought we'd both want the change.'

When they walked to an elevator, the security man at the desk came to attention, snapped out, 'Sir.'

Roarke gave him a nod, then swiped a card. When they stepped into the small, muted gold elevator, he said, 'Triplex West, top level.'

'Triplex, as in three floors?'

'I thought we'd use the third floor as HQ. That way we can lock it off, even from housekeeping if you want. Use a droid there. First level's living space, second's bedroom areas. I ordered the top as I thought you'd want to see the setup, leave your file bag. Then I want a bloody drink.'

'I could use a bloody drink myself, and a bloody shower, and a bloody suspect I can hammer into the ground.'

He smiled. 'Missing New York. How about a bloody meal to go with it?'

'I had a burger.'

'Fuck me, it's more than I've had.'

The door opened. She blinked.

A murder board sat center of the room, just as she liked it. It wasn't precisely arranged as she would do, nor updated, but images, data, a partial time line – it was all there.

As was a desk, a sleep chair, three screens, two D-and-C units – in addition to what looked like a fully equipped kitchen, bath, and she noted after a quick circle, a second office.

'How did you do this?'

'I have a man here, one I could trust with your board. He has top security clearance. Saves you time.'

'It really does. Yours?' she asked with a gesture to the second office.

'It is. Not quite like home, but, well, adjustments.'

160

He'd made it as easy for her as he could, given her all the tools to work the way she liked best.

She stepped to him, laid her hands on his face and her lips on his.

'That's just like home,' she murmured. Then because it felt so damn good, hugged him hard. 'Let's have a bloody drink.'

# 9

She sat on the terrace, drinking some wine, ignoring the view.
Roarke was prettier to look at anyway. And looking at him, she
saw the signs she'd missed in her hurry to get to the hotel.

'You're pissed off.'

He lifted his shoulders in a careless shrug. 'Not at you, at
the moment.'

'At who? Or what?'

'Let's just say I've had enough of cops – but again, not you.
At the moment.'

She tracked back out of her own work to his end of it.
EDD.

'If EDD's that annoying, don't go back. You don't need to
go in when you've got your setup here. You can coordinate
with Feeney if and when you want.'

'As you'll be going in there's every reason. I'm with you as
long as we're in this place,' he reminded her. 'And a bit of
annoyance isn't much in the larger scheme, is it?'

'Depends. What's the annoyance, specifically? It's not just
being around cops.'

'Believe me, it's no champagne picnic for someone with
my . . . predilections.'

He could read her, often too well for comfort. Tit for tat, she thought, reached over, took his hand. 'Roarke.'

'Ah, bugger it. It's nothing, really. Ricchio's father – another cop – had a part in the investigation on mine. He made a point of telling me, with the Texas version of the beady eye you're so fond of.'

Her hackles rose. 'Out of line.'

'Was it? Wouldn't you have done the same in his place?'

'Maybe. Probably. I'd have been out of line. You're here to help, a consultant duly designated by the NYPSD. And Patrick Roarke has dick-all to do with it. One of Ricchio's consultants is being held by a violent predator. That's his fucking focus, and he's got no business messing with your head when lives are on the line.'

'Well then, we can agree in part. But there's always going to be a smudge, isn't there? It's the way of things.'

'Things suck.'

'Often. But now that you're annoyed along with me, I feel better. I want food.'

Not in the least mollified, she shoved up, paced away. 'This fucking place. I hate it. I don't care if it's unfair. Probably there's good things about it, good people in it. I don't care. They met up here, your father and mine.'

'Eve, Ricchio has no reason, and no accessible data to make a connection between Patrick Roarke, Richard Troy, and Lieutenant Eve Dallas.'

'But it's there. It's always going to be there, that smudge.'

She swung back toward him, letting out what had been grinding inside her since they'd touched down.

'We're never going to get out from under it, not all the way. No matter what we do, who we are, what we make, they're part of it. We can't change that. It's always there, and it's more there here.'

'It is, yes. It is.' He rose, went to her. 'So, we'll have to find Melinda Jones quickly, deal with McQueen, and go home.'

She closed her eyes when he rested his brow against hers. 'Sounds like a plan. Simple, straightforward.'

'I have every faith.'

'Then I'd better get back to it. Tell you what, to make up for cop bullshit, I'll deal with your dinner before I write up my reports. How do you feel about Texas beef, burger style?'

'I could feel very agreeable to that.' But he took her hands. 'Think about this. Without the smudge we wouldn't be just who we are, and wouldn't be so damn determined to keep scrubbing at it. In our own ways.'

'I guess not. Still . . .' She stopped when her 'link signaled. 'Peabody,' she said with a glance at the readout.

'Deal with it. I can handle getting my own dinner.'

'Good. Sorry. Peabody. Did you get him?'

He went in, kept an eye on her as he selected from the AutoChef. She paced, one hand jammed in her pocket. Talking fast, eyes narrowed, cop flat.

Back to scrubbing at the smudge, he thought.

When she came in, fresh energy came with her.

'They picked Civet up, got him cold with his pockets lined

with baggies of poppers, Zing, zoner, and what all. Collared him within a block of a youth center, which adds weight. Adding up how many times he's been in, he's looking at ten to fifteen without the PA breaking a sweat. He'll deal. He'll talk. She just has to play him right.'

She started pacing again, around her case board. 'She's got to let Baxter go in hard and low while she takes the soft, let's-work-this-out method.'

'Do you trust her to get it done?'

'Yeah, I do. But I'd trust her more if I was there.'

'You just want to sweat a suspect.'

'Oh God, yeah. Peabody gets Stibble, Lovett, now Civet. I get Really Fat Vik, the completely cooperative bartender with the super memory. How is that just?'

She plopped down at the desk. 'Still, I want to go roust the UNSUB's neighbors at her old apartment. Maybe one of them will give me some game.'

'You're certainly due. I'm going to take my meal in the other office and play Find the Van without cops sneering over my shoulder.'

While he did, she settled into writing her report, read the progress on others. They'd eliminated some of the real estate, some vehicle transactions. Still a long way to go.

Big city, she mused, lots of apartments and condos, lots of vans. What else? What else did he need, did he want?

She sat back, put her boots on the desk, shut her eyes.

Likes good wine, she remembered. He'd had a nice selection – heavy on the Cabernet – in his New York hellhole.

She put herself back there, using her mind, her memory rather than the crime scene photos.

Wineglasses lined by type in the cabinet. She hadn't known good crystal from crap back then, but she did now. Good glasses. Dishes – four-piece place settings, nice quality – simple, classic white with a raised pattern around the lips.

Fresh fruit and vegetables in the market bags. Nothing processed. Some cheese, a – what was it? – baguette. Eggs in the fridgie. Not egg substitute.

Good food, good wine, and good dishes and stemware to enjoy it. He'd have missed that in prison.

He'd want what he wanted now.

She roamed the apartment in her head, eyes closed, boots up.

Not much furniture, and no clutter. Clean, tidy, organized.

Organic cleaning products, she remembered. Unscented.

His bedroom had posts and rungs on the headboard. He'd needed those to secure the ropes, the cuffs, his restraints du jour.

Good sheets – two spare sets – all white, organic cotton.

He'd always used the beds, always raped his prey on good, clean sheets.

Good sheets had to be laundered.

Bathroom. Organic cotton with the towels, too, and white again. Always white. Soaps, shampoos, grooming products. All natural again, no additives, no chemicals.

He'd need shops that carried his preferences. He'd have

given his partner his requirements. Local shops, online? Maybe a mix of both.

Security cameras, soundproofing, shackles and restraints. The locals and the feds already had those, were already running those elements.

But they needed to work the other details.

She swung her boots to the floor, rose to circle the board as she dictated the additional list to the computer.

'Advise search for retail venues carrying these products in the Dallas area and online. Purchases of linens, kitchenware, cleaning products within the last six weeks. Grooming products, wine within four. Foodstuffs within the last two to three days.

'Also check on laundry services – white organic cotton linens.'

She circled again as Roarke came in. 'Copy and send memo to all listed partners. Mark priority.'

**Acknowledged, working ... Task complete.**

'I wasn't thorough enough,' she said to Roarke. 'And I've been so focused on the woman herself, I didn't think about the little things, the everyday things. Dishes, towels. Fuck! It's part of his pattern, part of his profile.'

'Then it's in the file, which every team member has.'

'Yeah, but every team member wasn't *in* that apartment, didn't see the dishes, the bottles of expensive wine. The tub of Green Nature cleaner under the sink.'

Fascinated, he lifted his eyebrows. 'You remember the actual brand of cleaner?'

'Yeah, I remember it, and while that's buried somewhere in the list of items found and logged in his place, who's going to pay attention unless you put it all together? We'd have had men on this today if I'd just thought of it sooner.'

'And how soon did you think of it once you had an actual opportunity to sit down, clear your mind, *and* think?'

'Pretty quick, actually. It's probably been trying to kick through all damn day.' Dissatisfied, restless, she rocked on her heels. 'Still slow. Another problem is she probably got most of this, if not all, online. It'll take longer to track down transactions.'

'You believe she's in love with him.'

Eve stared at the ID shots, felt that little trip again. 'I believe she believes it.'

'I'll wager she bought locally for some of it. The linens particularly. She's setting up house, isn't she? She'd want to touch them, examine them, fuss a bit.'

'Really?'

'Not everyone objects to shopping on almost religious grounds.' Like Eve, he studied the woman's ID shots. 'She's hard, you say, tough, experienced. But he's found a weak spot. And that part of her might enjoy taking the time, in person, to select – especially what she imagines touching his body, and hers.'

'That's good. Almost Mira good. Well, it'd be a break if she did, and if some clerk recognizes her. Meanwhile—'

'Meanwhile, I have a line on the van, or what I think may be the van.'

'Already?'

'I started earlier, in EDD. But find I work much better without that itch between my shoulder blades. A 'fifty-two panel van, blue,' he continued as he walked over to program coffee for both of them. 'Registered to the Heartfelt Christian League – which is bogus, by the way. I thought, if Sister Suzan made the purchase, she might use some church-type organization for the registration, so I started there.'

'Good start.'

'Well, you'd be surprised how many church-type organizations have vans, and have bought same in the last year or so. I tracked this one back to its previous owner, a Jerimiah Constance – who's a devout Christian, by the way, in a little town called Mayville, just this side of the Louisiana border. As Sister Suzan had a Baton Rouge address on that ID, it's a nice link. Cash transaction,' he added. 'Sister Suzan Devon's signature's on the transfer papers.'

'God, that feels good. I need everything you've got.'

'Already copied to your unit.'

She spun on her heel, went back to the desk. 'We'll get this out. It's probably been painted, but that's another avenue there. And she'll have switched the tags, but it's good. I'm going to nudge the feds to verify, have somebody interview God-fearing Jerimiah.'

'I'm still working on the money. McQueen's covered himself well in that area.'

'He's good,' she said as she sent out the new data. 'You're better.'

'Yes, of course, but thanks all the same.'

'We're on a nice roll here. Let's keep it going. Let's go harass some apartment-dwelling Texans.'

Roarke toasted her with his coffee. 'Yee-ha.'


The building showed some wear, squatting in the lowering light. The patch of parking on the side apparently doubled as a playground as a bunch of kids ran between and around cars, shouting the way kids always seemed to at play.

Security was just shy of adequate, but as several windows were wide open to the nonexistent breeze – just inviting a visit from thieves – she assumed nobody cared.

As she got out of the car one of the kids barreled straight into her.

'Tag! You're It!'

'No, I'm not.'

He grinned, showing a wide gap where, hopefully, his two front teeth would grow in at some point. 'We're playing Tag. Who are you?'

'I'm the police.'

'We play Cops 'n' Robbers, too. I like being a robber. You can arrest me.'

'Get back to me in about ten years.'

She eyed the entrance, eyed the kid. What the hell, you had to start somewhere. She pulled out the ID of Sarajo Whitehead. 'Do you know her?'

'She don't live here anymore.'

'But she did.'

'Yep. Uh-huh. I gotta go tag.'

'Wait a minute. Did she live by herself?'

'I guess. She slept a lot. She used to yell out the window for us to stop all that noise 'cause people are trying to sleep. But my ma said that was just too bad 'cause it's the middle of the day and kids get to play loud as they want outside.'

'Who's your ma?'

'She's Becky Robbins and my pa's Jake. I'm Chip. We live on the fourth floor, and I've got a turtle named Butch. You wanna see?'

'Is your mother home?'

'Course she's home. Where else? Ma!'

He shouted, loud and high-pitched so Eve's ears rang.

'Jesus, kid.'

'You shouldn't oughta say "Jesus." You should say "*Jeez* it."'

'You really think *zzz* makes a difference?'

'Ma says so. *Ma!*'

'Christ!'

'Nuh-uh.' Gap-toothed Chip shook his head. '"Cripes" is okay, though.'

'Chip Robbins, how many times have I told you not to yell out for me unless you're being stabbed with a pitchfork?'

The woman who stuck her head out the window had her son's curly dark hair and an aggrieved scowl.

'But Ma, the police want to talk to you. See?' He grabbed Eve's hand, waved it with his.

Eve took hers back, resisted wiping off whatever sticky substance his had transferred. She held up her badge. 'Can we come up, Mrs Robbins?'

'What's this about? My boy's a pain in the behind, but he's good as gold.'

'It's about a former neighbor. If we could come up—'

'I'll come down.'

'Ma doesn't like to let people she don't know in the house when my pa's not home. He's working late.'

'Okay.'

'He drives an airtram, and Ma works at my school. I'm in second grade.'

'Good for you.' Eve looked to Roarke for help, but he just smiled at her.

'Are you gonna arrest a robber?'

'Know any?'

'My friend Everet stoled a candy bar from the store, but his ma found out and made him go pay for it out of his 'lowance, and he couldn't have candy or *nothing* for a whole month. You could arrest him. He's over there.'

He pointed, cheerfully ratting out his pal.

'It sounds like he's paid his debt to society.'

Jesus – jeez it – where was the kid's mother?

'Talk to him,' Eve suggested, desperately sacrificing Roarke.

'Okay. Are you the police, too?'

'Absolutely not.'

'You talk different,' Chip commented. 'Are you from French?

The lady at the market is, and she don't talk like us either. I know a word.'

'What word?'

'Bunjore. It means hello.'

'I know a word.'

Chip's grin widened. 'What word?'

'*Dia dhuit*. It's *hello* where I was born.'

'Deea-gwit,' Chip repeated, mangling it a bit.

'Well done.'

'Chip, stop pestering the police and go play.'

Becky Robbins had taken time to tame back her hair. She hurried now, her flip-flops flapping as she reached out to tuck an arm around her son's shoulders. After a quick hug, she made a shooing motion.

'Okay. Bye!' He raced off, and was immediately absorbed into the running and shouting.

'What's going on?' Becky demanded. 'A couple of the neighbors said the FBI was here before when we were out. Now the police.'

'Do you know a woman calling herself Sarajo White-head?'

'Yeah, the neighbors said the FBI asked about her. She used to live here. Second floor. She moved out a while back. Eight, ten months, maybe. Why? She did something, didn't she?' Becky continued before Eve could speak. 'The FBI people didn't really say, but Earleen – my neighbor – she could tell. And now you're here, too. I never liked that woman – Sarajo, I mean, not Earleen.'

Chip came by his talkative nature honestly, Eve decided. 'Why is that?'

'She could barely be bothered to say a friendly hello. I know she worked nights, mostly, but I don't appreciate anybody yelling at my kid – all the kids.'

Becky put her hands on her hips as she looked over the racing, shouting kids with the mother's version of the beady eye.

'They got a right to play out here in good weather, and in broad daylight for heaven's sake. Told her that myself, after she yelled and used swears at those kids one too many times. Told her she ought to get herself some earplugs or whatever.'

Becky looked back at Eve. 'What did she do?'

'We'll know more about that when we locate her. Did she have any visitors?'

'The only person I ever saw go in or out of there except her was another woman. Young, pretty.'

'This woman?' Eve showed her Melinda's photo.

'Yeah, that's the one. She's not in trouble with the police, is she? She seemed so nice.'

'No, she's not. You don't remember seeing anyone else?'

'Well, yeah, a man came once. A really fat man. Said she worked for him, and he was looking for her. But she'd already gone by then. Just left one day. Left the furniture, too. Turned out it was rented. She paid it up-to-date though, rent, too. The landlady told me. Anyway, I wasn't sorry to see her gone.'

Eve waited a moment. 'There's something else.'

Becky glanced around, shifted. 'It's just something I think. I can't swear to it.'

'Anything you know, think, saw, heard. It's all helpful.'

'I don't like accusing anybody – even her – of something, but the FBI, for heaven's sake. Now the police. Well ... I think she was on something. At least sometimes.'

'Illegals.'

'Yeah. I think. I had a cousin who got sucked into that scene, so I know the signs. Her eyes, the jittery moves. I know I smelled zoner on her, more than once. When we got into it about the kids, I said she oughta take a little more of whatever she was popping or smoking so she'd pass out and wouldn't hear them. I shouldn't have said it, but I was riled up.

'She gave me such a look. I have to say, it scared me some. She shut the door in my face, and I went home. The next morning, I go out to my car to go to work. My husband's rig's parked next to me. Every one of his tires is slashed. I know she did it. I know I'm accusing her again, but I just know it. But how're you going to prove that? Besides I'm the one had words with her, not Jake. He doesn't get riled up like I do. If she'd slashed my tires maybe I could've gotten the cops on her.

'Jake, he needs that rig to get to work. He lost a whole day getting new tires.'

'Did you report it?'

'Sure. You've got to for the insurance, though it didn't cover it all. Jake didn't want me to say anything about her, so

I didn't. She'd have denied it anyway, and maybe done something worse. I stayed clear of her the best I could after that. So I wasn't sorry when she took off.'

Eve talked to a few more neighbors, but she had everything she needed from Becky Robbins.

'The ball's still rolling,' she said to Roarke as they headed back to the hotel. 'She could pull off the hardworking, no-trouble-here woman at work. But at home, well, that's home.'

'Where you want to relax,' he commented. 'And be more yourself.'

'Yeah. You're entitled to some of your illegals of choice in your own home, entitled to some quiet when you want it, entitled to have your bitch of a neighbor leave you the hell alone. And when she gets in your face, you're entitled to payback. You know how to get it, too. The best way. Go after the primary breadwinner's ride to work. Fuck with that, fuck with the whole family where it hurts. In the money bag.'

'She has a temper,' Roarke added, 'and a mean streak. No fondness for children, I'd say, and saw no need to foster any sort of relationship with the other people in the building.'

'She didn't need them. But she's also smart enough not to skip out on the bills. No point in having anybody looking for Sarajo, even when she stops being Sarajo.'

'You've confirmed she didn't, while here, have personal transpo. So she walked or took public. No one visited but Melinda. No one came looking for her but her former employer.'

He latched on, Eve thought. She never had to refine the

lines for Roarke. 'So, whoever her dealer is, he or she didn't do business at the apartment. No men – and one of the neighbors would've seen or heard – so she's being true to McQueen. At least at home. Some dealers will trade junk for sex. But that's business,' Eve mused. 'That wouldn't be cheating. Sex is business.'

'Well then, I love doing business with you.'

She leaned back. 'And still . . . I didn't get to strong-arm or flex the muscles with anybody. They're all so damn cooperative. They just talk, talk, talk – especially that kid. It's like being in a foreign country.'

'Like going to French?'

That got a laugh. 'Maybe there's something in the water down here. Maybe we shouldn't drink the water, or we could start talking to everybody, telling complete strangers more than they could possibly want to know.'

'There's water in coffee.'

'Yeah, but it's, like, boiled, right? That kills the microbes that trigger all this cooperation and chattiness. It has to. It's getting dark. I know we're making progress, but it's getting dark. He's had her for more than twenty hours now.'

She took a long breath. 'Getting dark,' she murmured. 'He likes to hunt at night.'

# 10

Dark. He liked to keep them in the dark so they couldn't know if it was day or night. So they couldn't see each other, have even that horrible, small comfort.

Unless he blasted the lights, hours and hours and hours of bright lights. Then they could see too well. All those eyes, as empty and hopeless as the pit of her own stomach. The shackles and chains, like something out of an old vid – but real, so real, the weight and the bite of them on the wrists, the ankles.

But it was worse when he took them off. Worse when he took you out of the room, and into his.

She'd fight when he came again. Bree said they *had* to fight, no matter what. Bree was right, she knew Bree was right, but it was so hard. He hurt her so much.

But she'd try, she'd try to fight, try to hurt *him* if he came for her again.

In the dark she reached out, wanting her sister's hand, the contact of skin.

And remembered.

It was dark, but she was alone. And she wasn't a child this time. But he'd come back for her, as he had in every nightmare that plagued her.

He'd come back.

Melinda shifted, felt that weight, that bite on her ankles and wrists. In her head she screamed like a wounded animal, but she didn't let the sound come out.

Stay calm, stay calm. Screaming won't help. She had to think, to plan, to find a way out.

Bree would be looking for her, along with the entire force of the Dallas police.

But she didn't know if she was in Dallas. She could be anywhere.

The hysteria wanted to froth up in her throat, vomit out in a scream.

*Think.*

Sarajo.

On the 'link, desperate, urgent, asking for help. What had she said? Important to remember every detail, to get through the fog of whatever they'd given her and remember.

She'd claimed she'd seen the man who'd raped her. Needed help. So scared. Couldn't go to the police, couldn't go through it again.

Had to help, of course, even though she'd put in a long day and had hoped for an early night. Left the note for Bree, locked up. Always careful to lock up, to keep the doors on her car locked. Careful. Always careful.

And yet.

So sure, Melinda remembered now, that she'd be able to talk Sarajo Whitehead through the fear, convince her to go to the police with details. So confident she could help, she could handle.

*Of course,* she'd said again. *Of course* when Sarajo had dashed to the car when Melinda had pulled into the lot of the twenty-four-hour eatery. *Of course* we can go somewhere else, somewhere not so crowded and noisy.

Sympathy, empathy, eye contact, a touch of the hand. Reassurance. She'd let Sarajo into the car, sat for a moment, talking quietly, hoping to settle the nerves – what she took as nerves, she thought now.

The woman didn't look well, no, didn't look well at all, so she hadn't hesitated to pull over when Sarajo claimed to be sick.

Reaching out again, to help. She hadn't seen the syringe, but she'd felt the pressure on the side of her neck. Another bite.

Then, for just a moment as the gray rose, as it edged into black, she saw Sarajo smile.

*Stupid bitch,* she said. *Stupid, know-it-all bitch.*

And he was there, just there.

Going, going, fading, fading. Can't scream, can't fight. Just his voice, the sharp, ugly joy in it as they dragged her into the backseat.

*Hi, Melinda! Just like old times.*

Then nothing, just nothing, until the dark.

When he came, the lights came with him, stinging her eyes. Groggy, so groggy, and sick. But it was Bree on the 'link. Her face, her voice. She tried so hard to stay calm, to think clearly through the thick dregs of the drug.

Sarajo, she thought again. His partner. He always worked with a woman. Oh, she'd read and studied everything
on Isaac McQueen. Made herself read it, watch it, know
it.

And still, she'd walked right into his hands. Again.

He hadn't raped her. But he wouldn't be interested in her
that way now. She wasn't a young girl.

Thank God there were no young girls here. At least, she
prayed there were none.

He wanted her for another reason. Revenge? But she'd
been one of many. He couldn't possibly plan or hope to collect all the survivors again.

No, no, too much time and risk, and for what?

She tried to find some comfort on the floor of the room,
tried to clear the smear on her mind from the drug. There
had to be a reason for taking her, specifically her. For God's
sake her sister was a cop now, sharing the apartment with her.
Surely one of the others would have been easier prey.

Yet he'd targeted her, specifically, again. Sarajo had
reported the rape months before. Nearly a year, yes, almost
a year before. So he'd set the wheels in motion long before
the abduction.

Why?

Something she'd done, something she was.

She and Bree had been his last? Was it as simple as that?
Picking up somehow where he'd left off? It didn't make any
*sense*, she thought. Why waste time with her? Once he'd
gotten out, why waste time?

So she served a purpose, he always had one. Or represented something. Was she bait to lure Bree, so he'd have them both?

Oh God, Bree. Bree, Bree.

This time the panic won, stealing her breath, pounding hard in her blood. The shackles cut into her skin as she fought against them in blind fear and rage.

Not her sister. Not again.

She heard the locks click and slide, and fought a bitter, painful war for control. Remembering, she closed her eyes an instant before the lights flared on. Still, the hot red haze burned against her lids.

The woman, she realized, hearing the click of heels, catching the scent of perfume.

She'd dressed for him, Melinda thought, groomed for him.

And I'm the stupid bitch, she thought, digging for some grit. She's not smart enough to know she's as disposable for him as an empty tube of Coke.

She opened her eyes slowly, looked into the face of the woman she'd thought wanted and needed her help.

Yes, groomed for him, with lip dye and blond hair freshly fluffed around her shoulders.

Older than McQueen, trying to be younger in the short, snug red dress and high heels.

Melinda buried the disdain.

Sarajo – *think of her as Sarajo* – carried a sandwich on a plate – disposable, just as she was – and a cup of water. Might be drugged, Melinda thought, but put gratitude on her face.

'He doesn't want you to starve to death.'

'Thank you. I'm hungry. Is it very late?'

'Too late for you.'

'Please, Sarajo, I don't know what you want. What he wants. If you'd tell me I could try to get it for you, or do it for you.'

'We've already got what we want from you. Bleeding hearts like you, you're all the same. Weak and stupid.'

'I only tried to help you.'

'I only tried to help you,' Sarajo repeated in a nasty singsong. 'Marks like you are all the same, always whining. You think you're so smart, and look at you. Nothing but an animal in a cage.'

'What did I do to make you hate me?'

'You exist for starters. You put Isaac in jail for twelve years.'

'You know what he did to me, to all of us.'

'Asked for it, didn't you?' The boldly dyed lips sneered. 'Little whores.'

'I was twelve.'

'Yeah?' Sarajo cocked a hip, angled her head. 'When I was twelve I fucked plenty of men. They just had to pay for it first. That's where you're stupid. Seeing you in here's almost worth the time I had to spend with you.'

'If you help me, I'll get you money.'

'We've got money now.' The woman ran a hand down her side, sliding it along the dress. 'And we'll have more when we're done.'

'If you're after a ransom, I—'

'You think this is about you?' She threw back her head and laughed. 'You're nothing. You're just a way to help us get to something worth a hell of a lot more. She's going to pay for what she did to Isaac. And when we're done we'll have more money than anybody can dream of. Me and Isaac, we're going to live the high life.'

'He'll kill you,' Melinda said, her voice dull now. 'You'll help him get what he wants, and when he has it, he'll kill you and move on. You're the mark, Sarajo. You just don't see your cage.'

Sarajo kicked the plate across the room, upended the water on the floor.

'Uh-oh!' Isaac came in, all smiles. 'Cleanup on aisle six.' He laughed, obviously tickled as he draped an arm around the woman's waist, tugged her in. 'Are you girls talking about me?'

He pressed a kiss to Sarajo's temple, all the while sending Melinda a cocky, conspirator's wink.

'She's just running off at the mouth. It's what she's best at.' Sarajo turned into him, rubbed her body to his. 'Come on, baby, let the bitch lap at the floor. You can lap on me.'

'Sounds delicious. But we've got something to take care of, remember? And you have to change for it. Not that you don't look *amaaazing*.'

'Why don't we make it just you and me tonight?'

'It'll be even better,' he promised in a whisper. 'Promise. Go on, baby doll, go put on your Aunt Sandra clothes. It's going to be fun!'

He gave her a playful swat on the ass. With one last vicious glance at Melinda, she went out.

'Isaac, you've gone to a lot of trouble to get me here.'

'More than you know, sweetie pie, but worth every minute just to see your pretty face again.' His eyes, a brilliant blue now, sparkled with delight. 'We have to make time to catch up. I want to hear every little thing you've been up to.'

'I think you know. I think you've kept up since I saw you last.'

He smiled at her, handsome in his pressed jeans and casual shirt. His hair was blond, his face tanned, as if he spent his days working outdoors in the sun.

'It was so considerate of you to visit.'

'Is that why I'm here? For being considerate. Am I the only one who came?'

'And isn't that a sad commentary on manners in today's society.' He hefted out a sigh. 'Then again, so many bad girls.'

Melinda forced herself to maintain eye contact, to keep her voice mild. 'You and I know you don't take them because they're bad, but because they're innocent. You can be honest with me, Isaac.' She held up her shackled arms. 'You're obviously in control of this situation. In control of me, of Sarajo – or whatever her real name is.'

'I don't know if she remembers half the time. You're doing such a good job, Melinda, using your counselor's tone, the right words. I'm very proud of you.'

'Tell me why I'm here. What you're using me for. Don't you want to share that with me?'

'Tempting, but you know what would be more fun? And you know how much I love fun and games.' He came closer, cupped her chin in his hand, made her skin crawl. 'Figure it out. It's like a puzzle. Just put the pieces together. Now I'm going on a little adventure. You be good while I'm gone.'

'Won't you stay and talk to me? Or . . . we can do whatever you want. Anything. But don't go tonight.'

'That's just so sweet. No offense, honey, but you know you're not my type these days. Not that I can't make do.' He gave her another wink. 'The thing is, I've got plans for tonight.'

'They'll be looking for you.' She couldn't stop her tone from rising, her voice from shaking. 'If you go out, try to take another girl, they could catch you. Everything will be over before it begins. You don't need to do this. I'll be what you want.'

'Don't you worry your pretty head about me.' He blew her a kiss. 'I'll be back soon, and won't it be nice for you to have some company?' He glanced toward the ruined sandwich. 'Sorry about dinner, but I guess you've learned not to make the lady of the house mad. She's got a temper, that one.'

'Please, please, please. Wait!' No good, no good, nothing she could do to stop him. 'Please, just tell me where I am. Just tell me, are we still in Dallas or—'

'Dallas is the whole point. Be back soon.'

He left the lights blazing. Melinda dropped her head on her up-drawn knees, let out a keening wail for the child whose life would be forever scarred if McQueen had his way.

186

She rocked, she wept, she finally released the screams burning her throat until, exhausted, she lay curled on the floor of the horrible room.

She let her eyes track it now, let herself see where she was. A rectangle of walls, floor, ceiling, the single window barred and screened. Even if she could reach it, she'd need a tool of some sort to hack at the screening. No table, no chair, just a blanket tossed on the floor.

And four sets of shackles fixed to the walls.

He didn't mean for her to stay alone.

God, God, give her the strength to help whoever he brought in here. To help the children survive, to help her find a way to save them.

Help her save their hearts and minds. It's what she'd trained and studied for. And Bree, she had to trust that Bree would do the rest.

If they were still in Dallas, as he'd said, there was a chance, a good chance. Bree would never give up, never let up. And she was smart, canny, tireless. A cop through and through, Melinda told herself. She'd started to become one the day they'd been saved.

The moment Officer Eve Dallas had opened the door to that awful room in New York, Bree had set her path, and had followed it without detour.

To protect and serve, Melinda thought as she closed her eyes, the victims, the abused, the marks, the shattered. And she'd used the career of the cop who'd saved them as her template. Setting the goal high, that was Bree. That was ...

She shoved up to sit, eyes open.

Dallas was the whole point. Eve Dallas?

Was it all just about revenge after all?

Eve paced in front of her board, juggling the details, making patterns, taking them apart, reforming them. She constantly checked the time.

It hadn't been that long, not really, since they'd picked up Civet in New York. Pressuring solid information out of a dealer with his record and experience took finesse, effort, sweat.

But why the hell hadn't they pressured anything out of him?

She stepped to the connecting door where Roarke worked three comps, muttering at all of them, in his search for McQueen's accounts.

'Maybe you could holo me in to New York, into Interview.'

He paused, rolling his shoulders as he sat back to study her. 'If that's what you want, we can set it up.'

'If I'm there it adds weight, and maybe I can hit him from another angle.'

He said nothing for a moment, only watched her.

'And completely screw up their rhythm,' she said. 'Undermine their progress and fuck Peabody's confidence to hell. I know what you're thinking because I'm thinking it, too. But waiting here, it's ...'

'Hard. Waiting is hard, and frustrating, even when you know it's what you have to do. Maybe especially then.'

188

He'd know, she thought. A cop's spouse knew every layer of waiting. 'Does it piss you off, too?'

'More than a little at times.'

'There's nothing else for me to do tonight. Nothing else to dig at. All I can do is keep going over and over what we have, and fucking wait for somebody else to give me more.'

'Then take a break, let it settle awhile. I'll give you more on my area when I get it.'

She retreated, got more coffee.

She circled the board, told herself they had every area covered that could be.

She checked the time.

While Eve circled and studied, Darlie Morgansten tried on the most icy jacket ever. It was pink, her favorite color, and had sparkles all over the collar. Completely vid star.

It also cost more than three months' allowance, and since she'd already spent most of this month's on a too totally mag purse, and last month's plus on stuff she couldn't quite remember but wanted *so* abso-complete, she was awesome short.

Still, she modeled and admired herself in the mirror, ignoring the watchful eye of the salesclerk, who'd given her and Simka – her best friend since ever – the eyeball treatment since they'd walked in.

'Darl, you *have* to get it. It's, like, mag to infinity on you.'

'Maybe Dad will give me an advance. Mom won't.' She rolled her lively green eyes. 'All I'll get from her is—'

'The Lecture,' Simka finished, rolling her eyes in solidarity. 'You could tag him up, show him how super-frosted you look in it.'

'Too easy to say no over the 'link. Sheesh, that lady's still hawking us. It's not like we're shoplifters. Here, take my picture.' She handed Simka her 'link. 'Then I can go home, soften him up, show him when he's in a really good mood.'

'But somebody might buy it before you give him the works.'

'I've got a little left. I can put it on hold.'

She angled herself, smiled brilliantly for the shot, a pretty young girl with long brown hair, temporarily streaked with vivid purple, which had earned her The Lecture just that morning.

In fact, the hair deal had meant she'd had to wheedle her butt off for this trip to the mall, and she'd only copped it because her mother was shopping, too.

And she had to meet The Warden – her most current term for her mother – at nine forty-five on the dot right under the clock tower. And tomorrow was a free day and everything, with no school due to teacher-planning sessions.

She'd wanted to shop with Sim, go to the vids, have pizza after, but *no*. Home by ten, in bed by ten-thirty.

You'd think she was three instead of thirteen.

Mothers were such a pain.

'I'm going to put it on hold. We've still got a half-hour before we have to meet The Warden.'

'Check. I'm going to try on this top and the pants, too. I'll

190

come out so you can tell me the abso-total truth about how they look.'

'I will, but I already know they'll look complete on you. Cha.'

Darlie hurried to the counter, gave the watchful clerk a haughty stare as she paid the holding charge. She started back toward the dressing area when a fabo skirt caught her eye.

'Excuse me.'

Startled, Darlie jumped back. 'I wasn't doing anything.'

'I'm sorry.' Sarajo – now Sandra Millford – put on an easy smile. 'I didn't mean to scare you. I just wondered if you could help me out. My niece is about your size, your coloring, your age. Fifteen?'

Flattered, Darlie lied cheerfully. 'Yeah.'

'Do you think she'd like this? I want to get her something special for her birthday next week.' Sarajo held up a pink party dress.

'Oh, wow. I was looking at that before. It's so, just *so*. It's way expensive.'

'She's my favorite niece. Can I just hold it up against you, to see how she might look?'

'Sure. Oh, it's just frosted extremely.'

'You think?' Sarajo slid the pressure syringe under the material, shifting as she'd practiced to shield the movement from view. She jabbed it quickly into the side of Darlie's throat.

'Ow. What was—'

'Must be a pin in it.'

She watched the girl's eyes glaze.

'I don't guess it suits her after all.' Supporting Darlie with one arm, she hung the dress up. 'Time to go.' She spoke clearly, smiling, walking the girl out. 'School night!'

'No school tomorrow.' The words slurred.

'You're right about that.'

She walked Darlie toward the south entrance. McQueen picked them up on the way, tucked his arm around Darlie from the other side. 'How did the shopping go, ladies?'

'We had fun,' Sarajo said easily. 'But our girl's not feeling very well. Overtired, I guess.'

'Aw, well, we'll be home soon.'

Looking like a family, they went outside to the lot, McQueen jamming security as they went. Even as Simka came out of the dressing room to show off her outfit, they lifted Darlie into the van.

Eve walked into the shop with Roarke. It was a ground-level shop in a three-level mall. Dozens of ways in, she'd already noted, dozens of ways out.

Bree broke out of a huddle of cops, hurried to her.

'Darlie Morgansten, thirteen, brown and green, five-three, a hundred and ten. She was with her friend.' She gestured toward another girl, sitting on the floor, crying. 'The friend was trying something on in the dressing room. When she came out, Darlie was gone. They were to meet Darlie's mother, Iris Morgansten, at twenty-one forty-five. The mother' – she gestured again to a woman talking rapidly to Bree's partner – 'was shopping elsewhere in the mall.'

Bree took a breath.

'One of the clerks noticed Darlie with a woman, assumed it was her mother. They were looking at a dress. Then they left together. No struggle, no sign of duress. We've got people going over the security discs now.'

'Nearly an hour ago,' Eve calculated. 'They're gone. They won't be anywhere in here. Have them check the logs for the last few days. The partner would have cased the place for him, taken pictures. He'd have to know the best way out, where security is inside and out. Why the hell did it take this long to get out the alert?'

'The other girl looked around for Darlie, then asked one of the clerks. They told her Darlie left with her mother. So Simka – the other kid – went down to the meeting spot to wait. It was nearly thirty minutes before the mother got there, and realized something was wrong.'

'All right. I want to talk to the store employees, the kid, the mother.'

'The father's here, too, now.'

'I don't need him if he wasn't here when it went down. I want—'

She broke off when Nikos came over.

'You were right. You were right about this. I didn't trust your instincts, went with the percentages. Now that kid's . . .'

'If not her, someone else,' Eve said, cold now. 'You put your weight in, yeah, and that was a mistake. But either way, there aren't enough cops to watch every girl in Dallas.'

'Maybe not, but it's not going to help me sleep at night.

You were right about the van, too. The seller remembered her as Sister Suzan. We didn't get anything out of him because there just wasn't anything to get. Straight cash transaction, sign the transfer, and she drives off. Alone. We recorded the entire interview. You'll have a copy.'

'All right.' She saw Laurence sit down beside the weeping girl, hand her some tissues. And saw him put an arm around her when she turned her face into his chest to sob there.

'Laurence should take the friend,' Eve decided. 'She's already turning to him, so he's got a jump there. Maybe you can use the federal badge, give security a push. I want to see everything from the last week. Detective Jones, I want the clerk first.'

'Yes, sir.'

'We're going to get her back,' Nikos said. When her eyes met Eve's again they were full of regret, knowledge, cold rage. 'But not soon enough.'

'No.' No point in pretending otherwise, Eve decided. 'No, it's already too late. Now we concentrate on getting her back alive.'


At some point, despite the lights and the fears, Melinda slept. The sound of the locks shot her awake, hands balled into fists. Those hands went numb when Sarajo dragged the girl inside.

'No, no, no, no.'

Sarajo shoved the naked, trembling girl to the floor. 'Shut the fuck up.' She backhanded Melinda, sent her sprawling, added a vicious kick when Melinda tried to get up.

'Stay down, facedown, or I'll bloody her. That's how it works with you, right?' Grimly, Sarajo shackled the limp girl, let her drop as Darlie's head lolled. 'Yeah, that's how we get you to behave. You start something with me, bitch, she pays. Remember that.'

'Did you have a part in this? In what he did to her?'

'My part starts now.' Sarajo shook her hair back. 'Her?' She gave a half-laugh, a shrug. 'She was foreplay.'

'I'll kill you if I get the chance.' Melinda spoke quietly, and from a place in her heart she'd never known existed. 'You remember that. I'll kill you for what you did to her. You're worse than he is.'

'You don't worry me. Why don't you and the baby whore compare notes.'

She shut the door, locked it. As the lights went out, the girl moaned, cried for her mother. Melinda crawled over, did her best to comfort – soothing, singing, stroking.

She'd protect, somehow, she'd protect. Even though it was too late to shield.

Before the lights had gone to black, she'd seen the tattoo on the girl's small breast. Number twenty-eight inside a perfect heart.

# 11

Laurence stepped into mall security, glanced at the multiple playbacks Eve watched.

'I let the kid go home. Simka Revin,' he added. 'I showed her the pictures we have of the female UNSUB. She can't be sure. Jones reports same with the vic's parents, but two of the clerks on tonight recognized her. Said she'd come in a couple times a week over the last month or so.'

'Yeah, I've spotted her on here a few times – same look. Tells me she wanted mall employees to recognize her, think of her as a regular.'

'We got people showing the pictures, clearing employees and the shoppers who were here before the lockdown. Place was crowded, with plenty of kids Darlie's age milling around. Public schools are closed tomorrow.'

'Yeah, I got that already.' She turned to him. 'You can be sure he knew it when he picked his spot. There'll be other spots, and she'll have cased them just like this. He's having a real good time, Laurence.'

He nodded, hands in his pockets, eyes on the security monitor. 'I've been doing this awhile.'

'Yeah, I read your file.'

He smiled a little. 'Ditto. The way I see it, if Darlie had gone in the dressing room, Simka wouldn't be tucked into her own bed tonight.'

Eve gestured to the screens. 'That shop, and a couple others, particularly draw his vic type. Sometimes they go in with an adult, but more often in little packs. That's what he likes. Likes to separate one from the pack, like a lion with an antelope. Abduct in plain sight. It adds to the thrill, and makes him feel more important. A lot of girls went through that shop tonight, and she could've lured any one of them for him.'

'Bad luck for Darlie Morgansten.'

'Yeah. Bad luck.'

After two in the morning, with the initial search protocol complete, the alerts issued, the search active, Eve and Roarke returned to the hotel. The smudges of fatigue under her eyes blurred like bruising against her pallor. A sure sign, he knew, she'd passed the point of exhaustion.

She needed sleep but, as he expected, objected when he stopped the elevator on the bedroom level.

'I'm not done.'

'Oh, but you are.'

She stripped her jacket off, tossed it on a bench in the foyer. 'Look, I need you to do something.'

'Fine. And I need you to do something. We'll trade.'

She stood, weapon harness over shirtsleeves, her whiskey-colored eyes ripe with a combination of fury, sorrow, and stress he understood very well. He felt the same himself.

'Goddamn it, Roarke.'

'And that's not the way to get something from me, particularly at half two in the morning. Tell me what you need, and I'll try to get it for you.'

'The female, she cased that mall in her 'I'm just a harmless woman' gear. She even bought stuff for girls who fit the age spread, things the vic would go for. She knew the place, so I'm betting she used it for her own shopping.'

'Good bet.' He shrugged out of his own jacket, sat on the bench to pull off his shoes. If he'd be working a bit longer, he'd damn well work comfortably. 'I see where you're going.'

'She'd probably dress as who she is or who she wants to be for McQueen, wouldn't she? Hitting shops that cater to adults, women's stores, sexy gear stores. You want to bang, you buy the sexy underwear.'

He glanced up. She roamed the foyer, moving, moving, moving because she knew – as he did – once she stopped she'd go out.

'You don't.'

'I don't have to buy the sexy underwear when you buy enough for an entire gaggle of high-class LCs.'

'It's a weakness. A gaggle is it? Darling Eve, you're very tired.'

Frustration flickered over the tension in her face. 'Look, if we can just set up and run a face-and-body-recognition program, something that will give us some probables, we—'

'No, you said you wanted me to do it, and I will.' He rose, barefoot now and in shirtsleeves as she was, and pulled a thin leather tie from his pocket. 'In exchange you'll go to bed, the bed neither one of us has so much as seen yet. That's the master,' he added, gesturing.

'I want to get this started.'

'I'll get it started, and we'll both take a couple hours down while it runs. I'm pretty fucking fagged myself, but if you push it, I promise I'll put you down.'

'You're going to stand here and threaten me?'

'You know it's not a threat.' In a smooth, unhurried move, he tied back his hair. 'It's a simple fact, and one I'm not going to waste time arguing over. Go lie down, now, or it'll get ugly.'

He watched anger flood temporary color into her face, lifted his brows when her hand balled into a fist. She wasn't above throwing a punch under the circumstances, and he knew from experience she had a damn good right cross.

He almost hoped she would follow through on it, give him an excuse to manhandle her into bed, pour a tranq down her throat, and relieve some of his own temper in the process.

Apparently she thought better of it, as she spun around and stomped off toward the bedroom.

'You're fucking welcome,' he called after her.

She answered by stabbing her middle finger into the air before she slammed the bedroom door.

'Oh aye, back at you, darling.'

She'd wanted to give him a shot, one good shot. The problem was, she thought as she yanked off her weapon harness, she wasn't at her absolute best – which meant he'd have more than likely followed through on his threat.

'Oh, excuse me,' she muttered to the empty room, 'his *simple fact.*'

God, she hated when he ordered her around like she was an idiot infant at nap time.

She just needed coffee. Just some coffee to break through the fog. So she was tired, she admitted, dropping her clothes where she stripped. Cops worked tired. *That* was a simple fact.

One of his minions in his fancy, high-priced (no doubt) hotel had unpacked and put away the things Summerset had packed. She didn't even have control over her own damn clothes.

She yanked open drawers. Damned if she'd sleep naked and give that bossy bastard any ideas. She sniffed at the soft, pretty nightclothes, shoved through them until she found a practical, definitely unsexy nightshirt and dragged it on.

But she wasn't going to bed. Not to sleep, that is. She'd stretch out for ten minutes, and consider her part of the bargain met.

Then he could shove it.

She snatched the gold-foiled chocolates off the pillows, tossed them on the night table. She'd have that with her coffee after her ten down. It ought to be enough caffeine to keep her revved for another few hours.

She dropped down flat on her face on the neatly turned-down sheets, thought fleetingly that she missed the cat.

She thought of Darlie Morgansten. The pang as her belly twisted was the last thing she felt before going under. She never heard Roarke come in twenty minutes later.

The chill of the room kept her awake. She wanted to sleep, wanted to go away, but the cold and the gnawing hunger in her belly wouldn't let her.

She wasn't supposed to get food. She ate when he told her to eat, and ate what he gave her or there would be hell to pay.

She knew hell to pay meant a beating – or worse. She knew what hell was because she lived there.

She was eight.

She shivered in the cold, squeezed her eyes shut because he'd left the lights on when he went out. She couldn't make them go off. Bright, bright and cold with the dirty red flash from the sign coming through the window.

LIVE SEX. LIVE SEX. LIVE SEX.

He'd forgotten to feed her before he went out. Business. Places to go, people to see.

She never had places to go, and never saw anyone but him.

Maybe he'd forget to come back. Sometimes he did, and she was a long time alone. It was better alone, mostly better alone. She could look out the window at the people, the cars, the buildings.

She had to stay in the room. Little girls who tried to go out or talk to anybody got taken by the police and tossed in a dark pit or sometimes a cage with snakes and spiders that ate through their skin to their bones.

She didn't want to get thrown in the pit. Didn't want to have to pay hell. But she was so hungry.

She knew there was cheese. If she got just a little cheese – like a mouse – he wouldn't know. Eyes darting around the room, she scuttled over in the flash of red light, got the little knife.

She meant to cut off just a tiny bit, but it was so good.

If he didn't come back, she could eat all the cheese. And when he did come back, he'd be drunk, probably. Maybe he'd be drunk enough not to notice her, not to hurt her. Not to care that she ate the cheese.

The door opened, a crash of sound that startled her into dropping the knife.

She saw, with a terror that ate the bones like spiders, he wasn't drunk enough.

She tried to lie, to pretend – and for a moment, just one moment, thought he'd leave her alone.

He hit her so hard. As she fell, the blood she swallowed into her yawning belly roiled there.

*Please don't. Please. I'll be good.*

But he hit, and hit and hit no matter how she cried or begged. Then he was on her, the brutal weight of him. On her, smelling of whiskey and candy – the terrible smell of father.

She knew, knew, knew it was worse when she fought, but she couldn't stop the screams, the wild struggles as he pushed himself into her.

The pain ripped, tore, and still she begged.

And all around in the cold, bright room with the red light flashing were other little girls. Dozens of eyes watching as he panted and grunted, those terrible sounds mixing with her screams as he raped her.

She clawed his face, felt his skin tear as he tore hers. Over his shocked howl came a sudden harsh snap, and the agony followed like a flood.

No thought, all pain, and the eyes watching, his face twisted over hers. Her fingers found the little knife on the floor.

No thought, all pain. She struck.

The sound of his cry – his pain, his shock – rose through hers, and sounded in her desperate mind like triumph. She brought the knife down again, felt the warm wet on her hand as she crawled out from under him.

She fell on him like an animal, hacking, slicing while the blood splattered on her face, her arms, her body.

Red, like the light. Warm against the cold of her skin.

And the other girls chanted in one feral voice.

Kill him.

Kill him.

Her father's face, eyes wide. The other face, smeared with blood.

Kill them.

The girls, all the little girls, closed in around her as she plunged the knife into him. Into them. Hands stroked at her, arms tried to lift her.

She fought, snarling.

'Stop! Eve, stop!'

Roarke knew he hurt her, but the gentle, then the firm hadn't pulled her out of the nightmare. Fear clutched at his throat that this time she wouldn't come back.

'Eve. *My* Eve. Goddamn it, wake up.' He pinned her arms, held on even when her body arched on a wild, high scream.

'No. No, you come back to me now. Eve. Eve.'

He kept saying her name, a fierce repetition he prayed would get though whatever hell had her. 'I love you. Eve. I'm right here. You're safe. Lieutenant Eve Dallas.' He pressed his lips to her hair, her temple. 'My love. *A ghra*. Eve.'

When she began to tremble, relief left him weak.

'Shh now, shh. I have you. You're safe now. You're back now.'

'Cold. It's cold.'

'I'll warm you.' He rubbed her arms, like ice against his palms. 'I'll fetch a blanket. Just—'

'Sick.' She pressed a clammy hand to his chest. 'I'm sick.'

He picked her up, carried her quickly to the bathroom. Felt helpless while she was viciously ill. But when he started to soothe her face with a cool cloth she took it from him.

'Give me a minute.' She didn't meet his eyes, but sat, knees drawn up, her face pressed to them. 'Please. Just give me a minute.'

He rose, took the plush hotel robe from its hook. 'Put this on.' He laid it over her shoulders, wanted to bundle her into it. Hold her. But she wouldn't look at him. 'You're shaking with cold. I'll ... I'll get brandy.'

Walking out of the room, leaving her there, tore him to pieces.

His hand shook when he poured brandy into snifters. He wanted to heave the glasses against the wall. Break them, break everything he could reach. Beat it, rend it.

He stared out the window, imagined the city in flames, consumed to ashes.

And still it wasn't enough.

Later, he promised himself, later he'd find some way to vent at least part of this terrible rage clawing inside him. But now, he only stood staring out the window until he heard her come out.

Pale as the white robe, he thought, and her eyes so big, so tired.

'I'm okay.'

He turned to bring her one of the brandies.

'Oh God.' First shock, then tears filled her eyes. She lifted her hand, fingers brushing the livid scratches on his chest, his shoulders. 'I did that.'

'It's nothing.'

She shook her head, eyes flooded, touched an ugly bite mark. 'I'm sorry. I'm so sorry.'

'It's nothing,' he repeated, taking her hand, bringing it to his lips. 'You thought I was . . . You thought I was hurting you. I did hurt you. Drink some brandy now.' When she only stood, staring down at the glass, he touched her cheek. And still, she didn't look at him. 'I didn't doctor it. I promise you.'

She nodded, turned away, sipped a little.

'Why won't you look at me? I know I hurt you. I'm sick for it. Sick I reminded you, even for a moment, of him. Forgive me.'

'No, no, not you.' She turned back, met his eyes now. She hadn't let the tears fall so they swam there, pools of sorrow. 'Not you,' she said again, and pressed a hand to her heart.

She set the brandy aside. 'I can't drink it. I'm sorry.'

'Do you want water? Coffee? Anything? Tell me what to do for you. I don't know what to do.'

She sat on the side of the bed. He always knew, she thought. Somehow he always knew what to do. Now, it seemed he was as lost as she. 'I thought it was over. I haven't gone back there in a while. I thought I was past it, that I'd resolved it, and it was done.'

Careful not to touch her, he sat beside her. 'Being here, dealing with what's happening here. It's no wonder it triggered this.'

'It was more. It was worse.'

'I know.' He started to reach for her hand, then dropped his. 'I know it was. Can you tell me?'

'At first, it was the same. The room, the cold, the light. So hungry. The same, getting the knife, eating the cheese. And he came in, drunk but not enough. And it starts. He hits me, so hard. So hard, and he's on me. It hurts.'

He rose, had to, walked back to the window, stared out blindly. 'You were screaming.'

'I couldn't stop, and he wouldn't. But . . . they were there,

206

all around us. All the girls. The girls like me, all those eyes watching him rape me. So sad, so empty. All those eyes.

'And my arm.' Instinctively she wrapped it close to her body. 'The snap and the pain when he broke it. And I'm crazy with pain and fear. The same, that's the same. And the knife in my hand. And the blade's in him. The blood runs over my hand. It's so warm. So warm, a comfort. No, no, not a comfort. A thrill.'

When he turned, she'd gripped her hands together in her lap. 'Not like it was, not like I remember. Not that mindless defense, not just survival. I wanted the blood. And so did they. The girls, all the girls telling me to kill him. To kill him. And his face – then McQueen's – his then his then his. Kill them.

'I wanted . . . I felt . . . horrible, ugly pleasure. I don't think I put those marks on you because you hurt me. I think, oh God, I think I fought you because you tried to stop me.'

She pressed a hand to her face, wrapped her arm around her body, and broke with a shuddering, wrenching sob.

She tried to turn away when he came to her, but now he knew what to do.

He held her, stroked her hair, her back, and when she went lax, lifted her into his lap to rock.

'Why do you suffer for that? Baby, why do you make yourself pay for that? A dream, a nightmare of the nightmare you lived. Only a child.'

'I wasn't a child, not at the end. All the girls, Roarke, bruised and bloody and calling for death. But I wasn't a child when I gave it to them. I was me.'

'You were a child when he brutalized you. And now you work yourself to breaking for those girls, and for one you saved once already.'

'I can't be what I need to be if I kill, not that way. Not in defense, but because I want it over. I can't be if I enjoy it. Then I'm what they are.'

'You could never be.' He swallowed back a fresh spurt of rage, fought to keep his voice, his hands gentle. 'They tried to make you nothing, those obscene excuses for a mother and father. And you made yourself everything they weren't.'

'It scared me. It . . . shamed me. What I felt.'

'You went to bed exhausted, and angry. That part's on me.'

'I might've had a little to do with it.'

He managed a smile as he brushed tears from her cheeks. 'Maybe a little at that. Don't punish yourself for a dream, baby.'

When she rested her head on his shoulder, he closed his eyes. 'Do you want Mira?'

'No. Yes. Maybe.' Her voice broke again as she tightened her arms around him. 'I want you. I want you.'

'You have me, always. Don't cry anymore. Don't cry now.'

'Her face is in my head. Darlie. I knew he'd take another, but now her face is in my head. I know what she's feeling now – the shock, the shame, the fear. She'll have nightmares, too. It'll happen over and over again, long after we stop him. We have to stop him.'

'We will.'

She let out a long breath. 'We will. Let me fix those scratches.'

'It's all right.'

'No, let me.' She drew back, framed his face, looked into his eyes. 'Let me.'

'Well, I expect knowing us, Summerset packed a first-aid kit. It's likely in the bathroom.'

'I'll find it.' She got up, paused. 'You stopped me. I know it was just a dream, but you stopped me. It sounds weird, but I think by stopping me, you saved me. So thanks.'

He could see her, his Eve. He could see what she'd made herself. 'We've saved each other all along, haven't we?'

'I guess we have.'

She brought out the first-aid kit – ever-efficient Summerset – and sat to tend the wounds. 'Jesus, I really went at you. That's bad enough, but scratching and biting like a girl. It's mortifying.'

'You got a couple of punches in, if it makes you feel better.'

'I'm a crappy person, because it does a little.'

'Rang my bell once.'

'And still a little more.' She looked up at him. 'Do you ever wonder who the hell we are, that somehow we'll be okay that I bloodied you?'

'We're exactly who we're supposed to be.'

'I don't know what I'd do if you weren't who you're supposed to be with me. I just don't know.'

'I wouldn't be, without you.'

She set the kit aside, touched her lips to the wound on his shoulder. 'Does it hurt?'

'Now what sort of man would admit a few girl scratches hurt?'

She laughed a little, put her arms around him. There, she thought as he did, we're okay. Somehow we're okay. 'It's nearly time to get up.'

'We didn't get much sleep.'

'No, not much.' She eased back, met his eyes. 'And still.'

'And still,' he said before their lips met.

The need was like breath, simply there. Quiet as a whisper, soft as the light just eking through the windows. Comfort now, he thought, for both of them. Solace and an understanding no one else could give. She tamed the ferocious, tearing rage that reared inside him, channeled it to tenderness. For the moment.

For their moment.

He stroked her now, amazed, humbled, she would welcome him after the horror she'd known. Grateful if he couldn't stop the horror, he could bring her peace and pleasure.

With each long, dreamy kiss, that horror faded.

Taking care, they touched each other – gentle hands to soothe and stir. His lips roamed her face – pale, he thought, so pale – soft brushes along her cheeks, that endearing dent in her chin, the strong line of her jaw. And beneath to the delicate skin of her throat where her pulse beat for him.

She heard him murmur to her, a mix of English and Irish that so lifted her heart. The words, the sound of his voice, moved her beyond passion, beyond need and held her in the open arms of love.

She'd hurt him, more, so much more than the ugly scratches. She'd seen his face, the shattered look in his eyes when she'd come back to herself. He suffered, she knew, when she went to that place. Those wounds needed tending, too. Helping him heal, feeling him take what she could give, closed her own wounds again.

For the moment.

She sighed under him, and her skin warmed under his hands. Now she trembled, not from cold but from the slow and steady rise of heat. When her breath caught, it snagged on the bright edge of sensation. He carried her over it, delicately, as he would a fragile and precious jewel.

Her arms drew him closer, closer as she rose to him, joined with him. Here was beauty after the monstrous, the joy after the grief.

Wrapped in it, in him, in them, she found his lips with hers and poured into him what flooded her.

'Stay with me,' she whispered. 'Go with me. I love you, I love you.' She caught his face in her hands, let it fill her vision, let herself fall into the wild blue of his eyes. 'I love you.'

He went with her, up, over. And held her as they took the long, sweet glide down.

'Sleep awhile,' he said when she curled against him.

'I can't. I'm all right.' She tipped her head back as she spoke. 'I'm better. I need to work now. Work's . . . I guess it's a kind of first aid.'

'All right. But you'll eat. For me.'

'I could eat for me, too. A shower, coffee, food, work. Routine. That's what gets the job done.' She pushed to sitting. 'Maybe coffee first.'

'I'll get it. Have it in bed. It's early yet,' he added. 'I'll grab a shower. There are some things I have to see to, then I'll check on the search I programmed for you.'

'Okay. Roarke,' she said as he got out of bed, 'don't contact Mira. I'm all right, and I'd rather she work with Peabody and the New York team. Getting Melinda and the girl back, getting McQueen and his partner, that's what we all need.'

He got the coffee, brought it to her. 'Will you talk to her when we get back home?'

'When this is done, yeah.'

'All right, then. Drink your coffee. I won't be long, then we'll have breakfast and get to work.'

After he'd showered and dressed, he gave her time alone, heading to the office to check in with Caro, and with Summerset. Nothing urgent from either, he thought, and that was a blessing. A few details to deal with later in the day, more yet when he returned. But for now, he could leave those aspects of his world in the capable hands of his admin and Summerset.

He started to call for the search results when the house 'link signaled.

'Roarke.'

'Good morning, sir. Peterson at the desk. There's a Detective Jones for Lieutenant Dallas. I've scanned and cleared her credentials. Sending a visual now.'

Roarke watched Bree, standing at the security desk, come on screen.

'You can send her up.'

'Right away, sir.'

He clicked off, started down to the main level. Apparently everyone was getting an early start that morning.

# 12

And, he thought as he opened the door, someone else hadn't gotten much sleep. She'd done her best to hide it, he noted, covering the shadows under her eyes, adding color to her cheeks. But enhancements couldn't hide the underlay of worried exhaustion.

'Good morning, Detective.'

'It's early. I'm sorry. I didn't think of it until I was already here.'

'No problem. The lieutenant will be down any minute. We'll have breakfast.'

'Oh. I should have—'

'The three of us,' he said smoothly as he took her arm, drew her in. 'You haven't eaten.'

'No, I . . . How do you know?'

'I'm married to one very like you.'

'That's the biggest compliment you could give me. I shouldn't have come without checking first.'

'There's no need. I can promise you a working breakfast is what Eve has in mind. Isn't it, Lieutenant?' he asked as Eve came down the stairs.

'That's the plan, Detective.'

'I was hoping you had a little time before everything gets rolling today.'

'Why don't I go up,' Roarke suggested, 'set things up in your office.'

'That'd be good.'

He brushed his fingers over Eve's arm as he went by.

'I apologize, Lieutenant, for intruding, for overstepping.'

'I'll let you know when you've intruded or overstepped. Get any sleep?'

'Not really. I'm staying with my parents. I couldn't stay at my place with Melinda . . . And our parents need me there.'

'How are they holding up?'

'They're scared.' Bree's fingers worried at the ring on her finger. 'I keep telling them we're going to get her back, and they're trying to believe me. I told them I was going to the gym before I went in, to loosen up. It's the first time I've been dishonest with them since the night Melinda and I snuck out of the hotel in New York. Gotta see Times Square at night. My idea. Melinda went along because I harped on her, told her I'd go alone. I know what we put our parents through now. I thought I knew, but I didn't. Couldn't.'

She stopped herself. 'And none of that matters.'

'It all matters.' She hadn't gone to her partner, Eve thought, so she wanted or needed something her partner couldn't provide. 'Why don't we go up and eat? He'll nag the crap out of us otherwise.'

'If I could just have coffee.'

'Yeah, that's what I always say.' Eve led the way.

'It must be nice, being married.'

Eve thought of clawing out of the nightmare, and Roarke there, right there, holding her. 'It doesn't suck.'

She stepped into the office, noticed the door connecting to his place was closed. She'd known when he'd brushed her arm, exchanged a look, he intended to give her time with Bree.

She looked past the case board to the little table by the window set with two covered plates, mugs, juice, and best of all a jumbo pot of coffee.

'He's always feeding cops,' she said half to herself. 'He can't seem to help it.'

'He works with you a lot.'

'Sort of. He consults. He's got good instincts and extreme e-skills.'

'It's good to be with someone who understands being on the job. I had this thing for a while, but it didn't work out. He didn't like the hours, the missed dates. Figured I gave too much time to the job, not enough to him. He was probably right.'

'You have to be crazy or stupid to hook up with a cop.'

'Which is Roarke?'

'I'm still working on figuring it out.' She lifted the lids off the plates. Sighed. 'I should've known. He went for the full Irish.'

'Holy Jesus.' Bree goggled at the eggs, bacon, sausage, potatoes. 'What happened to bad coffee and a stale donut?'

'Exactly my pre-Roarke breakfast.'

'Isn't he eating? There may be two plates, but there's enough on them for three. Or four.'

'He's got some work to catch up on.' She gestured. 'Another office.' Eve studied Bree as she sat, poured coffee. 'No point letting it get cold.'

'I look at this, all this food, and I think, what's Melinda eating? Is he giving her any food? He didn't always give us food. Is she cold and hungry? Is she—'

'You need fuel, Detective.' God, she sounded like Roarke. 'You need it to help you get through, to help you think and act and do what needs to be done to bring your sister and the girl out.'

Obediently, Bree picked up her fork.

'Why did you come here, and not to your partner, or your lieutenant?' Eve asked what she already knew, to give Bree the springboard.

'Annalyn, she's the best. But . . . I can't stop thinking about before, the first time. She understands. She's worked SVU a long time, and with me, training me. She understands, but she doesn't know. Nobody does unless they were there, part of it.'

Bree lifted her gaze to Eve's. 'You were there. You know what he did to us because you saw. What happened then, it's important to what's happening now. You know him better than I do, I think. Even though . . .' She trailed off, one hand going to her heart.

'I kept it.' Deliberately she undid a few buttons of her shirt to show the tattoo. 'Melly had hers removed. Everyone told me to do that, have it erased. But—'

217

'You want to see it. When you pick up your badge and your weapon before every shift, you want to see it. You want to remind yourself why you're picking them up.'

Bree closed her eyes a moment, nodded. 'That's why I came here. You know.'

'He'll put it back on her.' Eve saw Bree jerk a little, but it was better to know, to be prepared. 'His pride, her punishment. He won't starve her, but he'll keep her hungry, and uncomfortable. He'll keep her alive until he's finished with me. And since I'm not going to let him finish with me, he'll keep her alive.'

Eve ate as she talked, primarily so Bree would follow suit. 'He won't rape her. Even the slim possibility of that lessens since he has the girl. He's already raped the girl. He feels more powerful now, more in control, more focused with that release.'

Pain shimmered over her face, but Bree nodded. 'He'll think hurting the girl will make Melly weaker, more malleable, will push her to grief and despair. He used us on each other that way.'

'You told me you felt sick with relief whenever he didn't take you, or Melinda out of the room in New York. You were one pissed off kid when you told me that.'

'I stayed mad as much as I could, so I wouldn't go crazy. But Melly would beg him not to take whoever he came for. She'd plead with him not to hurt his choice of the night – or day. And when he was finished, threw her back in, locked her up, Melly would just fall apart. That's what he thinks she'll do now.'

'But she's not a little girl now.'

'No, she's not.' Bree firmed her lips. 'She'll get stronger, put everything she has into helping Darlie get through this. She'll talk to him if he lets her, try to bargain and negotiate, stall. If she can find or make any kind of weapon, she'll use it. She'd kill him to protect the girl.'

She clasped her hands in her lap. 'And that's what scares me, more than anything.'

'He'll contact us today.'

'You sound so sure.'

'I am. He has to brag about the girl. And if he wants to get his hands on me, he has to start that maneuver soon. When he does, we start our next maneuver.'

'Which is?'

'We play him and the woman against each other, the way we do suspects in Interview. I'm just hoping for a little more meat first. And this might be it,' she said as Roarke came out of his office.

He held up a disc. 'You were right.'

'Damn straight. Let's see her.'

He passed her the disc. 'Once I had her, I ran for ID. She's going by Sylvia Prentiss, who's clean as the proverbial whistle.'

'Why is a whistle clean? I've seen whistles that weren't. Or is it the—' She curled two fingers between her lips, released a quick, high sound suitable for hailing a Rapid Cab on Fifth.

'If I'm using a whistle,' Roarke considered, 'I insist on it being clean.'

'I don't understand,' Bree said as Eve loaded the disc. 'There's a whistle?'

'Only in metaphor. And there's Sylvia Prentiss, who's been dead six years and was originally from Oregon, where she worked as a travel agent before . . .'

'Eve?' She'd lost her color again, had a hand clutched at her belly. 'What's wrong?'

'What – nothing.' For a moment, both pain and panic had stabbed her. 'Not enough sleep.' She rubbed her eyes, studied the ID shot again.

'You should sit down, Lieutenant,' Bree told her.

'I think better on my feet. Just went off for a minute. This is her, the real her. Or who she's made herself into for him. This is what she looks like when she's with him, when she's in her own place, when she's in her routine.'

'More attractive than the others.' Unable to help himself, Roarke rubbed her back as he studied the image. 'Lists her age as forty-six.'

'Shaved that some, I bet. Probably had some work done, too, but this is the face she sees in the mirror now.'

'How do you know? How did you find her?'

'Mall security discs,' Roarke answered when Eve said nothing, only stared and stared at the image on screen. 'The lieutenant believed, correctly, as she'd grazed that area with her more maternal aspect, she used it for herself as well. As herself, to shop for a proper wardrobe and the like.'

He waited again, this time running a hand gently over Eve's

220

hair. 'Do you want to see her movements at the shopping center?'

'I can't find it,' Eve muttered.

'What, darling?'

'I – I don't know. Something. Doesn't matter.' She tried to shrug it off, then bore down and shoved until she was clear of the feeling that dogged her. 'Yeah, let's see her – how she moves, where she goes.'

'There's an address on her ID.' A tremor shook lightly in Bree's voice.

'Yeah, I saw it. She might have listed her actual address here, might not. But we'll check it out. Let's get all we've got first.'

'I need to call it in. We need to get over there.'

'Detective, we don't rush this. She's smart. She's worked games for years. If we go charging after her before we lay out some strategy, we could lose her.'

She checked the time. Early still. 'And I'm waiting for my partner who's working another source. Let's look at the security.'

'Once I got the match,' Roarke said, 'I isolated her a number of times, various shops, dates, times of day.'

'Going for enhancements – upscale types,' Eve noted. Blond now, hair worn long and loosely waved. Dress, brilliant blue, short and tight. Good manicure.

'Jesus, do they watch these things? She palmed that lip dye and the other thing, whatever it is, right under the clerk's snooty nose.'

'Eye smudge,' Bree supplied. 'Top-drawer brand. But she's paying – cash – for the skin cream, and that costs more.'

'Maybe habit. Stealing for some's like a hobby.' She shifted her gaze toward Roarke, watched him smile at her cheerfully.

'She's good hands for it,' he commented. 'Quick ones.'

'She's using. Oh yeah, got a nice buzz on. Feeling good.'

Eve watched her walk, sort of breezily. Enjoying herself.

At a lingerie boutique she bought and lifted several sets – bras and matching panties, a couple of sex-me outfits, and a robe that would hide nothing.

'She's peeling off the cash in the best stores,' Bree commented, 'but if you ask me she's not paying for class. Her taste leans toward tacky.'

'Shoes,' Eve muttered. 'Had to be. Women always go for the shoes, especially if trying to walk in them makes your feet cry like a baby.'

'Actually I like that one pair, the green ones.'

'She's loving it,' Eve said, 'clerks fawning over her. Shoes, bags, clothes, sex-wear, face and hair gunk. Oh yeah, she's stockpiling for McQueen. Her shopping safaris run from two weeks prior to his escape, to two days. I'm going to want stills of some of these.'

'I have something I think you'll want more,' Roarke told her. 'I have the van.'

'What the fuck?'

'Apparently she didn't see any reason to, or perhaps didn't have the capability to jam security when she parked as

Prentiss. I took a chance, did a few scans. She also decided to give herself a break, and parked with the valet.'

He toggled something on the keyboard.

'Oh thank you, Jesus.'

'It's Roarke.' He tapped a finger on Eve's head. 'You really shouldn't forget your own husband's name.'

'There it is. Make, model, year. A dark, dull brown now. You got the fucking license plate.'

'A job not done well is just buggering around.'

'Nailed the bitch,' Eve said, and felt an uneasy mix of satisfaction and trepidation. 'Jones, run that plate, contact your people. Briefing in thirty. Shit, contact the feds, too.'

She turned, grinned fiercely at Roarke. 'You've earned more than a cookie.'

'I'll remember that come payday. Your color's back, Lieutenant.'

'Yeah, I'm feeling more like myself. I want to run the address on her ID, see what we've got there.'

'I'll do it. I would have sooner, but I wanted to get you her face, then there was the van.'

'The van's the killer. If you find the address, I can tag Peabody. At this rate, I could've walked to New York, sweated Civet, and walked back.'

She yanked out her 'link.

'Plate's registered to Davidson Millford, with the same address as her Prentiss ID. I'll run Millford after I set up the briefing.'

'Good enough. Once I contact my—' The 'link beeped

in her hand. 'Peabody,' she snapped. 'It's about fucking time.'

'Sorry, Dallas, Civet was a cashew, or whatever nut's really tough to crack. Apparently he did some studying during his last stretch and considers himself a jailhouse lawyer. Pain in the ass.'

'Did you go bad cop?'

'No.' On screen, Peabody sulked. 'I wanted to, but Baxter pointed out he has more evil genius. We worked him until nearly midnight. Civet kept calling for breaks, tossing out crazy loco trades. At one point he wanted a walk on the illegals charges, free ice cream for life, and season tickets to the Yankees.'

'How the hell did you let him play you that way?'

'Dallas, I swear he wouldn't be squeezed last night. Said we could toss him back in the cage, no problem. This time he'd come out a judge.

'I think he meant it. He could cite all these weird regulations and laws and bullshit.' As she spoke Peabody rolled her dark, tired eyes. 'He was enjoying the whole deal. I figure he was trying out his bullshit lawyer chops.'

'Did you get anything?'

'We broke at midnight, then went back at him this morning, bright and early. He took the deal. He was going to take it all along, the little bastard. He knows of McQueen, swears he never had direct dealings with him. We don't believe him.'

'No kidding?'

Peabody offered a wan smile. 'We made like we bought it

224

to get the rest. He admitted he'd had regular transactions with
a Sandi Millford, who—'

'Did you say Millford?'

'Yeah. M-I-L-L—'

'I know how to spell it.'

'Okay, then. She claimed – this would be if and when he
took payment in trade, and they partied together – that she
was McQueen's woman, and they had big plans. He was getting out, and they were going to fuck up who fucked with
him, then they'd be swimming in money. He figured she was
full of it. I believe him there. He's a reptile, but once he got
the deal – in writing, in trip – he talked for a freaking hour.
We ran Millford and got a Sandra, showed him the pic with
a handful of others. He picked her out first shot.'

'This is good. It's good. Run Millford,' she said to Bree,
'Davidson and Sandi and/or Sandra.'

'Who's that? Is it Roarke? I miss you guys. Can I say hi
before—'

'It's not Roarke.'

'No Davidson Millford in Dallas or New York,' Bree told
her. 'But I've got Sandra at a New York address.'

'I guess you're working with somebody else.' Peabody went
back to sulking. 'Is she pretty?'

'Oh, Jesus. I want you to dig on Sandra Millford, and a
Davidson Millford. Get me some data, Peabody.'

'Sure. I'll send you a copy of the interview with Civet
now, and my report once I write it up. We were going to
check out the New York address after I connected with you.'

'Do that. I'll send you an update from here asap.'

'Can you just tell me what—'

'Not now. I've got a briefing – and then I'm going to bag me a bitch.'

'I want to bag a bitch with you, Dallas.'

'There are plenty more. Later.'

She clicked off, saw Roarke watching her from the doorway. 'We should take her a souvenir. Maybe cowboy boots.'

'What? Who? Peabody? For God's sake. What did you get?'

'It's a duplex, with the lease in the name of Davidson Millford – signed in absentia – ten months ago. It's about a ten-minute drive to the mall where the girl was taken, by my calculations.'

'It's her place.' Fresh energy buzzed through Eve's blood. 'She's there. McQueen won't be far away. Let's put it together, take it in.'

'Lieutenant—'

'I'm contacting your LT on the way,' Eve told Bree. 'We need eyes on that location. He can work with the feds to decide whose eyes, but that's it. Just eyes. We don't want to move on her.'

'She could lead us right to Melinda and Darlie.'

'You bet your ass she could, and if we work it right, she will.'

Who was in charge? That was the sticking point in Eve's mind. The Dallas LT was good, was solid, but too damn polite. And the feds, well, they just assumed they were taking over. It was ingrained. But Nikos skewed a little too much by the manual and numbers for Eve's taste.

So she was taking point. If the rest didn't like it, they'd have to muscle her aside. And she wouldn't move easy, not on this one.

She said as much to Roarke as he drove and she worked out her operation strategy on her PPC.

'Ricchio knows the area, and the men,' Roarke pointed out. 'That's where he'd best lead.'

'Agreed, and that's what I plan to outline. I don't know how he works an op, how he lays things out, puts it together. And I don't have time to find out. The feds . . . Nikos knows her take on McQueen snatching a kid was off, and she's dealing with that. She may be more cooperative because of it. Laurence, he's got the best eye, nose, gut in my opinion. And he takes in the big picture fast. But I don't want the federal group-think system crowding me on this.

'Do this right, we end it today. All I want when we do is a piece of McQueen and the woman, in whatever box they choose.'

'I'm closer to his accounts,' Roarke told her, 'if that's any help at this point. I've found his pattern, and there's always a pattern. His is a very good one, with lots of tricky lures and dead ends. But I'm close now.'

'It all helps. If you can keep on that while we set up this op. We need to cut off his revenue stream once we have him. He's not going to bankroll his way out of the cage again.'

She tagged Bree. 'Eyes on?'

'The LT put four men on the duplex, orders to observe only. The van's there, Dallas. She's in there.'

'Eyes only. Make it clear, Detective. If she moves, we need an experienced tail. Don't approach, don't get twitchy.'

'The lieutenant ordered just that. I'm two minutes from the house. We're setting up in the briefing room.'

'We're right behind you.' She clicked off, tapped her fingers a moment, then tagged Peabody.

'We're en route to the New York address,' Peabody told her. 'Baxter and Trueheart say hey.'

'Yeah, yeah. I'm going into a briefing within minutes. At some point I'll need to bring you in.'

Peabody pumped a fist in the air. 'I'm going to Texas!'

'On com, Peabody, for Christ's sake. I want you to organize your notes. You're going to reel off data, names, facts, statements. Every fucking thing you've got, and I want clipped, cop precision. No amusing sidelines. Straight, hard. Tough cop.'

'I can be tough.'

'Right. You'll address me as "Lieutenant" or "sir."'

'Got it. You want them to think you're a hard-ass.'

'I am a hard-ass.' Eve scowled at the 'link screen. 'You've got that flippy deal going with your hair. Pull it back and get rid of the lip dye.'

'But I look really good today. Yes, sir, Lieutenant,' she said quickly. 'When will you pull me in?'

'I don't know yet. But be ready.'

'I appreciate it.'

She turned then, scanned the faces of the men and women standing, sitting, moving.

'Everybody sit. Knock off the chatter. Here's the situation.'

Out of the corner of her eye she saw Nikos start to rise, and Laurence put his hand on her arm, shake his head.

First problem solved.

'You.' She pointed to a Texas version of McNab – gaudy colors, a dozen pockets in baggy red pants. 'EDD?'

'You bet. Detective Arilio.'

'Run the screen, Arilio, and keep up. Get the surveilled location on screen one.'

He scrambled to obey the order. 'We found the UNSUB's hole,' she began, rattling off the address as Arilio fed the video. 'We have eyes on it now. We've identified and found the vehicle purchased by the partner for McQueen. Images of UNSUB's last two aliases – on screen two. Sandra Millford is the persona used to troll for McQueen's vics, and used in the abduction of Darlie Morgansten. Sylvia Prentiss, we believe, is the UNSUB as she looks when not using a disguise. This is her preferred appearance in what we'll say is her own time. She lives at this location under one, more likely both, of these IDs. We have another ID to add.'

She tagged Peabody.

'Put this on screen, Arilio.

'Detective Peabody, send ID image of the UNSUB identified by Civet during Interview.'

'Yes, sir. Sending.'

'Give us the salients on this ID.'

'Lieutenant,' Peabody began, and with her face sober as stone, her hair pulled back, gave the data quickly.

'In addition, sir, we are currently at the location where the UNSUB resided under this ID while in New York. We are in the process of interviewing other residents of the building, and have a name and address for her place of employment while she resided here.'

'Good work, Detective.'

'Thank you, sir.'

'Contact me with further data as it comes. Dismissed.'

She cut the transmission. 'I want everyone in this room as familiar with every one of these names, faces, salients as they are with their own. If, by chance, the UNSUB goes on the move under one of these IDs, she is to be followed. Not approached.

'Whether she's on foot or using the vehicle, we'll tail her until she leads us to McQueen.'

'Why don't we put a homer on the vehicle?'

She glanced at Detective Price. 'We have no way of knowing if said vehicle has sensors or security that would alert either the woman or McQueen if any attempt at tampering is made. As his vehicle we confiscated in New York did. Four-vehicle tail,' she continued. 'Five with me. Your lieutenant will assign the teams, and select the best location to wait until she's on the move. Air backup. EDD coordinating switchoffs and visuals throughout. We give her a clean path to McQueen. To his location, and straight to him. She so much as smells cop, we

232

lose her. Lose her, and we lose McQueen, Melinda Jones, and Darlie Morgansten.

'Nobody, absolutely nobody goes near the vehicle or the house, not when she's in or out. There may be alarms set on the residence. We wait.'

'Heat sensors identified a single hit inside the residence,' Ricchio told her. 'Moving around.'

'Excellent. She's there, she's up. Surveillance at that location is to be changed hourly. If she's spending some time at home, I don't want her noticing unfamiliar vehicles in place for long. I want a team of four ready in softclothes in case she leaves on foot.'

She waited a beat. 'Now, McQueen.'

Tough to refine an op when the location remained unknown, but she laid out basic strategy for recovery and apprehension.

'When she leads us there, we'll refine and adjust for specific location. We take this a step at a time. We're careful and we're smart. And we get it done.'

She answered questions, but kept it short. Time, she thought. The bitch was no housewife, who'd putter around half the day.

Nikos waited until she'd finished to approach. 'We can work the air surveillance and tail. Laurence and I will stay on the ground, part of the ground tail.'

'That'll work.'

'I've got some concerns about the recovery and apprehension.'

'Let's work that out when we have the location. Once she's with McQueen, we'll have time to nail it down. But I don't want to lose her now, so let's get where we're going.'

She turned away, went to Roarke. 'I need you in EDD on the financials. I know you'd rather stick with me.'

'My first and last priority, Lieutenant.'

'I get it, but I need those accounts. I'm going to be with two dozen cops, federal agents, SWAT. I'd say I've got plenty of backup there. Plus, I'll tag you the minute she's on the move. And again when she goes to McQueen. I'll give you the location, and you can come in then. You can come in before we take him.'

'That's fair enough.'

'I'm good,' she said, because he was studying her just a little too carefully.

He touched his fingertips, just a skim, to hers. 'I can see that.'

'I've gotta go. I'm taking the car. Nobody tails in a rig like that, so she'll never smell cop. I'll arrange for an officer to bring you to McQueen's location when we've got it.'

'No, you won't,' Roarke corrected, with feeling. 'I'll arrange for another car, and get myself there.'

'Have it your way.'

'That's the way I like best.' This time he took her hand, but very briefly. 'Go nail her down, Lieutenant.'

'Count on it.'

# 13

Nice neighborhood, Eve mused. Solid middle-class, with a selection of young families if the kid shit in the yards was a gauge. Little playgrounds with a lot of stuff to swing on, climb on, fall off, and break your arm on. A whole slew of bikes. Bikes not locked away, she noted, which meant nobody was too worried about theft.

A safe neighborhood – according to Ricchio's data and her own observations – where the people didn't know they had a predator sipping nightly cocktails right next door.

Mostly older vehicles sat in the drives and at the curbs, but with a sprinkling of shiny new ones so her ride didn't stand out. In any case, she sat a full block away from the target and well out of sight.

She studied the duplex on her dash screen, listened idly to the chatter in the EDD van and the other vehicles on surveillance.

Nice little yard in the front, shared with the other half of the house. The slim two stories appeared all neat and tidy on the exterior. Sizzling red and purple flowers flourished in emerald-green pots on the stoop of the connecting house. Most of the houses sported gardens or flowerpots. Apparently the UNSUB wasn't interested in posies, as her entrance remained bare.

A pint-sized bike in vivid blue rested on its kickstand in the front yard of the house one unit up from target. Boy's bike, she figured, given the style, and with those training-wheel deals.

Not a kid McQueen would be interested in, so his partner probably didn't give him a thought.

Did she get along with her neighbors? Probably. Didn't know how long she'd have to stay, wouldn't want trouble. Kept to herself, the neighbors would say when interviewed after the fact.

Nice, quiet, pretty woman – women, she thought. She had to be able to come and go as either, didn't she? They'd be college pals, living together, or sisters or something. Roommates. Never seen together, but who noticed? One worked days, say, the other nights. Different days off.

Not hard to run a game like that if you stayed smart and careful.

Top-line security, doors and windows. Well, a couple women, living alone. Who'd question that? Privacy screens drawn.

Come on, come out. Take a walk, take a drive. Don't you miss him? You're obsessed with him. Addicted. You think about him all the time.

Who are you? How do I know your face – your faces? Did you spend some time in New York before you hooked up with McQueen?

Maybe she'd busted one of her aliases. But then, she'd have run her. Wouldn't she have felt some buzz there the way she felt it now?

Way back, maybe, Eve considered, gnawing on the sensation. Maybe busted her under her real name. Or interviewed her.

Maybe she'd crossed paths with the woman when she'd been riding the system in foster homes or state institutions and schools. That was more likely, she decided. That would explain the dread. All those years, trapped in the system that, at its base, tried to help. But most of those years had just been another kind of torture.

She hadn't lived, hadn't felt real, until she'd gotten out, gone to New York. The Academy.

She shifted, sat straighter when the door on the far side of the next unit opened. A kid ran out. Yeah, a boy, she thought. Maybe too young for school. Didn't matter, no school today anyhow, she remembered. She watched as he zipped to the bike as if it was his one true love, his face shining with joy.

She eased back again, watching the boy pedal like a demon up and down the sidewalk. She saw him wave and shout, got a look at the guy in the shared yard. Older guy, ball cap, coming around to the front yard with gardening tools. The man set them down, planted his hands on his hips, and grinned at the boy.

Friendly neighbors. Yeah, just another day in the neighborhood. Kid playing, yard work. And here comes woman walking dog. Some weird little dog, all hair, pulling at the leash, jumping a lot, running in circles and yapping.

Why did anyone want something that yapped all the damn time?

Now Yard Work Man and Yapping Dog Lady stop to chat. How's it going? Hot, isn't it? Blah blah.

Thank God she didn't live in a place where she'd have to make conversation with people about the weather, little hairy dogs, and how the garden grew.

She'd want to stun every one of the neighbors inside a week.

Now Yard Work Man has to show Yapping Dog Lady his flowers. Yeah, it's a flower all right, growing right there on a bush.

And the dog jumps and sniffs and pulls and chews at the stupid leash while the kid keeps riding as if life itself hangs in the balance.

No, if she had to live here, she'd stun herself inside a week.

She came to full alert when the duplex door opened.

There you are, she thought. There you are. All dressed up for him. Sylvia this fine morning, hair all blond and shiny, pink sundress showing lots of skin, plenty of cleavage. Matching sunshades, high pink and white heels, big-ass pink purse.

All dolled up for him.

'We got her,' she said into her com. 'Give her room. She's going for the van.'

It happened fast. From her screen angle she couldn't see it all. But she saw enough.

The dog snapped the leash, and off balance, Yapping Dog Lady landed on her ass. Yard Work Man reached down to her.

And the dog raced straight for the kid. Even from her post, Eve could hear the wild, high-pitched barking.

The suspect turned as she opened the driver's side of the van.

The boy, startled, let out a yelp and swerved the bike, bumping it off the sidewalk, veering straight out into the street. And into the path of an oncoming car, one moving too fast for a quiet, family neighborhood.

'Shit, oh shit.'

As the kid did a header off the bike, one of the surveillance team – Price – bolted out of his vehicle, sprinted like an Olympian toward the kid while the oncoming car hit the brakes. The cop scooped the boy up, never breaking stride until he hit the sidewalk.

The car sent the bike flying as the cop and boy went down.

Price's jacket fell open. Eve clearly saw his badge, his weapon.

And so did the suspect.

'She made us!' Eve shouted. 'Move in, move in!'

Even as the woman leaped into the van, Eve was punching the accelerator.

'Cut her off. Abort op and apprehend.'

She swung around the stalled, damaged car and flattened bike with a harsh squeal of tires on hot pavement. Screams and shouts and the little boy's wails followed her. And the van had her by half a block.

She tuned into the chatter now – the directions, the street names, and kept her eye on the van.

The woman would contact McQueen, Eve thought, as soon as she got a little distance. And that couldn't happen.

Take her now, right now.

She hit vertical, pushed for more speed, and took back everything she'd said about Roarke and his fancy rides as the car soared. Sirens ripped through the morning air as she yanked the wheel, made the turn with the van, then edged over it.

A little more, a little more, she thought, gaining, gaining.

She nipped over the van, took the car down fast and hard, yanking the wheel again to block the road.

She saw the woman's face, just for an instant, saw the lips peel back in shock and rage. The van swerved, but there wasn't time.

It rammed into the rear of the car, sending Eve into a shrieking three-sixty while air bags exploded. She heard the crash as she shoved the seat back, pushed free.

The van tilted half on the street, half on the sidewalk where it had jumped the curb after smashing into a parked car.

Weapon drawn, Eve walked toward the van.

'Hands! I want to see your hands.'

She moved closer as other cops, other weapons joined her.

'Put your fucking hands on the wheel, now.'

'I'm hurt!'

'You're going to be more hurt if I don't see both your hands on that wheel.'

She saw them, and blood.

Head wound, she noted as she wrenched open the door, saw blood running down the woman's face. Without pity, Eve yanked her out of the van, spun her around to face it.

'What are you doing? I'm hurt. You wrecked my van. I need an ambulance.'

'Call for a bus,' Eve ordered.

'My chest.' The woman wheezed breath in and out. 'Oh God, my ribs. My head.'

'Yeah, yeah. You're under arrest.' Eve cuffed the woman's hands behind her back, then was forced to hold her up as she swayed.

'What are you talking about? I didn't do anything.' She added weeping to the wheezing. 'You drove me off the road.'

'What name should we start with? Sister Suzan? Sarajo Whitehead? Should we go with Sylvia Prentiss since you're her today?'

She turned the woman around. Broke her sunshades in the crash, she thought fleetingly. 'Whatever name you're using, we've got your ass. And we'll get McQueen's.'

Eve pulled off the broken sunglasses, tossed them to another cop.

The woman looked at her with such fierce, bright hate.

'Fuck you. You've got nothing. You are nothing!'

Eve's knees went loose, nearly buckled as the edges of her

vision grayed, wavered. The heat rolled up, a wave from her toes to the crown of her head that coated her skin in a thin layer of sweat.

And she knew.

'LT, Lieutenant Dallas.' Annalyn took Eve's arm. 'You should sit down. You took a pretty hard knock.'

'I know you,' Eve managed, her voice low and harsh with shock. 'I know you.'

'You don't know shit.' Then the woman's eyes rolled back. She'd have hit the street in a dead faint if Eve hadn't yanked her up again.

'I know you. I know you.'

'Dallas, Dallas. Ease back. Take the bitch, Jay.' As he did, Annalyn pulled Eve back. 'You're in shock, Dallas. She's out cold, and you're in shock.'

'What? What?' She pushed at Annalyn's hand, stumbled to the curb and sat. Put her head between her knees.

Couldn't get sick. Wouldn't.

Had to be wrong.

Everything kept spinning around, and rolling heat had turned to bitter, blowing cold. She couldn't get her breath.

Shocky, yes, Detective Walker was right. A little shocky from the crash.

'The bus is on the way, Lieutenant.' Bree crouched in front of her. 'Suspect is unconscious. She's banged up pretty bad. No safety bags in that van, so she took a hard hit. You, too, even with them.'

'I'm all right. Just got a little shaken up.'

'The MTs will look you over, but you should go in to the hospital.'

'Yeah, I'm going in. With her. I'll ride with her.' Pull it together, Eve ordered herself. Remember who you are. She lifted her head, bore down when the air seemed to shimmer and sway around her. 'Jesus, what a clusterfuck.'

'She didn't contact him. Didn't have time. We've got her 'link. Price already checked it and the dash 'link, and she didn't use either in the last half-hour. He doesn't know we've got her.'

'Silver lining.'

'We'll get McQueen's location out of her. We will.'

Tears in the corners of Bree's eyes, Eve noted. She wasn't the only one fighting to pull it together.

'We will. And we've got her coms. Make sure EDD starts on them asap.'

'We can take it from here.' Laurence stepped up to her. 'We'll work the van, the electronics, the duplex. You get checked out. That was some kick-ass driving, Dallas. Kick-ass.'

'Yeah.'

'Your lip's bleeding some.'

She swiped at it, looked at the smear on the back of her hand. 'Just smacked it on the air bag. I'm good.'

Blood, she thought, studying the smear. Blood on her hand, blood in the van.

Blood didn't lie.

She got to her feet, waved Bree aside. 'I'm okay. Just need to walk it off.'

She walked to the car as if to study the damage. Roarke knew her; she knew him. As she expected he'd had a field kit stowed in the trunk.

Don't think, she ordered herself, just do. Just do it.

She took out swabs, used one on the cut on her lip, capped it. Hands steady, she marked it, pocketed it.

She moved through the cops, around the MTs who'd just arrived to work on the suspect.

She stared at the blood on the wheel. Head wound, she thought dully. Always plenty of blood with a head wound.

She used the swab, capped and marked it.

After a few calming breaths, she walked back to where the MTs worked. 'What's the damage?'

'She's got the head laceration, probably concussion,' the MT told her. 'Contusions on her chest and arms, and a couple ribs either broken or cracked. Internal injuries likely. We've got to get her in.'

'I'm riding with you. What hospital?'

'Dallas City. If you're coming, you've got to come now. We're about to load her.'

'I'm coming.'

She stepped aside, took out her 'link.

'That was fast,' Roarke began, then stopped, smile dropping away. 'You're hurt.'

'Just a couple bumps from the air bags. I wrecked the car.'

'Typical,' he said, but the smile didn't reach his eyes. 'What happened?'

'Later. We have her. It got fucked, but we have her.'

244

The shakes wanted to start again, and the heat began its next roll over the ice.

'She's being transported to Dallas City Hospital. I need you there. I need you to . . . I need you to come there. I didn't get the address.'

'I'll get it. Eve, tell me what's wrong.'

'I can't, not now. I'm not hurt. It's not that. Roarke, I need you to come.'

'I'll be there.'

'Now or never,' the MT called out.

'I have to go.'

'Whatever it is, we'll handle it. I'm on my way.'

Eve slid the 'link into her pocket, climbed into the back of the ambulance.

She sat, studied the face of the unconscious woman.

Open your eyes, damn it. Open your eyes and look at me again.

Because, she admitted, she hadn't been wrong. It hadn't been shock, not from the crash. She knew McQueen's latest partner.

And it was just another nightmare.

But the woman didn't wake up, not on the short ride to the ER. Eve kept pace with the medicals, one foot in front of the other, and saw her prisoner's eyelids flutter, heard her moan as they rushed her down and through to a treatment room.

'Outside, please.'

Eve gave the doctor in charge, a young, harried black man in scrubs, one glance. 'She's in my custody. I stay.'

'Keep out of the way.'

She stepped back, but watched every move while the doctors, nurses, MTs rattled off in their strange language, transferred the woman to the table.

She moaned again.

'What's her name?' the doctor called out to Eve.

'Which one? She's got a lot of them.' She nearly gave him the one flashing like neon in her mind, then thought better of it. 'Try Sylvia. It's current.'

'Sylvia. We've got you now. Look right here. Can you tell me what day it is?'

'It fucking hurts! Make it stop. Give me something.'

'Just hang on now, we're going to take care of you.'

'Give me something for the goddamn pain, you fuck.'

'Classy,' Eve said mildly. 'She's an addict.'

'Keep that fucking cunt of a cop away from me. She tried to kill me.'

'She's lucid.' The doctor cut his eyes toward Eve. 'Is she on anything now?'

Eve kept her eyes on the bruised, bloodied face. 'Can't say, probability high.'

'What did you take, Sylvia? How much did you take?'

'Fuck you. I'm dying. She tried to kill me. Give me something.' She lashed out, tried to claw at the doctor's face.

'Strap her down,' he ordered.

Dispassionately, Eve watched the struggle, listened to the screams, the curses. One of the nurses moved over to her.

'Would you step outside with me? Just outside. She's

secured, and believe me, Doctor Zimmerman can handle her. We've got to get her stabilized, access the injuries.'

With a nod, Eve stepped outside the door, but faced the porthole window, continued to watch.

'Do you know what she might have taken?'

'Not at this time. They'll bring in the contents of her purse, whatever she had at her residence, in her vehicle. You'll have to run a tox yourself to determine. She's danger-ous,' Eve added. 'She's to be under guard at all times. She is not to be allowed any communications, and must be kept in restraints.'

'What the hell did she do?'

Eve glanced over, saw Annalyn and Bree coming at a fast clip. 'These officers will tell you what you need to know.'

'What's her status?' Bree demanded. 'Has she said any-thing?'

'Nothing helpful. Ask the nurse re status.' Eve went back to watching.

She'd live, Eve thought. She'd damn well live because there were questions to be answered.

Machines and scanners on her now, Eve noted, taking pic-tures of what was inside her. She'd stopped screaming and turned on the tears.

'Messed up, but not critical.'

Eve nodded at Annalyn's interpretation of the nurse's run-down. 'EDD's scanning the duplex for alarms and trips. When they clear it, we'll go in, take it apart.'

'What about her coms?'

'Last communication was a text.' She pulled out her notebook.

*U wore me out last night. Going to salon, some shopping. B there about 3. CU later.*

'Gives us some time. Any chance of a trace?'

'If he contacts her, we'll trap and trace. They're working on the code she used to send. I don't know yet.'

'Did the van have navigation? I didn't see.'

'Disabled,' Annalyn reported. 'All her 'links are disposable clones, juiced up with filters. But EDD will cut through.'

'She knows where Melly is,' Bree murmured. 'She knows.'

'And we'll get it out of her,' Annalyn assured her. 'He won't miss her until after three. We've got time to work her.'

'Send another text,' Eve said. 'After fourteen hundred, send another. It took longer at the salon, she booked a massage, or whatever the hell. Out shopping. Bought him a present. Something. Running late. Might be six. Buy us a few more hours.'

'That's an idea.'

'I'm full of them,' Eve muttered.

'I got word on the way over. We nailed down the salon. If we need to we can cover that in case he tries to contact her.'

'Cover it,' Eve ordered. 'We're not taking any chances.' She turned away from Annalyn when she spotted Roarke. 'Stay on her. If they take her out, stay with her. I need to take care of something.'

She intercepted Roarke. 'Let's go outside. I could use some air.'

He touched the abrasions on her cheek, the cut on her lip.

'Just the air bags. Hers didn't deploy, so she's banged up pretty good. She'll live, but she's going to hurt for a while.'

'McQueen?'

'She made us, tried to rabbit. So no. Not yet.' She went out, kept walking. Away from people moving in and out. 'She didn't have time to warn him, and we've got a window to work her.'

'That's not what's wrong.'

'I need you to do something for me, fast and private.'

'All right.'

She pulled the swabs out of her pocket. 'I need DNA. Need these two samples compared. I need to know if . . . One's mine. One's hers.'

She saw it come to him, first the shock, then the sorrow. 'Christ. Christ Jesus, Eve.'

'I recognized her from the first on some level.' Her voice wanted to shake, but she feared if she let it, it would never stop. 'Down deep where I couldn't – or wouldn't reach it, I knew her. It made me sick. Then I pulled her out of that van, and she looked at me, and I knew. It was the same look. The same as the day I remembered when I was two or three – who knows – and I'd been playing with her face stuff. She was so angry, hyped, violent. And she looked at me with such hate. Murderous hate.'

She took a shuddering breath. 'My mother.'

'You'd just been in an accident,' he began.

'Roarke.' She made herself meet his eyes, made herself let him see. 'I know. She was Stella then, but the name doesn't matter. She sticks with names starting with S. Maybe she's got monogrammed sheets or some shit.'

She didn't tremble, not until he touched her. Then she shook, her body, her voice. 'I know. I just need it confirmed.'

'I'll take care of it.' He drew her in. 'I'll see to it, don't worry about that. Did she know you?'

'No. Why would she? I was nothing to her.' *You're nothing*. She'd said it even now, Eve thought. 'A potential meal ticket, a punching bag. Just another long con.'

He eased her back, took her face in his hands. 'You need to step back from this, from her.'

'Never going to happen.' Reaching up, she wrapped her fingers around his wrists, felt his pulse beat against her palms. 'I won't let who she is, what she did get in the way of finding McQueen. It's only more important now. I'll think about that after it's confirmed. Think about what to do, how to do it. It's not going to break me.'

'I want to see her.'

'Seeing her's not what you have in mind.' She drew away to stand on her own, to prove she could. 'There'll be time to deal with her, to figure all that out. She's going to be caged for the rest of her life. But now, we need her. She's the solid link to McQueen.'

'Maybe not the only link. I found two of his accounts.'

'You – why didn't you *tell* me?' She lifted a hand. 'Sorry. Obvious.'

'He tapped one of the accounts on the day he first contacted you in New York. He had two hundred thousand wired to a bank in the West Indies, and from there to one in South Africa, and then here to Dallas.'

She lifted her hand again, needing a minute to sort it through. 'You're telling me you have the name of his bank here, in Dallas?'

'I do. He's using a South African passport and address for this account, one he tapped yesterday for seventy-five thousand. In person. Prairie Bank and Trust, their Davis Street branch.'

'Let me think, let me think.' Rubbing her head, she paced away and back, away and back. 'Too much clutter. Why does he go, withdraw that much in cash, in person? He doesn't want her to know. He's about done with her, so he's stockpiling traveling money. How did he get to the bank? Does he use the van? I don't see how without her knowing. Public transpo, maybe. Or maybe he's got another vehicle. One he'll drive when he puts that traveling money to use.

'We need to get to that bank, check their security cams.'

'I expect so.'

'The other, that other.' She glanced back toward the ER doors. 'It can wait. This is more important.'

'I said I'd take care of it. Don't worry about that part.'

'I need to update Ricchio and the feds on this. We need to move on it.'

They started back in. She stopped when she saw Detective Price standing just outside the doors, looking lost.

'Detective.'

'Lieutenant. Lieutenant Ricchio wanted to speak with you. He's here. He's . . . inside.'

'Roarke, will you find him, give him what you've got? I'll be right there.'

She waited a moment, standing there with Price, saying nothing.

'I know it's my fault. She would've led us right to Melinda, and I fucked up. We had it down cold, and I broke protocol.'

'Do you think any of us wanted to see that kid pancaked on the street, Price? Do you think Melinda would want that?'

'I don't know. God, we'd have her back by now. We'd have her.'

'If you hadn't reacted, that kid would probably be dead. Now he's home and safe and whole. You saved a life today, Detective. You did the job.'

'At what cost?'

'Nothing's free. We've got the partner. We've got other leads, and we've got some time. So shake it off and keep doing the job.'

She went inside, started back toward the treatment room. This time the nurse stopped her. 'We've got her stable. She needs some minor surgery. She's got a concussion, two broken ribs, whiplash—'

'She's conscious and stable,' Eve interrupted.

'That's right.'

'I want to talk to her.'

'She needs a little repair. As soon as—'

'No. Now. If she's not critical, she can wait for her repair. There are two lives on the line, and neither of them are hers. Is she still in there?'

'Yes. She's being monitored, then she'll need to be prepped.'

'Prepping can wait, too.'

Eve pushed past, shoved through the doors. She studied the woman on the table for a moment.

'Pay attention,' she snapped, and watched the woman's eyes open, go feral. Stepping forward, she Mirandized her mother.

# 14

You get that?' Eve asked her.

'I want a 'link, and I want one now.'

'You're not in a position to make demands. Give me your name. Your real name.'

'Sylvia Prentiss.'

'The longer you bullshit, the longer it'll be before a medical's cleared to come in here and give you a hit. Name.'

'Sylvia Prentiss, and I'm going to sue you inside out. You get me a 'link. I know my rights. I get to tag a lawyer.'

'Fine. Give me the contact and I'll arrange to have your lawyer come in. What's not going to happen is you making contact with anybody outside of this room. What's not going to happen is you tagging McQueen with a heads-up.'

'I don't know what you're talking about, and I don't give a shit. You nearly killed me. I'm not going to talk to you. I want a doctor, and I want a 'link.'

Eve stepped closer. She'd changed her eyes, she thought dully, gone a vivid, unearthly green. Once they'd been the same. In her last real flash of her mother, they'd shared the same eyes.

Wondering what else they shared made her sick.

254

'You know who I am, but you don't know me. You don't know me,' Eve repeated, calming herself. 'But I know you. Your name doesn't matter. You're the same under all of them.'

So many questions, Eve thought, but they had nothing to do with now. With Melinda or Darlie. With McQueen.

'You left a child with a monster.' Again, she thought, but this time it was different because . . . 'A child whose parents love and care for her. A child who'll never be a child again because of what you've done. You left her and a woman who tried to help you with this monster. In my book that makes you worse than he is.'

Pale, bruised face coated in a light sheen of sweat, the woman who called herself Sylvia bared her lips in a sneer. 'You've got me mixed up with somebody else.'

'I know you,' Eve repeated, leaning close so the woman could see the truth on her face. 'You're done. We know Stibble sent you to McQueen in prison. We know you've been in contact with McQueen for more than a year. We know you bought the van under your Sister Suzan Devon ID.'

Eve leaned back, kept eye contact. 'We know as Sarajo Whitehead you worked at the Circle D bar, faked a rape to draw in Melinda Jones for McQueen.' She saw the blows land, turn the pale face sickly gray. 'We know you rented the duplex as Sandra Millford – a slight variation on your New York Sandi Millford. Oh, Civet says hey. We know you rented and outfitted McQueen's apartment.'

Stella – Sylvia – moistened her lips. 'If you know so much you wouldn't be wasting time hassling me.'

'We're going to do more than hassle you. I see you as worse than McQueen, but the law looks at you as the same. You're going down for the kidnappings, for accessory to rape, enforced imprisonment. You're going down as accessory to murder, aiding and abetting. It's a smorgasbord of charges that'll keep you in a cage for the rest of your life.'

'You've got nothing.' But fear lived in those unearthly green eyes now.

'We've got it all. We've got Stibble and Lovett. We've got Civet. We've got your fake IDs, and witnesses. We've got you on the security discs at the mall with Darlie Morgansten – Sandra.

'He used you, left your ass swinging in the wind. And he doesn't give a rat's ass what happens to you.'

Fury burst over fear. 'You don't know anything about it.'

'I know *everything* about it, and him. I know all the others he used before, and what he did when he was finished with them. I know what he planned to do to you. He's sitting in the apartment you found for him, furnished for him right now, counting down the hours till he slits your throat.'

The nausea rolled again; Eve forced it down. 'You've got a chance to help yourself, make a deal so maybe you do your time on-planet, maybe you deal down some of the charges so you see the light of day again.'

'I don't know what you're talking about. And you're the one going down. Believe me, you're going to pay.'

'For what?' Rage spurted through her so she white-knuck-led the safety guard as she leaned closer. 'I don't owe you. I don't owe you a goddamn thing but pain and misery. You believe *me,* nobody wants to see you go down, all the hard way down, more than I do. I'm giving you a chance, and the door's closing. We'll have him in a matter of hours anyway, we're that close. Tell me now, tell me where he is, where he's keeping Melinda and Darlie, and I'll help you deal it down.'

'You're a liar, just like all cops. You've got jackshit.'

'We found his accounts. All that money, and neither of you will ever see it now. That's right,' she said when she saw the flicker in her mother's eyes. 'You'll be tapped out. And tapped out in prison, with nothing to deal with. Did you know he's pulled out a nice pile for his running money once he ditches you?'

'Liar.'

'He'll kill you, just like all the others, when he's done. You're the one being used now, after all the years of using. With him, you're dead. With me, you've got a chance to live. Where are Melinda and Darlie?'

'Fuck them. Fuck you.'

'He killed his own mother, and all the substitutes who came after. He'll do the same to you. Slit your throat and toss you in the nearest river.'

'He loves me!'

It shocked Eve to hear that passion, that desperation. Just for a moment she felt something close to sympathy.

'Who's doing all the work, taking all the risks? Not him. Who's strapped to a hospital gurney jonesing for a hit? Not him. He won't even let you stay with him, and if he touches you, it's just another way to use you. He likes little girls. You know about that, don't you? About men who like little girls.'

'Get the hell away from me.'

'What made you this way?' Desperation scraped at her. God, how she wanted that single answer. 'Does it go back even further? Your mother, your father? Is all the blood just poisoned?'

'You're crazy.' Despite the pain, Sylvia pushed up, strained against the restraints. 'He's going to make you pay, you and that Irish bastard you married. Pay and pay and pay.'

She panted, rearing up, bucking, face contorted. Withdrawal, Eve concluded. Withdrawal, fear, pain, fury.

'How? How will he make me pay?'

'You won't get to him. But he'll get to you. Roarke will pay a lot to get you back, but he won't get you back whole. And I'll watch while Isaac makes you scream, while he makes you beg.'

'Is that how you get off? Watching? Do you like to watch while men rape children? While they hurt the innocent?'

'Nobody's innocent! Some are just luckier than others. Get me drugs or I'll kill you myself.'

'Melinda Jones and Darlie Morgansten. Tell me where they are. It's your only chance.'

'They're where you're going to be. You won't be so lucky this time. You'll beg him to kill you. The asshole you married will bleed money every time Isaac cuts you. And we'll swim in a river of it.'

'If he's so good, he doesn't need Melinda and Darlie to get

me. Tell me where they are, unless you don't think he's man enough to take me on again.'

'I hope they're *dead*. Martyr bitch and whiny brat. I hope he lets me kill you when he's finished.'

Hated me then, hates me now, Eve thought, tired of it, unspeakably tired of it. Had there ever been anything but hate? Even for a moment?

'You're the one who'd be dead if he had his way. It's what he does, what he's always done. What makes you think you're any different than the others? Or is it you? Are your others no different?'

Risky, Eve calculated. Last ditch. 'What pulls you toward men like him? What's the draw? He's not your first. You can change your name, your looks, but it's all the same. Richard Troy, he was the same. Stella.'

Her mother's eyes narrowed, then cut away. 'Fuck off.'

'You remember him. Long time ago, but you remember. It didn't end well, did it? It never does. Who screwed who over that time?'

'You think I'm stupid? I get my share and I walk when I'm ready to walk. You got Rich to say any different, he's a liar, too. I took what was mine and walked.'

'Left something behind, didn't you?'

Her lips twisted into an ugly smile. 'Nothing I wanted. Rich is nothing but a fuckup with big dreams. Isaac knows how to get things done, and how to treat me right. Nothing you can do'll make me roll over on him.'

'Yeah, I can see that.' Love, she thought, even perverted

259

love could be unassailable. 'We'll get him without you. We'll get Melinda and Darlie back to their families without you. And we'll do you the favor of keeping you alive so you can spend the rest of the life we saved for you in a concrete cage.'

'He'll get me out.'

'He won't give you another thought.' But I will, Eve admitted to herself. I'll think about you for a very long time. 'You've got until the doctors put you back together to change your mind.'

She walked to the door, stopped, turned around. 'You had a kid once.' The medical exam would show that, and the data would be on her chart. 'What happened to it?'

'How the fuck should I know?'

Cold inside, colder and steadier than she'd have believed possible, Eve nodded. 'That's what I figured. You're just what you seem to be, Stella,' she said, using the name she remembered from glimmers of her childhood. 'Exactly what you seem.'

She walked out.

'Anything.' Bree grabbed at Eve's arm. 'Did you get anything?'

'She won't budge.'

'We'll take a pass at her.' Nikos stared at the porthole in the door.

'Be my guest. I don't think we need her. Roarke's got the accounts, and he's tracking them back. We've got a better shot at McQueen's location through that than through her.'

'We didn't get that information,' Nikos began.

'I got it right before I went in there, and you're getting it now. Let him fucking work it for an hour.' Okay, not as steady as she'd thought. 'Listen, Roarke's better at this than anybody you've got. Give him some room. McQueen's got to make contact, has to play the game with me. We need to be ready for that. Go ahead and take a whack at her.' She shrugged toward the door. 'But I'd give her a few minutes to settle in, think about things. The doctors have some fiddling to do with her.'

'We'll let them have her first,' Laurence decided, 'go at her after they've finished. She may be ready to talk a deal by then.'

'Good luck. Where's your LT?' she asked Bree.

'He went back to the house. We have to issue a media statement. Too much has gotten out, and he has to tamp down any possible leaks. If McQueen's monitoring the media, we don't want him getting wind we've got his partner.'

'He will be. I want a man on the prisoner, wherever they take her, whatever they do. I need to coordinate with EDD. When McQueen contacts, I need him sent to my 'link. I have to be mobile.'

'I'll sit on her.'

'Not you. She knows who you are, and she'll use it to shake you. Believe me,' Eve said when Bree's face went stony, 'if I wasn't sure you're the last person she'd spill to, you'd be in there working her now. Keeping a plug in leaks not only through the house but here is priority.'

'Ricchio has Annalyn laying it on that she's a suspect in a

series of robberies, injured during a chase after a botched B-and-E.'

'That should work for now.'

'I'll coordinate with EDD. The lieutenant said Annalyn and I should be at your disposal.'

'How many men has Ricchio stationed here, discounting you and your partner?'

'Three, on three-hour shifts.'

'That should cover it. You and your partner head in. Start working the area around the duplex. We're looking for an apartment, at least two bedrooms. Mid-range, remember, in a building with a garage. Good neighborhood. It won't be ground level. It'll have been rented within the last year. Follow up on the soundproofing. It's going to be within a thirty-minute drive. More than five or ten, less than thirty. He doesn't want her too close, but close enough.'

'Duplex, town house, condo?'

'Apartment,' Eve repeated. She'd gotten a good sense of how the split building worked that day. 'A setup like she had? It's too intimate. Too many people to see your comings and goings. And he needs parking for his other vehicle. Roarke said he made a personal in-bank withdrawal of funds from Prairie Bank and Trust, Davis Street branch. Use that for tri-angulation. I'm going by the bank, check out the security discs.'

'Roarke relayed that information. Ricchio had EDD pick up the discs.'

'Good. Have them sent to my unit at the hotel. I'll head

there with Roarke. I have a couple things to take care of from there, then I'll be in.'

'If she gives us McQueen's location—'

Like Bree, Eve glanced at the door of the treatment room. 'She won't. Your sister and the girl, they're less than nothing to her. The only things that matter are herself and him, and he's another drug to her. She's hooked. If I'm wrong, the feds will get it out of her. But for now, work the search.'

She turned away from the hope and despair Bree struggled to keep off her face. She got Roarke on the 'link, kept her own face schooled.

'Did you get new transpo?'

'I did, yes.'

'I need to go back to the hotel, work some angles there before I bounce back to Ricchio's house.'

'I'll pick you up where we spoke earlier.'

The minute she got in the car, she put her head back, closed her eyes. 'Just a minute, okay?'

'Take what you need.'

It hurt, she realized, now that she let it, everything hurt. Her head, her gut, her chest. Raw, wet wounds that throbbed with every heartbeat.

'I don't know if I did the right thing, talking to her. I don't know if I did it for me or the vics.'

'You never forget the victims, Eve.'

'She wouldn't flip. And she won't. She knows me – not the connection to her, but to McQueen. She knows he hates me, needs to teach me a lesson. So that's what she wants, even more than any sort of deal we'd offer. It's what she does, I think. Becomes addicted to a certain type of man, then puts him in control. Until she finishes, for whatever reason. She had a child she didn't want because Richard Troy wanted the investment. Now she's doing what McQueen wants. There have probably been others between.

'Doesn't matter,' she added, 'except as a pattern. But she's a dead end. If there's any chance I'm wrong and she can be flipped, it can't be me. I'm the mark, that's how she sees it. The mark, and worse, a cop. I'm the enemy and the mark. Or we are. It's for money. Still looking to make money off me. It's ironic, I guess.'

'Ransom?'

'Yeah. That's what he's told her. They get me – and he gets to punish me, play with me, and extort big piles of money from you. There may even be some truth in it, though he doesn't intend to share any of the take with her. It's a job for her. A labor of love. Melinda and Darlie, they're just incidental.'

'The withdrawal means he's on the clock.'

'Yeah, yeah.' She rubbed her hands over her face, shoved them back into her hair. 'He hopes to have me within a couple of days. Sooner if he can. He'd need her for that. A decoy, a lure. So we've fucked that up for him.'

She drew a breath, turned to study him. 'I'd be really pissed off if he'd made this work and you'd paid.'

'Would you now?'

'Flushing money away. He'd kill me anyway.'

'Aren't we matter-of-fact,' he said, very quietly.

'Just the way it is.'

'And this is your way of telling me, should he get lucky, I should sit on my big piles of money and simply consider my wife's fate sealed. Ah well, it was fun while it lasted.'

She knew that tone of voice, so cool, so pleasant. And dangerous as a snake. At the moment, she simply couldn't care.

'Not exactly. More or less. It's nothing to get steamed over since it's not going to happen.'

'But I should take note for the future. Your point of view is so noted. Now let me tell you just the way it is. If McQueen, or anyone, got lucky, I'd pay whatever I had to pay to get you back. And while I paid, I'd hunt him down. And I'd find him. When I did, he'd come to wish I ended him.'

He glanced at her. 'What would you do in my place?'

She looked away again, shrugged. 'It's your money. No skin off mine to flush it. It's stupid to talk about, anyway. He doesn't have me. He has Melinda and Darlie, and within a few hours he's going to realize something's wrong. He'll go under. He may leave them alive when he does, or he may not.'

'And you'll still have a target on your back.'

'Right now, that target is keeping those two people alive. The minute he has to change angles, all bets are off.'

At the hotel, she got out of the car, started inside. 'I wanted to come back here primarily because you'll work

265

better. No cops to bitch about, including me as I'll stay out of your way. You stay out of mine. He'll contact me and soon. I need to be ready for it. I need to write things out, sift through them – in the quiet. When I'm done I can have Ricchio send someone to pick me up so you can keep at it here.'

Rather than respond, Roarke rode up with her in silence. Bubbling silence, he thought. Right at the boil.

They got off on the office level, but before she could reach hers, Roarke took a good grip on her arm.

'As you're spoiling for a fight, I'll oblige you. But you'll take a blocker for the headache first.'

'I don't have time for a fight.'

'Then you shouldn't take a swing at someone ready to take one back.' He pulled a small case out of his pocket, opened it.

She scowled at the little blue pills.

'Simpler for you to take it,' he said all too easily, 'than for me to stuff it down your gullet.'

'Why do you *do* that? Push and order and threaten.'

'Because you're in pain, and too much of a bloody mule to admit it. Because I'm in the often maddening position of loving you beyond all reason, so you can infuriate and rip me to pieces at the same time. Now take the fucking pill.'

She snatched one, swallowed. 'I don't have time for emotional dramas.'

'Then don't set the stage for one by telling me to sit on my arse as you'll be dead anyway. I live with the reality of what you are and what you do every bleeding day, and don't need to have it shoved in my face.'

'I was only—'

'Don't.' He whipped out the word, and the end of the lash was ice cold. 'Don't tell me you were only being rational. You're trapped in a brutal situation, working to save lives while a piece of your own slashes your heart. I'm trying to cut you a break though you're denying both of us the comfort of sharing an impossible load.'

The fact that she wanted to weep, to just curl up in a ball and wail appalled her. Sympathy, one kind word from him would break her.

So she lashed out.

'I don't have time for comfort, or to examine my feelings, explore my goddamn psyche. While we're standing here discussing why you're pissed off, two people, one of them a thirteen-year-old girl, are being tortured or worse. So comfort and bruised egos just have to wait.'

'Bruised ego, is it? All right, then. You do what you must, and I'll do the same. When we're done we'll have that drama. We'll have a bleeding opera.'

He turned, walked into his office. Shut the door.

She took one step toward the door, stepped back. She wasn't going to play the talk-it-out, fix-it-up routine. Her personal problems had no bearing on the case. The fact that her mother was McQueen's partner meant nothing to anybody but her.

If they didn't find McQueen in a matter of hours, they'd

lose whatever advantage they held. He could decide to dispose of his two prisoners before he went under.

She couldn't be responsible for that. She couldn't let emotional turmoil over something that was over and *done* bog her down when lives were on the line.

She stepped to her case board, made herself look at the photos of the woman she remembered as Stella. Whatever Stella had done thirty years before had nothing to do with Melinda Jones, Darlie Morgansten, their families, their friends.

At this point she was Sylvia, and Sylvia was only a tool they might be able to use to save two people, to bring McQueen to justice. And she would spend all the years she had left in a cage.

However that made Eve feel, however it might haunt her, didn't apply to now.

She went to her desk, angling herself so she could see those photos as she worked.

She replayed the interview, making notes, looking for key words, any mistakes. Melinda and Darlie were still alive – it became clear Stella – no, Sylvia, Sylvia now – Sylvia hated them, wanted them dead and gone. Wanted McQueen to herself. Also clear Sylvia hadn't known that McQueen had withdrawn a large amount of cash.

Eve brought up the security discs from the bank, began to study them.

She made him immediately. He'd gone very blond for his South African ID. His movements precise, his suit perfectly cut.

Where'd you get the suit, Isaac? Did Sylvia buy it for you? Or did you go shopping in New York? Good briefcase, good shoes, too. Somebody did the shopping.

She watched him handle the transaction, flash the teller a charming smile. She followed him out of the bank, picked up the exterior cam. Crowded outdoor mall, she thought, and wondered why the hell people needed so many stores and restaurants. But he walked directly through the parking area.

An all-terrain and a pickup obstructed the view of his vehicle. She ordered the computer to enlarge a section, freeze, and got enough to identify a dark blue sedan, late model. As he pulled out, she enlarged again, froze again, thought she had enough for a make. Only part of the license plate, she thought, but still enough to start a search.

'Where'd you get the car, Isaac? Not a lot of time to wheel and deal, but plenty to set it up in advance.'

She turned to her 'link.

'Hey, Dallas.' Peabody beamed at her. 'How'd it—'

'Roust Stibble. He plays middleman. McQueen's driving a new Orion sedan, dark blue. If Stibble brokered the buy, shake it out of him. I've got a partial plate, Texas, Baker, Delta, Zulu. I'm going to run it here, but you do the same. If he didn't buy, he stole it. I want to know where and when he did either.'

'Okay, I'm on it. Is there anything else new?'

She hesitated, just a beat. 'We have his partner in custody.'

'Holy shit! That's great.'

'She's not giving anything up. Not yet. We're on the clock, Peabody. If she doesn't show at his place by six, he's going to smell something off.'

'I got an update from EDD just a few minutes ago. They're starting to pull transmissions off Stibble's wiped 'link, and they're digging out coms from his comps. You should have a report, including the data, pretty quick now. I know Roarke's close on the accounts because he's been keeping Feeney in the loop there. The dam's breaking, Dallas.'

'It can't be soon enough. He's got transpo and running money, and we can be damn sure he's got an escape route. If he gets wind of the partner, he'll use them. Drain Stibble dry, Peabody.'

'He's dust.'

Closing in, Eve thought as she rose to study the board again. But would it be soon enough?

Melinda stroked Darlie's hair. She'd wrapped the girl in both blankets, but Darlie continued to shiver from the aftermath of the nightmare.

Melinda's own throat raged with thirst. She'd risked drinking from the bottle of water the woman had tossed into the room, but after a few swallows she'd felt woozy.

Staying alert, staying aware was vital.

Darlie needed her.

He'd had the woman bring Darlie in the night – she thought it had been night – before. He preferred having the women he used deal with the chores. He'd think of the water, the blankets, snapping those restraints on trembling wrists and ankles as chores.

She'd done what she could for the girl – held her, rocked her, cocooned her in blankets while Darlie cried for her mother.

'Will he come back? Will he?'

Melinda couldn't count the times Darlie had asked, so she answered the same way.

'I'm going to do everything I can to keep him from hurting you again. My sister's looking for us. Remember, I told you about my sister, Bree?' She kept her voice soothing, like the stroke of her hand. 'She's a police detective. And there's another. The other I told you about, remember? The one who saved me? Eve Dallas. They'll find us, Darlie. We just have to hold on until they do.'

'He said I was a bad girl. He said I liked what he did, but I didn't. I didn't.'

'He lies, sweetie. He lies because he wants you to feel ashamed. But you didn't do anything wrong. None of this is your fault.'

'I tried to stop him.' Darlie burrowed into her. 'I tried to fight, but he hurt me so bad. I screamed and screamed, but nobody heard me.'

'I know.' Melinda had to close her eyes, close them tight to block off the memory of her own wild struggles, her own screams. 'I'm here. Help's coming.'

'He put the number on me, and now my mom's going to be mad. She said – she and Dad said I couldn't get a tattoo until I was eighteen. She's going to be so mad.'

'No, she won't.' Melinda held Darlie tighter when she started to weep again. 'I promise she won't be mad at you because it's not your fault.'

'I said mean things about her. I was mad and said mean things. It's bad. I'm bad.'

'No.' Firmer now to cut through the rise of grief and guilt. 'No, it's normal. It's what every girl does sometimes. You're not bad. You listen to me now. Don't let him get in your head. Whatever happens, remember who you are, that it's not your fault.'

'I'm not allowed to have sex.' Darlie wept.

'You didn't. He raped you. That's not sex. That's attack, assault, abuse. It's not sex.'

'Is he coming back?'

'I don't know.' But she did. Of course she did. 'Remember they're looking for us. Everyone's looking for us. Darlie, I'm going to do everything I can, but if I can't stop him—'

'Please.' The shackles rattled as Darlie shot up in panic. 'Oh please, don't let him hurt me again.'

'I'll do everything I can, but . . .' Melinda turned, cupped Darlie's pale, wet face in her hands. 'If . . . you have to, remember it's not your fault. If you can, go somewhere else inside your head. Don't let him get inside your head.'

'I want to go home.'

'Then go there in your head. Go—' She heard the locks give, felt Darlie cringe and shudder.

'Don't, don't, don't.'

'Shh, shh. Don't cry,' she whispered. 'He likes it better when you cry.'

The monster opened the door.

'There's my bad girls.'

His smile beamed indulgence, affection, but Melinda saw the hot glint in his eyes.

'Time for your next lesson, Darlie.'

'She needs a little more time. Please? She'll do better if she has a little more time to absorb the first lesson.'

'Oh, I think she absorbed just fine. Didn't you, Darlie?'

'Take me. I need to learn a lesson.'

He spared Melinda a glance. 'It's too late for you. Past your prime. Now this one—'

'I'll be anything you want,' Melinda said as he stepped forward. 'Anything. Let you do whatever you want. You can hurt me. I've been bad. I deserve it.'

'You're not what I want.' He struck out, a brutally casual backhand that rapped her head against the wall. 'Keep it up,' he warned Melinda, 'and she'll pay.'

'How about conversation? The woman you're with? She doesn't seem like she has a lot to say. It's obvious she doesn't have your intellect. We're not going anywhere,' Melinda added, gripping Darlie's hand hard under the blankets. 'Wouldn't you like to talk for a while? The day I came to see you, you wanted to talk and I didn't let you. I'm sorry. I'd like to make up for that now.'

He angled his head. 'Isn't that interesting.'

'I can't give you what she does, but I can offer something

273

else. Something you must have missed, something you can't get from her – or the woman.'

'And just what would we talk about.'

'Anything you like.' Her heart beat like a drum in her throat, and the beat was hope. 'A man like you enjoys the stimulation of conversation, debate, discussion. I know you've traveled a great deal. You could tell me about the places you've been. Or we could talk about art, music, literature.'

'Interesting,' he said again, and she could see she'd intrigued him, amused him.

'You have a captive audience.'

He gave a bark of a laugh. 'Aren't you the sassy one?'

When he walked out, Melinda let out a breath. 'Hold on,' she murmured to Darlie. 'And be very quiet.'

He came back in with a chair, set it down, dropped into it. 'So,' he said with a grin, 'read any good books lately?'

# 15

She thought of herself as Sylvia. It was the name she used when she and Isaac were alone, the name she'd like to use when the game was done and they were living the high life. Sylvia was classy, elegant, and Isaac liked class.

The cop bitch called her Stella, but Stella was long ago. Another game, but that one had left her more dry than high. Richard Troy. Now that was a name from the past. How had that bitch of a cop known about Stella and Rich?

Rich's flapping mouth, that's how. It was the only way she could angle it. He must be doing time somewhere, the fucking asshole, and worked some sort of deal for flipping on her.

But how had he known to flip?

Didn't matter. Not as long as Rich was jerking off in a cage somewhere.

She'd given the son of a bitch her best, too. More than her best. For Christ's sake, she'd carried that sniveling brat of a kid in her belly for nine months. For Rich.

Train it, he'd said. Train it and sell it. Plenty of men like young meat, and plenty of them paid top dollar.

But he hadn't been the one carting that weight around. He

hadn't been the one strung out for months, because drugs were off the menu.

He hadn't wanted the kid coming out fucked up – damaged goods didn't rate top dollar – so who'd paid that price?

Maybe it had been useful for a while, even though it cried half the goddamn day and night. Still, marks went even softer when you added a baby to the mix.

They'd made a good living running baby scams the first couple years. But then what had she gotten out of it? A whiny brat, that's what.

Then a bloody lip when she'd found out Rich had been skimming the take and called him on it. But she'd played it right, hadn't she? Going along, playing the game with the bastard and the brat until she'd pocketed a cool fifty large and walked.

Run maybe, because Rich would've beat the shit out of her if he'd caught her. Instead, he'd been stuck with the kid, and she had the take. Lived pretty damn well off it until it had run out.

She'd loved the cocksucker once.

Not like Isaac. Everything was different with Isaac. He treated her good – like Rich had in the beginning, and a couple others along the way. He *appreciated* her. He'd even sent her flowers. Imagine thinking of that when he was in prison.

And he told her she was beautiful, and sexy, and smart. He made *plans* with her.

Maybe they didn't tear up the sheets as often as she

wanted, but he had a lot on his mind right now. And what did she care if he banged the kid she'd found for him? The kid deserved it for being stupid.

And it put him in a really good mood. After he'd finished with the brat, they'd drink his fancy wine, she'd take a couple pops, and they'd talk and talk.

Big plans, big money, and they'd pay the cop back for screwing with him in the first place. Bitch would never have gotten the drop on her if she hadn't been lucky.

Her luck was about to run out.

It burned her ass the way the cop had talked about Isaac, how that cunt had tried to turn her against him. They had a future, and they were going to build it using the cop's blood for glue.

Isaac would make that bitch pay double now.

She slit her eyes open. The watchdog cop sat at the door, a big, burly lump of shit, in her eyes.

Whatever they'd done with her ribs helped her head. And so did the little dose of juice they'd finally given her. Better yet, when they'd taken her down to work on her, they'd had to loosen the restraints.

She hadn't lost her touch, she thought, running her thumb over the laser scalpel she'd palmed while faking a seizure. Smooth as the Samaritan gambit she'd worked as a kid – and the scalpel was worth a hell of a lot more than some do-gooder's wallet.

Time to make the move, she told herself. She didn't believe that crap the Dallas bitch had spewed about closing in on Isaac. But she had to warn him, had to get to him. And he'd take care of her.

Maybe he'd buy her flowers again. Then they'd deal with Eve Dallas.

She moaned, tossed from side to side.

'Help.' She made her voice weak, putting herself into the part.

'Settle down,' the cop suggested.

'Something's wrong. Please, can you get the nurse? Please, I think I'm going to be sick.'

He took his time, but he stepped over, pushed the call button. A few seconds later, the nurse's face came on screen.

'Problem?'

'She says she needs a nurse. Says she feels sick.'

'I'll be there in a minute.'

'Thank you.' Sylvia closed her eyes, just left the slit under her lashes. 'It's hot. I'm so hot. I think I'm dying.'

'If you are, it'll be hotter where you end up, end of the day.'

He turned as the nurse bustled in.

'Says she's sick, says she's hot, says she's dying.'

'Nausea's not unusual after the procedure she had, and the meds.' Laying the back of her hand on Sylvia's brow, the nurse raised the bed.

On a moan, Sylvia tried to turn, straining against the cuff on her right hand. 'Pain. There's a pain.' When she began to gag, the nurse grabbed a bedpan.

'Can't. Can't. Cramp. Need to – I can't.'

'Just breathe. I need to take off the right restraint, ease her over. She'll boot all over both of us otherwise.'

Muttering, the cop unlocked the restraint. In one vicious swipe, Sylvia slashed the laser across his throat. Even as he stumbled back, spurting blood, she pressed it to the nurse's cheek.

'One peep, one sound, and I carve your face off.'

'Let me help him.'

'You'd better help yourself and unlock the other cuff. This thing will slice you open at five feet. You'd know that, being a nurse. Get the cuff off. Hurry.'

To get her moving, Sylvia gave her a shallow nick. Freed, she flexed her fingers. 'Got some blood on you,' she commented. 'But that happens in hospitals. Strip.'

She thought about killing the nurse, but it might involve more blood. Too much on the scrubs might cause too much attention. Instead she used the restraints, gagged her with medical tape.

'You got big feet,' she commented when she put on the nurse's shoes. She pulled her hair back, fixed on the ID card, then grabbed a tray, tossed some supplies into it.

'Give Dallas a message for me. Tell her Isaac and me, we'll be coming for her.'

She walked out, walked briskly with her tray – and remembered belatedly she should've taken the nurse's 'link. But by the time she walked out the exit, she was smiling.

Cars had 'links. It'd been a while since she'd boosted a car. Just like old times.

Melinda kept him engaged, considered every moment he focused on her rather than Darlie a gift. The nights she'd spent studying him as she might a disease that had infected her had paid off. She knew his profile, his pathology, all of his background that had been discovered and published.

She knew he was well-read, considered himself an erudite man with exceptional taste. She discussed classic literature, segued into music – classical, contemporary, trends, artists.

Her head throbbed like a rotted tooth, but Darlie stopped shivering and eventually went limp in sleep.

When she disagreed with him she walked a tightrope, carefully navigating the shaky line between opinion and argument, conceding, flattering, even forcing out a laugh now and then as if he'd scored a point.

'But I like a good, silly comedy now and then,' she insisted. And thought she'd have sold her soul for one cool sip of water. 'Complete with pratfalls. Especially after a long, hard day.'

'Without wit it's mindless.' He shrugged. 'If it doesn't make you think, it's not art.'

'Of course you're right, but sometimes mindless is just what I want.'

'After a long, hard day. Counseling all the bad girls.'

Her heart tripped, but she nodded slowly. 'It's good to tune out and laugh. But as I said, you're right about—'

'And do you spend all day telling them it's not their fault, like you told our little Darlie here?'

She deliberately looked up at the camera above the door. 'We both understand I knew you were watching, listening. I wanted to keep her calm. To help her adjust.'

'So you lie and lie and lie some more. Because we both know, too, that they want what I give them. You did.'

'It's difficult to understand at such a young age, the—'

'Women are born understanding.' Something dark passed over his face and had her stumbling heart slamming against her ribs. 'They're born liars and whores. Born weak, and devious.'

He set his palms on his knees, angled forward, his tone mild and lecturing. 'The young ones, they need to be trained, educated, controlled. They need to learn they're here for a man's pleasure. Toys, really, he winds up at his whim. That he brands, like cattle.'

He smiled as he wagged his finger back and forth. 'You erased my brand, Melinda.'

'Yes. But you put it back.'

'That's right. That's absolutely right.'

He leaned back, waved a hand in the air. 'The older ones have their uses. You just might be useful with another couple decades of seasoning. They like to serve, or pretend to like it. They want to be flattered and petted, want pretty, shiny things. And promises.'

He let out a sigh, a shake of his head, but his eyes sparkled with an ugly glee. 'They're so pitifully grateful for the attention. So calculating in their attempts to manipulate a man. They need to be used – all while flattered and petted, of course. A woman will do everything she's asked if you dangle the bright and shiny, if you give her some poetry – and a good fuck now and then.'

He shifted in the chair again, wrapping his hands around his knee, smiling his smug smile until Melinda wanted to beat his face bloody with her fists.

'Then, they have to be ended because they're so *unspeakably* boring. Which you're not – yet. You will be, but for now you've been very entertaining. You working so hard to make this connection with me, Melinda, has given me a delightful time. So unnecessary, though, as we made a connection so long ago. Erasing the brand doesn't sever that connection. Nothing can. You'll never forget what I did to you. Never forget what I taught you.'

'No, I won't.'

'Well now.' He slapped his hands on his thighs before he rose. 'Time to move along to the younger generation. I have to thank you, honey. You really did *stimulate* me. I know I'm going to enjoy giving Darlie her next lesson.'

Melinda braced. It would be useless, end badly, but she wouldn't let him take Darlie without a fight. She had her teeth, her nails. At the least she'd give him pain.

His 'link sounded. He paused to pull it out of his pocket. 'The old bad girl checking in,' he said, then frowned at the unfamiliar display.

'Do you know a Sampson Kinnier? Neither do I,' he said

before Melinda could answer. 'Crossed transmission, I suppose, but we'll let it go to v-mail, see what Sampson has to say.'

When Sylvia's voice came on, McQueen's eyes went flat as a snake's.

'Isaac, baby, it's me. Answer the 'link! There was trouble. That fucking bitch Dallas tracked me to the other place. I made the assholes, but she crashed the van. She hurt me, baby – but not like we're going to hurt her. Come on, answer the goddamn 'link! I got patched up at the hospital. I got out – took a cop down doing it. I'm on my way to you. I need a boost, baby, need one bad. They wouldn't give me any decent shit at the hospital – had me tied down like a crazy person. I fixed it. Mama needs some candy, baby. Fix me some candy, will ya? I'll be there soon. And we'll make her pay. We'll make her bleed.'

Isaac studied the 'link, held his silence. Watching him, Melinda thought she saw confusion in his eyes, and felt another blossom of hope.

Then he sighed. The smile returned; the eyes stayed flat. 'We seem to have a change of plans.'

He pocketed the 'link. And he unsnapped the sheath on his belt, drew out his knife.

Eve snatched at the EDD reports the instant they came in. Video was toast, Feeney reported, and audio was fragmented. But they got solid chunks of the transmissions and more would come.

Eve closed her eyes, played them out.

McQueen's voice, smooth as cream, hinting of seduction. And Stella's – no, Sylvia's, she reminded herself – excited, flirtatious.

*Don't know what I'd . . . without you doll. Can't wait . . . won't . . . longer.*

*. . . come up to see you. Everything's set . . . could come back with you when . . .*

*Be patient . . . need to check security at our place. Don't want to . . . problems once we get started.*

*. . . just there yesterday. Soundproofing's finished . . . can't hear that baby crying half the damn night down the . . .*

*. . . security cams tested . . . count on you sweetheart.*

*You can . . . stalled last week. Tech tested all three . . .*

*Good girl. You've got your eyes on the prize?*

*Check her every day. Miss you, baby.*

*Miss you right back.*

*Can you send some money? Rent's . . . on our place in a couple days.*

*. . . run through your spending money already? . . . buy yourself something pretty?*

*Gotta look pretty for you, baby.*

*I'll take care of it. We don't want Maxwell's credit getting any black marks. My time's up. Just a couple more weeks and . . . with you.*

*It's killing me to wait . . . so close.*

*Soon doll.*

She noted down the date and time of the transmission, and on the text copy highlighted key words and phrases.

'Copy and send file to Detectives Jones and Walker, to Agents Nikos and Laurence, marked urgent. Orders to narrow search using highlighted text.'

**Acknowledged. Working . . . File copied and sent.**

'Begin search for apartments within a twenty-mile radius of listed address. Search for rentals with payment due on the fifteenth of the month. Further narrow to leases under the name of Maxwell – first or last name. Unit will be two or three bedrooms. Building will have direct access to parking garage.'

**Acknowledged. Working . . .**

She emailed Roarke the names, the dates. Easier than actually speaking to him right now, she decided.

The minute she'd done so, her 'link signaled.

'Dallas.'

'She's loose.'

'What?'

'She killed Malvie – Officer Malvie,' Bree said quickly. 'Forced the nurse on duty to give her her scrubs. Took the ID and walked out. They've locked down the hospital, have an alert out for her, but—'

'She's headed straight to McQueen.' Fury and frustration

would have to wait. 'She won't be on foot. She'll boost a vehicle, hail a cab.'

'You don't hail cabs here.'

'What do you – never mind. Have security check for a missing vehicle out of hospital parking, nearest her exit point. How long does she have?'

'An hour, maybe a little more.'

Too long, Eve thought. Too long.

'I'm on my way in.'

She broke transmission, shoved up to bang on Roarke's office door.

'It's not locked for Christ's sake.'

She pushed it open. 'She's out. She killed the cop on duty, got nurses' scrubs and walked. I need to go. Now.'

'Two minutes.' He hunkered over his comp. 'Two bloody minutes. I'm nearly there. She'll go to McQueen. Let me find the bastard.'

'Add Maxwell to the search. Don't ask,' she snapped. 'Just do it. Add Maxwell and look for a transfer of funds on the twelfth of the month.'

'Feeney sent me the same data. It's in. Be quiet.'

She gritted her teeth, fisted her hands. But she knew that look – the cold, clear eyes, the scowl. If he said he was close, he was close.

He snapped out orders even as he worked the keyboard and the screen manually. From her angle she could see data – incomprehensible to her – flashing by.

She answered her signaling 'link with a snarl. 'What?'

'A Sampson Kinnier just reported his all-terrain stolen out of the first-level visitors' lot. A red 'fifty-nine Marathon,' Bree continued, 'Texas plates, Charlie-Tango-Zulu-one-five-one. BOLO's issued.'

'Roarke thinks he's closing in on a location. I'm taking another couple minutes here. If he hits, I'll relay on the way.'

'Don't bloody think,' Roarke muttered. 'Bloody know.'

She went with instinct. 'It's going to hit. Advise your lieutenant we'll need SWAT, tactical, crisis negotiator – all the bells and whistles, Detective – on alert.'

'Yes, sir. Dallas, if he runs – Melinda.'

'The best thing we can do for her is the job. Now go.'

She shoved the 'link away. 'Roarke—'

He shot up a hand, clearly telling her to be quiet again.

Do the job, do the job, she told herself, rolling to the balls of her feet and back. When doing the job meant waiting, it could tear pieces off the guts.

'Got him, buggering bastard. Copy location to vehicle navvy,' Roarke ordered. 'And get the bloody vehicle out front now.'

As the computer acknowledged, he picked up a holstered weapon – one he'd had no business transporting over state lines – strapped it on as he moved.

'Where?' she demanded as she jumped into the elevator with him. 'Where?'

He rattled off an address as he shrugged his jacket over the weapon. 'It's only minutes from here according to the computer.'

'She's already there.' Eve relayed the address to Ricchio.

The adrenaline and whatever mild blocker they'd given her at the hospital burned off before she sped into the parking garage. The way pain radiated from her ribs she feared she'd snapped the fused bone. Her heart beat so hard she could barely get her breath as she headed toward the elevator in a limping run.

They'd said something about a hairline fracture in her ankle. Hairline, my ass, she thought. She could feel it puff out like a pus balloon over the nurse's ugly shoes.

She just needed to get to Isaac, just needed to get some candy. Oh God, yes. Needed him to take care of her, like he promised, like nobody else ever had.

He'd give her what she needed – the drugs, the drugs – and buy her flowers.

Tears of pain, rage, withdrawal leaked from her eyes as she stumbled into the building. Sweat poured down her face.

A couple of days, she thought, just needed a couple of days to heal up. Then they'd go after Dallas. God, she couldn't wait to get her hands on that bitch. She wouldn't look so fucking tough when they got through with her.

And she wanted to go first, wanted to pay the bitch cop back for the pain, for the fear.

Her breath came in wheezes as she limped into the elevator.

'Hold the elevator!' someone sang out.

'Fuck off!' she snarled at the woman and her snot-nosed kid when the doors shut in their faces.

She only had to ride one floor, but every second was its own separate agony. Teeth clamped, she dragged herself down the hall.

'Isaac.' Voice hoarse, she punched at the security plate. She couldn't remember the code; everything jumbled together in her head.

She needed a hit. God, God, she needed a hit.

Needed Isaac.

When he answered, she wept out his name, fell into his arms. 'I'm hurt. She hurt me.'

'Aw, baby doll.'

He rubbed her back.

She stank, he thought, stank of sweat and hospital. Stank of stupidity and age. Even her hair stank, the tangled, matted mess of it.

Her face was pinched, white – old again.

'You didn't answer. You didn't answer.'

'I was . . . involved. I didn't hear the signal, and I didn't want to tag you back in case. How did you get here, sweetheart?'

'I stole a car, right out of the hospital lot. Right under the cops' noses. They were waiting for me, Isaac, waiting for me outside the duplex. But I got away. Fix me up, Isaac. They wouldn't give me anything.'

'Fix you right up.' He helped her to the sofa where he'd already prepared a pressure syringe. 'Quick and good,' he told her. 'Poor baby doll.'

Her hands shook as she snatched at it, and he watched her jab it in the crook of her elbow, as he'd watched his mother countless times.

Like his mother, she let out a harsh, guttural grunt – almost sexual – as the drug punched into her bloodstream.

'Gonna be better now.' Eyes glazed with pleasure, she smiled at him. 'Gonna be better.'

'Absolutely. What did you tell her?'

'Tell who?'

'Dallas.'

'Didn't tell her shit. She tried to turn me against you. Lying whore. I spit in her face, told her you were going to pay her back good. You pay her back, Isaac.'

'Of course.'

'I want to cut her.' Cruising now, Sylvia leaned back, face going slack. 'I want to cut her first. She looked at me – you know how she looked at me? Like I made her sick. Tried to tell me she didn't need me anyway 'cause they were close to finding you. Lying cunt.'

'Said that, did she?'

He rose, wandered.

All the work, he thought, the time, the money, the preparation. And worse, all the hours he'd spent with this dried up, *stupid* junkie.

He wanted to beat her face to pulp with his fists. Saw himself doing just that. Caught himself turning toward her with his fists bunched, his breath coming fast.

She sat, glassy-eyed, smiling, unaware.

Bringing himself under control made him shudder.

'How did they find you, sweetheart?'

'I dunno. They were just there. Want more candy.'

'In a minute.'

The van, he decided. They'd managed to track the van. He'd really thought he'd had at least another week there. He *should* have had another week.

Ah, well, on to Plan B.

'Suitcase,' she muttered.

'Hmm?'

'We going? We packing up, and going somewhere nice?'

He followed her stare. He hadn't meant to leave the suitcase out in plain sight. He'd just been so rushed. Had so many things to think of, to decide on.

'Mmm,' he murmured, strolling behind the sofa.

'Get a nice new place, and when we get that Dallas bitch, you'll let me have her first. Bleed her good. Make some money off her, right, Rich? Make a whole lot of money off her.'

He lifted his brows at the name she called him. That was women for you, he supposed, couldn't keep their men straight.

'I'm going to have to disappoint you there.'

He yanked her head back, slit her throat with quick, almost surgical precision.

Good, he thought. Good. Now he felt *much* better.

When she gurgled, tried to clutch her throat, he shook his head, let her slide to the floor. 'You're useless to me. Absolutely useless.'

He pulled off his shirt, tossed it aside as he went to the kitchen to scrub his hands and arms.

He'd already carried most of what he needed to the car, though he intended to travel light. He changed his shirt, brushed a hand over his hair. Slipped on his sunshades.

Picking up the suitcase, he blew a kiss toward the door, toward Melinda and Darlie.

'Fun while it lasted,' he said, and strolled out without a backward glance toward the woman bleeding on the floor.

# 16

As Roarke drove, Eve worked the 'link, coordinated with, strategized, updated the team Ricchio put together.

'Four uniforms on scene, pulled a block back from target,' she muttered, while Roarke roared through the gap between a truck and a Mini with a stream of spit to spare. 'He doesn't know we have this location. Has to know she wouldn't go back if we did – and they've spotted the stolen car just inside the apartment's garage. So she's there.

'We need to keep them back,' she said into the 'link. 'Right now he has bait, a new start to his collection. If he sees cops, the bait become hostages. And he only needs one.'

'SWAT's ten minutes out,' Ricchio told her. 'We're right ahead of them.'

'We're under two. We need a way in. He'll have security. He's on guard now, wondering what we know. Or he's already poofed.'

'We'll ascertain with EDD on arrival.'

'Heat sensors won't show them in the room he's prepped for them. If they're all in there – On scene now. I'll get back to you.'

She leaped out before Roarke braked at the curb.

'Status.' She snapped it out, flashed her badge at the uniforms.

'No visible activity in the subject's apartment from the exterior. We got the stolen car in the garage.'

'He's got another vehicle. Dark blue Orion sedan.'

'We got that data, Lieutenant, and have no confirmation on it. There's an underground level. We'd have to approach the building and go in to ascertain. Orders are to hold here.'

She nodded.

'I need to get in there.'

'I can certainly get us in,' Roarke said, but she shook her head.

'If he's watching he'd make you in two seconds flat.'

'And not you?'

'That's a problem.' She kept scanning, kept thinking. 'Wait. Hey, you. Kid.'

Near the corner, the teenaged boy executed a smooth half-pipe on his airboard.

'Yes, ma'am?'

Christ, even boarders were polite here. 'This is police business. See?' She held her badge up.

'I didn't do anything.' He shoved his flop of hair out of his eyes. 'I'm just—'

'I need to borrow your hat, your sunshades.' And God help her. 'Your board.'

'Oh man, I just got the board.'

'You see that guy over there, with the cops? The one who looks rich?'

'Yes, ma'am.'

'He's going to give you a hundred for the loan. If you stay right where you are.'

'Well, yes, ma'am, but the board cost—'

'Two hundred, for a loan. If I'm not back in ten minutes, he'll make it three. Now give me the goddamn stupid hat and shades. I need that shirt, too.'

His face went pink. 'My shirt?'

'Yeah. And don't say "yes, ma'am" again.'

'No, ma'am.'

'What are you doing?' Roarke demanded as he joined them.

'Going boarding.' She stripped off her jacket, tossed it to him. Then pulled the oversized black shirt with its wild-haired music group on the front over her head. 'I need to get in.'

'If you think you look like a teenaged boy,' he began, then reconsidered when she cocked the hat on her head, fixed the rainbow neon shades on her face. 'Not that far off, actually. But you've got no business going in there.'

'Going in there is my business. He's on two,' she added, giving the building a good study. 'I'm not going above ground level. I can get down to the garage, verify his vehicle's there – or that it's not. We have to know, and may have to do what we can to evacuate civilians.'

'I'll go in from the rear.'

'Roarke—'

'You want me to trust you to take the front, and go unrec-ognized. Do me the same courtesy.' He gave the bill of the cap a flick with his finger. 'Keep your head down. And slouch.'

'Excuse me, sir, but the lady said you'd pay me two hundred for the loan.'

'Two ...' Resigned, Roarke pulled out his wallet. 'Do you know who owns that truck there?'

'Sure, that's Ben Clipper's truck.'

'If Ben comes looking for it, tell him it's on loan. There's two in it for him as well.'

Eve gave a glance back, signaled the uniforms. She wondered how the hell she was supposed to slouch on a goddamn airboard. Knees loose, she ordered herself, and for God's sake don't run into anything.

She kept her head down, as much to keep her eye where she feared she might plant it on the sidewalk as to block her face from any cams.

She didn't risk any flourishes, but hopped off at the building's entrance, and shouldered the board at an angle to shield her face.

She palmed her master, bopping her head and shoulders as she'd observed teenaged boys did for no good reason.

Inside she reached a hand under the shirt for her weapon, glanced up the stairs.

Nothing and no one moved.

'Single elevator,' she muttered into her com, tossed the sunshades onto the single chair beside the elevator. 'Both it and stairs right of entrance. Elevator's coming up. Stand by.'

She kept her weapon low, moved to the far side of the car, back to the wall.

A woman and two kids got out, making enough noise to raise the dead.

Eve stepped forward. 'Please stop where you are.'

'Oh! You startled me.' The woman's surprised laugh cut off as she spotted Eve's weapon. In a finger snap she had both kids shoved behind her.

'I'm the police,' Eve said quickly. She held up her free hand, then dug under the shirt for her badge. 'Do you know the residents of apartment two-oh-eight?'

'I'm not sure. I—'

'Big guy, good shape, late thirties. A lot of charm. Just moved in a few days ago. He'd be with a woman now and then, and she'd be in a lot. Blond, mid-fifties, attractive, a little flashy.'

'You must mean Tony, Tony Maxwell. He's the nicest man. Is he all right? I just saw him a little while ago when he was leaving.'

'When?' *Damn it*, Eve thought as she pulled off the borrowed shirt, tossed it on the chair. 'Exactly when?'

'Ah, maybe a half-hour ago. I had to go pick up the kids, and I saw him in the garage on the way out, stowing his suitcase. He said he had to go away on business for a couple days. What's this about?'

'Was he alone?'

'Yes.'

'Did you see him leave – actually drive away?'

'No, I left first, but he was getting in his car.' She wrapped her wide-eyed kids to her sides. 'I want to know what's going on.'

'I want you to take your kids, go outside, turn left, and keep walking until you get to the uniformed officers down this block.'

'But—'

'Go now.' She heard the elevator start its rise. 'Right now!'

She swung back, lifted her weapon as the woman grabbed both kids by the hands and fled. She lowered the weapon again as Roarke stepped out.

'His car's not there.'

'He's gone. Neighbor saw him leave – alone, and with a suitcase. Fuck! He told her he'd be gone a couple days.'

She pulled off the cap, raked a hand through her hair. 'We've got to go up.' She reached for her 'link as it signaled.

'Dallas, what's your status?'

She filled Ricchio in.

'EDD finds no heat sources in the target location. We've got the building hemmed in, and SWAT's moving into position now.'

'We're going up to try to verify whether the suspect is still in this location.'

'Backup's coming in.'

'Can you hold them, Lieutenant? Two minutes. On the off chance he's still here, his captives will be safer if he doesn't see us coming.'

'Two minutes, counting now.'

She shoved the 'link in her pocket. 'He's gone, but we

can't take the chance. Can you jam his security long enough for a quick, quiet entry?'

'You know I can.'

'Stairs.'

They went up fast. She swept the second-floor hallway.

'Hold here,' Roarke murmured, keying codes into his jammer. 'He's got several layers. And there.'

He moved ahead of her now, pulling a small case out of his pocket. 'A number of layers here as well.' He mumbled it as he crouched and got to work. 'They only look like standard locks. Very nicely done.'

'You can compliment him when he's in a cage. Just get us in.'

'So I have.' He met her eyes. 'Ready?'

She nodded, held up one finger, then two. They burst in on three, her low, him high.

She smelled the blood, smelled the death instantly. Swinging left, she saw the body, saw her mother and the pool of blood.

'God. God. God.'

'Eve.'

'We have to clear.' Her voice came out thin through the narrow opening the burn of shock left in her throat. 'We have to clear the area, take your side.'

When she swung the other way she saw the keys on the high table by the door, and the memo cube with them.

Gone, she thought. Gone, and walked over to pick up the keys.

She could hear the backup pushing through the door

downstairs. If Bree was with them, and if he'd left more death, she'd need to be prepared.

Eve unlocked the door. She breathed deep, braced herself. Opened it.

They were on the floor, the girl wrapped in a blanket, the woman's body shielding her.

Melinda stared at her. Blinked.

'Officer Dallas.' The words broke on a strangled sob. 'Darlie, it's Officer Dallas. I told you they'd come for us.'

'It's "Lieutenant."' Her voice sounded distant and tinny to her ears. Eve looked at the girl, at Darlie. And another pair of shattered eyes etched themselves into her head. 'You're safe now.'

Alive. She reminded herself what she'd told Tray Schuster on a morning that seemed years ago. Alive was better.

'You're safe now. They're safe,' Eve said as Bree burst through the door.

'Melly.'

'I'm all right.' But she dropped her head on her sister's shoulder and wept when Bree wrapped her arms around her. 'We're all right. I knew you'd find us.'

Eve stepped back, shifted away as Detective Price pushed his way through to Melinda.

'Let's go outside.' Roarke took her arm. 'There's nothing for you to do here.'

'Yes, there is.' Sweat, icy and thin, ran in a line down her back. 'There is,' she repeated, and turned to Ricchio. 'Your scene, Lieutenant.'

'Ambulance is on the way. We need to get them out, Melinda and the girl. Get them medical attention before we take statements. I want this scene secured and every inch of it gone over. We've issued a BOLO for the vehicle he's driving.'

He won't be driving it long, Eve thought, but nodded.

'We've got agents at every transpo station in the city,' Nikos added. 'If he ditches the vehicle and tries to get out of Dallas by other means, we'll find him.'

'He had to leave in a hurry.' Laurence glanced at the body. 'He could've left something behind besides his dead partner. If he's going to make a mistake, this would be the time. I'll start on the scene with a couple of your men. Lieutenant Ricchio, continue when your CSU arrives.'

'Good. I'm going to notify Darlie's parents, get some people knocking on doors.'

They watched as Detective Price lifted Darlie into his arms. He murmured to her, and she closed her eyes; he pressed her face to his shoulder as he carried her out.

Didn't want her to see the body, Eve thought, the blood. Spare her from that anyway. She'd have enough horror in her head already.

Melinda came out, leaning on her sister. She looked at death, then at Eve. 'Thank you. Again. He said to tell you to stick around. He said, 'Tell Dallas to stick around. More fun to come.' He's . . .'

'Later, Melinda.' Bree gripped her tighter.

'I need to stay with Darlie. She needs me to stay with her.'

'I'll be around,' Eve told her. 'We'll talk later.'

'Come on, Melly, come with me. We need to tell Mom and Dad you're okay,' Bree said as she led her sister out.

'Bad as it is,' Ricchio said, 'it's a good day.'

But it wasn't over, Eve thought. Not nearly over. 'I'm Homicide. I'll take the body if you have no objections.'

'I'd appreciate it. We'll inform the ME. Do you want an aide or assistant?'

'Roarke's done it before.'

'Then I'll leave it to you.' His glance at the body, the blood, held no pity. 'It looks pretty straightforward.'

'Yeah. Yeah, I guess it does.' She stepped over to the body again. 'I'll need a field kit,' she said to Roarke, then looked at him, held his eyes when he said nothing. She reached up, switched off her recorder. 'Please. I need to do this. It'll be easier if you help me do it.'

'Then I will. But Eve, there's a great deal to say when this is done.'

'I know it.'

'I'll get the kit.'

The room buzzed with cops, but she was alone, very much alone when she crouched by the body, the toes of her boots at the edge of a river of blood.

What should she feel, she asked herself. She didn't know, only knew what to do.

Routine.

She switched on her recorder.

'The victim is female, Caucasian, approximately fifty-five.

Facial bruises and contusions were incurred in a vehicular accident earlier on this date, and treated at Dallas City Hospital. Other injuries so incurred are on record. Initial visual shows a single deep gash across the throat, which severed the jugular. Blood-spatter patterns consistent with same.'

She sat back on her heels, let her gaze scan the floor, the walls, the sofa.

Work the scene, she ordered herself.

'She was sitting on the sofa, facing out into the room. Pressure syringe on the cushion. Needed a hit. He gave her a hit. Tox screen hereby ordered to determine substance and amount. Talking to her, taking time to talk to her, placate her, until she told him what she'd spilled, what we knew. Already packed, ready to go. Sure, all packed and ready because she'd tagged him from the stolen car. Note to check the in-dash 'link in the vehicle stolen from hospital lot for communications from vic to McQueen.'

She tagged him, Eve thought. Warned him, gave him time to pack up, plan, and plot. She set up her own murder.

While she waited for Roarke and the kit, Eve imagined it. The frantic rush in the stolen car from the hospital, after she'd done murder. After she'd killed in the same way she'd be killed so soon after. By the man she ran to.

Was that irony? she wondered. Some sort of brutal poetic justice.

She'd have been hurting, Eve thought. Head, ribs, chest.

Eve let her eyes track over the body. Badly swollen left ankle. That had to give her pain. Limping, trying to run, jonesing, sweating, heart racing, head pounding. Sick and hurt, a cop's blood on her hands, and thinking only of getting back to the man who'd kill her.

Thinking, too, no doubt, of another cop. Thinking of payback and paydays, of causing pain, spilling blood.

Was it more irony that her mother's last thoughts had revolved around her? Hateful, violent, murderous thoughts.

She straightened when Roarke came back with the kit.

'Easy enough to see how it played out,' she began, and kept her eyes on his face. Kept them on him until she felt centered again.

'We're going to find she contacted him from the stolen car. That gave him time to pack up what he wanted or needed to take with him. There aren't enough electronics in here, not for McQueen. He's got what he wanted there with him. Clothes, personal items, cash, alternate IDs. He had time. Most likely he already had a go bag stashed with the essentials.'

'He'd want the flexibility of being able to leave, move quickly, at any time,' Roarke agreed.

'I bet he kept that suit, the sharp one from the bank. He doesn't know you found the accounts. He doesn't know that yet. Can you trace any transactions he makes?'

'I can.'

'Set that up, okay? But I've got to play the team deal. Nikos! I need a minute.'

'You need help with her?'

'No. Roarke found McQueen's primary accounts. We've got his money.'

304

'That's good work.' Nikos gave Roarke a considering look. 'Our guys are still bouncing around. I need that data. We can freeze the funds, block him out, make him sweat.'

'You could,' Eve said, 'or you could track any activity, and maybe lock his new location.'

'And if he uses the money, manages to get someplace we don't have extradition, he's gone.'

'It's a chance. He's not finished, Nikos. He didn't get what he wants, what he's been working toward, planning. You better believe no matter how he rolls on this, under it he's pissed. He's furious. He wants another shot.'

'At you, maybe. Or he's smart enough to cut his losses. Look, I'll run this by my superiors – both ways. We'll make a decision, but I need the data.'

'I'll send you the files,' Roarke said. 'It's actually three accounts. He's not an eggs-in-one-basket sort.'

'Thanks.' Nikos pulled out her 'link, turned, and walked away.

'I can delay the data transfer, maybe an hour with a bit of a glitch in the routing.'

'Do that.' Eve nodded. 'Yeah, do that. I'll push harder if the feds opt for the freeze, because it's the wrong move. For now, we set it up – you should get Feeney in on that.' She took the field kit. 'I have to finish this.'

He laid a hand over hers on the handle. 'I can do this. You could assist with the search. You've a better sense of McQueen than anyone here.'

'You know I can't. She's mine now, whether I want it or not.'

She opened the kit, hunkered down again. And taking her mother's hand, checked prints. 'Victim is identified as Sylvia Prentiss, which has been determined to be falsified ID. Victim will be listed as Jane Doe until true identification can be verified.'

She fit on microgoggles, said nothing when Roarke stooped down beside her, took out gauges. Instead, she examined the fatal wound.

'ME to confirm. However, primary investigator's on-scene examination indicates a single cut, left to right with a sharp, smooth-edged blade. Both the angle and the blood-spatter pattern indicate the attack came from behind. He yanks her head back, slices. She slides down. He'd get some blood on him, on that shirt he tossed down there. Note to the sweepers to check all drains. He'd have washed up.'

She sat back on her heels again when Roarke read off the time of death. 'That's less than thirty – closer to twenty – before we had cops on the building. Yeah, like Laurence said, he had to hurry. TOD's about twenty-five minutes after she broke out of the hospital. So she was dead before we knew she was out. But . . . can you run a program, determine travel time from the hospital to here?'

'All right.'

She pulled out an evidence bag, sealed the syringe for evidence.

'Factoring in the most usual traffic patterns for that time of day, it would take about fifteen minutes.'

'Couple less,' Eve decided. 'She'd be driving fast, taking chances. But you have to factor in the time it took her to steal the car, the time it took her to get into the building from the lot – and on that bum ankle. We'll know more when we look at the 'link in the stolen car, get the time and location of her transmission to him. But putting it together, even though he's got to move, he takes at least four or five minutes with her. He doesn't just do her when she walks in. He lets her sit down, he gives her a fix. He talks to her.'

She fit the microgoggles on again, studied what she could of the face, the hands and wrists. 'I'd like to roll her, but I'd better wait for the ME. But the way it looks, he doesn't hurt her. He doesn't give her a good belt for fucking things up. He's going to kill her, and that's enough. He's got that strange sense of proportion, and he's got the control. He could have loaded that syringe with enough to kill her, but see, that's *not* enough.'

'It's too impersonal, too simple for her.'

'Yeah, exactly. When he kills, and he kills selectively, he wants to feel it. He likes the blade, the way it feels cutting flesh, the way the blood spurts. He doesn't mutilate. It's too messy, and it lacks the class he believes he has.'

She looked toward the room where he'd held Melinda and Darlie. 'With the girls, he likes to torture. It's part of that control and power game, part of the training. He'll take a lot of time with them – they matter. But with the partner? It's like taking out the garbage. You just get rid of it.'

'You have enough now,' Roarke said quietly. 'You know how, when, who, even why. It's enough now, Eve.'

'We need the ME to confirm, and to run the tox. Because if McQueen gave her more than a little buzz, if he gave her enough to put her under before he killed her it means something different.'

'Lieutenant Dallas?'

'Yeah.'

One of the crime scene investigators offered her a memo cube. 'McQueen left this for you. You're going to want to hear it.'

'Thanks.'

She activated it.

*Hello again, Eve. I hope I can call you Eve now, after all we've been through together. I'd planned to have a nice, long chat with you today, but plans change, and this will have to do.*

*Welcome to my home – former. I wish I could be there to offer you a glass of wine in person. I know you enjoy a glass now and again – the photographs of you in Italy sampling the local vintages were really quite fetching. Marriage agrees with you.*

*As you can see, I left a bit of a mess behind. But then I know you like tidying up those little misadventures, and I'm a bit rushed. I had hoped to entertain you here, to put you up for a few days. I so looked forward to some Isaac and Eve time. But we'll do it very soon, just the two of us.*

*You're probably wondering why I left the steadfast Melinda and the adorable Darlie alive. You know, I'm wondering that*

*myself. Perhaps I like knowing how well they'll remember me. No*
*one likes to be forgotten, to be ignored. Don't think for a minute*
*I'll do either with you.*

*You're in my thoughts, day and night. I'll see you soon.*


'Cocky bastard, but you can hear it in his voice. All that
fury, just barely restrained. He's thinking that bitch got lucky
again.' She carried the memo cube with her as she walked
over to study the holding room.

'Only four sets of shackles,' she noted. 'He wouldn't need
Melinda once he had me. He could eliminate her, start the
tidying-up process. He'd keep the girl, and want another.
He'd always want another. He'd need that rush. He could
take his time with me, take two or three days with me.
Maybe he was going to try to squeeze you for ransom. He's
too much a grifter not to look for a profit.'

'If he had you, stayed here, spent that much time and open
communications for a ransom, he'd risk his primary goal for
money.'

'Adds to the thrill. And he's got everything covered so
well – he thinks. He's arrogant,' she added. 'So fucking cock-
sure he's the smartest one in the room.'

'What does that make you?' Roarke asked her. 'The one
who beat him?'

Eve shrugged. 'Going down before, that was just a twist of
fate, just a lucky break for a rookie cop. He's not that wrong.
He eluded authorities for years. Years. He's absolutely certain
he can do it again. Takes me,' she continued. 'Kills Melinda.

He'd want me to see him do it, want me to watch him kill someone I saved. He'd want me to see him kill his partner, then when he'd had enough from me, kill the girl – or girls. I'd be last. He'd want me to watch him kill the kid, to know I was helpless to stop it. When he was done, he'd drift away. Set up shop somewhere else, far away. Maybe Europe this time. Somewhere urban and cosmopolitan enough for his tastes, where he could start a new collection.'

'Now he has to regroup, rethink, replan.'

So, Eve acknowledged, did she. 'He's got a contingency operation. He'll adjust, refine. He means it when he says it'll be soon. That must be the ME. I need to work with her, and I want to check with Laurence.'

Her 'link signaled.

'Dallas.'

'Lieutenant,' Bree began, 'sorry to interrupt.'

'What do you need, Detective?'

'Melinda – they're hydrating her and treating her injuries. They want to keep her overnight for observation. Darlie . . . you know what they need to do with her.'

'Yes.'

'But they want to talk to you, both of them. They've given us a statement, answered some questions. It seems important to them. Ricchio and the doctors, and Darlie's parents, have cleared it. If you could make the time, Lieutenant. We're at Dallas City.'

'When I'm done here.'

'I'll let them know.'

When she put the 'link away, Roarke reached up, switched off her recorder. 'You need a break.'

'I don't. The busier I am the better I am. I'll deal with the rest of it when I have to. But not now, not yet, because once I start dealing with it I just don't know. We don't even have the DNA match, so . . .'

She trailed off when he simply took her hand. And saw it in his eyes.

'You got it done?'

'The results came in when I went out to get your kit.'

Something sick and sour lodged in her throat. 'I was right.'

'Yes. It's conclusive.'

'Better to know,' she said, and stared hard at the wall.

'Is it?'

'I knew it – knew her – the minute we looked at each other. I thought I'd accepted it. Now . . . Hell, I just don't know.' She rubbed a hand over her face, pressed her fingers to eyes that throbbed. 'I need to work. I need to work and deal with this later.'

She walked to the medical examiner and the body. And Roarke stood for quite some time staring at the shackles fixed to the wall of the horrible little room.

# 17

Eve didn't wait for the bag and tag. What was the point? Instead, she walked into the bedroom where Laurence headed up what looked to her like a thorough and meticulous search.

'Anything?'

'High-dollar sheets, towels, nice fluffy duvet. We can trace them. Some he took with him. He's obsessively organized, everything in its place, so we can see some sheets and towels are missing. Some clothes, some shoes.'

He gestured toward the closet. 'He's got a dozen ties in there, and from the way he had them stored, took another dozen with him. Who needs two dozen ties?'

Eve crossed over to look for herself. 'He likes clothes, likes to collect. But . . . some of these ties are exactly the same. Or is that just my crappy eye for fashion.'

'If it is, it's mine, too. Same pattern, same designer.'

'That's not like him. And there's too much here, not just to leave behind but too much in the first place. This isn't so much collecting as it is—'

'Hoarding,' Laurence finished. 'That was my take. Could be he needed to hoard to compensate for a dozen years in prisonwear.'

'Could be. But it's another break in pattern. That's interesting.'

'Yeah, it is, isn't it. So. We'll take the laundry in. The only toiletries left are the partner's. Had to be a D-and-C there on that desk, so he took that. Had a monitor in the bathroom there so he could watch his holding room when he fucking jerked off. Sorry,' he said immediately. 'The kid, she got to me.'

'Understood.'

'He left a supply of syringes in the bathroom, again some missing.'

'He doesn't use, so he wouldn't need as many of them. He's not going to hook up with a partner yet.'

'Partner had a couple drawers, and it looked like he took a quick pass through, making sure she didn't have anything that linked back to him. He didn't check behind or under the drawers.' He gestured to the bags, sealed and tagged for evidence. 'She kept stashes – a freaking pharmacy.'

She'd done the same long ago, Eve thought, as quick, blurry flickers of memories ran through her head. 'She'd need to know it was there, in case he ran low or tried to cut her off.'

'And she liked variety. What we're finding, so far, is more of her than him. And we can judge where something was and isn't now, and what it likely would've been. Forensic-wise, we'll have enough to put the bastard away for twice as long as we already did, but nothing right yet to tell us where he's running.'

'Maybe he said something to one of the vics,' Eve speculated. 'Maybe he didn't figure on them getting out, not alive, and he likes to show his intellect. I'm going in to talk with them, maybe I'll get something.'

She walked out and up to Roarke who'd found a corner to work on his PPC.

'The feds should be getting the data about now,' he told her. 'Feeney and I have a long jump on them, though I'll do better when I'm back at the hotel office, using that equipment.'

'We're done here, for now. You can go back, dig into it.'

He tracked his gaze to hers, held it. 'I'm with you, Lieutenant. I've already made that clear. You need to stop at the hospital, talk with Melinda and Darlie.'

'Yeah, but I want to do something first.' She shook her head to hold off questions. 'On the way.'

Outside, she took a scan of the street. The lookie-loos and bystanders had dispersed – by boredom, she expected. Cop work was long and tedious, and most civilians lost interest pretty fast.

But not her civilian.

'Did you pay off the kid, the airboard kid?'

'I did, yes, and someone named Ben for the loan of his truck.'

'Put in a chit for expenses. I'll make it good.'

'One way or the other,' he said casually as they got in the car. 'Where are we going?'

'I need to go back to her place. They'll have done a search

by now, taken the electronics, whatever other evidence they turned up. But people miss things, especially when they're not sure what they're looking for.'

'And you do?'

'No, but I think I'll know it when I see it. I need to go there, for the job. And I need to go there for me.'

'Then why would you suggest I go back to the hotel?'

'I don't know. I don't know.' She felt that hard bubble pushing up toward her throat. 'I don't know. Don't make me think about it yet.'

He took her face in his hands. 'I'll take you wherever you want to go. I'll be with you wherever that is. All right?'

'Yeah.' She fought for composure and won it when he pulled away from the curb. 'I'm sorry about before. I don't even really remember what I'm sorry about. But just to clear it.'

'We're not something that needs to be cleared. You wanted to get under my skin so you could be angry with me, find some release there. And so I'd be angry with you and leave you alone.'

'I guess that's probably it.'

She stretched out her legs, rolled her shoulders, circled her neck. It felt as if her body and everything in it was coiled to the point of aching.

'I did okay with her, with the interview. I handled it okay. I've gone back over it, and over it, and maybe I could've done better. But you always look back when it doesn't work out the way you wanted and think you could've done it better.

It was after, when I was afraid something was going to break, I shored it up by taking a kick at you.'

'Well, I kicked back, didn't I?'

'I knew you would. I didn't even mean it, about the stupid money and dying anyway. It was stupid, and I knew it would hurt you. I didn't even think about it. It was like a reflex.'

He turned his head, looked at her tense, tired face. 'You've had a miserable fucking day.'

'Yeah, real red letter. I met my mother. I arrested her, put her in the hospital. I grilled her. I found her body, and started the murder book on her. Miserable fucking red-letter day.'

'I contacted Mira.'

She swiveled toward him. 'What?'

'I don't give a rat's damn if that pisses you off. You need her. She's on her way.'

'You don't—'

'I need her, goddamn it.'

Her eyes widened, blinked once at the short, violent explosion. Stupid, she realized, not to have expected it, not to have seen it coming. Stupid not to understand she wasn't the only one coiled like a spring.

'Okay.'

'I know what I want to say to you,' he said, calmer now. 'Do for you, but I don't know if it's right. I also know this isn't about me, but anything that hurts you pulls me in. And this . . . well, that's for later. You need to handle this, finish it. I understand that. Mira can help you. She can help both of us.'

316

She didn't speak for a minute, had to settle the storm inside her – a pretty close twin to his, she imagined.

'You're right. It's good she's coming. It's just ... once I start talking about it, it's real. There's no more sliding in this block that says it's a case to be worked. Nothing more, nothing less.'

She sat, studying the duplex, when he stopped.

'It's a nice place. I was thinking when we were watching for her, how it was a nice neighborhood. Not McQueen's kind of place. Too suburban, even though it's one good spit from the action. Not her kind of place either, with kids on bikes and guys fooling with flowers. But he wanted her out of her element, a little off balance. She'd be grateful every time he let her come to him.'

Let her think of it as a case for as long as she could, Roarke thought. A reckoning was coming soon enough.

'Why did she do it? Devote herself to him?'

'It wouldn't have lasted, even without the knife across the throat. She'd have gotten twitchy, moved on. But he made her feel important. He treated her good – she said. He bought her things, I imagine, and the illegals. I think we may find he set up her source here in Dallas, to keep her happy. Maybe paid for them, or a portion of them.

'Anyway.'

She got out of the car. She saw the door of the neighboring unit crack open, and held up her badge.

A woman Eve pegged as late twenties came out.

'There were other police here. They just left a little while ago. They said Sylvia was arrested.'

'That's right.'

'I just don't understand it. Bill up the street said there were cops all over, and little Kirk almost got run over. I was at work, and when I came home it was just crazy.'

'Have you lived here long?'

'Four years. My sister and I. What about Sandra?'

'Sorry?'

'Sylvia's sister. Sandra Millford. Is she in trouble, too?'

'You could say that. Were you friendly?'

'We try to be, Candace and I. And I guess we thought, when they moved in, being sisters like us, we'd get together a lot. Hang.' She shrugged it off with a glance toward the neighboring unit. 'But they were always too busy. We stopped asking them over. They didn't spend a lot of time at home anyway, not really.'

'Ever have any visitors?'

'I can't say I ever saw anybody come by and pay a call. But Sylvia was involved with someone.'

'Oh?'

'A woman doesn't dress like that unless it's for a lover. And I overheard her talking on the 'link just yesterday, now that I think about it. Sitting outside, and I was, too, having some coffee. The way she laughed, the tone of her voice. There was somebody. What did she do?'

'She aided and abetted in the escape from prison of a dangerous felon. She aided and abetted in the abduction of two people, one a minor female for this dangerous felon who is a violent pedophile.'

Eyes wide, mouth open, the woman rubbed at her throat. 'Well, oh my God.'

Eve took out her PPC, brought up McQueen's photo. 'I don't think he'll come around here, but if he does, stay inside and contact the police.'

'I saw him on the media reports! Oh my God. Sylvia's involved with him?'

'She was. He killed her a couple hours ago.'

'Oh. Oh.' She backed up a pace, slapping both hands to her heart. 'Sandra? Her sister?'

'There was no sister. Just one woman, two different identities. Tell your neighbors. If they see this man, contact the police immediately.'

'I will. I will.' She turned, bolted for her own door. 'Candy! Candy!'

'You scared the hell out of her.'

'I meant to,' Eve said as the door slammed, as locks snicked into play. 'Because he could come back here. He might start to wonder if she had anything that might point the way to where he's dug in now. And that one's just the type who'd come out, talk to him like she did with me. I flashed a badge, a New York badge from ten feet away, and she just accepted and came right out. I don't want to find out she's had her throat cut.'

She stepped to the door, used her master.

The sweepers had been through, she noted, leaving their fine layer of print dust.

'No need to seal up again,' she told Roarke.

'Small blessing.'

'Decent furniture, on the gaudy side,' she began as she walked through the living area. 'Not a lot of it, and no fussy stuff sitting around. Not home, not for her.'

She studied the couch fabric, and the purple and pink roses growing over it in wild abandon. 'Does that make your eyes sting, or is it just me?'

She needed to keep it light, then he'd keep it light. 'I was about to dig out my sunshades.'

'She could watch some screen down here if she was bored enough, privacy shades down. Don't want nosy neighbors peeking in. Had to be lonely, waiting for him to get out, but she doesn't have any men over. She went to them, took care of that somewhere else. As someone else, I imagine.'

She moved through into a powder room. A single towel, she noted. 'No guests. Just a place to pee if she was down here. If there'd been any trash, any paraphernalia, the sweepers would've bagged it. Nothing here.'

She moved on, dining alcove – empty – and the kitchen.

'Sits at the counter to eat.' She opened the fridge. 'Or drink,' she said, when she saw only four bottles of brew, one bottle of wine, open.

She opened cupboards. 'Glasses, a couple of plates, a stack of disposable ones.' She jerked her chin toward the pile of dirty dishes and unrecycled cartons in the sink, on the counter. 'Not much on housekeeping.'

'And no house droid,' Roarke observed, 'to tidy up after her.'

'Good appliances, nice counterwork, cabinetry, but she

doesn't care. It's not hers. Not what she wants. She wants a lot more than this little playhouse with its fenced yard and the two bitches next door who ask too many questions. She wants the high life Isaac's going to get her. Nothing here,' she said again, and walked back to take the stairs up.

She turned to the bedroom first. Too much perfume, she thought immediately. Too thick, too strong, too much. And the memory struck like a fist.

'Eve.' Roarke grabbed her arms when she swayed.

'Too much. Do you smell it? It's too sweet – dying sweet, like flowers left out too long. God, it makes me sick.'

But she pushed back when he tried to draw her out of the room.

'No. I remember. I remember. The bedroom – their room. Always smelled like this. Too much. Perfume, too strong. And sex. Old sex and perfume. All those bottles and tubes. Lip dyes and sprays and powders. Can't touch or she'll hurt me. She'll hurt me anyway because I'm ugly and stupid and always in the fucking way.'

'No. Baby, no.'

'I'm all right, I'm all right. Just need to breathe. God, open the window. Please, God, get some air in here.'

He yanked up the privacy screen, the window. She leaned out the opening, gasping air like the drowning. 'I'm okay. It just hit so hard. She wanted to get rid of me. I can hear them talking, arguing. I'm so scared. I want to hide so maybe they'll forget about me. Maybe she won't remember me. She wants to get rid of me, for Christ's sake. I'm useless, always hungry, always in her things. They should sell me now, get something out of the fucking little bitch.

'But he says no. They'll get more later, renting me out. Can't get top dollar for a six-year-old. But rent out, starting at ten, maybe sooner – rake it in for five, six years easy, then sell what's left.'

Undone, simply shattered, he laid his cheek on her back so they drew in the hot, fresh air together. 'Let me take you away from this.'

She reached back for his hand. 'I can't get away if I can't get through.'

'I know it.' He pressed his lips to the back of her neck. 'I know.'

'I didn't understand what they were talking about, not exactly. Not then. But I was so scared. And they fought. I could hear them beating on each other, then the sex. I think she left after that – or soon after. He'd already started to touch me, to do things to me, but soon after that night, he got so mad because she was gone, and she'd taken money and things – I don't know. He got mad and drunk, and he raped me for the first time. I remember.'

She took one last deep breath, eased herself back into the room.

'Is this what you were looking for?'

'No.' She swept the heels of her hands up her cheeks, annoyed tears had gotten through. 'No, I didn't expect to remember anything, not from this place. It's the smell. It's eased off with the window open.'

'Eve, there was barely a trace of perfume in the air here before.'

'I don't know, but it was the same.' She scrubbed her face dry. She'd come to work, she reminded herself, not to wallow.

'I want to toss this room, top to bottom. See if she had any hidey-holes. I think she used to have one, wherever we were. Extra stashes, hiding them from him. If she thought there was a chance McQueen would come here, she'd expect him to use the bedroom. If she was keeping something, she'd want it where he wouldn't see it. Illegals, running money, but more maybe. Maybe.'

'Such as?'

'She thought she loved him. What do you have in your pocket?'

He smiled, drew out the gray button that had fallen off her very ugly suit the first day they'd met.

'See?' She couldn't say why that stupid button moved her so damn much. 'People in love keep things. Sentimental things.'

'What do you have?'

She pulled the chain, and the tear-shaped diamond from under her shirt. 'I wouldn't wear this for anybody but you. It's embarrassing. And—'

'Ah, something else.'

'Shit. I'm tired. It makes me gabby. I have one of your shirts.'

His brow creased in absolute bafflement. 'My shirts?'

'In my drawer, under a bunch of stuff. You lent it to me

the morning after our first night together. It still sort of smells like you.'

For a moment, the worry on his face simply dissolved. 'I believe that's the sweetest thing you've said to me in all our time together.'

'Well, I owed you. Besides, you have enough shirts to outfit a Broadway troupe. So, help me toss the room?'

'Absolutely.'

Eve took the dresser first. The cheap, flimsy fake wood re-affirmed this had been no more than a stopping point, less personal than a motel flop. Not really a piece of furniture, she thought, but a big suitcase with drawers.

She opened one, saw her mother had spent more on underwear than she had on the container used to store it.

She reached in, immediately pulled her hands back. God, she didn't want to touch any of it, didn't want to put her hands on those hard, bright colors.

Stop thinking of who, she told herself. Who doesn't matter. Think of what, of doing the job.

She pushed through, examined contents, pulled out draw-ers to check the sides, bottoms, backs.

If she let herself, she could have put together a picture, one of a woman who shopped – or shoplifted – at boutiques, upscale stores and markets. And who still managed to select the trashy.

She found one drawer dedicated to the more subtle wardrobe of the alternate ID, found the simple shirt worn as Sandra on the night Darlie had been taken.

She switched to the tables beside the bed, and as she'd

expected she found the toys and tools of a woman who didn't stint on items for self-pleasuring.

They'd been through this, she thought, the cops, the sweepers. She imagined the careless comments, the lame jokes – then shut them out.

'Got something here,' Roarke called out.

She went to the closet where he worked, studied the disordered display of clothes, shoes, bags. He'd cleared a space and was removing a section of the floor, lifting it with one of the little tools he carried.

He set it aside, pulled a box covered with ornate, fake jewels and small circular mirrors out of the hole. He glanced at Eve, read her face very well. She didn't want to go in the closet, didn't want to surround herself with the clothes, the scents clinging to them.

'Why don't we take this downstairs?'

'Yeah, let's do that.'

She opted for the kitchen and the counter space.

'It's probably expensive, but it's still cheap and gaudy. It's not new.'

'No, it's got some travel on it, so something she likely took with her from place to place.'

'I don't remember it,' she said, answering his unspoken question. 'She wouldn't keep anything that long. What's inside's more important.'

She opened it.

'Variety of illegals, cash, some IDs with credit cards.' She pulled out a dried rose, carefully sealed in a small bag. 'But this is sentiment. See, she's drawn a heart on the bag, S and I in the middle. Isaac gave her this. And here, she took a picture of him when he was sleeping.'

She held it up, studied him, sprawled on his back under a tangled sheet. 'I bet he doesn't know she did this. That's the bed from his place. He's blond here, tanned – like the South African ID. So he got a flash or gave himself some fake sun. But he looks really tired, a little drawn, doesn't he? What's that on the nightstand? Champagne? A celebration. Maybe his first night in. Yeah, maybe.'

'That's Vie Nouveau. One of mine, and very exclusive. I wonder what vintage.'

'So, he – or she – buys a pricey bottle of bubbles.'

'More than that. You can't get it just anywhere. That's how you keep it exclusive and desirable. Hmm.' He took out his case again, opened it for a small magnifier.

'Handy.'

'Sometimes you need a closer look at things. I can just make it out . . . Yes, that's a limited premiere 'fifty-six. Not easy to come by. We had a bottle on our anniversary.'

'Yeah? It was good.'

'Good? Darling Eve, it's exquisite. He had some very nice wines at his apartment, but nothing at this level.'

'Maybe he took the top drawer with him.'

'Maybe he did. He'd need a top-drawer outlet to purchase this.'

'In Dallas,' Eve said. 'How many top drawers are there in Dallas?'

'I'll be checking on that.'

'He could go back for more. We can sit on the outlets once we have them. Jesus.' She lifted out a short stack of notes, postcards. 'Mother lode. Here, a postcard from Dallas, but it's stamped New York. Mail drop-box addy. Numbers. Code?'

He glanced at it. 'Measurements. Inseam, sleeve, waist, so on from the looks of it. He's ordering a suit.'

'The numbers and Baker and Hugh.'

'Men's shop,' Roarke told her, 'known for its excellent tailoring.' Roarke pulled out his PPC, did a quick run. 'There's only one in Dallas.'

'He wants clothes, good clothes. Doesn't have time to fiddle with fittings and all that. So he has her take care of it. Has his suits waiting for him when he gets here. No.' She closed her eyes a moment, brought New York back. 'He was wearing a suit, sharp-looking gray suit, flashy red tie, when I saw him in the crowd at the medals ceremony. He had her order the suits, and send at least one of them to New York. He wanted to look good when he let me catch a glimpse.'

'He went to a lot of trouble to impress you.'

'That's his problem now, that's his chink. He's complicating things to take jabs at me. Engage, taunt, humiliate, instead of just moving in for the knockout.'

She opened the first note. 'He'd kill her if he already hadn't. She printed out some of their e-coms. "Miss you, too, baby doll,"' she read. '"Countdown D-minus-30. Time to arrange my flight into your arms. Reserve private, Franklin

327

J. Milo. I'll need those docs, sweetheart, so you get that Cecil on the stick! I don't want to get to the drop and find an empty box.

"The wait's almost over. Milo needs his things waiting at the hotel so he can get cleaned up and changed before he flies to you. We'll go back there one day, stay in the penthouse and drink a champagne toast to us.

"Keep an eye on our Melinda, and take good care of my baby doll. I'll write next week with the next steps. Almost there!

"'SWAK times two.'" She frowned. 'SWAK?'

'Sealed with a kiss – times two.'

'Eeww. He wrote it out. He actually wrote this shit down. Didn't trust her to remember. Quick PS reminding her to wipe, but he got sloppy because he didn't think she was smart enough to remember the details. Maybe she'd dropped the ball a time or two.'

She opened another. 'They're little love notes with instructions sprinkled through the mush. Here he's telling her how to outfit what he calls the guest room. Sick fuck. Tells her to see Greek in Waco for the bracelets. Shackles. And Bruster B in Fort Worth for soundproofing.'

'Does any of this help you now? You've found his place.'

She looked up as pieces began to link together in her head. 'He's got another one. He's got another place in Dallas, and he'd want some of the same there. Would he use the same people? Maybe not. But ... We find them, we find out more.'

She pulled out her 'link, tagged Peabody.

'Franklin J. Milo – that's the ID McQueen used to book his transpo – private shuttle – and a hotel room. A hotel with a penthouse. Find them.'

'Okay, but—'

'It's just tying the ends, Peabody. It may not lead anywhere, but let's tie it up tight. And find Baker and Hugh, men's clothing in New York. See if he picked up any clothes there. And what transportation he used to get to the shuttle. I'll pick it up from here.'

'Okay, got it. Listen. Tray Schuster came back in. They didn't notice – pretty understandable – on the day they were attacked, but they're missing a duffel, an old 'link they hadn't gotten around to recycling, a new pair of navy blue skids, a shirt Julie had boxed up for her brother's birthday. A bunch of little things. I'm going to send you an inventory.'

'Things that would be useful for checking in a hotel. When you find the hotel, see if he left anything behind in his room. I've got to get on this from here.'

'You look beat,' Peabody commented.

'Not yet, I'm not.' She clicked off. 'Let's take this to Ricchio, let him and the feds start working on tracking down the names. We'd better go by the hospital first. We can probably pass the box to somebody there.'

Peabody was right, Roarke thought as she resealed the door. She looked beat. Pale and strained.

'You need a couple hours down. You know you do.'

'I'll take it when I can. I can't stop yet.' She got in the car. 'I'll down a booster if I need it.'

'A booster isn't what you need. I'm not going to press you, yet. Especially not if you agree once you've talked to Melinda and Darlie you'll go back to the hotel if there's nothing immediate. You'd rather work there anyway.'

Since she'd already planned to do just that, it wasn't hard to go along. 'If you agree to try not to tranq me.'

'That's a tough bargain, a hard line. Agreed.'

'That was easy. Too easy.'

'I'll let Mira tranq you.'

She managed a weak laugh. 'I can take Mira.'

'I imagine she's wily.'

So was he, he thought, as he pulled her directly to Vending at the hospital. 'Pick something.'

'I'm not really—'

'You may not think you're hungry, but you need food. I'll pick. Veggie-and-cheese pocket. Some protein,' he said as it slid out of the tray.

'I'd rather have the—'

'Candy bar, yes. And so you shall. When you eat that.' He ordered up the bar, wishing he could offer her some rich Belgian chocolate.

She stuffed half the pocket in her mouth. 'Why do I have to eat and you don't?'

'I'm considering my choices, which are all equally unappetizing. Ah, well.' He ordered up a second pocket. 'We'll suffer together.'

'It's not that bad.'

He took a bite. 'Yes, it certainly is.' Not wanting to risk the coffee, he ordered them each a tube of Pepsi.

'Food snob.'

'This barely qualifies as food. Give me some of that candy.'

'Get your own candy.' But she pulled credits out of her pocket, plugged them in. 'There.' She ordered it, offered it, and gave him a genuine smile. 'You look like a really well-dressed pirate carting around an ugly treasure chest. Thanks for lunch.'

# 18

Annalyn started to step on the elevator as Eve and Roarke got off. She moved back.

'I was just on my way in. I've been splitting time between Melinda and Darlie, Darlie's parents, Bree, her parents, the doctors.' She rubbed her eyes. 'You see it, you see it in this job. You never get used to it.'

'Good cops don't,' Eve said, and had Annalyn dropping her hands.

'Well, I'm a damn good cop today.'

'Do they still want to talk to me?'

'Yeah. Melinda convinced Darlie she should. She's made you out to be the monster slayer. It's a good thing,' she added when Eve winced. 'It's helping the kid. The idea there are slayers, since she knows monsters are real. Melly's ambulatory. They want her in bed, resting, but she's in and out of the kid's room. That helps, too. It's helping them both.'

She raised her eyebrows at the box Roarke held. 'If that's a gift, it's really sparkly.'

'It's evidence. We found it at the duplex.'

'What? Where? I didn't see anything like that on the evidence list. I've been keeping in touch.'

'She had a hide in the bedroom closet. I played a hunch,' Eve added. 'And we got lucky.'

'We could use some luck. Missing that son of a bitch today, losing Malvie.' She looked back down the hall. 'I keep reminding myself we got Melly and the girl back safe. But Malvie's dead, and McQueen's in the wind.'

'She's got some correspondence from McQueen in here.'

'No shit?'

'None, and some names, some data. If you're going in, you can start the runs. There's a photo of him, too. She took it while he was sleeping. There's a champagne bottle in it. My source here tells me it's pretty special.'

'There's only two outlets for that label and vintage in Dallas,' Roarke told her. 'Vin Belle and Personal Sommelier.'

'And he may get a yen for more.' Annalyn reached for the box. 'I'll get this in. If we hit anything, you'll be the first.'

'My people are working on some of the New York data in there. You can connect with Detective Peabody.'

'Will do.' She called for the elevator again, glanced back as she got on. 'You're a good cop,' she said to Eve. 'So the kid's going to break your heart.'

'I'm going to take Melinda first,' Eve told Roarke as she walked toward the nurses' station. 'She'll be okay with you in there if you want to be. With the kid, it's better if you stay out.'

'If you don't need me, I'll find a spot, see if Feeney and I can make any progress.'

'Better yet.' She offered her badge at the station. 'Lieutenant Dallas.'

'Yes, you're cleared. Melinda – Ms Jones – would like you to see her first. She's in six-twelve. We arranged for Darlie to be across the hall.'

'Thanks.'

She started down the corridor. She hated hospitals, hated the memory of being in one, in this city, broken and traumatized like the child across the hall from Melinda. And the cops asking questions she couldn't answer, the sorrowful sympathy the medicals couldn't hide when they worked on her.

She hesitated outside Melinda's door. Should she knock? she wondered. Instead she shifted to look through the small window, saw both sisters in the narrow hospital bed. Oddly it was the cop who slept, an arm around her sister's waist.

Eve eased the door open.

'Lieutenant Dallas.' Melinda spoke quietly, smiled. 'She's so tired. I don't think she slept since ... Our parents just went to get us both some fresh clothes, some things. They really want to see you again, to thank you again.'

'There are a lot of people to thank. I'm surprised Detective Price isn't hovering.'

A pretty little light came into Melinda's eyes. 'I said something about pizza. My favorite place is over in our neighborhood. He went to get me some – wouldn't take no.'

'It helps to have something to do.'

'I know. Just as I know Bree and Jayson will go back to

334

work when they're sure I'm all right. I'm all right, but they're not sure.'

'I can come back later. No point waking her up.'

'I'm awake.' Bree's eyes fluttered open. 'Sorry, I went out for a minute.' She sat up, took her sister's hand.

It was like looking at slightly altered dupes, Eve thought. Not exact, not identical, but damn near.

'It's like a replay,' Bree began. 'It's not, not even close for the two of us. But you came in the hospital room before.'

'And the two of you were in the same bed. I remember. You were asleep that time,' Eve said to Melinda.

'It was weeks before I could sleep without Bree holding on to me. You look tired.'

'I guess we all are.'

'Would you sit? We can get you some coffee, something to eat.'

'I grabbed something.' But she sat on the side of the bed as Melinda indicated. 'Do you want to go over it again?'

'Darlie needs to. I used you and Bree, over and over, to give her hope, to give her something to hold on to. He didn't rape me. He only hit me once in anger, and that was almost an afterthought. They kept me drugged at first, but I stopped drinking the water. He killed his partner. I saw—'

'Yes.'

'Sarajo – well, that's how I knew her. I keep asking myself why I didn't see she was a liar, that she'd duped me.'

'She was a pro.'

'I wanted to help her, and thought I had. When she

335

contacted me again, so shaky, so urgent, I didn't think twice. I played right into it.'

'Do you need me to tell you it's not your fault?'

'No. I had plenty of time to replay it, rethink it. You have to trust, or you're only living half a life. You have to try to help or even that half is empty. I believed her. I was concerned because I suspected she was on something, but I thought it was because she was so frightened. I let her into my car, I drove away from the diner where we'd agreed to meet because she asked me to. I pulled over because she asked me to.'

'I never saw it coming. I felt it.' Melinda lifted a hand to the side of her neck. 'And still I didn't understand. Not until he was there. Right there.'

She closed her eyes a minute, then laid a hand over Eve's. 'I thought of you. Of Bree, then of you when I woke up in that room. In the dark, like before. But it wasn't like before. I was alone, an adult.'

She opened her eyes. 'This time I was bait. He made that clear, let me know he wasn't interested in me like before. I wasn't . . . fresh enough. He had her bring me food most of the time. Once she stood there, ate it in front of me. She hated me. I think she hated me most of all because I'd tried to help her.'

'Sick, twisted bitch,' Bree stated, and Eve said nothing. Could say nothing.

'She hated everything about me, and you,' Melinda said to Eve. 'She taunted me with you. How they were going to lock you in there, how they were going to hurt you, teach

336

you a lesson for what you did. How they were going to make a fortune selling you – Are you all right?' she asked when Eve jerked.

'Yeah. Fine.'

'I should've said *pretending* to sell you. I think she wanted you dead as much as he did, maybe more. She was obsessed with him. And couldn't see, just couldn't see how he despised her. She couldn't see his contempt. He let me see it, like it was our little private joke. Then they brought Darlie.'

Tears shimmered now, and Bree brought Melinda's hand to her cheek.

'He made sure I knew he was going after a girl – that's a kind of torture. Sarajo threw her in after they'd finished with her. They left the lights on so I could see what they'd done to her.'

'Having you there helped her.'

'It's a horrible thing, but having her helped me. Someone who needed me, someone I could comfort and counsel and tend to. When he came back for Darlie the next day, I did everything I could to distract him. She wasn't there, the partner. I'd studied him, so I used that. I got him to talk to me – to *converse*. He enjoyed it, and sat there for a long time, showing off his knowledge of literature, art.'

'Did he tell you anything personal? Anything he planned, anything that could tell us where he'd go?'

'I don't think so. It was all this lofty, cocktail-party sort of conversation. I kept it that way. I was afraid if I asked him anything, he'd remember Darlie.'

'What was he wearing?'

'Oh ... ah.'

'Try to think back,' Eve prompted, 'picture him there.'

'A crewneck with the sleeves pushed up. Very classic, and navy blue. Casual pants, but good ones. Buff colored, I think. Yes, with an embossed brown belt and silver buckle.' Her forehead creased as she concentrated. 'Silver buckles on his shoes. They matched the belt. He had a leather sheath on the belt. Once I wondered if I could get him to come over, somehow get the knife out of the sheath.

'It had initials on it, the sheath. I'd forgotten that.'

'What initials?'

'His. I. M. I am,' she murmured. 'He must love that.'

'On it,' Bree said before Eve could speak, and rolled out of bed, already pulling out her 'link.

'Did you notice anything else? Jewelry?'

'Silver wrist unit. It looked like a good one. A monogrammed leather sheath. You can trace that. I *know* that.' Frustration vibrating, Melinda pressed a hand to the side of her head. 'I didn't think before.'

'Give yourself a break,' Eve suggested. 'You held on, and more, you held him off from taking the kid for another round.'

'He got bored. I'd amused him for a while, but he knew what I was doing. He would have taken her, but the partner contacted him. He looked puzzled at first, let it go to v-mail. Then he was furious. He didn't rage, but he was so angry. He took out the knife. I knew he meant to kill us, but he just stood there.'

'Stood there?'

'Just stood there for a minute, looking blank, looking like someone who'd lost their train of thought or forgotten what they'd meant to do next.'

Eve's eyes sharpened. 'He wasn't sure what to do?'

'Yes, but it was more like he couldn't remember, or couldn't decide. Then he just turned around and walked out, locked us in again. I kept waiting for him to come back, to come back with the knife. That was the worst of all of it. Waiting for him to come back with the knife, and knowing I wouldn't be able to stop him.'

She fought off a shudder. 'Why didn't he come back?'

'The extra time, extra mess, lack of interest. The sudden, unexpected change in plans.' Eve hesitated, then decided Melinda deserved the full truth. 'And he knows you won't forget him, either of you. That's important to him.'

'He marked her.' Melinda laid her fingertips on her heart. 'And me, again. We can have it erased, like I did before. But it's always going to be there.'

'You got through it. So will she.'

'I hope you're right. You never get over it. You can't. So you have to get through it. She's one of us now, poor little girl. One of his numbers.'

'You're not a number, Melinda, to anyone but him. You should remember that. Remember he tried to make you one twice, but he couldn't.' Eve got to her feet. 'And when he's back in prison, go see him again, and show him that.'

'Will you talk to Darlie now?'

'Yeah. If you remember anything else, just let me know.'

When she stepped out into the hall, Bree walked up to her. 'We're tracing the leather sheath. It's a good lead.'

'Look at the clothes, too. The belt and shoes especially. She bought some of the wardrobe for him, but he'd want to shop for himself after being caged. Browse, touch fabrics. Maybe he did a little shopping when he went to the bank. He might want to replace some of the things he had to leave behind.'

'I'll work from here. They're bringing in a cot so I can stay with her tonight. It's not likely he'll come back for either of them, but—'

'He won't be back, but why take chances? Stay with your sister.' She crossed the hall, turned back. 'He's not as smart as he thinks he is, not this time. He's caught up in being out, in being free as much as by the plans he made. He wants his fashionable wardrobe, his good wines. He needs them after being denied for so long. He can't stay under long, it's like being back in a cage.'

'And he'll want another girl.'

'Yeah.'

Thinking of that, Eve opened the door to Darlie's room.

The mother sat on the bed, an arm curved around Darlie's shoulder, with the father flanking the other side. Eve's entrance had interrupted. She could see the father desperately trying to make Darlie smile or laugh.

Tears shimmered in his eyes as he turned toward Eve.

'I'm Lieutenant Dallas.'

'I remember.' The mother stood up. 'You were at the mall

when . . . I remember. We're so grateful, my husband and I, and Darlie.'

'I saw you. You came in the room.' Darlie's gaze fixed on Eve. 'You came in, and you said we were safe.'

'You are safe now.'

'Melinda said you'd come.' Her fingers fretted with the hospital sheet. 'Where's Melinda?'

'She's right across the hall.'

'Did you find him yet? Did you find him and put him back in jail?'

'Working on it.'

Darlie took a little sobbing breath that had her father's face crumbling, and her mother moving in to take her hand.

'I'd like to speak with Darlie alone.'

'She's already gone over everything,' Mr Morgansten began. 'She really needs to—'

'It's okay. It's okay, Daddy. I want to talk to her. Melinda said. It's okay.'

'We'll give you a little time.' Mrs Morgansten stood up, hovered a moment. 'Let's go outside,' she suggested to her husband.

'I . . . We'll go get you that ice cream,' he said to Darlie. 'How's that?'

'Okay.'

'Fudge Sludge, right? Your fave. You're a slave to your fave.'

'That's the best.'

'We won't be long.' He bent down, kissed her. When he

turned to go, the look he sent Eve was a painful morass of guilt and grief and terrible hope.

'My dad's been crying,' Darlie said when they were alone. 'He tries not to, but he can't help it. He's trying to make it better, but he can't.'

Faced with the girl's misery and exhausted pain, Eve missed Peabody like a limb. Her partner would know what to say, how to say it, how to reach both the child and her parents.

'I can't tell my dad what he did to me. I can't talk about it, not to my dad. I want to tell my mom, but I don't know how. I was stupid, so it's my fault. I can't tell them.'

'How were you stupid?'

'I'm not supposed to talk to people I don't know, like that woman. If I hadn't—'

'She was nice,' Eve began. 'She looked nice, normal. And you were right in the store, with lots of other people around, your friend right in the dressing room.'

'She said she was going to buy a present for somebody – I can't remember. It was a really mag dress, and she just wanted to ask me if I liked it. It's all mixed up.'

'I bet your parents taught you to be polite to adults.'

'Sure, but—'

'And you were in a store you know, with other people, the salespeople, your friend. And a nice woman asked you a question. You weren't stupid to answer it, and she counted on you being polite, being raised well. It's not your fault she wasn't nice. None of it's your fault. You didn't do anything wrong. You didn't do anything to deserve what happened to you.'

'You don't understand.' The tears started, slow, thick drops sliding down her cheeks. 'The other police don't understand. You can't.'

'Yes, I can.'

Darlie shook her head, fierce now. 'You *can't*. You don't *know*.'

'I do know.'

Eve's tone had Darlie swiping at tears, staring at her. Then her lips trembled. 'Was it him? Was it Isaac?'

'No. It was someone like him.'

'You got away? They came and saved you?'

Blood on her hands, her face, her arms. Wet and warm. 'I got away.'

'How are you okay? How can you be okay? I'm never going to be.'

'Yes, you will. You've already started. You told your father you wanted ice cream, but you don't. You said it because you didn't want to hurt his feelings, because you want him to be all right.' She picked up a brush from the table beside the bed. 'I bet you let your mother brush your hair, because she needed to do something for you.'

'It felt good when she did.'

'You've already started,' Eve repeated. 'It won't be quick and it won't be easy. You'll want it to be. They'll want it to be. It won't. The ones who tell you it will are the ones who can't understand. I guess that's not their fault, but it's annoying and . . . it hurts some, too.'

Tears spilled as Darlie nodded her head, quick and hard.

'You'll be pissed, you'll be scared,' Eve continued in the same easy, matter-of-fact tone. 'Now and again you'll go back to thinking it's your fault, which is bullshit.'

'Everybody's going to look at me different.'

'Probably, for a while anyway. They'll feel sorry for you, and sometimes you'll hate that. Really hate it because you just want everything to be like it was. It's not going to be.'

'I can't ever go back to school.'

'That won't fly, kid,' Eve said, and made Darlie blink. 'Nice try though. You've got plenty of people to get you ice cream, brush your hair, hold your hand, and dry your tears. That's good, because you'll need them. I'm going to give it to you straight. You'll learn to live with what happened to you. What you do with that life is up to you.'

'I'm afraid he'll find me.'

'It's my job to see he doesn't.' Monster slayer, Eve thought. Maybe that would do, for now. 'I'm good at my job. You don't have to tell me what he did to you. But if you could tell me anything you remember about him and the woman, what they said to each other, or about the apartment, whether they talked to anyone else.'

'She said he should give her a tattoo, to give her a heart with his name in it. He laughed, and that made her mad. He was . . .' Like Melinda, she touched her heart. 'I couldn't move. It hurt. It burned, but I couldn't move.'

'You were awake?'

'I could see them and hear them, but it was like I was dreaming. She said he could go ahead and stamp his little

344

whores. She'd go get a real pro to give her a tat. He said not to do that. He didn't want anybody marring her skin. She liked that.'

Darlie took an unsteady breath when her lips trembled. 'He didn't have any clothes on, and when he finished with the tattoo, she started . . .' Darlie's color came up, rode high on her cheeks. 'She started touching him, you know, down there. And he started touching her, but he was watching me. I felt sick, and I closed my eyes because I wanted it to be a bad dream.'

'Is there anything else about the room, or what they talked about?'

'He told her to stop, you know, the touching, and she got mad again. He said it was time for a threesome. Time to set up the camera.'

'Camera?'

'He made her get it out of the closet. It was on a stand, a vid cam on a stand. He made me drink something, and I could move. But my hands. They were tied.' She held her arms up and back. 'I screamed. I was crying and trying to get away and she slapped me. Really hard. She told me . . .' Darlie glanced toward the door. 'She said, "Shut the fuck up." But he told her he liked hearing the bad girls scream. And then . . .' Tears flowed again.

'It's okay. You don't have to think about that or talk about that, unless you're ready. Tell me about the camera.'

'Um . . . He had it so he could take a vid of what they were doing. When – when he was—' She shut her eyes,

345

reached up. Understanding, Eve stepped closer, gripped her hand.

'When he was raping me,' Darlie said, eyes still closed, 'he told me to scream "help", to scream, "Help me, help me". I did, but he didn't stop. He said to cry, cry, sweetheart, and to scream "Dallas" over and over. I did, but he didn't stop. He didn't stop.'

So, Eve thought, sickened with rage, he'd thought of her when he'd raped Darlie. Even then he'd thought of her.

'Were you ever alone with him? Did the woman ever leave the room?'

'I don't – yes. I think. It was after the first time, or the second. It gets mixed up.'

'Doesn't matter.'

'I didn't think I could scream anymore. It hurt to scream. They were lying on the bed with me. She said she was hungry, and she wanted some candy, so he told her to go help herself. When she went out, he said maybe he'd keep me, his first new bad girl. Maybe he'd take me with him when he was done.'

'Where? Did he tell you where?'

'He wasn't really talking to me. He was looking up at the ceiling, sort of talking to himself, I think. He said he'd find us another mommy, and we'd live it up for a while with Dallas at our feet. But he missed New York and all the bad girls. Couldn't wait to go back home.

'Then he turned the camera back on.' Her breath started to hitch. 'And he got on me. I could still scream.'

'Give it a rest awhile. You gave me a couple of things I might be able to use to catch him.'

'I did?' Darlie swiped at her cheeks. 'Really?'

'What's the point of telling you if you didn't?'

'To make me feel better.'

'Hey, you're getting ice cream. You're already going to feel better.'

Whether it was surprise or genuine humor, a smile ghosted around Darlie's lips. 'You're funny.'

'I'm a barrel of monkeys, kid, though mostly I figure monkeys stuck in a barrel are just going to be pissed off.'

The laugh tripped out, a little rusty, a little weak, but it fell into the room just as Darlie's parents came back in. At the sound of it, Mrs Morgansten's eyes filled.

'Good timing.' Eve got to her feet. 'We're just finished here.'

'We got you a cone.' Mr Morgansten lurched forward, holding out a cone topped with a scoop of chocolate goo.

'Now you'll feel better, too,' Darlie told her.

'Looks like. Thanks.'

'Lieutenant Dallas?' Darlie took the cone her father gave her, but continued to stare at Eve. 'Will you tell me when you catch him and put him back in jail?'

'You'll be the first. That's a promise.'

She stepped outside, leaned against the wall a moment, just to breathe. She studied the door across the hall, but just couldn't face going back in. Enough, she told herself. Just enough for now.

She took out her 'link, noted the goo dribbling down the cone. What the hell, she thought, and licked at it.

Roarke came on screen.

'I'm done here, and have a couple things to follow up on. Where—'

'You have ice cream?'

'Yeah, it was a gift.'

'I wouldn't mind ice cream.'

'Anybody who does is just sad. I'm heading back to the car, so—'

'Why don't I walk with you,' he said, coming out of a room on the right as she walked to the elevator. 'And share your ice cream.'

'I think it's Fudge Sludge.'

'An unfortunate name.' He leaned down, sampled. 'But tasty. How's the girl?'

'Wounded, fragile, and stronger than she thinks she is. Between her and Melinda I got matching brown leather shoes and belt – both with silver buckles, a leather knife sheath, monogrammed I.M., and a vid cam with tripod. He never used a cam before. None of the other vics mentioned being recorded.'

'A recording can be found, and would incriminate. From what I read in his file, he didn't need that kind of thing. He doesn't have to relive what he can simply live again.'

'Exactly. He had the girls. If he wanted a replay, he could just pick one. He didn't document because he's smart.'

'But he's not attempting to hide what he's doing this time.

He's already convicted. So he needs the vid to relive the moment, at least between victims?'

'I don't think so. He made it for me. This thing's dripping.'

Roarke took out a spotless white handkerchief, sacrificed it by wrapping it around the cone. And took payment in ice cream before handing it back. 'For you?'

'He made her scream for me while he was raping her.'

'Christ. That's it for my appetite.'

In agreement, she tossed the cone in a recycler. 'I'm going to check the evidence list, but I didn't see any cam or tripod on it. So he took it with him, which says he means to use it again.'

'Another girl?' At her hesitation, his jaw tightened. 'No, you're saying he means to use it with you, not for you. To record you, once he has you. Perhaps for me, perhaps just for himself.'

'It demonstrates he's still confident. And she gave me another tidbit that confirms – in my mind – he's still here.'

She opened the car door, slid inside.

'When his partner left the room for a snack and a hit, he talked about keeping Darlie. Not to her, she said, and I think she was right about that. This was thinking out loud, not indulging in his sick version of pillow talk. He talked about getting them a new mommy, and that reinforces the profile. The partners are Mommy, in his very, very sick version. He mentioned having Dallas at their feet. I can't pin down whether he meant me or the city. Maybe both. But he did talk about going back to New York. Later.'

'You believe he already had his backup location set here.'

'I think he had it set for a long time. I've got to work it out in my head. I need to filter some of the excess out of my head and get to it.'

She pushed a hand through her hair. 'Anyway.' She contacted Lieutenant Ricchio, relayed the data.

'I should go back to his place, get a better feel for it, for what he took, what he left. What he—'

'And how is adding yet more helping you sift through the extra crap in your head?'

'Shoving more in there gives me more to work through, and with. I couldn't get a feel for the place before. It was too crowded, and . . . I wasn't at my best.'

He said nothing for a moment. 'Mira's at the hotel.'

'I'm not ready for Mira. I'm not ready to yank my mind and guts open. I need to feel I've done all I can. I need to do what I'd do under any other circumstances. What I'd do is go back to the scene.'

'All right, we'll go back to the scene. Then that's enough, Eve. That's bloody all for the day.'

Not if they got any sort of a hit, she thought, but didn't argue.

'Park in the garage,' she told Roarke when they approached the building. 'That's the way he'd have gone in and out routinely.'

She got out of the car. Minimum security, but still it was there. He'd have jammed the cameras when he brought

Melinda, then Darlie in. Dallas EDD would work with the discs. If they pulled anything out, she'd take a look. But for now . . .

'You know he may have kept the second ride here, right under her nose. How would she know? Why pay to store it somewhere else, and have to go get it? Plus, it's just like him. He loves screwing with people, pulling the con, making them a fool.'

'I asked for copies of the building security. We can review them.'

'Yeah, you never know.' She studied the area, the setup, and yes, began to get the feel of it. 'He'd bring them in late, reduce risk of running into another resident or visitor. But he'd jam the elevator. No one up or down but him until he was inside. He puts them in a kind of twilight sleep. Walks them right up. Uses the stairs, that's why he likes a lower floor.'

She started up. 'Quiet. Quick. Confident, but excited, too. Especially this time because it's been so long. The partner goes out first, clears the hall.'

Roarke obliged.

'And they walk the vic right in,' Eve said, stepping out, using her master to uncode the police seal.

'Melinda, straight into the holding room. But Darlie, into the bedroom.' She crossed to it. 'Put her down a little deeper, secure her hands to the headboard. It's a form of paralytic. The vic is aware, but immobilized. He can't have her squirming around when he does the tat. He's a perfectionist.'

She visualized it. Stripping the girl, touching her – but just a little, not too much now. Removing his clothes, putting them away. Neat and tidy. Then the tools, the tat.

'Camera's in the closet.' She walked over, opened it. 'He took the brown shoes,' she noted. 'The ones Melinda remembered. He took time to select what he'd pack. Nothing rushed or spur of the moment. Nothing carelessly discarded. Except the shirt with his partner's blood on it.'

She studied the ties again, the duplicates, thought of Melinda's statement. Just stood there – indecisive.

Considering, she fingered the sleeve of a jacket, a shirt. 'Nice. Nice material. He must've hated leaving some of this, especially since he couldn't have had time to wear a lot of it. He'll want replacements. Will he wait until New York? I don't know. Can't say.'

She stepped out of the closet.

'Dallas at their feet. If he means the city, he's got a place posher than this. He's tired of the middle-class scene. He bought too many swanky clothes to suit this neighborhood. Not just a few select pieces like before. So, he's planning, he's thinking it's time to move up, where he belongs. He'll need to bring me there now, so it's either set up for that or he needs to do it.'

She walked into the bath, stood there, studied, moved out and on, back into the living area where her mother's blood stained the floor.

Did she believe herself unaffected by it, Roarke wondered. Didn't she realize she looked at everything *but* the blood?

'He spends a lot of time out here. He likes the space. A cage is so confining. He can watch Melinda, then Darlie on the monitor, or catch up with some screen, listen to music, read. But he'd get itchy. He needs to be out and about. He needs the city. He'll go out, seek out places with people. Shops, restaurants, galleries, clubs. After he sends the partner away, he'd go out. He'd want to go out, get the smell of her out of his nose. Put on a new persona, sit at a bar or a table in some trendy club. Strike up conversations, flirt with some woman. If he could run a game, so much the better. Then he'd come back, lock up, check on his 'guests.' Maybe have a drink while he counted up his take. Then he'd sleep like a baby.'

She walked to the kitchen, checked the AutoChef, the fridgie, the cabinets. 'He left a lot of this behind, and you know, there's a lot of duplication here, too. Does anybody need a half-dozen jars of stuffed olives?'

'Hoarding?' Roarke suggested.

'Yeah, maybe.' But she wasn't so sure of that now. 'He has to leave a lot behind because it's too annoying and time-consuming to repack food. He can get more. Check gourmet food shops, that should be on the list. And clubs, the trendy ones. If we can find out where he went the nights he abducted Melinda, then Darlie, we'd know what he's looking for in late-night entertainment.'

'He wouldn't go back. He'd look for fresh,' Roarke said when she turned and frowned at him. 'And wouldn't go back on the off chance whoever he played as a mark came in as well.'

'You're probably right. Good thought. So if we can find, we eliminate. But we'd have a style.'

She walked to the window, looked out, looked down.

Dallas at our feet, she thought again.

'He talked about staying in a hotel penthouse. High life. Upper floors, higher price, higher life. If he changed his MO with this second location, we're looking for a top level, good view. Big windows, maybe a terrace. Lots of open. More, I think, in the center of things. The rest applies. At least two bedrooms, on-site garage.'

She shut her eyes, trying to think. 'One of those corporate apartments, maybe, or a long-lease rental? Or—'

'You're clutching now because you're tired. You're tired, Eve, and trying not to think you're standing a foot away from where your mother bled out hours ago. But you are thinking it. This isn't the place for you to think clearly or well, and you need to accept it.'

'I think,' she said slowly, deliberately, 'he left food, wine, clothes, equipment behind. But he took some of everything with him. I think he carefully selected the best of each category. I think he did that because he was moving to a better location. And, I think, if we focus on high floors – even top floors of more upscale buildings, more urban center areas, more luxury accommodations, we'll find him.'

'Then you should pass that on to your associates here so they can begin to do that.'

'I am. I will.'

'Good. You do that while I contact Mira. She can join us for a drink back at the hotel.'

'I don't want—'

'It's past that. You need to do this for yourself. If you won't, then do it for me. I'm asking you, please, do this for me.'

She pulled out her 'link, but she didn't look at him, or at the blood. She contacted Ricchio as she walked away from the crime scene.

# 19

Roarke understood her silence. It didn't matter that she'd agreed to talk with Mira, even acknowledged she needed to. He'd forced her hand – made her stop her forward motion and her focus on the crimes, the perpetrator, the victims, the questions and answers. Stopping the forward motion meant facing the past – her past.

Dealing with her feelings about her mother's life, and her mother's murder.

He could accept her need, and her ability, to turn her reluctance into resentment aimed at him. In her place he'd likely have done the same.

What a pair they were.

He expected, and accepted, her reaction when the elevator opened. And Mira turned from her place by the windows. The single glance Eve spared him, one ripe with the shock of betrayal stabbed him right through the heart.

'I've been admiring your view,' Mira said.

'It's good to see you.' Roarke walked over to greet her. 'How was the flight?'

'Very smooth.'

'And your room here?'

'It's lovely.'

Behind them, Eve's silence was a roar of fury.

'Why don't we have some wine?' Roarke began.

'You two go ahead with your social hour,' Eve interrupted in a tone like cracked ice. 'I need a shower.'

She stormed upstairs, had nearly slammed the bedroom door. Then she saw the cat sitting on the bed, blinking at her with bicolored eyes.

Pressure thudded into her chest, burned in her throat, behind her eyes as she rushed forward, dropped to her knees by the bed.

'Galahad.'

He bumped his head against hers, purred like a cargo jet.

'He had her bring you.' She rubbed her face against his fur. 'He had her bring you for me. God, God, I'm a mess.'

She sat on the floor, braced her back against the bed. Comfort flooded her when the cat jumped off the bed, padded into her lap. And circled there, digging thin claws into her thighs.

'Okay. Okay,' she murmured, giving him a long stroke down the back. She closed her eyes, and holding the fat, purring cat, tried to find her center again.

'I'm sorry,' Roarke said downstairs. 'I didn't tell her you'd be waiting for us. I knew she'd stall otherwise, and we'd end up . . . I thought it would be harder. I'm going to get us that wine.'

He chose a bottle at random from the rack in the bar area. While he uncorked it, Mira walked over.

'You look very tired. You rarely do.'

'I'm not particularly. Frustrated, I suppose. This should breathe a bit, but bugger that.' He poured two glasses.

'Frustrated with Eve?'

'No. Yes.' He swallowed wine. 'No. Not really. She has enough to deal with, more than anyone should. With myself. I don't know what to do for her, what to say to her. I dislike not knowing what to do for or say to the person who means everything to me.'

'I'm sorry, please, sit down. Have some wine.'

'Thank you.' She sat, and in her quiet way sipped and waited while he roamed the room as a wolf might a cage.

'What do you think you should do, or say?' she asked him.

'Well, that's just it, isn't it? I don't bloody know. Does she need me to just let her work herself into exhaustion? That can't be right. Yet I know very well she needs the work, the routine of it, the structure to get through the rest.'

He shoved a hand in his pocket, found the gray button, turned it over and over in his fingers. 'But it's not routine this time, is it? It's not simply another case, another investigation.'

'It's difficult, coming here. Being here.'

'Bad enough if it were only that, with all the memories it shoves down her throat. The nightmares, they'd eased off, until we came here. Now she's had one worse than anything

358

I know of since we've been together. She's made of courage, you know? And for her to be so terrified, so absolutely defenseless . . .'

'Makes you feel the same.'

He stopped, and the anguish lived in his eyes, on his face, in the set of his body. 'I couldn't get her back. For . . . it seemed forever, I couldn't pull her out. And this was before her mother. This was just being here, tracking a man who makes her think of her father.'

'You understood it would be difficult for her, physically, emotionally. Did you try to stop her from coming?'

'As if I could.'

'Roarke.' She waited until he again stopped his restless movements, looked at her. 'You know you could have. You're the only one who could have stopped her from coming to Dallas. Why didn't you?'

He stood for a moment, and when the storm in his eyes faded, sat across from her. 'How could I? If she hadn't come, hadn't done whatever she could and McQueen had hurt, worse, killed Melinda Jones, Eve would never have forgiven herself. It would have cut something out of her. Neither of us could have lived with that.'

'Now Melinda and the girl McQueen abducted are safe.'

'But it's not done, and not just because he's still out there. She stood over her mother's body today. God.' He rubbed at his temple. 'Could it only be today? There's been no time, you see, to deal with it, to understand it. To cope. She won't take it. Do I force her to? Pour a tranq into her so she gets some rest? Let her run until she drops? Do I just watch her suffer, and continue to do nothing?'

'You feel you've done nothing?'

'Tracking financials and making her eat a goddamn sandwich?' The brittle, brutal frustration snapped out of him. 'Anyone could do the same, so it's next to nothing. She needs more from me than that, and I don't know what it is.'

'You brought me the cat.'

Eve stood on the stairs, Galahad at her feet. Roarke stood as she crossed the room.

'Who else would think – would know – I needed the stupid cat? Who else would do that for me?'

'Maybe I did it for myself.'

She shook her head, laid her hands on his face, and watched everything – the sorrow, the fatigue, the love, swirl into his eyes. 'You brought Mira and Galahad. Why didn't you toss in Peabody and Feeney, add Mavis for comic relief?'

'Do you want them?'

'God.' She did what she rarely did in company. She took his lips with hers, let the kiss spin out, felt his hand fist on the back of her jacket. 'I'm so sorry.'

'No. No. I don't want you to be sorry.'

'Too bad. You needed to stop, and I wouldn't. Wouldn't let either of us take a breath. Routine, procedure, logic. It's necessary. And it's all fucked up.' She leaned on him a moment, let herself lean on him. 'It's so fucked up. So, I guess we'll take a breath now. I'd better use the first one to tell you I love you because there's going to be others that fuck it up again.'

He murmured to her in Irish, brushed his lips on her brow. 'We're used to that, aren't we? *A ghra,* you're so pale. She's lost weight, you see,' he said to Mira. 'It's only been a couple of days, but I can see it.'

'He worries. He nags like a' – she nearly said 'mother,' caught herself – 'wife. He's a damn good wife.'

'Now you're just trying to piss me off. But under the circumstances, I'll let it pass. Why don't you sit, and I'll get you a glass of wine?'

'Oh yeah, a really big glass of wine.' She dropped into a chair, let out a long, long breath. 'I know I was rude before,' she said to Mira. 'And I figure you know a defense mechanism when you see one. Still, sorry about that. I appreciate, a lot, that you came.'

'You're welcome.'

'I've work to catch up on,' Roarke said as he handed Eve her wine. 'I'll go upstairs, let the two of you talk.'

'Don't.' Eve took his hand. 'You should stay. You're part of this.'

'All right.'

'I don't know where to start. How to start. It's like trying to navigate a maze in the dark, and . . .' Then the cat sprawled weightily over her feet. And that was it, the start. 'I miss home. Roarke had you bring the cat, because the cat's home. I never had anything, didn't want anything until that cat. I don't even know why I took him, exactly, but I made him mine.'

She took a long, slow drink of wine. 'I missed him. I miss

Peabody and her smart mouth and steady ways. I miss Feeney and Mavis and my bullpen. Hell, it's so bad I even miss Summerset.'

When Roarke made some sound, she turned narrowed eyes on him. 'If you ever tell him I said that, I'll shave you bald in your sleep, dress you in frilly pink panties, and take a vid that I'll auction and sell for huge amounts of money.'

'So noted,' he said, and thought: *There's Eve. There she is.*

'It's not just being away. Since Roarke, I've gone away, from home, from work. It's here, and it's working here without my people, my place. And it's more than that,' she admitted when Mira waited her out. 'McQueen's another beginning for me. Not just the real start of the job for me. When I opened the door in New York where he had all the girls, when I saw them, knew what he'd done to them, I went back, for a minute, to that room in Dallas.

'I'd probably remembered things before, but that was the first time I couldn't pretend I didn't. He'd done to them what someone had done to me. I knew it. Even if I didn't know all of it, I knew that.'

'How did you feel?' Mira asked her.

'Sick, scared, enraged. But I put it away, could put it away for a long time. Maybe little parts would slip out, give me a bad time, but I could shove them back into the shadows again. Then, right before I met Roarke there was an incident. A girl – baby, just a baby really. And I was too late.'

'I remember,' Mira said. 'Her father was crazed on Zeus, and murdered her before you could get to her.'

'Cut her to pieces. Right after, I caught the DeBlass case, and Roarke was a suspect. He was so . . . he was Roarke, and while I could eliminate him from my suspect list, I couldn't shake him. And the case built, and everything turned around inside me.'

'How did you feel?' Mira asked again, and Eve managed a smile.

'Sick, scared, enraged. What does he want from me? I mean, look at him. What does he want from me, with me?'

'Should I tell you?'

She looked at him. 'You tell me every day. Sometimes I still don't get it, but I *know* it. And with everything turned around and opening up and breaking apart, I remembered. My father, what he did to me. It can't go back in the box anymore.'

'Is that what you want? To shut it away?'

'I did. I did,' Eve repeated in a murmur. 'Now? I want to deal with it, accept it, move on. I was, I think. When I remembered the rest. Remembered that night when he came in and he went at me, hurting me, raping me. He broke my arm.' She rubbed it, as if she felt the shock of pain. 'And I killed him. I didn't think I could live with that, get through that memory. I don't think I would have without Roarke. Without you. But I know more, coming back here again, this time. With McQueen and my father twisting together in my head.'

'Do they?' Mira asked.

'Yes. I guess they always did. I know I killed to survive. I know it was a child, striking out to save herself. But I know, too, I felt . . . joy in the killing. In driving that knife, that little knife, into him again and again and again, I felt euphoric.'

'And why shouldn't you?'

In absolute shock, Eve stared at Mira. 'I've killed since, in the line. There's no joy. There can't be.'

'But this wasn't in the line. This wasn't a trained officer acting in the line of duty. This was a child, one who had been continually, systematically, brutally abused, physically, mentally, emotionally. A child in terror and pain, killing a monster. And that joy, Eve, didn't last. It's only part of the reason you suppressed. It frightened you, that joy, because of who and what you are. He couldn't make you an animal, couldn't make another monster out of you. You killed a beast, and felt glad. You took a life, and punished yourself.'

'If I ever felt that again, ever felt glad again with blood on my hands, I couldn't come back from it.'

'Is that what frightens you?'

'It . . . disturbs me to know that's in me.'

'In all of us,' Mira said. 'Most are never put in a position where they experience, or choose to experience it. Some who understand it become monsters. Others who understand it become the ones who hunt the monsters, and protect the rest of us.'

'Most times I understand, and accept that. Here, it blurs.

'I attacked Roarke when I had a nightmare here.'

'It was nothing,' he began, and she rounded on him.

'Don't say that! Don't protect me. I clawed, and I bit. I drew his blood, for God's sake. If I'd had a weapon, I'd have used it. I'm afraid to sleep.' It jerked out of her. 'I'm afraid I'll do it again.'

'Have you?'

'No, but I looked into my mother's eyes this morning, and I knew her. I stood over her body this afternoon, and I remembered her. Some. I remember some.'

'And you're afraid, with those emerging memories, you'll become more violent when your defenses are down in sleep.'

'It follows, doesn't it?'

'I can't promise you there won't be more nightmares, or that they won't become violent. But I can tell you what I believe. Your first night here, under such strain, with your past so close to the surface, you ... overloaded.'

'Is that a shrink term?'

'It's one you understand. You couldn't hold any more, couldn't contain any more. You weren't attacking Roarke, but defending yourself against the person trying to hurt you.'

'I did hurt her,' Roarke admitted.

'And with the physical and psychic pain merging, you fought back.'

'What's to stop me from doing just that again?' Eve demanded. 'How long are either of us supposed to lie down at night and wait for the battle and the blood?'

'I could give you medications for the short term. Or,' Mira continued, 'you could consider something you haven't yet spoken of. If you recognized your mother, isn't it possible your subconscious already had when you studied the photos of the woman you suspected was McQueen's partner?'

'Yeah. I knew there was something, but I couldn't get down to it. I couldn't reach it.'

'Consciously. You're not only trained to be observant, Eve, you're naturally so. Often uncomfortably so. If you recognized her, added the strain of that to the rest, it's hardly a wonder it manifested in a traumatic and violent nightmare. She was part of what you hadn't yet come to terms with, what you continued to block out. The mother, the symbol of everything intended to nurture, to tend, to love and protect.'

'She hated me.'

'Why do you say that?'

'Because I saw it, I felt it. I knew it even when I was – who the hell knows? Three, four, five. She liked to knock me around. She had me because he got the bright idea to breed their own moneymaker. I was less than a dog to her, and the reality of me was more than she'd bargained for. She wanted to sell me, but he wouldn't. The investment wasn't ripe enough, not yet. She'd hit me when he wasn't there, or just shove me in a closet. It's dark, and there's nothing to eat. She didn't even give me a name. I was nothing to her. Less than nothing.'

She took a shaky swallow of wine. 'She didn't know me. When we were face-to-face again, and she looked right at me. She didn't know me.'

'Did that hurt you?'

'No. I don't know. I couldn't think. I just know that for a minute I was nothing again. Like they – she – took everything from me. Roarke, my badge, my life, myself. For a minute it was just gone because she was there. I can't be nothing again.'

'You could never be nothing.' Roarke spoke in a voice of barely controlled rage. 'You're what you made yourself against the impossible. Even when you were helpless they couldn't destroy what you are. You're a miracle. You're my miracle, and you'll never be anything else.'

'They're in me.'

'And what's in me? You know. You know how I chose to beat it back, and still you're mine. Of all the choices you could have made, you chose to protect. To stand for the victim. Even her. Now, even her.'

'I saw what she was, in that hospital bed, where I put her. Hurt and bruised and knocked around.'

'The way you'd been,' Mira prompted.

'The way I'd been. And I felt . . . maybe contempt or disgust, studying her like a bug, hoping I'd been wrong, that she wasn't the one. But I knew she was, and what she was.'

'What was she?'

'Selfish is too easy a word. Selfish and vicious and sly, and still I don't know how or why.

'So much blood,' Eve said quietly. 'At the end, so much blood, and I thought, what's in it? What's in the blood, hers, mine? Our eyes are the same.'

'No.' Roarke spoke with absolute certainty. 'You're wrong.'

'She changed the color, but—'

'No,' he repeated, looking into Eve's troubled eyes. 'Who

367

knows yours – and all their moods – better than I? Do you think I haven't studied those ID shots?'

He remembered what his aunt had said to him on their first meeting, and gave it to Eve, in his own words. 'Color changes on a whim. The shape of things counts for more. Your eyes are yours, Eve. The color, the shape, and more what's behind them. You got none of it from her.'

'I don't know why that's important, except I don't want to look in the mirror and see her. I don't want you to ever look at me and see—'

'Never.'

'It's stupid to pick at it,' Eve said wearily. 'I know, I do know I'm not like her. Melinda and the kid, they were just means to an end to her. Not human, not important. Her next hit, that was important. Fucking with the cops, that was important. Getting back to McQueen, that was the most important. Weak spot. A certain kind of man, that's a weak spot, makes her do what's unnatural to her. Have a child, run errands, fix a meal. Because he makes her feel like the drug makes her feel. She lives a lie, but that's second nature. Like using and exploiting. She stole another woman's child knowing what he'd do to her. She left me with my father and she had to know what he was, what he'd do. He'd already started doing it. But she left me with him.'

'As she left Darlie with McQueen,' Mira added.

'Yeah. I knew what she was, and I felt nothing but that contempt. Then I felt sick, then cold. Then I had to step out of it. Had to, because if we didn't find them, find

Melinda and Darlie, without her help, I'd have to work her again. Go back, knowing who and what she was and work her again. But she went to him. Killed a cop without a second thought to get to him. And when I walked into that place, his place, and saw her on the floor, the blood, the death, I felt . . .'

'What?' Mira asked her. 'What did you feel?'

'Relief!' It burst out of her. 'Relief. She didn't know me, and now she never would. God, the thought that she might realize . . . I wouldn't ever have to think of her somewhere in the world. Wouldn't have to think someday, somehow, she might remember me, might put it together, might know. Use that against me, against Roarke, against everyone I care about. She was dead, and I was relieved.'

In the silence, she pressed a hand to her mouth, struggling to hold back sobs.

'You didn't say you felt joy,' Roarke said quietly.

She stared at him, eyes wet, shoulders trembling. 'What?'

'You didn't feel joy.'

'No! God. He'd slit her throat like a pig for slaughter. Whatever she was, he had no right to take her life.'

'And that's who you are, Lieutenant.'

'I . . .' She swiped at tears, looked at Mira.

'It's an exceptional thing to have someone in your life who knows and understands you so well. Who loves who you are. A very exceptional thing. He asks the question, as I was about to do, already knowing the answer. You felt relief because a threat to everything you are, everything you have, and what you love ended. It ended in blood so you're struggling to treat her like another victim. She's not.'

'She was murdered.'

'And McQueen should pay for it. You need to have a part in that not because of the connection, but because she was murdered. She was murdered here, in Dallas, by a man you see as very like your father. You want to walk away from it, and you can't. Relief won't stop you from seeking justice for her. That conflict causes you stress, unhappiness, self-doubt. I hope by admitting what you felt, what you feel, some of that will ease.'

'I would've put her away, built the case to put her away. I thought there'd be some justice. Locking her up, the way she'd done to me.'

'She chose the monster, again.'

'She thought he was still alive. Richard Troy. I brought him up, testing, I guess. She thought he was still alive. I let her think he'd given us information on her.'

'Well played,' Roarke commented, then lifted his eyebrows at her frown. 'Sorry, was that cold? Am I supposed to feel otherwise?'

'No.' Eve looked down at her wine. 'No.'

'I wish she were alive, that's the God's shining truth. So I could imagine her in a cage for the decades to come. But we live with disappointment.'

'You hate her. I can't.'

'I've enough for both of us.'

'I feel disgust, and – God, I wish I had the words. I feel a little shame, and there's no point getting pissed off because I feel what I feel. I'd rather feel hate. If she'd lived, I might've gotten there. So maybe I feel a little cheated as well as relieved. I don't know what that says.'

'In my professional opinion?' Mira crossed her fine legs. 'It says you have a very healthy reaction to a very unhealthy situation. The two of you have been scraped raw by this, yet here you are. With your cat.'

Eve let out a weak laugh while Galahad continued to snore at her feet, all four legs in the air.

'You need sleep. If you want medication, I can arrange it.'

'I'd rather not.'

'I'll be here if you change your mind.'

'It's good to have a doctor on tap in case I bloody him again.'

'For now I prescribe food and rest.'

'I could eat,' Eve realized. 'It's the first time I've actually wanted to all day.'

'That's a good sign. I'm just next door if you need me.'

'Stay, have a meal with us,' Roarke began.

'Another time. I think the two of you should just be together awhile. If anything breaks on the case, I'd like to be informed.'

'Sure.' Eve stepped forward when Mira rose. 'It helped, a lot, you coming. Listening.'

Mira brushed a hand over Eve's hair. 'Maybe it's the influence of my daughter – the Wiccan. While I think we have to make the most out of our life while we're here, I believe we get more than one chance. When we get another chance, there are connections, people, recognition. I recognize you, Eve, and always have. That's unscientific, and absolute truth. I'll be right here.'

Roarke walked her to the door, then, leaning down, kissed Mira softly on the lips. 'Thank you.'

After closing the door, he turned to Eve. 'You're loved. One day, I hope when you think of 'mother' you'll think of her.'

'When I think of good I think of her. That's something.'

'It is.'

'I'm sorry. I made this harder on you than I needed to.'

'That goes both ways.'

'It'll probably still get screwed up before it's over.'

'Oh, almost certainly. So why don't we eat before it does?'

'Good idea.' But she walked to him first, wrapped her arms around him. 'I'd rather be screwed up with you than smooth with anybody else.'

'Again, both ways.' He drew her back, traced his finger over the dent in her chin. 'What do you say to spaghetti and meatballs?'

'I say yay.' She hugged him again, then let out a genuine laugh as Galahad wound between their feet. 'In a dead sleep he hears you say spaghetti and meatballs.'

'Three plates, then. If you can't spoil your cat, who can you spoil?'

'But no wine for him. He's a mean drunk.'

She held on another moment, taking comfort, giving it back. 'I want to say just one more thing about it, then set it aside, at least for now.'

'All right.'

'When I was a kid – after, I mean. When I was in the system, I used to imagine somebody stole me from my parents. They'd find me, take me home. Somewhere nice, with a yard and toys. And they'd be great, perfect. They'd love me.'

She closed her eyes when he tightened his grip. 'After a while I had to deal with what's real. Nobody was coming for me. There was no house and yard and toys. I did okay, and one day I did a whole hell of a lot better. I found you.'

She stepped back, gripping his hands in hers. 'I got really lucky because, Roarke, you're my what's real.'

He brought her hands to his lips. 'Always.'

He expected she'd go back to work after dinner, and she didn't surprise him. But Mira was right. He understood her.

She needed the work, the forward motion again. She needed to connect with Peabody again, like a touchstone, no matter how brief the conversation.

'They're still working on finding his New York hole. But we've sussed out his steps from the breakout to Dallas.'

She went to her board, started another time line. 'He picked up a package at the mail drop he'd arranged with his partner. The IDs, some clothes, the jammers, the 'link. From there, he goes to his old apartment. Secures Schuster and Kopeski, does his particular brand of torture. Has some breakfast, cleans up, takes what he wants. When he's finished there, he takes a stroll. He checked into the Warfield Hotel, reservation, early check-in secured, under Milo, picks up a package they're holding for him – which I'd say is the suit. Peabody tracked down the cab that dropped him off, and that's damn good work. He'd walked five blocks from his old place, hailed one. We've got the security disc from check-in.'

She ordered it on screen. 'See, working man – traveling. A duffel, a ball cap, sunshades – Tray Schuster's – skids,

Schuster's again. He makes contact with me from the hotel room, using the filtered 'link and jammer. He calls for the valet to press his suit, the one she sent him. He orders a hearty meal from room service. Gets suited up.'

She shifted the screen image, showed him coming out of the elevator, blond hair, sharp suit, briefcase he probably bought in New York. 'He used the in-room checkout. He'd arranged for private car service, which picked him up, took him a block from Central, where he ordered it to wait. Breezed by to see me, slipped back into the car, which dropped him off at the shuttle. He had a light snack and two glasses of Cabernet in flight. Stibble spilled he'd helped McQueen purchase a vehicle that was waiting at the transpo station here.'

She snorted. 'Claims, according to Peabody, McQueen told him it was a gift for an old friend.'

'He's a poor judge of people for a grifter,' Roarke commented.

'He wasn't. Prison's taken some of the shine off him, and he had a fairly murky pool to fish from. Stibble served his purpose well enough,' Eve added. 'McQueen didn't think we'd fish Stibble out of the pool so fast.'

'One of a number of miscalculations this time around.'

'Even miscalculating, he's killed two people, tortured two more, abducted Melinda, abducted and raped Darlie.'

'So don't underestimate him,' Roarke concluded.

'Never. We lose him once he picks up the car at the transpo center here, but I'll fill that in. What he did was go to the fancy wine store, run more errands before going to the apartment.'

She tucked her hands in her pockets as she tried to put herself in McQueen's head. 'I think he didn't give Sylvia his ETA. Didn't want her there to greet him. Had things to set up. He'd want to enjoy his alone time, check the cams, hide whatever he didn't want her poking into. Plus, she'd want a romantic reunion, wouldn't she? No time for that. He wants to get Melinda in before the champagne and caviar.'

She walked around the board. 'And maybe, most probably, one of the errands he ran was a stop-off at his second location. Check it out, set up whatever he wanted in the place, assure himself it was adequate when and if, if and when.'

She glanced over, saw the cat had found the sleep chair, and was putting it to his usual good work. Then she turned, saw Roarke drinking coffee, watching her.

'No comments?'

'Just watching my cop work. I like the look of her when she's on her game.'

'I feel on game – or close. Better.'

'I can see it.'

'Aired out the brain, and the belly. Then filled the belly part with spaghetti and meatballs. McQueen's toasted.'

He smiled at her. 'And what does all this tell you, his errands and caviar?'

'It's pattern, it's movement. The more you know, the more you know. He's had to take time to change his hair, subtle changes to the face, eye color. That means supplies. Wigs and rinses, enhancers. We didn't find anything at the apartment, so he took those with him. Which tells me he means to use them again.'

She stepped back to study the various photos, the IDs he'd used.

'You're always buying me jewelry.'

'Are you angling for a gift?'

'Jesus, no, I can't keep up as it is. She had jewelry at her place. A couple of nice pieces. She was wearing jewelry when I crashed her van. Wouldn't she have had some at his place? She had clothes, shoes, the face and hair gunk. Wouldn't she have left some baubles there?'

He considered. 'Yes. She wanted to be with him, hoped to live with him. When a woman's maneuvering to move in with a man she tends to leave pieces of herself behind. Get him used to it.'

'Really?'

Her tone made him grin. 'Something you were careful not to do initially. I had to make do with a stray button.'

'Living with you wasn't in the plans. Plans change. So saying she left some baubles, he took them. Which means he thinks he can use them, or sell them, pawn them. The locals could look at that.'

'Sounds like busywork, as you don't know what or when he might sell or pawn.'

'Investigations are loaded with busywork. The locals need to find the people he told her to contact for the sound-proofing, the security. He wanted them, specifically for the main apartment. Wouldn't he have used them for the secondary location? No,' she said before Roarke could comment.

'No,' he agreed. 'Because they might have mentioned the other job to his partner, even if he instructed them not to. She was a player, knew the games. Sex, money, or just asking the right question at the right time, and she could have found him out. Better to keep it all separate.'

'So, the locals dig up the first round, and we dig for the second. I need you to search for a second location. The higher level. Classier, more central. He had to arrange it from prison, and without an outside partner. I'll get Feeney on it, piecing through what he's getting on McQueen's coms, but everything coming through is patchy and fractured.'

'It takes time to piece jammed, wiped, and filtered coms back together.'

'I'm not saying otherwise. We work it here; they work it there. The locals and feds do what they do.'

'You want him now,' Roarke decided. 'Before, you wanted him, but it didn't matter who took him down. Now, you want it.'

She didn't answer at first, but walked to the AutoChef for coffee. 'It's not because he killed her,' she began, and turned back to Roarke. 'Not because of the connection.'

'All right.'

'It's because he killed. Because she killed a cop. It's because Darlie's father gave me ice cream while he was fighting back tears. And I guess it's because I remember when I was the kid in the hospital bed with a cop standing over me.'

'I don't care why unless you do. I'm just glad of it, because it's been personal, Eve, all along. And don't tell me it can't be, that you have to stay objective. It's both. It's always both for you. That's why you're so good at it.'

'I want to take him down, but I won't bitch if someone else gets it done.'

'Fair enough. I'll look for your centralized high-rise, high-end location.'

'With a good view of the city. No less than two bedrooms, two baths, attached garage. What time is it in New York?'

He shook his head. 'An hour later than it is here. The earth simply has to revolve, Eve, however annoying it is for you.'

'It can revolve all it wants. I just don't see why people can't settle on the same time.'

'I'll think about that when I'm running your search, and talking to Hong Kong.'

'What time is it there?'

'Morning.'

'See? Crazy.' She walked to her desk, settled down. And contacted Feeney.

It felt good, good and solid, just to see his face, hear his voice.

He said, 'Yo,' and took her right back to New York.

'I got an angle I want you to work. What's that noise?'

'Ball game. No score, bottom of the second. Two outs, runner on first. Mets don't screw up they can clinch the division tonight.'

'Shit, I wanted to see that game.'

'They got a ban on baseball down there?'

'No. Or probably not. Maybe I'll catch it on replay.'

He shook his head sadly. 'Not the same.'

'Better than nothing. Anyway, I'm working on the theory that McQueen's got a second hole down here.'

'Peabody's kept me in the loop. She's doing good. I know McQueen sliced the partner, slithered out. You got the woman and the kid back.'

'She killed a cop, walked right out of the hospital, stole a car out of the lot. She had an hour on us.'

'Yeah, I heard that, too.'

He shifted, paused the game. She realized he was home, not at Central. Which considering the time she should have expected.

Home, she thought. Beer and the ball game.

'I know you've been on this, hard.'

'We're running it round-the-clock, digging out bytes, cleaning them up, piecing them together. The guy's a fucker, but he's no amateur.'

'I'm looking for different bytes. If he's got this place ... and I know he does, Feeney. I know it.'

'I wondered if he had one here back in the day. A grifter has to grift. He couldn't take marks into the place on Murray. But we had him, so digging hard for that got pushed down the line.'

'Everything points to a second location here. So he had to find it, rent, or buy it. To do that he had to communicate

380

with some sort of real estate or rental company, right? Even if he used a go-between, he'd have to communicate. He'd have to wire funds.'

Feeney popped a couple candied almonds, washed them down with beer. 'He wouldn't be running games yet. No time to set them up. So how'd he know he'd need the other digs?'

Yeah, it felt good, Eve thought as she ran it through for him. If she tried hard enough she could imagine herself in his office at Central, bouncing the info, the theories back and forth.

'Makes sense to have an alternate, a safe zone if things go south. He's not going to want to leave Dallas, what with wanting to kill you so bad.' Feeney pursed his lips, tipped the beer back again. 'Yeah, he likes having all his frogs in a line. Always meant to slice the partner. You just made that sooner than later. From what he packed up he'd likely have more wherever he was going. The thing is, he's smart. It's smarter to lay low, take the hike, let you come back home. Wait you out some, then come at you when your guard's down.'

'He needs it. Needs to clinch the division. He can't move on and up until he's taken me. He took the kid because he needed to get off, and because he wanted to rub it in my face. Added to it, it gave him two lures or bargaining chips. Now he's got none.'

'You think he'll go after another kid?'

The possibility had been one more thing eating at her gut all day. 'I think we've got some time. A day, maybe two. He's got to regroup, and he doesn't have a partner running

381

interference. He's pissed, Feeney, and smart enough to know to take time to cool off. Plus, he's got the recording. It won't be the same for him – like watching the game on time delay – but it'll take the edge off.'

'Sick fuck. I'm going to program some key words – rent, lease, real estate, closing, down payment – that kind of thing. If we dig up anything that matches, it'll pop, and we'll focus on cleaning that com. Can't promise you we'll have anything in a day, but we'll be on it.'

'Roarke's searching for applicable units down here. I'm going to start on the security and soundproofing he'd need done. We got lots of pieces – exclusive champagne, his vehicle, make, model, tag, nailed down multiple IDs. The feds are going to freeze his accounts, Feeney. They're leaning that way.'

'Piss him off good.'

'Yeah, and maybe enough for him to screw up. Or maybe shake him enough for him to take the route you talked about before. Go under and wait.'

She hesitated. They'd covered it so she should let him deal with the work, then get back to his game. But she didn't want to let him go.

'So, how's your wife?'

'Same as always. She's out taking one of those pottery classes. Why?'

'No reason.' Jesus, she was actually making small talk. She needed to get the hell back to New York. 'I'll wait to hear from you.'

'Get some sleep, Dallas. A pair of B-and-E men could hide in the shadows under your eyes.'

'I'll get there.'

Since even the idea of sleep made her twitchy, she rose, walked over to Roarke's office. 'He has to have another account.'

'For paying the rent or the mortgage, the expenses of the unidentified second location,' Roarke finished. 'I'm looking.' He sat back, studied her. 'I need to deal with Hong Kong. That should give you time to start your search on the security and soundproofing.'

'That's next.' She left him to it, started her own work.

High-end location, high-end services. Everything above-board on this one, she mused. Everything clean and shiny.

New?

She thought of the cranes all over the city, the new buildings popping up like glossy weeds. Custom-build maybe. He could have the amenities installed as it was constructed, designed with his needs in mind rather than rehabbing, tearing out, patching up.

She started to get up again, give Roarke that angle. And remembered Hong Kong. Maybe he was faster, but she could handle the task.

'Computer, run search on buildings constructed in Dallas within the last two years. Central location, residential accommodations.'

She closed her eyes, went through her list of requirements.

He was there, she thought. Right now, sitting in his new

digs, stewing over the change of plans. But putting things in order, oh yeah, putting everything in place. And telling himself he liked it better this way. This added more challenge, more fun, would make the kill more meaningful.

But wishing, really wishing, he could start his latest collection.

Can't let that happen, she told herself. Can't have another pair of eyes in my head.

When she felt herself drifting, she straightened in her chair. And when the computer announced the results – what the hell was *with* this city that it couldn't make it work with the buildings it already had? – she got up for more coffee.

Roarke found her hunched over the machine. He could all but see the fatigue sitting on her shoulders like stones.

'Finished with Hong Kong?'

'For the moment.'

'I'm working this angle that he bought or leased something recently constructed. He could have the work done during the build, customize the design. The problem is they build too damn much down here, but I'm filing it down.'

'Good thought.' He'd had the same thought himself, and was doing an ancillary search. But didn't see the point in mentioning it. 'Come with me.'

'You got something.'

'It's running, and will continue to run – as yours will,' he said, leaning over and keying in a command, 'without both of us sitting here until blood tears out of our eyes.'

'I need to cross-reference the—'

'Which the machine will do.' He simply lifted her to her feet.

'Look I'm not ready to sleep yet.'

'All right. There are other ways to rest, relax, and take a break.'

'Yeah.' She smirked. 'You'd think that.'

'Sex, sex, and more sex. And you wonder why I married you.'

'You'll just have to put that program on hold,' she said, but he pulled her through the bedroom, bypassing the bed, and into the bathroom.

He'd filled the enormous tub sunk into the floor. She could smell the fragrance of the water, something slightly floral and earthy. Soothing. He'd lit candles so the light shimmered soft, and again soothing.

'A warm bath,' he began. 'Or as I know you, hot. Some quiet, and a VR program designed to relax and restore.'

As she'd taken off her jacket and weapon harness in the office, he simply lifted her shirt over her head. 'Sit and we'll deal with the boots.'

'I can undress myself.'

'There you are, denying me my small pleasures.'

So she sat on the padded stool, let him undress her. When she stepped down, then sank into the pale blue perfumed water, her sigh was long and deep.

'Okay, it's good.'

'Jets on low,' he ordered, and now she moaned as the water pulsed against her aching muscles.

'Okay, even better.'

'Let's shoot for best. Try the VR.'

She didn't want virtual reality, and though it made her feel weak and stupid, she didn't want to be alone. What she wanted was standing there watching her with far too much concern.

'You could stand to rest, relax, and take a break.'

'God, couldn't I.'

'It's a really big tub. You could practically do laps.'

'Then I'll join you. One minute.'

When he left she eased back, looked up. The ceiling wasn't mirrored – thank Jesus – but some sort of reflective material that caught the candlelight and sparked into little stars.

Nice touch.

He came back with two glasses of wine, which she eyed suspiciously.

'Only wine. My word on it.' He set the glasses on the lip to undress.

If he'd tranq'd it, he wouldn't lie about it. So she picked one up, tried a small sip.

'Beer and a ball game.'

'What's that?'

'Beer and a ball game,' she repeated. 'That's how cops wind down from the hard. Not with pool-sized jet tubs and wine.'

'It's terrible how I make you indulge me.'

'Tell me,' she murmured, watching him.

God, his body was so beautiful. Long, lean, carved with muscle. Disciplined, athletic, primal under the exquisitely tailored business suits.

All hers now. Only hers.

The wince and muffled oath he gave when he stepped into the water got a laugh out of her.

'It's not that hot.'

'If I had a lobster, we'd boil it and eat it.'

'You set the temp.'

'So I did, and now, with no lobster in sight, we're boiling my balls.'

He'd set it for her, she thought, so she could soak in the heat and the scent, turn off her mind with some relaxation program. She thought of what she'd overheard him saying to Mira, how he'd looked.

He needed this as much as she did.

'You've probably got more than Hong Kong to deal with.'

Eyes closed, he sipped wine. 'The advantage of holding the reins is you can choose when to put them down for a bit.'

'Maybe you should try the VR.'

He opened his eyes. 'Actual reality suits me fine here and now.'

As they faced each other across the bubbling water, she rubbed her foot along his leg. 'One way or another, we'll be going home within a couple days.'

'Couldn't be soon enough.'

'Oh, so right there with you. I guess we have to go find cowboy boots for Peabody. She'd get a charge, and Feeney said she was doing good.'

'I'm sorry, perhaps the wine's going to my head. Are you saying I'm going shopping with my wife?'

'Don't get used to it, pal.'

'How about a ten-gallon hat for Feeney?'

The image of Feeney in a cowboy hat released a laugh that nearly had her choking on her wine. 'You did that on purpose.'

'Spurs and chaps for McNab. Glow-in-the-dark.'

She laughed again, sank to her chin. 'And I don't even know what chaps are.'

But the laugh, he noted with pleasure, put a sparkle in her eyes.

'We'll take bolo ties back for the bullpen,' he continued.

'Oh, Jesus, the horror.'

'One of those little skirts with the fringe for Mavis.'

'She probably already has a dozen.'

Virtual reality, her ass, she decided as he tossed out more foolish suggestions – some of which he probably intended to follow up on. Soaking here in quietly churning water, candle stars sparking overhead, talking about nothing important, nothing tragic. *That* was restorative.

When she'd finished the wine, when the water began to cool, they stepped out. Before she could reach for a towel he wrapped one, warm and soft, around her.

'Why don't we watch some screen for a while?'

She turned, opening the towel, wrapping him in with her. 'We could do that. Is that the next step of spaghetti and meatballs?'

'That was the plan.'

She looked up at him; everything inside him yearned. 'But

apparently I missed a step,' he murmured, then laid his lips on hers.

'You never miss a step.'

So he deepened the kiss, let himself fall into the moment with her damp body pressed so eagerly to his, with the dreamy scent of the water clinging to her skin.

When he lifted her, the towel fell away.

No words now; they'd both had enough of them. Enough of storms and soothing. She stayed wrapped around him on the bed, holding on, holding on while her lips roamed his face. Already stirred, already lost, he took his hands over her.

Quick, quick, no time for thinking, he took her up, felt her body arch and shudder. Accept.

Strong mind, strong needs, he thought. He'd fill them, fill her and himself. For a little while the ugly stains of the day would be cleansed.

For a little while, pleasure and passion would smother pain.

His heart drummed against hers. It brought her a thrill, that hard, frantic beat. But more, it restored. His life, beating there against hers. Their lives.

Nothing could change that, no nightmare, no shame, no poison in the blood. She'd brought herself out of the dark, but she'd come to crave the light he'd flooded into her world.

That light shot through her like a thousand arrows when he pushed her to climax.

She cried out, and he heard the edge of triumph in the sound. And he understood. She could feel and want to reach and take, she could give, no matter what had been done to her. She could live and thrive. She could want him.

That she could, did, would, humbled him. Enraptured him.

She rolled, sliding over him, feeding and feasting until he was mad for her. When he dragged her up, she straddled him, took him deep. And rode, rode, rode him like a stallion under the whip.

He saw, before his vision blurred, the strong curve of her body, and the fierce joy on her face.

She collapsed on him, body limp, breath tearing.

'God,' she managed. 'Thank God, thank God, thank God.'

'I think I rate at least an "I appreciate it."'

'I appreciate it.' She kept her face buried against his throat. 'I thought I might clutch. You know, it's been . . . a day. But it was just the way it should be.'

'Darling Eve.' Smiling, he stroked her back. 'I was afraid I might clutch.'

'We didn't. We're just too damn good at it.' She shifted, tucked her head in the crook of his shoulder. 'It was a really excellent step.'

'Quite possibly better than the spaghetti and meatballs.'

'It's neck-and-neck.' She lay quiet for a moment. 'I know you want me to sleep. I'm just not . . . we should watch some screen, finish all the steps.'

'All right, then. How about some porn?'

She laughed as he'd meant her to, then elbowed him. 'Perv. Didn't you just have porn?'

'It shows what you know about fine art and lowly pornography.'

'Then let's leave that step on the high note. Feeney had the ball game on. The Mets could clinch the division tonight. They've got to have a replay, time delay, something.'

'Baseball it is.' He ordered the screen on, drew the throw at the foot of the bed over them.

She went under in the top of the fifth. He wondered how she'd held out that long.

He ordered the lights on low in case she woke, ordered the screen off. And holding her, let himself slip into sleep with her.


Closer than she knew, Isaac McQueen roamed his new spaces. It was, very precisely, what he'd wanted and arranged – the colors, fabrics, materials, layout.

And still he felt caged.

She'd put him in again, that bitch Dallas. Just another run of luck for her. And the total fucking stupidity of Sylvia.

At least she was dead. Her stupidity, her unending *neediness* wouldn't be a problem anymore. She'd had her uses, but he'd find another when the time was right. One he could be more sure of, one he wouldn't have to charm and train and instruct from prison.

That had been the problem. He hadn't made a mistake with his choice. Because of Dallas he simply hadn't had the opportunity to correctly train that choice.

*Next time,* he thought, circling his hand to keep his brandy moving in its snifter.

He was still in control of the situation. He'd planned for the unforeseen, hadn't he? Of course, without Sylvia's idiocy, he'd have bad little Darlie to entertain him right now. Nothing kept him more in tune than a bad little girl.

He walked to the window, looked down at the city, sipping his brandy, wondering how many bad little girls walked the streets. He only needed one for now. Just one.

He could find one, of course. He was so very much smarter, better, wilier than the cops. He could take one, just one, and christen his new home.

Better not. No, better not, he reminded himself. He felt too rushed, too upset. Too fucking *angry* to work properly tonight.

He'd have to make do with the pale, bloodless substitute of the recording.

He mulled it over. He'd watch it and imagine how he'd feel when he forced Dallas to watch it with him. That would perk things up.

He decided to make himself a little snack. For a time he simply wandered the kitchen, unable to choose. So many choices, he thought. Too many choices.

Ridiculous. He brushed off the uneasy sensation, the temporary lapse. He knew exactly what he wanted. He *always* knew.

He selected a few cheeses, some berries, carefully sliced rounds from a baguette, calming a little itch of panic at the base of his spine with the homey chore.

He did *love* this kitchen, he thought as he worked, the high sheens, the smooth surfaces. He'd enjoy using it for a week or two.

Really, this was a much better location, better plan. Things had worked out precisely the right way. Precisely.

Then soon enough, with Dallas floating in the river – a real pity he'd been denied that tradition with Sylvia – he'd move on. As much as he wanted New York, for spite if nothing else, he had to consider another venue altogether.

London perhaps, he thought as he carried his tray into the living area. He'd always planned to spend some time in London. He set his tray on the coffee table, unfolded a wide, white linen napkin. Ran his fingers over the spotless and smooth material.

Yes, London. Carnaby Street, Big Ben, Piccadilly Circus.

And all those rosy-cheeked bad girls.

'Screen on,' he ordered, trying out a public school British accent. Pleased with the sound, he laughed, and continued in character. 'Play Darlie.'

He swirled brandy, nibbled on cheese and berries. And discovered that the pale substitute worked quite well if he just had the right mind-set.

He decided then and there to make one titled 'Eve Dallas.' He imagined the staging, the props, the lighting. He considered writing some dialogue, for both of them.

Wouldn't it be fun to force her to speak his words?

He could barely wait to produce it, direct it. And view it, over and over after he'd killed her.

# 21

Near dawn she dreamed. Trapped in the dark, whispers and whimpers all around her. Cold, so cold, and the bite of the shackles clamped on her wrists and ankles.

He was out there, and the knowing carved a bleeding gash of fear in her belly.

Not like this, she thought as she yanked and strained against the shackles. A thousand ways to die, but not like this, and not at his hand.

Light oozed into the room, slipping dirty red through cracks and fissures to smear the dark like blood.

And she learned it could be worse to see.

They huddled all around her, all the girls, all those hopeless, empty eyes. They sat, staring and shivering in the icy room of her nightmares. All of them had her face. The child's face.

She fought harder, twisting, dragging against the restraints. She heard – felt – the bone snap. One of the girls shrieked, and each of them clutched her arm.

'It's not happening, not happening. It's not real.'

'It's as real as you make it.' Mira sat in one of the blue scoop chairs from her office, crossed her pretty legs.

'You have to help.'

'Of course. It's what I do. Now, how does being here like this make you feel?'

'Fuck feelings. We have to get out!'

'Angry then,' Mira said placidly, and sipped tea from a china cup. 'But more, I think. What's under that anger, Eve? Let's dig it out.'

'Get us out. Can't you see how scared they are?'

'They?'

'I'm scared. I'm scared.'

'Progress!' With a pleased smile, Mira lifted her teacup in salute. 'Now let's talk about that.'

'There's no time.' Her head swiveled side to side while panic gnawed at her, belly and bone. 'He'll come back.'

'He'll only come back if you let him. Well, that's all the time we have for today.'

'For God's sake don't leave us like this. Take the girls. Take them out of here. They don't deserve to be here.'

'No.' Her voice gentle as a kiss, Mira shook her head. 'You don't.'

'What about me!' The woman, the partner, the mother stood, her throat gaping and wet with blood. 'Look what you did to me.'

'I didn't kill you.' Eve cringed while the girls, all the girls curled into defensive balls.

'Stupid bitch, it's all your fault.' When she slapped one of the girls aside, Eve felt the blow. 'Stupid, ugly, worthless bitch. You should never have been born.'

'But I was. How could you hate what came out of you? How could you hate what needed you? How could you let him touch me?'

'Whine, whine, whine, all you ever did was whine. You're nothing but a mistake, and now I'm dead because you're alive.' The face changed, image over image. Stella to Sylvia, Sylvia to Stella. 'You deserved everything he did to you, everything he's going to do.'

'He's dead! He can't do anything because he's dead.'

'Stupid little cunt. Then how did you get here?'

'Boy, nobody lays the guilt on like a mom.'

With a sympathetic smile, Peabody crouched in front of Eve. 'How're you doing?'

'How the hell does it look like I'm doing? Get these kids to safety. Call for backup. Get me a weapon. I need a weapon.'

'Jeez, Dallas, take it easy.'

Incensed, Eve yanked at the shackles. 'Take it easy? What the fuck's wrong with you? Get off your ass and do your job.'

'I am doing my job. We're all doing the job. See?'

She could, like a dream over a dream, see her bullpen, cops at desks, in cubes. And Feeney in his rumpled suit in the middle of the clashing colors and constant movement of EDD. Above them Whitney stood, his hands clasped behind his back. Watchful.

'Officer needs assistance,' Eve murmured, dizzy.

'You're getting it, Dallas. Best we got, just like you taught me. Look at my guy.' She grinned and pointed to McNab,

396

who pranced around on wildly striped ankle skids, talking incessantly in e-geek. 'That's how he works. Doesn't he have the cutest skinny butt? Now your guy, he's got it rough right now.'

Eve saw Roarke behind a wall of glass. At his desk he worked a comp, two smart screens, a headset. His 'link signaled, and codes and figures whizzed by on the wall screens.

He had his hair tied back. His eyes were fierce and intense, and even from a distance she could see they were filled with fatigue and worry.

'Roarke.' Everything in her spilled out in the single word, the love, the fear, the anguish.

'It's hard to think really clear, catch the little details when you're that worried. He loves you. You hurt, he hurts.'

'I know. Roarke.'

'Gotta break the glass, I guess.' Peabody smiled. 'You're my hero.'

'I'm nobody's hero.'

Peabody gave the wrist cuffs a tap. 'Not like this, you aren't.'

'Get me out of these!'

'How?'

'Find the key. Find the goddamn key and get me out.'

'Wish I could, Dallas, but that's the whole thing. You've got to find it. Better find the key before he gets another one. Before he gets you. You've never been stupid. Don't let her make you stupid.'

'How am I supposed to find anything when I'm locked in?

How—' She broke off, cringing back when she heard the footsteps. 'He's coming.'

'He never left.' The mother walked to the door.

'Don't open it. Please!'

'Whine, whine, whine.' She opened the door.

McQueen walked in, flashed a charming smile. 'Hello, little girl,' he said in her father's voice.

And bleeding from a dozen wounds, he came for her.

She bolted up in bed, clutching at her throat. The breath wouldn't come, no matter how wildly her heart hammered, the breath wouldn't come.

She didn't even feel the cat butting his head fiercely against her side.

Roarke burst into the room. He leaped to the bed, clamped his hands on her arms. 'I'm here. Eve. Look at me.'

She did, she was. She saw his face, his eyes violently blue against bone-white skin. She saw fear, and struggled to say his name.

'Breathe. Goddamn it.' He shook her, hard, lifting her half off the bed.

The shock of it unlocked her throat. When her breath exploded out, his arms wrapped around her. 'It's all right. You're all right now. Just hold on to me.'

'He came for us.'

'No, baby, no. He's not here. It's just you and me. Just you and me.'

'You were there, behind the glass.'

'I'm here, right here.' He cupped her face so she could see him, feel him. 'You're safe.' His own breathing unsteady, he kissed her brow, her cheeks, wrapped the throw around her.

'The room. I was in that room. He locked me up. I don't know which one. They were all there. The girls. All the girls were me.'

'It's over.'

But it's not, she thought, and closed her eyes. It's not over.

'I'm sorry. I shouldn't have left you alone.'

She opened her eyes, looked around. The hotel, she assured herself. The bedroom with the lights low and soft. The cat – he'd brought her the cat – and Galahad sat at her side watchful as a guard dog.

'Where did you go?'

'I had some work. Bloody work.' He bit off the words, his voice raw. 'I didn't want to wake you, so I went up to the office. You'd slept quiet, so I thought . . . I shouldn't have left you.'

She studied his face now, looked beyond herself and into him. Guilt, fear, worry, anger. All that, she thought. All of that in him. 'Did I scream?'

'No. You started to thrash and struggle, and when I got here—'

'How did you know? How did you know to come?'

'I had you on monitor.'

'You were watching me sleep,' she said slowly, 'while you worked.'

'I'd hoped you'd sleep a bit longer. It's early yet, barely dawn.'

'But you were working, and watching me.'

'It was hardly voyeuristic.'

She waved him, and the edge in his voice away. 'You were worried about me, so you had to keep an eye on me while you tried to work.'

She thought of how he'd looked behind that glass wall, handling so many tasks at once with weariness on his face.

'Of course I was worried.'

'Because I might have a nightmare.'

'You *did* have a nightmare, so—'

She waved him off again, and this time shoved to her feet. 'So you have to monitor me like I'm some sort of sick kid, and feel guilty because you actually took a little time, before the fucking sun came up, to deal with your own work. Well, that's just enough. They've screwed us up long enough, and it's got to stop. It's going to stop.'

He watched her storm around the room and wondered if she knew she was gloriously naked, and absolutely shining with outrage. And watching her he felt more at peace than he had since she'd walked into his office in New York days before.

'I'm not putting up with this,' she continued. 'You can't even go out and buy up a solar system without worrying I'll fall apart. How are you supposed to get anything done?'

'Actually, I'm not in the market for a solar system right at the moment.'

'Bad things happen, who knows better? Bad, unspeakable, ugly things happen whether you deserve them or not. Your father was a bastard, and he put you through hell, but you don't sit around whining about it.'

'No. Neither do you.'

'That's right.' She jabbed a finger at him. 'That's fucking-A right, and it's just more crap that needs to be flushed. I am not a whiner. I'm not weak and stupid. I'm a goddamn cop.'

'To the bone.'

'Damn straight, so this subconscious shit better latch the hell on because I'm *done* letting it kick me around. I'm *done* letting it put that look on your face. I'm a goddamn cop, and it doesn't matter why I am or how I am. What matters is doing the job, doing it right, doing it smart, doing it all the way through. What matters is you and me. What matters is you, because I fucking love you.'

'I fucking love you, too.'

'Bet your ass, you do, and you wouldn't have fallen for some sniveling coward.'

'I wouldn't,' he agreed. 'I didn't.'

'So.' She took her first clear breath. 'That's it. That's settled.'

She slapped her hands on her hips, then looked down with a frown as flesh met flesh. 'I'm naked.'

'Are you really?' He felt a laugh in his chest, a marvelous sensation. 'Well, so you are. I don't mind a bit.'

'I bet.' She snatched up the robe he'd obviously laid at the foot of the bed before he'd gone off to try to work. She punched her arms through the sleeves. 'I'm so pissed off.'

'Is that a fact?'

She went to the AutoChef, programmed two coffees. Then, studying the cat, who studied her, added a bowl of milk. She set the bowl on the floor, carried the coffee to Roarke.

'Thanks.'

'I'm not saying you can't worry. Worry's part of the deal, I get it. But I don't want to be responsible for worry weighing you down like it has since we got here.'

'You're not responsible.'

'I let it screw me up, so it screwed you up. I've got to get a handle on it. My mommy didn't love me, well boo-frig-ging-hoo.'

He drew her down beside him. 'We both know it's a bit more complicated than that.'

'Whatever, I'm not letting her get me so tangled up I can't think straight. I keep you on edge. And no more guilt. If you're going to be guilty it's going to be about something I want to punch you for, not for getting some work done one flight up.'

'What matters is you – as you said to me. But I'll try not to feel guilty unless it's a punchable offense.'

He draped an arm around her as they sat drinking coffee. 'You slept well,' he commented, 'until the last.'

'Credit the full spaghetti-and-meatballs treatment. Who won the game?'

'I haven't a clue. I was right behind you.'

'So we both got some sleep, that's a good start. Let's make a deal. Let's get this son of a bitch and go home.'

'Gladly.'

'I need to suit up and look over what we've got again. Because if there's anything to this subconscious shit, I'm missing something. We're missing something.'

'Give us a minute,' he murmured when she started to rise.

So she sat with him, with him and the cat, drinking coffee and watching the sky lighten into day.

In her office, she had a second cup of coffee and studied her board. She hadn't wanted breakfast, and he'd decided not to push.

'Are you going in this morning?' he asked her.

'In? Oh, to Ricchio's house. I'm not sure. Here's the thing. We got Melinda back, and that was the lure. That was the specific reason to request I come here to work with them. Continuing to work with them wouldn't be a problem for Ricchio, and probably not the feds, though they've all had time to study up on McQueen and don't necessarily need me there. But unless we're idiots, it's very possible he'll snatch another kid, then hang her over my head to get me where he wants me. Why not just stay put and finish it?'

She shrugged. 'But I think we both work better from here, so why go in until and unless we have something solid to add?'

'Working from here suits me. That search you wanted on potential locations is in.'

'Okay. Look, why don't you take care of the half a million things you've been letting dangle in Roarke's Empire of Everything?'

'Catchy title. I may use it one day.'

'I'm going to go back to the beginning. I want to go over all the data, the interviews, time lines, the works. Basically do a solid review, and that'll take a while. You can send me the search results, and I'll add them in.'

'All right. But I have Summerset and Caro, and a number of other people dealing with the dangling half a million in REE. So if you come up with anything, or want something looked into, let me know.'

'Yeah.'

She went to her desk, called up the incident report and Bree's statement on the night Melinda was abducted.

The data remained fresh in her head, she admitted. She knew all the details here, just couldn't see anything she or the Dallas cops, the feds, had missed. But she rechecked the time lines, read over the interview with the bar owner on Sarajo, the statement from the neighbor.

She filtered in, sifted through all the information Peabody, Feeney, and the New York team had accumulated. She went step by step, stage by stage, retracing her time in Texas, reviewing every fact, speculation, and probability on McQueen and his movements.

She answered her 'link with her mind still steeped in it.

'Dallas.'

'McQueen's made contact,' Ricchio told her. 'He wants to talk to you. Should we link him up?'

'Give me a second.' She rushed over to Roarke's office. 'McQueen through Ricchio. Can you try a trace from here?'

'Yes.'

'I'll have him linked.' She went back to her desk, sat. 'I'm set.'

'Do you want to block your video?'

'No, let him see me.'

'We're linking.'

She angled in. She wanted him to get a good look at her. She was rested, alert. She was ready.

'Eve.'

'Isaac. Really sorry I missed you yesterday.'

'I feel the same. That's why I'm making arrangements for us to get together very soon.'

'How about now? I happen to be free.'

'Patience. I have a few more preparations to make so we can have a perfect reunion. As you know I had to dispose of the help, so I'm a little shorthanded.'

'Yeah, you were a little rushed, not so careful this time around, Isaac. When you go back to New York, it'll only be a jumping-off point. This time it'll be off-planet accommodations for you.'

'Oh, I have something else entirely in mind.'

'Such as.'

'Tell you what, I'll tell you all about it when you're gracing my guest room. Meanwhile, I thought you might enjoy a preview of an exciting home vid I produced recently.'

The screen flashed from blank to the obscenity in McQueen's bedroom. Darlie's screams and pleading sobs shattered the air.

Eve forced herself to watch, willed herself to give him no reaction while the child inside her wept as piteously as the child on screen.

It shut off abruptly.

'We'll watch the whole thing when you're here,' McQueen told her. 'I'll make popcorn. TTFN.'

She held on when Ricchio came on, his face like stone. 'Jammed and filtered. We're cutting through it.'

'Lovers Lane in Highland Park.' Roarke came on, split screen. 'He's moving.'

'Copy that!' Ricchio called out. 'I'll dispatch now. Dallas?'

She shook her head. 'I'll wait to hear from you.'

She ended the call, sat very still.

'I'm all right,' she said when Roarke came in, brought her a glass of water.

'You're not, and pretending to be isn't helpful.'

'I already had that in my head, already knew what he — they — did to her. I'm not going to let it mess me up.' But she drained the glass of water. 'I'm not heading out because he won't be there. They have to go, have to try, but he won't be anywhere near there.'

'No,' Roarke agreed.

'His new location won't be near there either, so we can eliminate that. Highland Park, right? Lovers fucking Lane. That was deliberate.'

'Yes. Do you want Mira?'

'Yes, soon – but not for me, for this. To help me refine the profile. All those years he kept what he did, what he could do locked in. He could only share his brilliance, as he sees it, with the women he intended to kill anyway. Now he's found release and enjoyment in bragging. He contacted me to shake me up, to make sure we're still connected, but also to share. His control isn't what it was, and that's an advantage for us. It also makes him more unpredictable.'

Steadier, she thought. She was steady enough. 'If you could send Mira all the updates, this 'link transmission. Ask her to review and reprofile. Then we can talk it through, pass it to the locals and feds.'

'All right. Don't watch it again.'

'You know I have to.'

'Then give it some time. You said he contacted you, with that, to shake you, to brag. Consider he may have also sent it to switch your focus, to have you spend time studying that brutality rather than pursuing other leads.'

'You're probably right. I'm going to finish my review, run some fresh probabilities. It's unlikely anything on that preview will help us nail down his current location. But he confirmed for me he has one, with a guest room.'

She nodded, slowly now. 'He's slipping, and I won't.'

She dug back in, reviewing notes, making new ones, checking maps. She ran a probability and got a high enough result to allow her to eliminate the Highland Park area. She adjusted the property list she and Roarke had compiled, then began the laborious task of checking with soundproofing companies.

'I'll help you with that,' Roarke told her when he saw what she was doing. 'But the deal is you take a break. It's nearly one, and you've been up since dawn without anything to eat.'

'I'm not getting anywhere. All of the locations on my list had soundproofing during the build. Most of yours, the same, or during a remodel. These sorts of buildings, people expect soundproofing, so he wouldn't have to hire it out.'

'Then we'll move on to security and electronics. After we eat.'

'Yeah. I'll get it. I need to let this sit and simmer some. If I missed something, if there's a key, I'm not finding it.'

'What are we having?'

'I don't know.' She checked the AutoChef's menu without much interest. 'They got nachos.' She perked up a bit. 'Nachos are supposed to be good here, right? And this tortilla soup. Not bad.'

'I'm in,' Roarke said, thinking that with a messy plate of nachos and the soup she'd have to sit to eat.

She ordered it up, got drinks out of the office fridgie. And wandered around her board again.

'The beginning, the beginning again.' She sat, scooped up a loaded nacho. 'He's settled in New York. Excellent hunting ground. He's got money stashed all over the place – good, solid money – but he's settled in his working-class building. We haven't found a second location in New York, but that doesn't mean he didn't have one. Higher end again. He gets caught, gets caged. But he finds people in the system to exploit. That didn't start with Stibble and the guard. People running errands, giving him unrecorded access to coms. That takes money.

You've got to keep the errand boys happy. So if he owned the second location, wouldn't he sell it? Invest the money?'

'Possibly.'

'Because if he had another, and I think he did, why didn't he go there, too? Why just where I took him down? He could've used that instead of a hotel. If someone else is living there, he just does what he did to Schuster and Kopeski. More fun anyway. But if he sold it, it doesn't mean anything. Reaching,' she said, pushing her hair back.

'Maybe, maybe not. Keep going.'

'I'm not sure where I'm going, but okay. He killed the New York partner before I took him down. Our best theory is he kills his partner before he switches locations. But there wasn't any sign he planned to leave that apartment or New York. He had his collection there.'

'He was bored with that partner.'

'Yeah, or she got on his nerves or screwed up. But say he was bored with her, wouldn't he have another on the string? A replacement, at least potentials?'

'I'd say yes. Yes,' he repeated, pleased they both seemed to be thinking more clearly. 'And wouldn't he want or need another place – one where he didn't have to worry about the partner dropping by, or the potential becoming too curious about that locked room. A place where he could entertain her, begin to train her, develop the bond.'

'A place more suited to his tastes.'

'I could find it for you, given time,' Roarke considered. 'But I don't see how it would help you at this point.'

'Just additional data. He's nested in New York. It's his kind of town, and he's having one hell of a run there. He's listening to the media reports on the Collector, how the cops aren't any closer. Oh, he's loving it, maybe about to get a new mommy, too. Life is excellent. Then some poor bastard gets mugged and murdered outside his building, and I show up at his door.'

'He couldn't have planned on that.'

'No, and that's what he does. He plans. Anticipates, prepares for contingencies while he' – she trailed off with a spoonful of soup halfway to her mouth – 'plans.'

'Someone got a buzz,' Roarke commented.

'He plans.' She pushed up, strode to the board. 'That control, anticipation. Routine, procedure. It's what made him so good at what he did. What did he have to do in prison but plan? Oh, he's going to get out. It may take time, but that's all right. He wants everything in place first. It takes time to groom the errand boys, time to get the rhythm of the prison, and show what a good boy he is so he gets a few perks. Time to find the partner, start the training. Time to set it all up, so he can move right ahead.'

Roarke saw precisely where she'd landed. 'We haven't been looking back far enough for the location.'

'No. We've been looking back a couple of years. Not far enough.'

'A dozen years is a long time, and clever. Who'd look that far back?'

'Not that far.' She laid a finger on Melinda's picture. 'Here, right here. She went to visit him. Whatever plans he made prior, he adjusted. She was the key. A sign from whatever perverted god he worships. He took her – the last he took – and I freed her. Melinda from Dallas. I knew that would trip his switch. I knew it had. How did I miss this?'

'Bollocks. You didn't miss a thing. You didn't even suspect he had another hole until yesterday. Why would you?'

He got up, went to her desk. 'When did she visit him?'

'August 'fifty-five.'

'Then we start there.'

'New construction. He had plenty of time, why not customize it, get exactly what he wanted?'

She pulled out her 'link, nearly tagged Peabody before she remembered. Dutifully, she contacted Ricchio. 'I might have something.'

She let Roarke handle the search while Ricchio set up a team to do the same from his end.

'The feds are about to freeze the accounts,' she told Roarke. 'This bought us a couple hours. They'll hold off that long.'

'But no pressure,' he muttered.

She started to snap back, then got a look at him. Hair tied back, working the comp, a smart screen, data flashing on the wall screen across the room.

But no glass wall, she thought. And no drag of worry and fatigue on his face.

Instead of snapping she walked over, leaned down, and kissed the top of his head.

411

He glanced up at her. 'I haven't found it yet.'

'But you will. I'm calling Mira in. She may be able to help us. And Feeney. I should let him know where we are.'

'Go do it somewhere else.'

When she brought Mira up, Eve gave Roarke another glance. 'Don't talk to him,' she warned. 'He can get bitchy when he's in this deep. I don't know if we have any of that tea stuff.'

'I had it stocked, and I don't get bitchy. Bloody, buggering *hell*.'

Eve just rolled her eyes and got the tea.

'Thanks.'

'We can take this downstairs.'

'No. The board's helpful to me, too.' But Mira spoke quietly as Roarke switched to Irish and mutters. 'He's devolving.'

'No, he just gets more Irish when he's frustrated.'

'Not Roarke.' Mira smiled a little. 'McQueen. He spent a long time in prison, and as many do, he grew used to the routine, the structure. Freedom after confinement can be frightening, overstimulating, leave you floundering. How do you make a decision when making decisions has been taken away?'

'But he made decisions in prison. He chose a partner, chose a location, chose his first victim with Melinda.'

'Yes, but even those were illogical. He's first and foremost a pedophile, but he risks his freedom with a plan to kill you.'

'I stopped him. He's also made of ego.'

'Yes. I would have expected him – and so did you – to go

under first, to hunt next, and to come after you last. He put you first. And since he's been out, he's acted on impulse, he's been impatient, broken pattern. His confidence is broken. He denies it, but his actions are rash ... inelegant. Contacting you today, showing you the video—'

Eve looked Mira in the eye. 'I'm okay.'

'Showing you tells me he's fighting to get his confidence back, to show you how confident he is.'

'Ties and olives.'

Mira simply stared. 'I'm sorry?'

'He's bought a lot of stuff, duplicated it, which doesn't go with his previous pattern. Like dozens of ties, multiple jars of olives. Other stuff. And Melinda said he went blank for a minute after he got the call from Sylvia. Pulled out the knife, then just went blank. Like he forgot what he wanted to do.'

'It fits.' Mira nodded. 'Freedom after a long confinement can be stressful even though deeply desired. Decisions are more difficult. Adjustments when a factor changes unexpectedly, even more so.'

Like Eve she studied the board. 'In my opinion, he'll continue to devolve. His actions will deviate more and more from the pattern he once carefully adhered to. And he'll become more violent. If he abducts another girl, he'll be more brutal. He may kill her because the rape and the violence won't be enough, not for much longer. Nothing will be enough but you. He'll take greater risks to get to you. As long as you exist, he can't feel complete. You punished him. In a terrible way, you're the mother now.'

413

'Jesus. I'd gotten some of the rest, but I hadn't gone there.'

'You don't fit the pattern. You're not old enough, you're not an addict, you're not weak or susceptible to his charms. But. His mother abused him, punished him, and more important, for many years had control of him.'

'So he had to eliminate her, replace her periodically with someone he controls.'

'It's most probable, and my opinion, you're the only woman to take control away from him since his mother.'

'And I'm damn well going to do it again.' She glanced at her wrist unit. 'Less than an hour till the feds freeze his money. What will he do when—'

'Moot point,' Roarke told her. 'I've got him.'

'You've got some locations that fit all the parameters?'

'No. Do you honestly think it would've taken me that long just to pull out possibilities? It's a wonder I tolerate your insults. I've got *the* location.'

'How did you determine?' She rolled her eyes when his narrowed. 'I'm not questioning your big, sexy skills. I have to be able to relay to Ricchio and the feds, convince them you're right.'

'I am right. He put a deposit on a projected two-bedroom, two-and-a-half-bath apartment, with gourmet kitchen and private elevator – sixty-sixth floor – in September of 'fifty-five.'

'Why didn't you see the transfer for the deposit before? It had to be a hefty chunk.'

'Because, as you suspected, he had another account.'

Since she could clearly see he was annoyed he'd missed it the first time, she kept it zipped.

'A corporate brokerage account,' Roarke continued, 'and he has a law firm handling the deposits and transfers. A law firm out of Costa Rica. I know that because when I found this location, I did another search, a bloody miserable one,' he added grimly, 'and was able to track it back to him. The apartment's leased by Executive Travel, yet another dummy corporation, which has made him a nice return by renting it to legitimate corporations for overnight or short-term stays or meetings.'

'Then it's—'

'However' – Roarke ignored the interruption – 'the apartment was taken off the market for refurbishing three months ago. Which is when he added the electronics. It remains unavailable for lease.'

'We got him.'

'As I said. Now, call off the feds, Lieutenant, and call in the dogs. Let's go finish this.'

# 22

Here's how I want it to go.' Once again Eve headed toward Ricchio's briefing room at double time. Roarke strode beside her; Mira scrambled to keep up.

'We have the data, so we run the show. While I'm sorting that out with Ricchio and the feds, I want Roarke to set up all the data – the building schematics you accessed, the blueprints for the apartment, everything we have on building security and his personal security. I'm going to have you break off with whoever Ricchio picks from his e-men, and head up the security team.'

'Are you now?'

'They're going to listen to you because unless they're idiots they've figured out by now you're better and faster than anybody they've got. And because I'm going to tell them to.'

'She's a team player,' Roarke said in an aside to Mira, and got the beady eye from his wife.

'We're going to take down his security, disable his elevator, and lock down the whole damn building without alerting him,' Eve pointed out. 'And we're going to need to do it slick, fast, and at exactly the right time. That's for you. I know you can do it. I don't know if Ricchio's men can.'

'You can do that?' Mira asked Roarke. 'Isolate McQueen's apartment, and shut down the entire building?'

'Just a hobby of mine.'

'I want Mira to start it off,' Eve continued, giving Roarke another, beadier eye, 'updating the profile. I want everybody on this op to know what they're going after. Take your time, punch it in. The last op went to hell, so some of them are going to be edgy, some overeager.'

'Understood.'

'Then let's do it.'

She headed straight to Ricchio. 'I need a minute, Lieutenant.'

'Sure.' He nodded at the detective beside him. 'Have them picked up. We identified and located the two people McQueen told the partner to contact for security and sound-proofing. I'm having them brought in for questioning.'

'Excellent.'

'We've also interviewed the clerk at the wine store where McQueen purchased the champagne, wine, caviar, and we have the security discs showing him in the store and making the purchase. The clerk carried the stuff out to the car, and confirms McQueen was driving the Orion.'

'Also excellent, and adds to the time line.'

'We also ran down the knife and sheath, purchased that same day.'

'Busy boy. Lieutenant, I've brought my profiler. I'd like her to brief everyone on the changes in McQueen's pattern and profile. It's important they understand the target and his current state of mind.'

'Agreed.'

'My consultant is setting up the data.' She paused as the feds came in, turned to include them. 'We have the building blueprints, the layout of McQueen's apartment, the security. He'll need some good men,' she said to Ricchio, 'to work with him. Disabling the security – McQueen's apartment as well as building security – shutting down his elevator, and the timing of it, will be key.'

'We have men for that,' Nikos put in.

'Good, send them to Roarke. He'll coordinate.'

'He—'

'He's the best there is,' Eve interrupted.

'I'm going to agree with that,' Ricchio put in. 'Stevenson isn't easily impressed, and he'd draft Roarke into his division if he could.'

Not an idiot, Eve thought. 'Roarke's already familiar with the layout, knows the security system as it's one of his makes. McQueen's personal security will be trickier, which also goes to timing and the skill of the tech. We wouldn't be having this briefing right now without the data accessed by my tech.'

'Agreed,' Laurence said before Nikos could speak. 'He'll have whatever he needs from us.'

'Good.' Eve waited a beat. 'We'll need to establish whether or not McQueen's inside before we disable and lock down.'

'It sounds like you assume you're heading this op, Dallas. The last one you headed ended up with a high-speed chase, a dead cop, and a dead suspect. Which brings up the matter of Detective Price.' Nikos glanced toward him. 'And the decision to include him on this operation.'

'My detective's actions saved a child from serious injury, possibly death. Don't you begin to question his actions or my judgment, Agent.'

'You want to hang the failure of that operation on someone, you hang it on me,' Eve snapped out. 'Or maybe you'd have just let that kid end up roadkill.'

'I do hang it on you, and also suggest Detective Price may not be mentally prepared to—'

'Oh give it a rest, Nikos. Seriously.' Laurence rubbed his forehead. 'If you've got to blame somebody, blame the goddamn dog. But the fact is, we did everything right, and it went south. We need to catch up on this second location. Dallas has the data.'

Nikos set her jaw. 'We have to analyze the data and confirm we've got McQueen's location in the first damn place.'

'It is confirmed,' Eve tossed back. 'You want chapter and verse?'

'I want facts. Verified.'

'McQueen's paying for the unit, and has been paying for it since September of 'fifty-five – a month after Melinda went to see him at Rikers. Construction of the building and the apartment was completed in February of the following year. I'm not finished,' Eve said as Nikos started to interrupt.

Tired, Eve noted, edgy, with the stress and strain of the last few days clear on Nikos's face. She'd just have to suck it up, Eve thought. Like the rest of them.

'The payments, money from the rentals from corporate tenants, the maintenance, and so on are handled and arranged by Ferrer, Arias and Garza, a law firm out of Costa Rica – Heredía, to be precise. That's something you might want to look into. The unit's owned by Executive Travel, which appears to conscientiously pay its taxes and fees – also through the law firm. He uses a local cleaning service, the same used by the partner at the duplex – both paid for through the law firm and billed to Executive Travel, which lists what turns out to be a mail drop as its address. Leases are arranged by building management, for a fee. They also report to the law firm.'

Well aware cops' ears were tuned in to her recitation, she kept her focus on Nikos and pressed her point. 'This is data my consultant accessed, a great deal of it in the travel time between our hotel and this room. If you want it, he can get you the name of every employee in the law firm and whether they wear boxers or fucking briefs. He's just that good. And he looked for said data because I deduced McQueen had the second location. I'm just that good, too. With what we're handing you, you can tack on all sorts of fun federal charges, potentially bust a criminal organization – i.e., the law firm, if you're not keeping up – that's certainly bent or broken a number of international laws, and confiscate a whole shit pile of money. Before that, there's the little matter of busting McQueen's ass.'

She turned to Ricchio who struggled to control a smile. 'With your permission, Lieutenant, I'd like to start the briefing, then coordinate with you on assignments.'

'Then let's roll it out.'

Nikos steamed her, but Eve didn't mind. It pumped her up.

After Mira finished the profile, Eve laid on operational strategy and procedure. Then she pulled Roarke and Mira aside.

'You're going to be working with e-men from DPSD and the FBI.'

'Quite the party,' Roarke commented, with no real pleasure.

'Ricchio is going to give you a space to coordinate. He's also getting the warrants for you to link up with building security and tamper with McQueen's. You're Team One.'

'So you said. Well, I'll go find my space. See you on the line, Lieutenant.'

'I'd like you to go out on this,' Eve said to Mira. 'We know McQueen was mobile when he contacted me. It's unlikely he's taken another girl, but it's not impossible. If so, we may need hostage negotiation, and it takes time to pull one in. Besides, you know him.'

'Yes. I'd like to go.'

'We'll keep you out of the hot spot, but linked in so you know what's going on.'

'Just tell me where you want me.'

Moving on, Eve thought as she climbed into the van with her team, fit on her earpiece. Step by step.

Link with building security, establish eyes and ears in and out. Establish target is on-site. If so, locate and disable his vehicle. All teams move into secondary hold positions.

Disrupt apartment security, disable elevator. Move into corridor, block stairwell, lock down building. Trap him like a rat.

Break in the door, go in hot. Take him down.

If target wasn't on-site, wait until he was and proceed.

Bree shifted over to her. 'I wanted to thank you for requesting me as part of your team.'

'Maybe I just wanted to keep an eye on you so you don't screw up.'

Bree offered a tight smile. 'I won't. My parents are with Melly, at our place. I didn't update them. Just in case.'

'That's best.'

'I want to be able to tell them we got him.'

'Then let's make it happen.'

'I know Nikos got in your face, and Ricchio's, about Price. Things get around.'

Cop shops, Eve thought. Some aspects had no geography. 'Yeah, they do.'

'I know you stood up for him.'

'He didn't screw up. It was bad luck, that's all. Nikos knows that, too. She's just pissed and frustrated.'

'Yeah, but still. It's appreciated.'

'You can buy me a drink when this is done.'

'You got it.'

Here we go, she thought as the van pulled over. 'Team Two in position,' she said into her mic. 'Sound it off.'

She listened as team leaders reported, gestured to the e-man on her team. 'Bring it up. Let's have a look.'

She studied the building, all shimmering gold and glass in

422

a wide curve. Railed balconies spread into longer, deeper terraces on the upper levels.

And McQueen's, the top level, east corner. 'Zoom it in on target.'

She edged forward. Unless he had a parachute or a personal jet lift, he couldn't escape by way of the terrace. With the elevator and stairs blocked, he wouldn't have access to the roof.

The only way out would be through a wall of cops. He wouldn't make it.

'Do a sweep, ground level,' she ordered.

She spotted the softclothed cops in position or moving into. The couple having coffee at the sidewalk café nestled beside the building, a man sitting on a wall above a bunch of flowers working a PPC. Still another window-shopping.

She counted off the rest.

She'd given strict orders not to approach or pursue should McQueen be spotted outside. The last thing she wanted was another chase, and any opportunity for him to slip the net.

'We're in,' Roarke said in her ear.

'Copy that. Show me.'

The monitor switched again, showing her the lobby area – glossy, elegant – droid at a long, low table to check in visitors, deliveries, cleaning crews. Lots of flowers in angled glass vases along one wall.

While he took her through maintenance areas, security stations, utility rooms, Team Four's leader sounded in her ear.

'Sensors read empty, Lieutenant.'

She thought, *Crap*. 'We hold. Team Five, move on the garage. Let's see if he's on the road or on foot. If you locate the vehicle, disable.'

She settled back. 'Roarke, let's see his floor.'

She studied the corridor, the placement of other apartments, the position of the stairs, the elevators. And the security on McQueen's door.

'Target's vehicle in assigned slot. Now disabled.'

'Acknowledged. We hold.'

And, she thought, we wait.


A few blocks away McQueen browsed the selections of a gourmet market. He'd missed this – missed the *time* to do as he liked, missed enjoying a meal of his own choosing when he chose to enjoy it.

He intended to make himself a very special dinner, the last before he had some company.

The last before Eve joined him.

It would work very well, he thought as he considered the artichokes. He knew just where to find her now.

The hotel security on communication was, as you'd expect from a Roarke property, perfection. But the Dallas police weren't quite so clever or well-funded. It hadn't been difficult to triangulate her signal during their last contact. And tonight, he'd pay her a visit. He would, undoubtedly, have to kill Roarke, which was a shame considering all that lovely money that might have come into his hands.

But Eve was worth the cost.

Just a few more details to iron out, which he'd do after marketing.

He found himself staring, unable to make a decision on olives. So many different choices, all those little jars. How was he suppose to pick one, to *know* what he'd want in an hour? In two?

Annoyed with himself, he grabbed one at random, then another, then two more. Of course he knew what he wanted, what he would want. He just had so many things on his mind. Gaining entrance to the hotel, then to Eve's rooms wasn't a snap, after all. Not that it was beyond his reach, but it did take careful planning. Hardly a wonder he couldn't decide on olives.

He took out his PPC, where he'd carefully noted down everything he'd need for his special meal. Calmer now, he continued to browse. Everything was so much better when it was noted down, organized.

He studied the little berry tomatoes for a long time.

'Something's going on at the Gold Door.'

McQueen came out of what felt like a trance. 'What did you say?'

'Cops.'

He jerked, fumbled, and nearly dropped his basket. With his head swiveling from side to side, he prepared to run.

Then he saw the stock boy talking to another one of the staff.

'Cops at that place?' the stock boy snickered. 'What, did somebody trip over their money and fall out the window?'

'Maybe bigger. I had a delivery over there. When I came out I see this cop.'

'So. Cops are everywhere except when you want them.'

'You took your cynical pill this morning. Not just a cop, a *detective,* and he must've been undercover.'

'Then how do you know he's a detective?'

'Because I know him. Detective Buck Anderson. He came in to talk to my criminology class a couple weeks ago. He's pretty chill, man, made me think about being a cop.'

This time a snicker and a snort from the stock boy. 'As if.'

'I'd be a mag cop. I spotted an undercover detective, right? He's sitting on the wall over there, jeans and a T-shirt, sunshades, but I recognized him.'

'Maybe it's his day off.'

'No way, 'cause when I said hi to him, he acted like he didn't know me. I talked to him after class for like twenty minutes. He gave me his card and everything. Like I said, he was chill, but he said I had it wrong. 'Do I look like a cop,' he says to me, and tells me to get lost.'

'Big whoop, Radowski. It probably wasn't even him. And so what if it was?'

'It was him. I bet he's on a stakeout or something. I bet we're going to hear something big goes down at the Gold Door.'

Very carefully, McQueen set the basket aside. He fixed on a smile, strolled up to the two young men. 'Excuse me, did I hear you mention the Gold Door? The police? I have a friend who lives there. I hope there's no trouble.'

'I don't know, sir. I just thought I saw somebody I knew.' The smile didn't go with the fury in the man's eyes, so the delivery boy edged away. 'I have to get back to work.'

The stock boy turned to McQueen. 'Can I help you find anything, sir?'

'No. No, you can't.' McQueen stormed out, shoving past a couple just coming in, then walked quickly in the opposite direction from the Gold Door and his perfect apartment.

Eve blocked out the bored chatter, stayed inside her own head, her own thoughts. An hour into the wait, Roarke spoke in her ear.

'McQueen's made contact again. He wants to talk to you.'

Something up, something wrong, she thought. 'Hold him. Keep that sweep going. I don't want to hear a sound from anybody in here. Can you track him?' she asked Roarke

'Possibly. It's more difficult on these mobile units.'

'Try to pin him. Link us up, block the video.'

'Use the com on your mobile. I'm crossing to give us two points. Try to give me some time with the track. Linking now.'

She changed positions, waited.

'Twice in one day. You must miss me, Isaac.'

'Not for long.'

Something wrong, she thought again. She heard it in his voice – not the usual controlled amusement, but temper, ripe as roses.

'So you keep saying.'

'But you just couldn't be patient. It's rude, very rude, Eve, to come to my home without an invitation.'

Fuck, fuck, fuck. 'Just dropped by. When are you coming back, Isaac? I have a housewarming present for you.'

His breath hissed in and out, in and out. 'You think you're smart.'

'Found your hole, didn't I?'

'Luck. Blind luck. It won't be luck when I come for you. I'm going to make you very, very sorry, so sorry you'll be grateful when I finally cut your throat.'

'Do you plan to use the knife you bought at Points and Blades? That's a lot of money for a sticker. I can't wait to see it.'

'You will. One day I'll just be there.'

'You know, you sound a little miffed. Why don't we—'

She swore under her breath when he cut her off.

'Working on it,' Roarke said before she could ask. 'I can't nail it, not from here. The best I can give you is somewhere on Davis Ave, between Corral and Kingston.'

Ricchio came on. 'I'm alerting dispatch. We have an all-points out.'

'He's not coming back here,' Eve said. 'We're going in. He's running now, maybe we can find something that tells us where he's most likely to run.'

She wanted to punch something, but kept it together as she got out of the van. She'd watched the sweeps, kept track of the cops they'd put on the street. Nothing should have tipped him off.

'How'd he make us?' she demanded when Roarke joined her. 'How the hell did he make us?'

'Instincts perhaps.'

'Nobody's are that good.' She shook her head at him. 'He knew we were here. I was here. And he is seriously pissed.'

She let Ricchio clear the road with the check-in droid, building security. By the time they'd reached McQueen's apartment and gained access, she found calm again.

'We think it was one of my men,' Ricchio told her. 'Nothing he did, or we did. Someone recognized him, a college student. My detective had spoken to his class recently, spent some time answering the boy's questions after. The kid came out of the building, spotted him. He got rid of him, but did a run on him anyway. He works at a gourmet market a few blocks away – just outside our perimeter.'

'Talk about luck.'

'He's down there now, speaking to the boy. It's possible McQueen was in there, the boy said something about the police.'

'Jesus.'

'No one could've predicted or foreseen—'

'No, no one could. It just swung McQueen's way, and that's all.' But she stiffened when Nikos strode up to her. 'If you're going to crawl up my ass on this, just save it.'

'Not this time. It was running like clockwork. But I want to know why you didn't deny it when he made contact. Why you confirmed.'

'Because he knew, so I chose to grind him up a little. He's

off center. Doctor Mira calls it devolving. Swiping at him should help that along.'

'Doctor Mira also said he's likely to become more violent and less controlled.'

'That's right. Freeze the accounts, now's the time.'

'Done,' Nikos told her. 'Five minutes ago.'

'Good. He's got no place to go, no way to get there, unless or until he steals a car. And he knows he can't ride around in a stolen vehicle for long. We need roadblocks, we need to cover all public and private transpo. He doesn't have any cash except what he's got on him. He only has the ID he has on him. He uses credit, we nail him, and he knows it.'

She turned around, gestured. 'Look at this place. He took a lot of time and care putting all this together, and from prison. Now he can't use it. When he goes to access more funds, he's frozen out.'

'He's going to try to get out of Dallas.'

'Maybe, but we don't have to make it easy for him.'

She crossed over to the locked door, glanced at Roarke. When he disengaged the locks, she stepped in.

He'd covered the walls with pictures of his victims. All the girls, all the eyes.

'These are case-file shots,' she stated. 'It mattered enough for him to get them. He wanted me in here, locked in with them.'

She studied the shackles, remembered how they weighed on her wrists and ankles in her dream.

Then she turned away, walked out. 'Let's see what else he left behind.'

The high life, she thought as they turned the apartment inside out. Sheets of Irish linen, towels of Turkish cotton. French champagne, Russian caviar.

Tranqs and paralytics and syringes all meticulously organized in an embossed case.

'Fresh flowers in every room,' she said to Mira. 'And enough food for months. A lot of it fresh, too. So it would spoil.'

'He needed to acquire – collect again – and purchase and have. And he's likely having trouble deciding what it is he wants.'

'So he buys too much. Too many flowers, too much food, too many clothes. He knew how to live light once – well, but light. I bet we find his prints everywhere, overlapping each other. He'd want to touch everything, over and over. He'd stand out on the terrace, feel like the king of the world. Then he'd come in here, lock up like a fortress. Where's he going now?'

'London was in the plans,' Roarke told her. 'We're getting through some of his blocks, and found where he's started researching accommodations and real estate in London.'

'He can't get there now.'

'He knows New York.'

Eve nodded at Mira. 'And expects I'll go back there. He'll need to ride the grift for a while, pump up his funds. He'll need to hunt, and that's soon. But he's got nowhere to take her, keep her. A motel maybe, something he can pay cash for.

He'd have to keep her under. No soundproofing this time. But he'll need that release.'

She paced. 'Or break into a home, a private residence. Take what he needs, regroup.'

'He's angry. He'll be rash,' Mira warned her. 'And violent.'

'The media should be useful. Blanket it with his face, his name, feed the media some of the data on the manhunt. If he catches it, he'll get more pissed, more shaken. He's alone now, and has to go back to living on his wits. It's been a long time.'

She had a pair of uniforms take Mira back to the hotel, watched EDD carry out the electronics.

'They could use you on that,' Eve said to Roarke. 'I know you'd rather not work at Ricchio's house, but that's where the equipment's going.'

'Yes. So we'll go there.'

'I'm going to stay here, keep looking. A dozen cops in here,' she said when he frowned. 'Not counting me. When I'm ready to go back to the hotel and work, I'll have a couple big bad cops take me to the door if you're still at it. Good enough?'

'Nowhere alone. Your word.'

'Don't worry. I'm not going to give him a chance to get me alone.'

'I'm going to nag you,' Roarke warned, 'contact you every hour.'

'Okay, fine, but I'm going to finish here, get an escort back, then close myself up and try to find a new angle on where he'd run, how, and how the hell he expects to get to me when the cops have Dallas – the city – sewed up like . . . whatever gets sewed up.'

'Tag me when you leave for the hotel. If I've done all I think I can do at that point, I'll meet you there. We can find the fresh angle together.'

'That's a deal.'

# 23

Reduced to shoplifting, McQueen thought, like a common street thief. One more thing Eve Dallas would pay for. Still, it didn't hurt his feelings to know he hadn't lost his touch. Three relatively quick stops, and he had what he needed.

Maybe it had been tedious to have to ditch one car, boost another, but he had to admit, just a bit exciting, too. Nostalgic.

He hadn't boosted since he'd been a lad at his mother's knee. Plus, the second car had netted him a briefcase – a nice stroke of luck. Props always added to the illusion.

It was time, he thought, to get to the *point*. Time to finish it, finish *her*, and get the hell out of Dallas. The city was bad luck, nothing but stinking bad luck. Back to New York. That would be like rubbing her dead face in it, wouldn't it?

But no, no, he'd had bad luck in New York, too.

Philly maybe, or back to Baltimore. Maybe Boston. No, no, winter was coming despite the vicious heat in this god-forsaken bad-luck city. He should head south. Atlanta, no, Miami. All those fresh bad girls on the beaches. Easy pickings. Like a vacation.

He'd take a vacation in Miami, he decided, and saw himself trolling South Beach in a white linen suit.

In the pretty roadster, in a happier state of mind with the prospect of sun and surf in his future, he pulled up in front of the hotel. Fussed a bit with his safety belt, the briefcase, to give the doorman time to open the door for him.

'Good evening, sir. Checking in?'

'Just meeting a friend at the bar.'

'Enjoy your visit, sir.'

'Oh, I will.' He didn't resent the tip. He intended to leave with more than he'd come in with, so he could afford to be generous.

He strode in, took a moment to glance around as any man would, noting the layout just as advertised on the webpage. Noting, too, lobby security – the cams and the manpower.

Swinging the briefcase, he strolled into the lobby bar, chose a table facing a bank of elevators.

He had some time, he considered. They wouldn't be back soon – they had work to do! Searching his apartment, going through his things. Coordinating their roadblocks and man-hunt.

They could arrange all the media bulletins they liked. He'd taken care of that, the snip, snip in the restroom of the pharmacy, the careful comb through of color, the use of his own shorn hair and some lifted spirit gum for a jaunty goatee, and he had a whole new look.

And not unattractive, he mused as he flirted with the waitress and ordered a club soda, extra lime. And she flirted right back. They always did, he thought. And what did she see? A man with short chestnut hair, a bit on the choppy side, with a trim and narrow goatee. The well-cut suit, the briefcase.

She didn't see a man the police chased their tails for. No indeed.

His hand flexed and unflexed under the table. He wanted blood, and soon. Wanted the just-budding body of a bad, bad girl. Wanted to see the life drain out of a certain bitch of a cop. But he had to take some time. He had to choose carefully.

His luck was up, he reminded himself. And gave the waitress a cheerful wink when she brought his drink, a dish of olives, and a pretty bowl of snack mix.

Olives, he thought, losing his thread a moment. What was it about olives?

The stock boy, the other, the cops. All those jars.

He took a slow sip. Club soda now, champagne later, he promised himself. Everything would go according to plan. He only had to wait for the mark.

He scanned the bar, the lobby, considering and rejecting as he sipped his club soda.

It took twenty minutes, but he spotted her. Pretty and petite in a short black dress. Costume jewelry, a bit too carefully made up, and brown hair that could've used some highlights and a zippier style.

But he gave her credit for the hot-pink heels.

Early twenties, he judged as she made her way to the bar. Small-town girl in the big city. When she sat at a table nearby, he considered it a sign.

He didn't even have to move to make it work.

She ordered a champagne cocktail. Living it up, he thought, watching her look everywhere at once. He made sure she'd glanced his way when he checked his wrist unit, frowned. Then he caught her eye, smiled at her.

She blushed.

'I think I've been stood up.' He shrugged, smiled again. 'I hope you don't mind, but I just have to say, those shoes are amazing.'

'Oh.' She bit her bottom lip, glanced around again. Plenty of people at the bar, excellent hotel. What was the harm? 'Thanks. I just bought them today.'

'Terrific choice.' He turned his wrist again as if checking the time. 'Are you visiting Dallas?'

'Um.'

'Sorry.' He waved a hand. 'I don't mean to intrude.'

'Oh . . . That's okay. I'm here to see some friends. We're having dinner, but they had to push back the reservation. So I thought, well, I'm all ready now—'

'And wearing amazing new shoes.'

She laughed, and he thought it was just too easy.

'I thought I'd have a drink down here instead of sitting in my room.'

'Can't blame you a bit.' He waited until the waitress served her, ordered another club soda. 'I'm supposed to meet a client, but as I said . . . So where are you from?'

'Oh, Nowhere, Oklahoma.'

'Seriously?'

'It might as well be. Just a little town – Brady – south of Tulsa.'

'You're kidding me! Tulsa,' he said, tapping his chest. 'That's where I grew up – until I was sixteen anyway, and we moved here. Broke my heart. I had to leave the girl I was sure was the love of my life. I can't believe it. Brady, Oklahoma, and she sits down with her amazing pink shoes right in the same hotel bar. I have to buy you a drink.'

'Oh, um—'

'Come on, Okies have to stick together.' Careful, he told himself, and simply shifted to face her more directly. 'Matt Beaufont.'

'Eloise. Eloise Pruitt.'

'It's a pleasure, Eloise. So, is this your first time in Dallas?'

He engaged her, made her laugh, made her blush. He paid for his drinks and hers when the waitress made the next round.

'Look, do you mind if I join you, just until you have to go?'

Before she could answer, he grabbed his drink, rose. He moved fast, sliding his chair over next to hers, boxing her in.

'I really should—'

'Sit very still, and keep smiling at me. You feel that, Eloise? That's a knife. If you make a sound, a move, I'm going to have to put it in you.' Her eyes were so wide, so shocked. Another thrill. 'It'll ruin the line of that dress, and get blood all over your amazing pink shoes. We don't want that.'

'Please.'

'Now, I don't want to hurt you, I really don't. I want you to give me that giggle, like you did before. Give me a giggle, Eloise, or I'll cut you.'

She managed it – a little high, a little shrill. He got his hand on the prepared syringe in his pocket. Leaned in as if whispering in her ear.

'Ow.'

'Oh, that didn't hurt. And it's just a little taste, to help you relax. That and the drink will do it.'

'I feel . . .'

'Drunk, oh yes, you do. What room are you in, Eloise?'

'I'm . . . sixteen-oh-three. I'm dizzy. Don't hurt me.'

'Don't worry. I'm just going to take you up to your room. I bet you want to lie down.'

'I need to lie down.'

'Put your arm around me, Eloise. Give me that giggle.'

She swayed a bit when he got her to her feet. Smiled when he told her to smile, leaned on him as they crossed the lobby.

'I don't feel right.'

'I'm going to make it all better. You just have to do what I tell you. Exactly what I tell you.'

He got her in the elevator, told her to put her arms around his neck with him keeping his back to the camera. 'Push sixteen, Eloise, and smile for me.'

'I have to meet my friends.' She missed the button twice, then hit it.

'That's for later.'

No one got on. His luck still ran true. In the corridor of sixteen, he danced her down the hall, her stumbling, him laughing.

'Need your key, baby doll.'

'Key?'

'I'll get it.' He braced her against the door, caging her in again as he took her purse, dug out the card. 'Here we go!'

The minute they were inside the room, he let her drop to a heap on the floor.

'Well done, Eloise! Now, we have more work to do.'


Carlotta Phelps got off on sixteen. She'd been with hotel security for three years, and this wouldn't be the first time she'd assisted a drunk guest. And since her shift ended in ten, unlocking a bathroom door and recoding a key wasn't a tough way to end the day.

She knocked briskly on 1603. 'Ms Pruitt, hotel security.'

There was some fumbling at the door. Carlotta kept her face blank, but inside she smirked, and hoped Eloise from Oklahoma had some Sober-Up with her.

The woman who finally got the door opened looked a little mussed, a lot drunk, but matched the ID on file. She said, 'Sorry. I'm sorry.'

'It's no problem. You reported a lost key and a locked bathroom door?'

'I . . . that's what I said.'

'May I come in?'

'I . . . please.'

Eloise took an unsteady step back, and Carlotta moved through the door.

As it shut behind her, she caught a movement out of the corner of her eye, had half a second to react before the syringe punched against her throat.

'There now,' McQueen said cheerfully. 'That wasn't so hard, was it?' He gestured with the point of the knife. 'Now get on the bed, Eloise, facedown.'

'Please.'

'You're so polite. Please, please, please. Sit down or I'm going to open that pretty cheek of yours all the way to the bone.'

She did as she was told.

'Duct tape,' he said as he used it to secure her hands behind her back. 'Low-tech, easily available, and so very versatile.' He continued on to her ankles while she shuddered and wept.

'I could smother you. No blood that way, but to be honest, Eloise, I'm just not that interested.' Tired of her blubbering and pleading, he slapped tape over her mouth. 'There now, some peace and quiet.'

Pleased, he turned to the woman on the floor. He rolled her over, took her master, her communicator, personal 'link, earbud, and as he'd done with Eloise, whatever cash and jewelry she had.

Waste not, want not, he thought.

He bound her, gagged her for good measure though he expected she'd be out for an hour, then replaced the tape roll in the briefcase. He'd have preferred to simply cut off her thumb, quick and easy. But so messy.

Instead he took the time to press her thumb to a strip of foil, carefully fixed it to his own, sealed it.

Pumped with success, he strolled over to the bed. 'Maybe I'll smother you anyway. Really with that hair, that pathetic use of enhancers you probably don't deserve to live. Just kidding!' he said, laughing uproariously as she squirmed and struggled to scream. 'Well, not about the hair and makeup. Bye-bye, Eloise – and you're welcome. You'll be dining out on this little adventure for years.'

He stepped over the guard, considered a moment. Taking out his jammer, he eased the door open a crack for line of sight. Best not to be seen, if anyone bothered to glance at the right monitor at the right time. He counted off a three-second disruption as he rushed down the corridor to the stairwell.

A long climb, he thought as he started up, but the prize at the end, so worth it.

He broke a sweat, but considered it a byproduct of good, healthy exercise.

He paused outside the stairwell door on fifty-eight. He'd need the jammer again. The master and print would get him in, but the use of it would trigger a record and alert.

Anything over a ten-second disruption would trip another alert and result in a standard check. So he'd have to move fast.

He hit the jammer and bolted. Swiped the card, pressed his sealed thumb. Nothing.

They'd just had to send a woman! One with small hands, little digits.

Cursing, sweat rolling now, he forced himself to steady, did the swipe a second time, and with more care, more delicacy, pressed the print to the pad.

The light went green.

He shoved inside, flicked the jammer off even as he shut the door.

He took a moment to catch his breath, realized there were tears in his eyes. Tears! Of joy, of course. He blinked them away and scanned the area.

How she'd come up in the world, he thought, just by opening her legs for money. Plush rugs over an exquisite tile floor, the dull gleam of silver chandeliers sparkling over the deep cushions of chairs, sofas in rich jeweled colors.

He wandered a bit, struck with a burning envy, noted the fully stocked bar in the same silver as the lights, a long dining table of genuine ebony, a small kitchen that made the one he'd designed pale.

Yet more exquisite tile in a powder room.

This was what he wanted, this luxury. This was what he deserved. His heart galloped as he walked up the graceful curve of stairs to the second level. He wandered the master bedroom, felt the rage vomit up from his belly to his throat.

She'd lived like this, like *this*, while he rotted in prison. Killing her hardly seemed payment enough. She'd taken everything, denied him everything. Even now she denied him the pleasure of torturing her, of taking the time he wanted to watch her suffer, to humiliate her.

Making her watch him carve up her meal ticket had to be enough.

He moved to the closet, felt that envy rise again. The man had taste, McQueen thought. The suits, the shirts, the shoes – even if he had none in his choice of wife.

Since the killing would be messy – as messy as he could make it – he'd need a change of clothes. A snug fit, he thought, fingering the material of a jacket. Jacket open, shirt out, it would do well enough. Or perhaps something more casual – snug again – but . . .

He lost time, swimming in indecision, then whirled when something hissed behind him.

He stared at the cat who stared back at him with bicolored eyes.

'Hello, kitty.' He smiled, reached for the knife.

The idea of carving up her cat filled him with delight. When it bolted, he pursued, charging up the stairs to the third level.

'Here, kitty, kitty!'

Laughing now, he walked into Eve's office.

And forgot about the cat.

The case board fascinated him, brought him a quick, warm rush of pride.

His girls, all his bad girls. And him, so much of him. Just look at how he'd become the center of her world. It was delicious. She'd spent hours – hours and hours and hours – thinking of him, trying so hard to outwit him.

But who was standing right here, right now, just waiting for her? Who had outwitted whom, again and again? She'd had her way for twelve long years. But now, he would have his.

'I was wrong,' he murmured, eyes sparkling on the board, 'and I so rarely am. Killing you is enough. Is exactly enough. And right here, right in front of all your hard work. Right in front of all the bad girls. It's perfect.'

'Heading out now,' Eve told Roarke via 'link. 'I've done all I can do here. I want to sift through it all, then have Mira take another pass.'

'I'll be close behind you. We've made some progress on the electronics, but it's slow going. I may do better on my own, with my own. How are you getting back to the hotel?'

Worry, worry, she thought. 'I'm about to get into an official vehicle with two strapping uniforms. We found the car he stole, and ditched, damn near halfway to Fort Worth. They're running any reports of stolen vehicles as he likely boosted another. Might've jacked one though, and kept heading west. They're covering the highways and byways and cow paths.'

She nodded to the uniforms, slid into the backseat. 'They're pumping out the media alerts. They're already flooded with reports of sightings, and they'll follow up on all of them. But the downside of that angle is it brings out the crazies and the easily spooked.'

'Why don't you have your escort bring you here? We'll go back together.'

'Roarke, I'll be in the hotel and in the room in ten, drinking a decent cup of coffee and putting my notes together. You know what we found in his dresser? A photo album. Pictures of his mother, then of the partners we knew about – and more we didn't. Numbered, just like the girls. Mira's going to love that.'

'He'd started to research shopping centers, vid complexes, arcades, youth clubs, in central London.'

'Well, he won't be having – what is it – bangers and mash for breakfast anytime soon. I don't know why anybody'd want to, but I like knowing he won't. I need to go over the timing again, but I don't think he had a big enough window to get gone – and I don't think he's in the frame of mind to get gone if he had. He's pissed and panicked.

'We're pulling in to the hotel. I'll see you when you get here.'

'I'm leaving now. You might have the cops go up with you.'

'I *am* a cop,' she reminded him. 'Thanks,' she said to the uniforms as she hopped out. 'And I'm now walking into the hotel. See you in a few.'

Wound up, she thought. McQueen, the almost-got-hims, her personal bullshit – it had them both too wound up. Time to unwind it, wrap it, and get the hell back to New York. Not that people wouldn't try to kill her there, too, but at least that was *normal*.

Nothing about this felt normal.

She scanned the lobby, the lobby bar, the shops as she passed through, alert for signs, for tingles. He couldn't know where she and Roarke were staying, but she supposed he could make an educated guess.

446

She walked to the elevator by the security post, nodded to the man on duty as she accessed it.

'Good evening, Lieutenant. I'll clear you up.'

'Thanks.'

She stepped in, leaned back against the wall. Coffee, she thought, and a couple minutes to let it settle in, loosen up. She got off on the bedroom level. What she craved was a long, hot shower to wash away the hours spent at McQueen's, the faint scent of chemicals clinging to her clothes from the sweepers' tools. She settled on pulling off her jacket, and after removing her weapon harness, changed to a fresh shirt.

Better, she decided, and got the coffee from the bedroom AutoChef. She drank the first sip where she stood, then decided, since he hadn't come to greet her, to hunt up the cat. Coffee and Galahad, her case board – almost like home.

She'd put her feet up on her desk, grab some thinking time before Roarke got in, then dive in. Since he wasn't sprawled on the bed, she expected she'd find Galahad on the sleep chair in her office – and expected he'd act as if he'd been starved as they'd left him alone all day.

She turned into her office, surprised not to see the cat. Probably sulking. She shrugged, started toward her board. Nearly smiled when Galahad poked his head out from under the chair. Would've smiled, ragged on him, but he bared his teeth in a hiss.

For the second time in their acquaintance, Galahad saved her life.

She spun around, led with a stiffened forearm. The knife bit a shallow stream down her arm, but missed carving into her back. She followed the block with a punch, and as McQueen dodged, she reached for her weapon.

Remembered tossing it and her jacket on the bed.

He came at her again, the knife arcing through the air. She leaped back, managed to kick his knife arm, but without enough juice to dislodge the weapon.

Clutch piece, she thought as she dodged another swipe. She still had her clutch piece on her ankle. But didn't have the room to get it.

Devolving, she thought. So push.

'You're losing it, Isaac.' She crouched, fighting stance. 'You'll never get out of here.'

'I got in, didn't I? Luck's on my side this time around. It's just too bad Roarke's not with you. But I can wait. Maybe I won't kill you – yet. I'll let you watch me slice him, piece by piece, first.'

'He'll take you apart. You have no idea.' She dodged the knife again, spun around, got a boot in his gut. The blade grazed her hip on the follow-through.

'I'm going to put so many holes in you.'

She shoved a chair at him, and the action, the reaction took her back to the room where they'd fought before. But she wasn't a rookie now. She was smarter, stronger. She only had to hold him off, get to her weapon.

'You're the one with holes where your control, your brains used to be. You should be gone, in the wind, living it rich on all that money you stashed by. But we've got it all now. You're going back in a cage, and this time there won't be any accounts to tap. You're just fucking *stupid.*'

Fury stained his face dull red as he charged. She leaped over the sleep chair, and the knife sliced down, leaving a vicious gash down the back of the chair. Momentum carrying her, she reached down for her clutch piece, tried to gain her feet, her balance as she swung back.

Both weapons clattered to the floor when he hit her like a battering ram. His weight bore her down, with her arm twisted under her. Something popped, but she registered the sound, the screaming pain as a snap.

And she was back in a room washed in dirty red light.

Roarke used the time sitting in traffic to run through some logistics. They'd broken through most of McQueen's filters – he hadn't been quite as obsessive about blocks and fail-safes on what he'd installed in the second location.

Felt safe, Roarke thought. Untouchable.

He'd learned differently.

Still, nothing they'd recovered thus far proved particularly helpful in finding him now. But the extensive data files McQueen had amassed on Eve had given Roarke some very bad moments. That kind of obsession wouldn't fade or be turned aside. That obsession was exactly why McQueen had changed pattern, pushed the boundaries of all sense, tumbled into a crazed sort of labyrinth of plot and plan.

He wouldn't give up, very likely couldn't give up.

The contacts he'd made with her, even the memo cube – so personal, so unnecessary. Somewhat like a spurned lover, Roarke concluded, as bored, annoyed with the stall, he began to weave through traffic.

And the last communication, he mused as he finally turned to the hotel. That last furious com, with cops only blocks away, when McQueen should have been thinking of nothing but escape. That was completely dead stupid, over-the-edge. Survival always came first, and didn't he know it. If you want to taunt – though he'd never seen the point of it himself – taunt from cover. But to risk the communication from only blocks away when McQueen had to know they were linked up, had to know they'd initiated a track and trace? That was . . .

It struck him, a hammer to the heart. Linked – then, linked when Eve had talked to him earlier from the hotel office.

Track and trace.

He jumped out of the car before he reached the hotel door. Dragged out his 'link. He tried her first, on the run, got her voice directing him to leave a message.

'Sir!' the doorman called after him as he bolted toward the doors. 'Your vehicle—'

'Contact the police,' Roarke ordered when he'd reached the security station at the elevator. 'Lieutenant Ricchio. Now! And send a team, armed, to my rooms. Now, god-damn it.' He flew into the elevator, drew the weapon from the holster at the small of his back.

He might've prayed, but only a single word sounded over and over in his head.

*Eve.*

She screamed. The pain was so huge, filled everything. He struck her, again and again, and pressed against her. Hard against where she knew he would push into her, tear her, hurt her. Again.

And this time he'd kill her. She saw it on his face.

Her father's face.

'That's right, scream. Nobody can hear you. You're going to scream when I fuck you. That's right, that's right.' He tore at her clothes. 'I'm going to fuck you, then I'm going to kill you. Who's lucky now, bitch? Who's lucky now?'

'Please, don't! It hurts.'

'Beg some more.' He panted it out, thrilled. 'Cry like a little girl. A bad girl.'

'I'll be good! Don't, please, don't.'

When he struck her again, her vision doubled. She tried to claw at him, wild with pain and terror. He howled when she raked her nails down his face. Howled, reared back.

In her mind she felt him shove himself inside her. In reality his hands closed around her throat, shutting off her air.

Her free hand flailed out – helpless, hopeless – and closed over the knife.

She brought it down, felt the warm blood run. Coughing, choking, gagging, she brought it down again.

Then she was free, somehow free, kneeling beside him, her

451

injured arm hanging uselessly, and the knife clutched in her hand. The knife poised over him.

'Eve!'

Roarke's heart stopped. Later he would think that for an instant his heart simply stopped beating in the violent collision of relief – she was alive – and the horror of what he saw in that room.

'Eve!'

Her head whipped toward his, her face bruised, bloody, and the eyes he knew so well feral. Once again the cat, loyal to the last, stood beside her butting his head to her bloody hip. When Roarke stepped forward, she bared her teeth, made a sound like a snarl.

'I know who you are. Dallas, Lieutenant Eve.' He prayed now, prayed he wouldn't have to stun her to save her. 'Look at me. See me. He can't hurt you now, Eve. Dallas, Lieutenant Eve. That's who you are. That's who you made yourself. Eve. My Eve.'

'He comes back.'

'Not this time.'

'He hurts me.'

'I know. Not anymore. Eve. I'm what's real. We're what's real.'

If she brought that knife down, put it in him, she'd never be able to live with it, never come back from it. They'd have beaten her – her father, her mother, the excuse for a man bleeding on the floor.

'He's Isaac McQueen. He's not your father. You're not a

child. You're Lieutenant Eve Dallas, NYPSD. You need to take charge of your prisoner, Lieutenant. You need to do the job.'

'The job.' She sobbed in a breath. 'It hurts. It hurts.'

'I'll fix it.' Slowly, watching her eyes, he knelt on the other side of the unconscious McQueen. 'I love you, Eve. Trust me now. Give me the knife.' Gently, he closed his hand over hers on the bloody hilt.

'Roarke.'

'Yes. Give me the knife now, Eve.'

'Take it. Please take it. I can't let it go.'

He pried it out of her trembling fingers, tossed it aside.

As he reached out, lifted her into his arms, his security team rushed in. He started to snap out orders, and realized the ones that came first to mind were the wrong ones – restrain McQueen, an ambulance for his wife. The wrong ones for her.

'Doctor Charlotte Mira, room fifty-seven-oh-eight. One of you go, tell her Lieutenant Dallas needs her, and her medical bag. Now. The rest of you go down, wait for the police.'

He carried her to the sleep chair, where the cat immediately leaped to crawl into her lap.

'No,' she said when Roarke started to nudge him aside. 'He saved me. He saved me. You saved me.'

'You saved yourself, but we had a part in it. Let me look at your arm.'

'Is it broken?'

'No, baby, not broken. It's dislocated. I know it hurts.'

'Not broken.' She closed her eyes, shuddered out another breath. 'Not this time.'

She took his hand with her good one. 'I wanted to kill him. But I couldn't. I need you to know.' She hissed between her teeth, struggling to think, to speak through the pain. 'I need you to know.'

'It doesn't matter.' He laid his fingertips over the purpling bruise on her cheek. 'Let's wait for Mira.'

'It matters. I couldn't do it. There was something inside me – I was inside me, I guess. Just a child, and she was screaming. But I was there, too. Me. It was like being frozen between. I don't know how to explain it. I couldn't do it, but I couldn't let go, not until you came. Until you touched me. I couldn't do it, Roarke, but I couldn't move, and finish it the way I need to finish it, until you came.'

'Can you finish it now?'

'I have to. I think, if I don't . . . I have to.'

'Let me have your restraints. I'll do that part.'

While she cradled her injured arm, he took the cuffs off her belt, and rising, shoved McQueen over, knelt, and snapped them on. Mira ran in as Roarke dragged McQueen faceup again.

'Oh, dear God.'

'She'll keep.' Roarke got to his feet, moved to block Mira's dash toward Eve. 'Give him something to bring him around.'

'She needs—'

'She needs to read her prisoner his rights. She needs to know he sees her, hears her while she does.'

With one long look at Eve, Mira nodded. Roarke turned to the door as the room filled with cops, security, feds. 'This is for her to do. This is Lieutenant Dallas's job.'

He wanted to give her his hand, but she shook her head, got shakily to her feet as Mira brought McQueen around.

'Can you hear me?' she demanded.

'You're bleeding.' He spoke through gritted teeth while Mira put pressure on the gash in his side.

'You, too. Isaac McQueen, you're under arrest for the murder of Nathan Rigby, for the murder of the unidentified subject known as Sylvia Prentiss, for the kidnapping and forced imprisonment of Melinda Jones. For the kidnapping, rape, and forced imprisonment of Darlie Morgansten. For the assault with a deadly on a police officer. For the attempted murder of a police officer. And for other charges yet to be determined.'

'I'll find you again.' Rage burned like acid in his voice. 'I'll get out and find you again.'

'Look how scared I am. Isaac McQueen, you have the right to remain silent.' The churning sickness in her belly ebbed as she read him his rights.

'Detective Jones, would you take charge of the prisoner?'

'Yes, sir.'

'You can tell your family we got him.'

'What the hell happened here?' Nikos demanded.

'I did my job.'

'How did—'

'Lieutenant Dallas needs medical attention.' Before Roarke

could, Mira strode forward. 'Questions have to wait. Roarke, help me take her upstairs. We'll use the elevator.'

Cops parted for them. 'I have to tell Darlie. I promised. We need to secure the scene,' Eve said just as the elevator doors shut. Then thought – *Uh-oh*.

'Shit. I think I'm going to pass out.'

'Go ahead. Nobody can see but us.' As she did, he lifted her into his arms. Then just pressed his face to her throat.

When she came to, she was on the bed, her arm in a stabil- izer, with Mira working on the gash on her hip.

'Nothing hurts.'

'Not for the moment.'

'But I feel ... Crap, you gave me something. I feel weird.'

'It'll pass.'

'How bad is it?'

'Bad enough. You've been stabbed, beaten, choked, and had your arm nearly twisted off. But you'll heal.'

'Don't be mad.' Eve smiled at her. Drugs always made her stupid. 'He was going to rape me. For a minute when it was crazy, I thought he was raping me. But he didn't get the chance.'

'No.' Mira laid her hand on Eve's cheek. 'You stopped him.'

'You got blood on you. You always look so pretty, and you got blood on your dress, suit, skirt. Whatever. Sorry.'

'It's all right. I'm nearly done.'

'Okay. Am I naked?'

'Not quite.'

'Good, 'cause that's just embarrassing. Roarke? Where's Roarke?'

'I convinced him I could take care of you while he spoke with the police, gave a statement. He's contacting Darlie for you. You can speak with her a little later if you like.'

'He loves me. Roarke, I mean. He loves me.'

'Oh, so very much.'

'Nobody did before. Before Mavis, she just wouldn't give up and leave me alone. And Feeney. But he'd feel weird saying the whole love thing, so . . .' She mimed zipping fingers over her lips.

'But Roarke doesn't feel weird about it. He's full of it, the love, I mean. And when he loves me, things that never worked in me did – do. It was easier when they didn't work, but it's better when they do. You know?'

'I do. You should rest now.'

'Want to finish, give my report. Is my face messed up? I hate when that happens. Not like I'm pretty or anything, but—'

'You're the most beautiful woman ever born,' Roarke said from the doorway, and Eve sent him a woozy, drugged smile.

'See, told ya he's full of it. Gonna give my report, then let's go home, 'kay? Let's all go home.'

He walked over, sat on the side of the bed. 'Let's.'

# Epilogue

Mira refused to clear her for travel for twenty-four hours, and Mira was a nut that wouldn't crack. Still it gave Eve time to sort out all the details and tie them off.

'McQueen's being transferred to off-planet max-security facilities on a prison transport,' she told Roarke. 'But the Dallas PSD and the feds have filed the additional charges. He'll stand trial by holo.'

'You'll have to testify.'

'With extreme pleasure. How's your hotel security woman, and the guest?'

'Recovered. We'll be implementing some changes in our security procedures in that hotel.'

'Nobody could've foreseen what he'd do. It was lunacy.'

'But it worked, didn't it?' And that he'd never forget. 'He got to you.'

'You and I both know that with some skill, a lot of determination and luck, anybody can get to anybody, anywhere. That's why we have cops.'

She leaned back. God, she hated to fly, but at least this time, the shuttle headed in the right direction.

'And how's my cop?'

'Feeling pretty good, actually. The arm's the worst of it.'

'You slept well last night.'

'Hard not to, loaded up with tranqs.' She took his hand. 'I know I'm going to have to think about it, deal with it. The whole ugly mess of it. But I can, because in the end I did the job. You helped me to do it.'

'I always wondered, if such things were possible, if I'd go back, kill your father to spare you that. Then I stood in that room in Dallas and saw so clearly what happened that night, what he'd put you through, what he'd done.'

He brought her hand to his lips, the hand he'd covered with his on the knife, sharing the blood with her. 'I could have taken the knife from you and put it into his heart. McQueen, your father. I could have done that.'

'You didn't.'

'No. You loved me, and things in me that didn't work did, and do.'

'You heard me,' she murmured. 'With Mira.'

'I did. And I can say to you it was easier when they didn't work, but it's better, very much better, when they do.'

She leaned her head on his shoulder. 'For two people who started out so fucked up, we're okay.'

Beside him, she watched out the window, ignored the pitching in her stomach on descent. The cat leaped onto her lap, circled with his questing claws, settled.

And beside Roarke, with the cat snoring, she watched New York break through the clouds.

Dallas to New York, she thought. Where she belonged.

EXCLUSIVE EXTRACT

Read an extract from

# CELEBRITY
# IN DEATH

The new J.D. Robb thriller
## Out now

# 1

With frustration and some regret, she studied murder. It lay in the quiet room on a sofa the color of good merlot, with heart blood staining a pale gray shirt beneath the silver bolt of a scalpel. Her eyes, flat and grim, tracked the body, the room, the tray of artfully arranged fruit and cheese on the low table.

'In close again.' Her voice, like her eyes, was all cop as she straightened her long, lean frame. 'He's lying down. He's deactivated the droid – leaving it and the house security programmed for do-not-disturb. But he's lying here and he doesn't worry about somebody coming in, leaning over him. Tranqs maybe. We'll check the tox screen but I don't think so. He knew her. He didn't fear for his life when she came into the room.'

She stepped to the door. In the corridor outside the pretty blonde sat on the floor, head in her hands with the sturdily built, newly-minted detective smirking beside her.

And she stood, framed in the doorway with murder at her back.

'And cut! That's the money shot.'

At the director's signal, the area – dressed as the late

Wilford B. Icove Junior's home office – became a hive of sound and movement.

Lieutenant Eve Dallas, who'd once stood in that home office over a body that did not – as this one did – sit up and scratch his ass, felt the weird sense of *déjà vu* shatter.

'Is this iced or what?' Beside her, Peabody did a restrained little dance by lifting and lowering the heels of her pink cowboy boots. 'We're on an actual vid set watching ourselves. And we look good.'

'It's weird.'

And weirder yet, Eve thought, to watch herself – or a reasonable facsimile – coming toward her with a big, happy smile.

She didn't smile like that, did she? That would be yet another weird.

'Lieutenant Dallas. It's so great you made it on set. I've been dying to meet you.' The actress held out a hand.

Eve had seen Marlo Durn before, but as a sun-kissed blond with dark green eyes. The short, choppy brown hair, the brown eyes, even the shallow dent in the chin that matched her own gave Eve a little bit of the wigs.

'And Detective Peabody.' Marlo passed the long leather coat she'd worn for the scene – a twin of the one Eve's husband had given her during the Icove investigation – to a wardrobe person.

'I'm a huge fan, Ms Durn. I've seen everything you've been in.'

'Marlo,' she told Peabody. 'We're partners, after all. Well, what do you think?' She gestured at the set, and a twin of the wedding ring on Eve's finger flashed on Marlo's. 'Are we close?'

'It looks good,' Eve said. Like a freaking crime scene still with people tromping around.

'Roundtree – the director – wants authentic.' Marlo nodded toward the burly man hunched over a monitor. 'And what he wants, he gets. It's just one of the reasons he insisted we shoot everything in New York. I hope you've had time to look around, really get a sense of things. I wanted this part the minute I heard about the project – even before I read Nadine Furst's book. And you, both of you, lived it. Now I'm babbling.'

She let out a quick, easy laugh. 'Talk about a huge fan. I've steeped myself in all things Eve Dallas for months now. I even did a few ride-alongs with a couple of detectives when even Roundtree couldn't budge you or your commander to let me and K.T. ride with the two of you. And,' she continued before Eve could respond, 'having steeped myself I completely understand why you put up the block.'

'Okay.'

'And babbling again. K.T.! Come over and meet the real Detective Peabody.'

The actress, deep in discussion with Roundtree, glanced over. Annoyance showed in her eyes before she put on what Eve assumed was her meet-the-public smile.

'What a treat.' K.T. shook hands, gave Peabody the once over. 'You're letting your hair grow.'

'Yeah. Kind of. I just saw you in *Teardrop*. You were totally mag.'

'I'm going to steal Dallas for a few minutes.' Marlo hooked an arm through Eve's. 'Let's grab some coffee,' she said, drawing Eve out of the crime scene set and through the mock-up of the Icove home's second story. 'The producers arranged for me to have the brand you drink, and now I'm hooked. I asked my assistant to set us up in my trailer.'

'Aren't you working?'

'A lot of the work is waiting. I guess that's a similarity to police work.' Moving quickly in boots and rough trousers, her prop weapon -- Eve assumed -- in a shoulder harness, Marlo led the way through the studio, past sets, equipment, huddles of people.

Eve stopped at the reproduction of her own bullpen. Desks – cluttered – the caseboard that took her back to the previous fall, the cubes, the scuffed floor.

The only thing missing were the cops – and the smell of processed sugar, bad coffee and sweat.

'Is it right?'

'Yeah – some bigger, I guess.'

'It won't look it on screen. They reproduced your office, in the same layout, so they can shoot me or one of the others going through this area and in, or out. Would you like to see it?'

They walked through, past the false wall and an open area Eve assumed wouldn't show on screen either, and into a near perfect model of her office at Cop Central, right down to the narrow window. Though this one looked out on the studio instead of New York.

'They'll CGI in the view – buildings, air traffic,' Marlo said when Eve walked over to look out. 'I've already shot some scenes in here, and we did the conference room scene where you lay out the conspiracy – Icove, Unilab, Brookhollow Academy. That was intense. The dialog was straight from the book, which we're told stuck very close to the actual record. Nadine did a brilliant job of merging the reality with a page-turning story line. Though I guess the reality was page-turning. I admire you so much.'

Surprised, mildly uncomfortable, Eve turned.

'What you do, every day,' Marlo continued, 'is so important. I'm good at my work. I'm damn good at it, and I feel strongly what I do is important. It's not uncovering a global cloning ring important, but without art, stories and the people who bring those stories to life, the world would be a sadder, smaller place.'

'Sure it would.'

'When I started researching this part, I realized I've never had another role I wanted so much to do justice to. Not just because of the Oscar potential – though the shiny gold man would look great on my mantel – but because it's important. I know you only watched the one scene, but I hope if there was anything that didn't ring true, didn't feel right to you, you'll tell me.'

'It seemed right to me.' Eve shrugged. 'The thing is, it's strange, I guess a little disorienting, to watch somebody being you doing what you did, saying what you said. So since it felt strange and disorienting, it must be right.'

Marlo's smile exploded. And no, Eve thought, she absolutely did not smile that way.

'That's good then.'

'And this.' Eve did a turn around the office set. 'I feel like I need to sit down and knock out some paperwork.'

'Carmandy would be thrilled to hear that. She's the head set designer. Let's get that coffee. They'll need me back on set soon.'

Marlo gestured as they went out. 'If we go this way, you'll see some of the Roarke/Dallas house set. It's spectacular. Preston, our AD, told you they were going to want some publicity shots while you and Peabody are on set? Valerie Xaviar, that's the publicist, is handling it. She's on top of everything.'

'It was mentioned.'

Marlo smiled again, gave Eve's arm a quick, light rub. 'I know it's not something you'd choose to do, but it'll be great publicity for the vid – and it'll make the cast and crew happy. You're going to make the dinner tonight, I hope. You and Roarke.'

'We're planning on it.' Couldn't get out of it, Eve thought.

Marlo let out a laugh, shot Eve a look. 'And you're wishing you had a hot case so you could skip it.'

'I guess you are good at your work.'

'It'll be more fun than you think. Which won't be hard because you think it'll be torture.'

'Have you got my office wired?'

'No – but I like to think I'm wired into you.' Marlo tapped her temple. 'So I know you'll enjoy yourself a lot more than you think. And you'll love Julian. He's nailed Roarke – the accent, the body language, that indefinable sense of power and sex. Plus, he's gorgeous, funny, charming. I've loved working with him. Are you on an investigation now?'

'We just closed one a few days ago.'

'The Whitwood Center case – at least that's what the media call it. As I said, I'm steeped. Still, even when you're not working something active, you're supervising other investigations, testifying in court, consulting with the offi-cers and detectives in your division. It's a full plate. Dealing with—'

Marlo broke off when Eve's communicator signaled.

'Dallas.'

*Dispatch, Dallas, Lieutenant Eve. See the officer at 12 West Third. Possible homicide.*

'Acknowledged. Dallas and Peabody, Detective Delia en route.' She clicked off, signalled Peabody. 'We caught one. Meet me at the vehicle.'

Pocketing the communicator, she glanced at Marlo. 'Sorry.'

'No, of course. You caught a case, right when we're stand-ing here. It's probably a stupid question, but how does it feel when you're contacted, told someone's dead?'

'Like it's time to go to work. Listen, thanks for showing me around.'

'There's so much more. Big Bang Productions basically built Dallas World here at Chelsea Piers. We'll be shooting for at least two more weeks – probably three. Maybe you can make it back.'

'Maybe. I've got to go. I'll see you tonight, work permitting.'

'Good luck.'

Eve wound her way around to the VIP lot and her vehicle. She wasn't happy somebody was dead – but if they were going to be dead anyway, she wasn't *un*happy to have picked up the case, *before* the stupid photo shoot thing. She'd found Marlo Durn personable, maybe a little intense, but personable, smart, and not an asshole. But she had to admit it got to be a little unnerving to keep looking at somebody who looked so much like you. And to do it in surroundings that looked like your surroundings.

Dallas World.

Huh.

'Wouldn't you know we'd catch one.' Peabody hustled up. 'That was fun! And Preston – Preston Stykes, the assistant director – said I could do a cameo! They're going to be shooting some street scenes next weekend, and I get to be a pedestrian – with a close up, and maybe even a line. I bet I get a zit.' She patted a hand around her face, checking. 'You always get a zit when you have a close up.'

'Had many – close ups, not zits. I don't want to know about your zits.'

'It'll be my first.' She settled into the passenger seat while Eve got behind the wheel. 'And tonight we get to hob with the nob at dinner. I'm having dinner with vid stars, with celebrities, at the swank Park Avenue residence of the hottest director in Hollywood, meeting the most powerful and respected producer – and founder of Big Bang Productions.' Peabody stopped checking for potential zits to press her hand to her belly. 'I feel a little sick.'

'Then you can boot in the swank john of the hottest director in Hollywood.'

'He was looking for you – Roundtree. He was about to send a go-fer to find you.'

'I was having the surreal experience of having myself show myself around my office and bullpen.'

'Oh! My desk. I could've sat at my desk. I could've sat at *your* desk.'

'No.'

'It's a vid set.'

'Even then, no.'

'Mean. The other you is nice. I can call her Marlo. The other me is kind of a bitch.'

'There you go. Type casting.'

'Funny, ha ha. Really, she talked to me for about thirty seconds, then brushed me off. And do you know what she said?'

'How can I know when I wasn't there?'

'So, I'll tell you.' Scowling out the windshield, Peabody stuck on her rainbow-lensed sunshades. 'She said if Nadine's book was an accurate portrayal, she suggests I take an assertive course. Otherwise I'm never going to be anything but an underling, or a sidekick at best. But with my subservient attitude I'd never be in charge.'

Eve felt a claw of annoyance scrape down the back of her neck. Her *partner* had been assertive enough to spring-board the investigation and downfall of an organization of dirty cops.

'She isn't kind of a bitch. She's essentially a bitch. And you're not an underling.'

'That's right. I'm your partner, and okay, you're my lieutenant, but that doesn't make me some kiss-ass underling with a subservient attitude.'

'Following orders in the line isn't subservient, it's being a good cop. And you have a smart-ass attitude half the time.'

'Thanks. I didn't like me very much.'

'I don't like you a whole lot. Neither does the other me.'

'Now I'm confused.'

'Marlo and K.T. don't like each other much. It shows when the camera's not on them. Once the director called cut, they went separate ways, didn't speak or look at each other until Marlo called K.T. over to you.'

'I guess I had Hollywood stars in my eyes because I didn't notice. But you're right. It must be rough to work with somebody so closely, have to pretend you like and respect each other, and you really don't.'

'That's why they call it acting.'

'Still. Oh, and I think the other me has a bigger ass.'

'No question about it.'

'Really?'

'Peabody, I didn't actually look at her ass, and I rarely have occasion to look at yours. But I'm willing to say her ass is bigger if it makes you happy and we can stop talking about the Hollywood people.'

'Okay, but just one more thing. The other me is also a lying sack. She told me she had to go prep for her next scene, but when I cut across where the trailers are to get to the VIP lot, I saw her – and boy, I heard her. Banging on one of the trailer doors, yelling. "I know you're in there, you bastard, and open the fucking door." Like that.'

'Whose trailer?'

'I don't know, but she was pissed, and didn't care who heard because there was crew milling around.'

'It's like I've always said. You're a bitch with a nasty temper and no class.'

Peabody sighed, smiled. 'But not an underling.'

'With that settled,' Eve said as she pulled behind a black and white, 'maybe we can check out this DB.'

'A visit to a vid set, a DB, and dinner with celebrities. It's a really good day.'


Not for Cecil Silcock.

His day had ended early on the leopard print tiles of his elaborate kitchen. He lay there, blood from the head wound running river to lake over the black-spotted gold. It made the floor look a little too much like a terminally wounded animal, in Eve's opinion.

Cecil was definitely terminally wounded. Blood also soaked into the tissue-thin white cashmere robe he'd put on some time before his head had made contact with a blunt object of some weight, then the unfortunately patterned tiles. From the gash down his forehead, Eve figured Cecil also made contact with the edge of the gold-topped black cooking island.

The rest of the kitchen, the dining and living areas, master bedroom, guest bed and bath were as spotless, accessorized and *arranged* as a upscale home decor showroom.

'No sign of forced entry,' the officer on the door told Eve. 'We got the vic's spouse in the bedroom there. He says he was out of town the last two days, got home – early, wasn't supposed to come in until this afternoon – and found the body.'

'Where's his suitcase?'

'In the bedroom.'

'Let's get the security discs.'

'The spouse said the security was off when he arrived. He claims the vic often forgot to set it.'

'Find their security station, check anyway.' Eve tossed her Seal-It back in her field kit and crouched by the body. 'Let's confirm ID, get TOD, Peabody. He took a hard blow here, left side of the head, across the temple, eye socket. Something wide, heavy and flat.'

'Vic is confirmed as Cecil Silcock, age fifty-six, of this address. Married to Paul Havertoe, four years. He's the owner operator of Good Times – party planning company.'

'No more good times for him.' Sitting back on her heels, Eve looked around. 'No forced entry. And the place looks like it's been cleaned and fluffed by magic fairies. He's wearing a – bet it's platinum – wedding band with a big-fat diamond. Robbery unlikely as a motive here. The jewelry, plus I can see plenty of easily carried top-scale electronics.'

'TOD ten-thirty-six. Dressed like this, no forced entry, he had to know the killer. He let the killer in, walked back here, maybe to make coffee or something. Whack, and good-times Cecil is no more.'

'Could be just like that. Or could be, dressed like this, Cecil had company while his spouse was out of town – which out of towning we will confirm. Comes out to make a nice breakfast, company whacks him. Or spouse returns, realizes Cecil has not been a good boy, whacks him.'

The uniform came back in. 'The security's been off for twenty-eight hours, Lieutenant. We've got nothing for last night or this morning.'

'Okay. Start the knock-on-doors. Let's see if anyone saw anything.'

Fitting on micro goggles, Eve took a careful study of the body. 'Cecil's as clean as the house. Smells like lemons.' She leaned her face to the face of the dead, took another sniff. 'But there's a little coffee here, too. Had himself a shower and a cup before the whack. No visible defensive wounds, or other trauma. Takes the hit, goes down, smacking the edge of the island here, then takes another hit, other temple, on the tiles. It's odd, isn't it?'

'It is?'

'Everything's so clean, so tidy.'

'The vic was neat?'

'Maybe. Probably.' Eve took off the goggles, stood.

'There's no AutoChef. What kind of place is this?' She poked in the fridge. 'Everything very fresh here, and also sparkly clean.' She began opening cupboards, drawers. 'Lots of pots, pans, gadgets, matching dishes, wine glasses, blah, blah.' She pulled out a large, heavy skillet. Wide and flat-bottomed. 'Got weight.'

'Oh, my gran's got one of those. Cast iron. She swears by it – came down from her gran.'

Eve studied the skillet, crouched again, goggles on to study the wound on the side of Cecil's head. Pulling out another tool from the kit, she took a quick measure. Nodded.

'Betcha. Seal and tag for the sweepers. Let's see if there's any of Cecil on here. So, Cecil has company – or gets it – then they come in here, behind the cooking island. But there's no sign of cooking – and since there's no AutoChef like any other civilized kitchen in the known world, he'd have to use a pan, tools. And what about coffee?'

'That's a espresso type machine there. You put the whole beans in, water, and it grinds and brews.'

'But it's clean and empty.'

'Maybe he didn't have time before the whack to prep.'

'Uh-uh. He's got a touch of coffee breath. He didn't just come in here with the killer, and get smacked with a heavy object – and I'm betting the cast-iron deal is the murder weapon. If he got that out, where's the other stuff – whatever he was going to put in it to cook? If he's arguing with some-body, is he thinking about making breakfast? Why doesn't the killer leave the murder weapon out – or take it with him?

Instead he cleans it up, stores it – and in what appears to be its proper place.

'If you're getting breakfast, what's the first thing you do?'

'Get the coffee,' Peabody said.

'Everybody gets the coffee, and Cecil's breath tells me he did just that. But there's no coffee made, no cup or mug.'

Lips pursed, eyes scanning, Peabody tried to see it as Eve did. 'Maybe he or they had already eaten, cleaned up. Then had the argument.'

'Could be, but if so, why was this pan still out – handy for the whack? Everything's put away all perfect, but this is within handy reach. Because this?' She lifted the now-sealed skillet. 'It's a weapon of opportunity. Get pissed, grab, whack. You wouldn't open the drawer, take it out of the stack, select the weapon then whack.'

Peabody followed the dots. 'You think the spouse did it, then cleaned up, then called the cops.'

'I wonder how Havertoe got home. It's time to have a chat.'

Eve released the uniform sitting with Havertoe to join the canvass. Like the kitchen, the master bedroom could have stood as an ad for Stylish Urban Home. From the sleek silver posts and zebra-print spread – with its carefully arranged mound of black and white pillows – the mirror gleam of bureaus, the strange angled lines of the art to the sinuous vase holding a single, spiky red flower that looked to Eve's eye as if it might hide sharp, needle-thin teeth under its petals.

In the sitting area in front of the wide terrace doors, Paul

Havertoe huddled on a silver-backed sofa with red cushions, and clutched a soggy handkerchief.

Eve judged him about twenty years his dead spouse's junior. His smooth, handsome face carried a pale gold tan that showed off well against the luxurious sweep of his caramel-colored hair. He wore trim, pressed jeans and a spotless white shirt over a body that Eve assumed put in solid health-club time.

His eyes when they lifted to Eve's were the color of plums and puffy from weeping.

'I'm Lieutenant Dallas, and this is Detective Peabody. I'm very sorry for your loss, Mr Havertoe.'

'Cecil's dead.'

Under the rawness of the tears, Eve caught hints of molasses and magnolia.

'I know this is a difficult time, but we need to ask you some questions.'

'Because Cecil's dead.'

'Yes. We're recording this, Mr Havertoe – for your protection. And I'm going to read you your rights so you're clear on everything. Okay?'

'Do you have to?'

'It's better if I do. We'll make this as quick as we can. Is there anyone you'd like us to contact for you – a friend, family member – before we start?'

'I ... I can't think.'

'Well, if you think of someone you want with you, we'll arrange it.' She sat across from him, read off the Revised Miranda. 'Do you understand your rights and obligations?'

'Yes.'

'Okay, good. You were out of town?'

'Chicago. A client. We're event creators. I got back this morning, and . . .'

'You returned from Chicago this morning. At what time?'

'I think, about eleven. I wasn't due until four, but I was able to finish early. I wanted to surprise Cecil.'

'So you switched your flight and your car service?'

'Yes, yes, that's right. I was able to take an earlier shuttle, arrange an earlier pick-up. To surprise Cecil.' Choking on a sob, he pressed the damp handkerchief to his face.

'You've had a terrible shock, I know. What car service was that, Mr Havertoe? Just for the record.'

'We always use Delux.'

'Okay. And when you got home,' Eve continued as Peabody stepped quietly out of the room, 'what happened?'

'I came in, and I brought my bag in here – but Cecil wasn't in the bedroom.'

'Should he have been home at that time of the day?'

'He was scheduled to work from home today. He has a client coming in this afternoon. I should contact them.' He looked blankly around the room with streaming eyes. 'I should—'

'We'll help you with that. What did you do next?'

'I . . . I called out for him – um – the way you do. And I thought he must be in his office. It's off the kitchen, with a view of the courtyard, because he likes looking out at our little garden when he works. And I saw him on the floor. I saw him, and he was dead.'

'Did you touch anything? Anything in the kitchen?'

'I touched Cecil. I took his hand. He was dead.'

'Do you know anyone who'd want to hurt Cecil?'

'No. No. Everybody loves Cecil.' With some drama, he pressed the soggy handkerchief to his heart. 'I love Cecil.'

'Who do you suppose he'd let in, while he was wearing only his robe?'

'I . . .' Havertoe struggled to firm his trembling lips. 'I think Cecil was having an affair. I think he'd been seeing someone.'

'Why do you think that?'

'He'd been late getting home a few times, and – there were signs.'

'Did you confront him about it?'

'He denied it.'

'You argued?'

'Every couple argues. We were happy. We made each other happy.'

'But he was having an affair.'

'A fling.' Havertoe dabbed at his eyes. 'It wouldn't last. Whoever he was seeing must have killed him.'

'Who do you think he was seeing?'

'I don't know. A client? Someone he met at one of our events? We meet so many people. There's a constant temptation to stray.'

'You have an impressive home, Mr Havertoe.'

'We're very proud of it. We often entertain. It's what we do – it's good promotion for the business.'

'I guess that's why you cleaned up the kitchen,' Eve said

conversationally as Peabody came back in. 'You didn't want people to see the mess.'

'I . . . what?'

'Was Cecil fixing breakfast when you got in – earlier than he expected? Or had he finished? Were there signs he hadn't been alone? Cheating on you when you were away. He was a very bad boy.'

'He's dead. You shouldn't talk about him that way.'

'What time did you get home again?'

'I said – I think – about eleven.'

'That's odd, Mr Havertoe,' Peabody said. 'Because your shuttle landed at eight-forty-five.'

'I – I had some errands—'

'And the driver from Delux dropped you off at the door here at nine-ten.'

'I . . . took a walk.'

'With your luggage?' Eve angled her head. 'No, you didn't. You came in at nine-ten, and you and Cecil got into it while you – one of you or both – made coffee, fixed breakfast. You wanted to know who he'd been with while you were in Chicago. You wanted him to stop cheating on you. You argued, and you picked up the cast-iron skillet, swung out. You were so mad. All you've done for him and he can't be faithful. Who could blame you for losing your temper. You didn't mean to kill him, did you, Paul? You just lashed out – hurt and angry.'

'I didn't – you have the time wrong. That's all.'

'No, you got it wrong. You got home early. Did you think you might catch him with someone?'

'No, no, it wasn't like that. I wanted to surprise him. I wanted things to be the way they were. I fixed him his favorite brunch! Mandarin orange juice mimosas and hazelnut coffee, eggs Benedict with raspberry French toast.'

'You went to a lot of trouble.'

'Everything made by hand, and I set the table with his favorite china.'

'And he didn't appreciate it. All the time and effort you went to, just to do something special for him, and he didn't appreciate it.'

'I . . . then I went for a walk. I went for a walk, and when I came back he was dead.'

'No, Paul. You argued, you hit him. It was like a reflex. You were so mad, so hurt, you just grabbed the skillet and swung out. And then it was too late. So you cleaned up the kitchen, put everything away.' While he lay there, dead on the floor, Eve thought. 'You scrubbed the cast-iron skillet.' With his blood staining the bottom. 'You made everything neat and tidy again, just the way he liked it.'

'I didn't mean to do it! It was an accident.'

'Okay.'

'He said he wanted a divorce. I did everything for him. I took care of him. He said I was smothering him, and he was tired of me looking through his things, going through his schedule and calling him all the time. He was tired of it. Of me. I made him brunch, and he wanted a divorce.'

'Harsh,' Eve commented.

# Have you read them all?

## Go back to the beginning with the first three In Death novels.

### Book One
### NAKED IN DEATH

Introducing Lieutenant Eve Dallas and billionaire Roarke. When a Senator's granddaughter is found shot to death in her own bed, all the evidence points to Roarke – but Eve senses a set-up.

### Book Two
### GLORY IN DEATH

High-profile women are being murdered by a knife-wielding attacker. Roarke has a connection to all the victims, but Eve needs his help if she's going to track down the real killer.

### Book Three
### IMMORTAL IN DEATH

With a new 'immortality' drug about to hit the market, Eve and Roarke must track down a vicious and evil drug dealer and killer – before it's too late.

# TREACHERY IN DEATH

## J.D. Robb

*'There's another body on a slab, Dallas. Dirty cop or not, he's dead, and she's responsible. She has to be shut down before she decides to clean house again.'*

Lieutenant Eve Dallas is about to come up against her most formidable criminal yet: Lieutenant Renee Oberman. Oberman runs a tight ship in the Illegals department of the New York Police and Security Department; she's also the daughter of a NYPSD legend. After eighteen years on the force, Oberman is efficient, decorated – and utterly corrupt.

When Eve's partner Peabody overhears a damning conversation between Oberman and one of her flunkies, Peabody, Eve and her husband Roarke are soon on her case. Together, they must track down the hard evidence needed to bring Oberman and all her dirty cops down – knowing all the while that she will kill anyone who gets in her way.

'This series gets better with every book' *Publishers Weekly*

978-0-7499-5395-9

# CELEBRITY IN DEATH

## J.D. Robb

*'We've got a corpse that looks like one of the investigators,
a houseful of Hollywood and a media machine
that's going to eat it like gooey chocolate.'*

Lieutenant Eve Dallas is panicking – and she's not at a crime scene.
Forced to attend a celeb-packed party for a new movie based on her
most famous case, she is surrounded by actors who look like everyone
in her life. Just as the end is in sight, brutal reality crashes
through the sparkly façade.

There's been a murder.

The obnoxious actress playing Eve's partner, Peabody, has been found
face down in the pool. As Eve hastily interviews the guests, it's hard
to find anyone who didn't have a motive for the crime. But with a
murdered Personal Investigator, a missing tape recording and
a hugely expensive movie in the mix, Eve must fight
to keep a clear head and stop a calculated killer.

'I hope Ms. Roberts continues to write new stories for this pair
for a long time to come . . . Long live Eve and Roarke!' *Bella*

978-0-7499-5591-5